The Northern Light
From The German Of E. Werner

by

E. Werner

The Northern Light
From the German of e. Werner
by E. Werner

Copyright © 2024

All Rights reserved.

No part of this publication may be reproduced, stored in a retrieval system, or transmitted in any form or by any means, electronic, mechanical, photocopying or Otherwise, without the written permission of the publisher.
The author/editor asserts the moral right to be identified as the author/editor of this work.

ISBN: 978-93-64282-61-1

Published by
DOUBLE 9 BOOKS
2/13-B, Ansari Road
Daryaganj, New Delhi – 110002
info@double9books.com
www.double9books.com
Tel. 011-40042856

This book is under public domain

ABOUT THE AUTHOR

Elisabeth Bürstenbinder, better known by her pseudonym E. Werner, was a prolific German author who wrote during the late 19th and early 20th centuries. She gained considerable popularity for her romantic novels that often explored themes of love, mystery, and social issues. Under the pseudonym E. Werner, Bürstenbinder published numerous novels and short stories. Her works were known for their intricate plots, strong character development, and vivid descriptions of settings, particularly in northern European landscapes. She often incorporated elements of mystery and drama into her romances, which captivated readers and contributed to her widespread popularity. Notable Works. "The Northern Light": One of her most famous novels, known for its blend of romance, mystery, and drama set against a northern European backdrop. "Under a Charm": Another well-received work that explores themes of love and societal expectations. "Good Luck": A novel that reflects on the complexities of relationships and personal growth. Elisabeth Bürstenbinder's novels continue to be appreciated for their engaging storytelling and insightful exploration of human relationships. Her works contributed significantly to the genre of romantic fiction in the late 19th century, appealing to readers with their blend of romance and mystery. While details about her personal life are sparse, her literary legacy endures through her enduring novels that continue to attract readers interested in historical romance and drama. Elisabeth Bürstenbinder, writing under the pseudonym E. Werner, remains a notable figure in German literature for her compelling narratives and exploration of love, mystery, and societal complexities.

CONTENTS

CHAPTER I 7
CHAPTER II 25
CHAPTER III 45
CHAPTER IV 62
CHAPTER V 72
CHAPTER VI 87
CHAPTER VII 101
CHAPTER VIII 114
CHAPTER IX 138
CHAPTER X 156
CHAPTER XI 169
CHAPTER XII 183
CHAPTER XIII 205
CHAPTER XIV 224
CHAPTER XV 237
CHAPTER XVI 263

CHAPTER I

The grey mist of an autumn morning lay upon forest and field. Through its shadowy vapors a swarm of birds were sweeping by, on their Southward way, now dipping low over the tops of the tall fir forest, as if giving a last greeting to their summer homes, and then rising high in the air; turning their flight due South, they disappeared slowly through the fog.

At the window of a large manor-house, which lay at the edge of the forest, two men stood, watching the course of the birds and conversing earnestly with each other. One was a tall, stalwart figure, whose firm and erect bearing betokened the soldier fully as much as the uniform he wore. He was blonde and blue-eyed, not handsome, but with a strong and speaking countenance; a typical German in form and feature. Yet something like a shadow lay upon the man's face, and there were, wrinkles, on his brow which surely were not the result of age, for he was yet in the prime of life.

"The birds have started already on their journey to the south," said he, after watching the flight attentively until they had finally disappeared in the cloud of mist. "The autumn has come to nature and to our lives as well."

"Not to yours yet," objected his companion. "You are just in the hey-day of life, in the full strength of your manhood."

"True enough, as to years, but I have a feeling that age will overtake me sooner than others. I often feel as if it were autumn with me now."

The other man, who might have been a few years the speaker's senior, was slender, and of middle height, and clad in civilian's dress. He shook his head impatiently at his companion's last observation. He appeared insignificant when compared with the strong, well-built officer near him; but his pale, sharply cut face wore a look of cold, superior repose, and the sarcastic expression around the thin lips, together with his aristocratic air and bearing, suggested a hidden strength behind a feeble exterior.

"You take life too hard, Falkenried," he said reprovingly. "You have changed strangely in the last few years. Who would recognize in you now, the gay young officer of other days? And what's the reason of it all? The shadow which once darkened your life has long since disappeared. You are a soldier, heart and soul, and have repeatedly distinguished yourself in your profession. A high position awaits you in the future, and the thing above all others is—you have your son."

Falkenried did not answer; he folded his arms and looked out again into the mist, while the other continued: "The boy has grown handsome as a god in the last few years. I was quite overcome with surprise when I saw him again, and you yourself, told me that he was unusually gifted and in many things showed great talent."

"I would that Hartmut had fewer talents and more character," said Falkenried, in an almost acrid tone. "He can make verses quick enough, and to learn a language is child's play to him, but as soon as he tries some earnest science, he's behind all the others, and in military tactics I can make nothing of him at all. You cannot comprehend, Wallmoden, what iron severity I am constantly compelled to employ."

"I fear you accomplish little by this same severity," interrupted Wallmoden. "You should take my advice and leave your son to his studies. He has not the qualifications for a soldier. You must see that for yourself by this time."

"He shall and must acquire those qualifications. It is the only possible career for such an intractable nature as his, which revolts at every restraint and to which every duty is a burden. The life of a student at the university would give him unrestrained liberty; only the iron dicipline of the service will force him to bend."

"The only question is, how long will you be able to force him to do your will? You should not deceive yourself; there are inherited tendencies which will not allow themselves to be repressed or eradicated. Hartmut, now, is in appearance the counterpart of his mother; he has her features and her eyes."

"Yes," assented Falkenried gloomily, "her dark, demoniacal, glowing eyes, which cast their spell upon all who knew her."

"And were your ruin," supplemented Wallmoden. "How often did I warn and advise you then; but you would not listen. Your passion had seized you like a fever and held you like chains. I declare I never have been able to understand it."

Falkenried's lips were drawn in with a bitter smile.

"I can readily believe that you, the cool, calculating diplomat, you, whose every word is weighed, are protected against all such witcheries."

"I should at least be cautious in my choice. Your marriage carried unhappiness on its face from the very beginning. A women of a foreign race, with strange blood in her veins and the wild, passionate Sclave nature, without character, without understanding of what we here call duty and morality; and you with your rigid principles, with your sensitive feeling of honor, it could ultimately lead to but one end. And I believe you loved her in spite of all, until your separation."

"No," said Falkenried, in a hard tone, "the fire burned out in the first year; I saw that only too clearly. But I shrank back from publishing to the world my household misery by a legal separation. So I bore it until no choice remained, until I was forced. But enough of this."

He turned abruptly on his heel and looked from the window again; but the quick movement betrayed rather than concealed the torture which he with difficulty repressed.

"Yes, it takes a great deal to tear up a nature like yours by the roots," said Wallmoden earnestly. "But the divorce freed you from the unhappy bond, and why should you not bury the memory as well?"

Falkenried shook his head and sighed heavily. "One cannot bury such memories; they are forever rising from their supposed sepulchres, and just now—" he broke off suddenly.

"Just now; what do you mean?"

"Nothing; let us speak of other things. You have been in Burgsdorf since day before yesterday; how long do you expect to remain?"

"About two weeks. I haven't much time at my disposal, and am for that matter only nominally Willibald's guardian, for my diplomatic position keeps me out of the country most of the time. The guardianship really rests in the hands of my sister, who rules over everything."

"Well, Regine is equal to the position. She governs the great estate and the numerous servants as though she were a man."

"And gives her orders like a cavalry officer from morning to night," put in her brother. "Recognizing all her excellent qualities, I, nevertheless, feel a slight creepy sensation whenever I am constrained to visit Burgsdorf, and I always leave the place with shattered nerves. They live in a most primitive fashion over yonder. Willibald is a perfect young bear, and of course at the same time the apple of his mother's eye, and she, by the way, is doing her best to bring him up as a bluff country squire. It's useless to enter any protest, and, for the matter of that, it seems just what the youngster's good for."

Their conversation was interrupted at this moment by a servant, who entered and handed his master a card. Falkenried glanced at it. "Counsellor Egern? I am glad of that. Tell the gentleman to come in."

"You have a business engagement I see," said Wallmoden rising. "Then I'll not disturb you."

"On the contrary I beg you to remain. I have had an intimation of this visit and its purpose, and know what will be the result of our conversation. The question is—" He did not finish, for the door opened and the lawyer entered. He seemed surprised not to find the officer alone, as he had fully expected, but Falkenried took no notice of his ill-concealed astonishment.

"Herr Counsellor Egern—Herr von Wallmoden, secretary of legation," said the host, presenting them. The man of law bowed with cool politeness as he took the seat offered him.

"I have the honor of being known to you, I believe, Herr Major," he began. "As your wife's attorney at the time the suit for divorce was in progress, I had the opportunity of making your acquaintance." He paused as if expecting an answer; but Major Falkenried gave no sign beyond an affirmative nod.

Wallmoden was all attention. He could understand now his friend's irritation on his arrival.

"I come to you to-day in the name of my former client," continued the counsellor. "She has authorized me—have I your permission to speak freely?"

He glanced at the diplomat, but Falkenried answered shortly: "Herr von Wallmoden is my friend, and knows all about this affair. So you may speak freely."

"Very well. The lady has, after an absence of many years, returned to Germany, and naturally enough wishes to see her son. She has already written you about the matter but has received no answer."

"I should think that was answer enough. I do not wish any such meeting, and I will not permit it."

"That sounds very blunt, Herr Major. Frau von Falkenried, in that case, has—"

"Say Frau Zalika Rojanow, if you please," interrupted the Major. "I believe she assumed her maiden name again when she returned to her own country."

"The name does not signify on this occasion," responded the lawyer composedly. "The question concerns only and alone a mother's natural desire, which the father neither can nor dare refuse, even though, as in this case, the son has been unconditionally adjudged to him."

"Dare not? But suppose he does dare?"

"In so doing he will overstep the limit of his rights. I beg you, Herr Major, to consider the matter quietly before giving so decided a no. A mother has rights of which no judicial decree can ever divest her, and one of those rights is the privilege of seeing her only child again. In this case my client has the law on her side, and she will appeal to it, too, if my demand meets with the same refusal as did her written request."

"Very well, she can make the attempt. I'll run the risk. My son does not know that his mother is living, and shall not learn it now. I will not have him see her or speak with her, and I will know how to prevent it, too. My no is absolute under all circumstances."

This declaration left nothing to be wished for as regarded energy; but Falkenried's face was deathly pale, and his voice had a hollow, menacing sound. One could see how fearfully the interview had excited him. He was scarcely able to preserve the semblance of outward composure.

The attorney seemed to see the uselessness of further endeavor, and only shrugged his shoulders.

"If this is your last word, then my errand is at an end, and we will determine hereafter what our next step will be. I regret having troubled you about the matter, Herr Major." He bowed himself out with the same cool, indifferent manner with which he had entered. As the door closed upon him, Falkenried sprang up and began pacing excitedly up and down the room; there were a few minutes of oppressive silence, then Wallmoden said, half aloud: "You should not have done that. Zalika will not resign herself readily to your no; she made a desperate struggle for her child in the beginning."

"But I obtained the victory. It is to be hoped she has not forgotten that."

"At that time the question concerned the possession of the child," objected the secretary. "Now the mother only asks permission to see him again, and you will not be able to refuse her that, if she demands it peremptorily."

The Major stopped suddenly, and his voice was full of undisguised contempt as he answered:

"She will not venture to do that after all that has happened. Zalika learned to know me in the hour of our separation; she'll be cautious about driving me to extremes a second time."

"But perhaps she will seek to accomplish secretly what you have openly refused."

"That is impossible; the discipline of our institution is so severe there could be no intercourse here of which I should not learn at once."

Wallmoden did not seem to share his friend's confidence. He shook his head doubtfully.

"To speak openly, I regard it as a great mistake that you are obstinately silent toward your son concerning his mother and the fact that she is living. When he learns it from some other source, what then? And sometime you must tell him."

"Perhaps, in a couple of years, when he'll have to enter the world. Now he's only a student, a half-grown boy, and I cannot disclose to him the drama which was once played in his father's house—I cannot."

"So be it. You know the woman who was once your wife, and know what to expect from her. I fear there is nothing impossible for this woman to accomplish."

"Ah, I know her," said Falkenried with intense bitterness, "and because I know her I will protect my son from her at any price. He shall not breath the poisonous breath of her presence; no, not even for an hour. I do not under estimate the danger from Zalika's return, but as long as Hartmut remains at my side he is safe from her, for she will never come near me, I give you my word for that."

"We will hope so," answered Wallmoden, as he rose and reached out his hand at parting. "But do not forget that the greatest danger with which you have to contend lies in Hartmut himself; he is in every trait the son of his mother. You are coming over to Burgsdorf with him day after to-morrow, I hear?"

"Yes, he is to spend his short autumn vacation with Willibald. I shall be able to remain a day only, but I'll surely come for that time. Good-bye."

The secretary left the house, and Falkenried returned once more to the window, but he only gave a fleeting glance after his friend, who waved him a parting greeting, then returned gloomily to his own thoughts.

"The son of his mother." The words rang in his ears, but the thought was not new to him; he had known it a long time, and it was this knowledge which had furrowed his brow so deeply, and wrung from him many a deep sigh. He was a man who could brave any outward danger; but against this unfortunate heritage of blood in his only child he had battled with all his energy for years, but in vain.

"Now I tell you for the last time that all this noise and confusion must come to an end, for my patience is finally exhausted. Such goings on as we have had for the last three days are enough to make one think that all Burgsdorf is bewitched. That Hartmut is full of mad tricks from his head to his feet. When he once gets loose from the reins which his father holds tight enough, I'll admit that, there's no getting on with him, and of course you follow after him through thick and thin, and obey your lord and master's slightest behest. Oh, you are a fine pair."

This philippic, which was delivered in a loud tone, came from the lips of Frau von Eschenhagen of Burgsdorf, while sitting with her son and mother at breakfast. The great dining-room lay on the ground floor of the old mansion, and was an extremely simple room, with glass doors leading out upon a broad stone terrace, and to the garden beyond. On the brightly tinted walls hung a number of antlers, which bore witness to the sporting tastes of former possessors, but these were the only adornments of the room.

A dozen high-backed chairs, arranged stiffly in rows like grenadiers, a cumbrous dining-table and a couple of old-fashioned sideboards constituted the entire furniture of the room; and one could see at a glance that they had already done service for several generations. Such luxuries as wall-paper, paintings or carpet could not be found here. Evidently the occupants were contented to live on just as their ancestors had done, although Burgsdorf was one of the richest estates in the district.

The appearance of the mistress of the house was in keeping with her surroundings She was forty years old or there abouts, with a large, strong figure, cheeks glowing with health, and firm, solid features, which could never have been called beautiful, but denoted great energy. Very little escaped the sharp glance of her gray eye, her dark hair was brushed back smoothly, her gown was of coarse texture, simply made, and looking at her hands, you saw at once that they were made for work.

There was nothing attractive in her appearance, and her manner and bearing were thoroughly masculine.

The heir and future master of Burgsdorf, who had just been reprimanded so sharply, sat opposite his mother, listening, as in duty bound, while he helped himself liberally to ham and eggs. He was a handsome, fresh-looking youth, about seventeen years old, whose appearance indicated no great intellectual strength, but he seemed to beam with good nature. His sun-burned face was the picture of health, but otherwise he showed little resemblance to his mother. He lacked her energetic expression, and the blue eyes and blonde hair were not from her, but were an inheritance from his father. With his large, but very awkward limbs, he looked like a young giant, and formed a striking contrast to his more delicately formed, aristocratic looking uncle, Wallmoden, who sat next him, and who said now with a slight *soupcon* of irony in his tone: "You certainly cannot hold Willibald answerable for all these mad pranks; he certainly is a model son."

"I would advise him not to be anything else; who lives with me must obey orders," cried Frau von Eschenhagen, as she struck an emphatic blow upon the table, which made her brother wince.

"A man is bound to obey orders under your government," he answered. "At the same time I would advise you, dear Regine, to do something more for the intellectual development of your son. I have no doubt that under your guidance he will become, in time, a most excellent farmer, but to the education of a future landed proprietor, something more than that is needed. Willibald has outgrown home instructors and should be sent away now."

"Sent a—?" Frau Regine laid down knife and fork in unbounded astonishment. "Sent away," she exclaimed, greatly irritated, "and in the name of common sense, where?"

"Well, first to the university, and later to travel, that he may learn something of the world and of men."

"That he may be altogether ruined by this world and these men, and no comfort to me at all! No, Herbert, I'll never do that, and I tell you so now, once for all. I have educated my son to be honest and fear God, and do not think I shall turn him loose in your Sodom and Gomorrah which the dear Lord in his forbearance has yet spared from the fire and brimstone which it so richly deserves."

"You only know this Sodom and Gomorrah by hearsay, Regine," interrupted Herbert, sarcastically. "You have lived in Burgsdorf ever since your marriage; you must acknowledge that yourself!"

"I acknowledge nothing at all," declared Frau von Eschenhagen, obstinately. "Will shall become a capable farmer; he is qualified for that, and for that he needs no cramming at your universities. Or perhaps you'd like to educate him in your own school, and make a diplomatist of him? That would be too great an honor."

She began to laugh loudly, and Will, to whom the whole conversation had appeared very comical, joined in in the same key. Herr von Wallmoden took no part in this sudden explosion of gaiety; he only winced again, as though his nerves were affected, and shrugged his shoulders.

"No, I had not thought of that. I know full well I should have my trouble for my pains. But Willibald and I are the only representatives of our family, and if I should not marry—"

"Should not? You are not thinking of marrying in your old age?" interrupted his sister, sharply.

"I am in my forty-fifth year, dear Regine, and a man is not usually considered old at that age," said Wallmoden, somewhat vexed. "Above all things I consider marriages made late in life by far the happiest; one is not influenced then by passion, as Falkenried was, to his lasting wretchedness, but gives to reason the decisive word."

"The saints protect us! What if Willibald should wait to marry until he is fifty years old and gray-headed?" cried Frau von Eschenhagen, greatly vexed.

"As an only son and future heir he will have to consider such matters; as for the rest, the main point will be his own inclinations. What do you think, Willibald?"

The young heir, who had disposed of his ham and eggs by this time, and with undiminished appetite was now attacking the sausage, was evidently much astonished that his opinion had been asked. Such a thing had never happened before, and he was obliged to reflect deeply before he could answer at all.

At length he reached a conclusion. "Yes, of course I must marry some time, but mamma will choose a wife for me when the right time comes."

"She will indeed, my boy," assented his mother, warmly. "That is my affair, so you need not trouble your head about it, and until then you will remain here in Burgsdorf where I can have my eye upon you. As to the university and traveling, that matter is—settled."

She threw a defiant glance at her brother, but he was gazing with a look of horror at the enormous sausage to which his nephew and ward was helping himself for the second time.

"Have you always such a large appetite, Will?" he asked.

"Always," Will assured him complacently, as he helped himself to a large slice of bread and butter.

"No, we don't suffer thank God, with indigestion or any other stomach trouble," said the mistress of the house tartly, "but we earn our bread honestly here. First pray and work, then eat and drink, but what we do, we do thoroughly, and that keeps body and soul together. Just look at Will, now, and you will see that what I say is true." She gave her brother a friendly slap on the shoulder with her last words, but this token of her good will was so energetic that Wallmoden shrank back in his chair, and immediately moved it sidewise to be out of the reach of that muscular hand.

The expression of his face showed clearly that the "creepy sensation" was coming over him again. In the presence of these patriarchial conditions, he thought it best to forego any attempt to enforce his prerogative as guardian, an office, moreover, which, so far as he was concerned, had always been purely nominal. It was plain from Will's manner that his mother's praise was highly gratifying to the young man's feelings.

"And Hartmut is not here for breakfast again, this morning. He seems to think there is no necessity for being punctual at Burgsdorf, but I will enlighten the young gentleman when he comes and make it clear to him that—"

"There he is now," exclaimed Willibald. On the clear sunshine which flooded the room through the open windows, there fell a shadow, and a tall, slender figure appeared suddenly at the window and vaulted upon the high sill.

"Well, what kind of an imp are you anyway, that you can only come in through the window?" said Frau von Eschenhagen indignantly. "What are the doors for?"

"For Will and all other well-ordered human beings," laughed the newcomer good-naturedly. "I always take the nearest way, and that led this time through the window." So saying he gave one spring from the high seat into the middle of the room.

Hartmut Falkenried, like the young heir of Burgsdorf, stood upon the boundary line where boyhood and manhood meet, but it needed only a glance to recognize that he was his friend's superior in every respect. He wore a cadet's uniform which became him well, but yet there was something in his whole appearance which seemed to be at war with the military cut and fit. The tall, slender boy was a true picture of youth and beauty, yet there was something odd about this beauty, something wild in his motions and appearance, with absolutely nothing to remind one of the martial figure and earnest repose of his father. The luxuriant, curly locks which crowned the high forehead, were of a deep, blue black, and the warm, dark coloring of the skin betokened rather a son of the south than of German parentage. Neither did the eyes, which flashed in the youthful countenance, belong to the cool, earnest north; they were enigmatical eyes, dark as the night, and full of hot, passionate fire. Beautiful as they were, however, there was something uncanny hidden in their depths, and though the laughter which accompanied Hartmut's words was free and unrestrained, it was not a hearty, merry boy's laugh.

"You certainly conduct yourself in a very free and easy manner," said Wallmoden, sharply. "You evidently take advantage of the fact that the inmates of Burgsdorf think little of etiquette. I have no doubt, however, that your father would protest against such an entrance into the dining-room."

"He would not do it if his father were here," said Frau von Eschenhagen, who did not seem to notice the stab intended for herself in her brother's remark. "And so you have come to your breakfast at last, Hartmut. But laggards get nothing to eat; did you know that?"

"Yes, I know that," replied Hartmut, quite undisturbed, "so I got my breakfast some time ago from the housekeeper. You can't starve me, Aunt Regine. I stand on too good a footing with your people."

"And so you think you can do as you please and go unpunished," cried the irate lady. "Break all the rules of the house, leave no one and nothing in peace, and stand all Burgsdorf on its head; but I'll soon stop all this business, my lad. To-morrow I'll send a messenger over to your father requesting him to come and take home his son who knows neither punctuality nor obedience."

The threat had its effect. The youth was frightened, and thought it well to surrender at discretion.

"Oh, you are only jesting; shall I not enjoy my short vacation with—"

"With all manner of folly?" Frau von Eschenhagen added for him. "Will has not done so much mischief in all his life as you have accomplished in the last three days, and you'll spoil him with your bad example and lead him into all manner of misdoing."

"Oh, Will is not the kind to be spoiled. I could not do it if I tried," said Hartmut very warmly.

The young heir, who certainly did not look as if he could be led into any impropriety, ate on, untroubled by these personal allusions, until he had finished the last slice of bread on the table; but his mother was highly incensed at this remark.

"That must grieve you greatly," she retorted. "It is certainly not your fault, for you have tried hard enough to ruin him; but as I just said I will write to your father to-morrow."

"That he is to come and fetch me away? You won't do that Aunt Regine, you are far too good. You know how very strict papa is, how severely he can punish; you won't complain of me to him; you have never done it yet."

"Leave me alone, don't bother me with your flatteries." Frau Regine's face was as inflexible as ever, but her voice had a certain unsteadiness which made Hartmut feel he had won the day. He laid his arm upon her shoulder with the freedom of a child.

"I believe you do love me a little, Aunt Regine, and I—I have been happy for weeks over the thought of my visit to Burgsdorf. I have been sick with longing for woods and sea, for the green meadows and the far blue heavens. I have been so happy here; but of course, if you really do not want me, I'll go away from the place. I won't wait to have you send me."

His voice had sunk to a soft, seductive whisper, while his eyes spoke more eloquently than his tongue. They could plead more powerfully than the lips, and Frau von Eschenhagen, who yielded to no one, from her only son to the lowest tenant on the estate, permitted herself to be persuaded by them now.

"You are incorrigible, you merry-andrew" she said, brushing the curls from his forehead. "And as to sending you away, you know only too well that Will and all my people are always ready to make fools of themselves for you, and I, too, for that matter."

Hartmut laughed aloud at the last words, and kissed her hand with impetuous gratitude, then he turned to his friend, who, having finally ended his meal, was looking on in silent wonderment.

"Have you finished your breakfast at last, Will? Come, we'll go to the Burgsdorf fishing pond—don't be so vexatiously slow. Good-bye, Aunt Regine, I can see Uncle Wallmoden does not approve of your having pardoned me. Hurrah, now we're off for the woods." And away he rushed over the terrace and across the garden. There was something attractive in his exuberance and enthusiasm. The lad was all life and fire. Will trotted after him like a young deer, and in a few moments the two disappeared behind the trees.

"He comes and goes like a wind storm," said Frau von Eschenhagen, gazing after them. "That boy is not to be restrained once the reins are slackened."

"A dangerous youth," said Wallmoden. "He even understands how to manage you, who usually have all your commands obeyed. It is, within my knowledge, the first time you have ever forgiven disobedience and lack of punctuality."

"Yes, Hartmut has something about him which bewitches one," exclaimed Regine, half angry at her own irresolution. "If he did not look at me with those big black eyes of his while he begged and flattered, I might be able to resist him. You are right, he is a dangerous lad."

"Well, we've had enough of Hartmut for this morning. The question which interests me concerns the education of your own son. You have really decided—"

"To keep him here. Don't bother yourself about him, Herbert; you may be a great diplomatist, and have the politics of the whole country in your pocket, but I wont give my boy into your keeping; he belongs to me alone, and I intend to keep him, and—that's enough."

A sounding blow on the table accompanied the "that's enough." Then the ruling lady of Burgsdorf rose from her chair and left the room. Her brother shrugged his shoulders and said half aloud: "He can grow up an ignorant country squire for all of me—perhaps it's the best thing for him after all."

Hartmut and Willibald had, in the meantime, reached the tolerably extensive forest which belonged to the estate. The Burgsdorf fish pond, a lonely, reedy sheet of water in the middle of the wood, lay glittering in the sun in the still morning hours. Willibald had chosen for himself a shady place upon the bank, and gave himself up, with as much perseverance as comfort, to the delights of angling, while the impatient Hartmut wandered here and there, now scaring a bird, now breaking off a branch for the blossoms, and at last, after a series of gymnastic performances, seating himself on the trunk of an old tree which lay half in the water. "Can you never be quiet in any place? You frighten the fish away every time," exclaimed Will, out of humor. "I've caught nothing at all to-day!"

"How can you sit for hours on the one spot waiting for the stupid fish to bite?" retorted Hartmut. "Ah, you can spend the whole long year in the woods if you desire, you are free, free."

"Are you a prisoner, then?" asked his friend. "You and your comrades are out daily, are you not?"

"But never alone, never without supervision and control. We are always and eternally in the service, even in recreation hours. O how I hate it, this service, and the whole slavish life."

"But Hartmut, what if your father heard you?"

"Oh, then he would punish me again as he always does. He has nothing else for me but force and punishment, all for my own good—that goes without saying."

He threw himself full length on the grass, but hard as the words sounded, there was a tremor in his tone which told of pain and passion. The young heir only shook his head soberly while he put a new bait on his hook and for a few minutes there was perfect silence.

Then suddenly something black swooped down like a flash of lightning from the height above them into the water, and a second later rose again in the air with the slippery, glittering prey in its beak.

"Bravo, that was a good catch!" cried Hartmut, rising. But Will spoke angrily.

"The wretched robber robs our whole pond. I will speak to the forester and tell him to fill him full of lead."

"A robber?" repeated Hartmut, as his glance followed the heron who was just disappearing behind the high tree tops. "Yes, of course, but how fine it must be to live such a free robber's life up there in the air. To descend like a flash for your booty and be up and off again where no one can follow; that's a hunt that pays."

"Hartmut, I verily believe you'd take pleasure in such a wild, lawless life," said Willibald, with the repugnance of a well-trained boy for such sentiments.

His companion laughed, but it was the same bitter laugh without the joyousness of youth in its sound.

"Well, if I had any such desire, they'd take it out of me at the military academy. There obedience and discipline is the Alpha and Omega of all things. Will, have you never wished that you had wings?"

"I, wings?" asked Will, whose whole attention was again directed to his bait. "How ridiculous! Who would wish for impossibilities?"

"I only wish I had them," cried Hartmut excitedly. "I would I were one of the falcons from whom we take our name. Then I would mount higher and always higher in the blue sky towards the sun, and never come back again."

"I believe you're crazy," answered his listener good-naturedly. "Well, I wont catch anything, if I sit here all day, for the fish wont bite. I must move to another place."

With that he gathered up his fishing tackle and crossed to the other side of the pond, while Hartmut threw himself on the ground again.

It was one of those autumn days which during the midday hours recall thoughts of early spring. The sunshine was so golden, the air so mild, the woods so fresh and odorous. Upon the glistening little lake danced thousands of shining sparks, and the long grass whispered softly and mysteriously to itself whenever a breath of wind passed over it.

Hartmut lay stretched out motionless on the grass as if listening to the secrets it told to the autumnal wind. The wild passion and excitement which flashed from his eyes when he spoke of the bird of prey had all vanished. Now the eyes which looked into the heavens above were sad and dreamy, and there rested in them an expression of ardent longing.

A light step, almost unheard on the soft ground, approached, and the low bushes rustled as if against a silk garment. Then they parted and a woman's figure appeared and stood looking intently at the young dreamer.

"Hartmut!"

The boy started and sprang up instantly. He knew neither the voice nor the apparition which stood before him, but saw it was a lady, and he made her one of his courtly bows.

"Pardon, Madame—"

A slender, trembling hand was laid quickly and restrainingly on his arm.

"Be quiet, not so loud; your companion might hear us, and I want to speak to you, and to you alone, Hartmut."

She stepped back again into the thicket and motioned him to follow. Hartmut hesitated a moment. How came this heavily-veiled and richly-attired stranger into the lonely wood, and why did she speak so familiarly to him whom she had never seen before? But the mysteriousness of her behavior beginning to charm him, he followed.

She stood now in the shadow of the low trees, where she could not be seen from the lake, and slowly threw back her veil. She was not very young, a woman of more than thirty, but her face with its great burning eyes, possessed an indefinable witchery, and a certain charm lay in her voice, which, though she talked in whispers, had a soft, deep tone, and an odd intonation, as though the German which she spoke so fluently was not her mother tongue.

"Hartmut, look at me. Do you really not know me any more? Does no memory of your childhood come back to you, to tell you who I am?"

The young man shook his head slowly, and yet some dreamy and obscure memory did come to his recollection, of having heard this voice before, and of this face which had looked into his at some far distant period. Half shy, half fascinated, he stood looking at this stranger, who suddenly threw her arms around him.

"My son, my only child! Do you not know your own mother?"

"My mother is dead," he answered, half aloud.

The stranger laughed bitterly, shrilly, and her laugh seemed but an echo of the hard, joyless sounds which had come from Hartmut's lips a few moments since.

"So that's how it is. They would even say I was dead and not leave you the memory of a mother. It is not true, Hartmut. I live, I stand before you; look at me, look at my features, are they not your very own? That at least they could not take from you. Child of my heart, do you not feel that you belong to me?"

Still Hartmut stood motionless, looking into that face in which his own was so faithfully mirrored. He saw the same lines, the same luxuriant, blue-black hair, the same dark, flashing eyes; and the same demoniacal expression which was a flame in the eye of the mother, was a spark in the eye of the son. Their close resemblance to one another was witness enough that they were of one blood. The young man felt the influence of the mysterious tie.

He demanded no explanation, no proof; the dreamy, confused recollections of his childhood were suddenly clear, and after a second's hesitation he threw himself into the arms which were stretched out to him.

"Mother!"

In this cry lay the whole fervid intensity of the boy, who had never known what it was to have a mother, and who had longed for one with all the passion of his nature. His mother! And now he lay in her arms, now she covered him with warm kisses, and called him by sweet, tender names, which had been strangers to his ear until that moment—everything else seemed forgotten by him in this flood of stormy ecstasy.

After a few minutes Hartmut loosed himself from the arms which still enfolded him.

"Why have you never been with me, mamma?" he asked vehemently. "Why have I always been told that you were dead?"

Zalika stepped back, and in an instant all tenderness had died out of her eyes, and in its place was a wild, deadly hate, as the answer came like a hiss from between her set lips.

"Because your father hates me, my son—and because he wishes to deny me the love of my only child since he thrust me from him."

Hartmut was silent. He knew well enough that the name of his mother dare not be mentioned in his father's presence, and that he had been sharply reproved once for doing so, but he had been too much a child at the time to ask "why." Zalika gave him no time to do so now. She brushed the thick locks back from his brow and a shadow crossed her face.

"You get your forehead from him," she said slowly. "But that is the only thing that reminds me of him, all the rest belongs to me and me alone. Every feature tells that you are mine—I always knew that."

She suddenly clasped him in her arms again with unspeakable tenderness, and Hartmut returned the embrace with ardor. It seemed to him like the fairy tales which he had so often dreamed, and he gave himself up unresistingly to the spell of happiness which some wonderful magic had cast over him.

Just at that moment, Will called loudly to his friend from the opposite shore to come on, that it was time to go home. Zalika spoke at once.

"We must part now. Nobody must learn that I have seen and spoken with you; above all things your father must not know it. When do you return to him?"

"In eight days."

"Not for eight days?" The words sounded almost triumphant.

"Until then I can see you daily. Be here by the pond to-morrow at this same hour; make some pretext for leaving your friend behind, so that we may be undisturbed. You will come, Hartmut?"

"Certainly, mother, but—"

She gave him no time for any objection, but continued in a passionate whisper:

"Above all things maintain absolute silence toward every one. Do not forget that. Good-bye, my child, my own dear son, good-bye."

Another kiss and she had retreated in the woods as noiselessly as she had come. It was high time, for Willibald appeared at this moment, though not noiselessly by any means, for he broke the twigs with many a crackle as he stepped heavily on them.

"Why didn't you answer me?" he asked. "I called you three times. You have been asleep; you look as if you were dreaming."

Hartmut did have a dazed look as he stood gazing at the trees behind which his mother had disappeared. Now he straightened himself and drew his hand across his forehead.

"Yes, I have been dreaming. A very strange, marvelous dream," he said slowly.

"You had better have been fishing," returned Will. "See what a fine catch I have made. A man should never dream in daylight—that's the time to be at something serious—mother says."

CHAPTER II

The Falkenried and Wallmoden families had been on friendly terms for years. Living upon adjoining estates, their intercourse was frequent, and their children grew up together, while many common interests united the bonds of friendship still more closely. Neither of the families were wealthy, and the sons, after completing their education, always had to make their own way in the world, and this in their turn Major Hartmut von Falkenried and Herbert von Wallmoden had done.

They had played together in their youth, and as men had remained true to their boyhood's friendship. At one time it looked as if they would be more closely allied, for their parents had planned a marriage between Lieutenant Falkenried, as he was then, and Regine Wallmoden. The young couple seemed to understand one another fully, and everything stood on the happiest footing, when an event occurred which put an abrupt termination to all their plans.

A cousin of the Wallmoden family, an incorrigible idler and spendthrift, who had made his longer residence at home an impossibility by his wild conduct, had gone out into the world years before, and after much wandering, and an adventurous career, had finally turned his steps in the direction of Roumania, where he obtained the management of a wealthy Bojar's estate. After the Bojar's death he succeeded in winning the widow's hand, and once more regained the position among the nobility which he had lost earlier in life, through his own folly. And now, after an absence of more than ten years, he returned with his wife to make a long visit to his kinsfolk.

Frau von Wallmoden was by no means a youthful bride. She had long since reached maturity, but she was accompanied by her daughter by her first marriage, Zalika Rojanow; and this young Sclave, scarcely seventeen years old, turned the heads of the simple country gentry, who after all had seen but little of the world, by her grace and strange beauty, and the fascination of her warm southern temperament. She was a strange enough figure in this little circle, whose forms and customs she set aside with such sovereign indifference. But there was many an earnest shake of the head, many a word of blame, which was not outspoken, because they only considered the girl a fleeting guest; she would vanish again as suddenly as she had appeared on their little horizon.

Then Hartmut Falkenried came home from his garrison on leave, and met the new family in the house of his friends. He saw Zalika, and his life's destiny was sealed. It was a sudden and blinding passion, for which one too often pays with the peace of a whole life.

He forgot the wishes of his parents, their plans for his future, and his quiet, warm attachment for his youth's playfellow, Regine. He had eyes no longer for the simple woodland flower, which yet bloomed young and fresh for him; but, inhaling the fragrance of the strange and beautiful exotic, all else sank into insignificance. In an unguarded hour he threw himself at her feet, and told her of his love.

Strangely enough, Zalika returned his affection. Perhaps it was according to the old adage of extremes meeting, for this man was, in every particular, her opposite; perhaps it flattered her to see that a word, a glance from her, could so powerfully effect this earnest, quiet officer, who, even then, had a touch of melancholy in his disposition. Enough, she accepted him, and with joy he clasped his affianced bride in his arms.

The news of their betrothal aroused a storm in the family circle. From all sides came objections and warnings. Zalika's mother and step-father were sorely opposed to it, but resistance only increased the ardor of the young lovers. The engagement, in spite of kinsfolk, was soon an established fact, and six months later Falkenried took his young bride to his own house.

But the voices which had foretold unhappiness from this marriage were prophetic.

It was not long before the brief intoxication of joy was followed by bitter disenchantment. It had been a fatal error to believe a woman like Zalika Rojanow, who had grown up in the unrestrained freedom of a disorderly, extravagant Bojar family, could accommodate herself to the rules and restrictions of a settled German household.

The only life she had ever known, and the only life which suited her temper, was one of excitement and outward splendor. A house full of guests, horses, cards, hunting, racing, and the utmost liberty of conversation with the men of her acquaintance; this was the life she had led in her Roumanian home.

She had no notion of duty and no understanding for the obligations and requirements of her new position. And this was the wife who must adapt herself to the narrow life of a little German garrison town, and direct the household of a young officer with but limited means at his command. That it was impossible for her to do so, was shown within the first few weeks. Zalika began at once; regardless of all prudent considerations, to order her house after the same fashion as her father's, and squandered her large marriage portion right and left.

In vain her husband pleaded with and admonished her; she paid no heed to him. She had nothing but jeers for forms and ceremonies which were sacred to him, only a shrug of the shoulders for his strict ideas of honor and propriety. Soon there were violent quarrels, and Falkenried recognized, too late, what his precipitancy had done for him.

He had had great faith in the power of love, notwithstanding all the warnings he had received about Zalika's foreign birth, and the seal which her erratic education had stamped upon her character. But he had now to learn that she had never loved him; that it was the whim of the hour, or, more probably, the fleeting passion of a moment, which had made her throw herself into his arms. And she saw in him only an uncomfortable companion, who spoiled all her pleasure in life with his foolish pendantries and his laughable notions of honor with which he wished to bind her hand and foot. But with it all, she feared this man, who, in his energy and force, was striving to bend her characterless nature to his will.

The birth of little Hartmut did nothing to relieve the strain of this unhappy marriage, but it was a tie which, outwardly at least, still bound them together. Zalika loved her child passionately, and she knew her husband well enough to recognize fully, that if it ever came to a separation between them, he would demand the boy. That thought alone kept her by his side, while Falkenried suffered intensely, hid his misery in his own breast, and gave a brave front to the world.

But, in spite of all, the world knew the truth; it knew things of which the husband had never dreamed, and was only silent out of compassion for him. But at last there came a day when his eyes were opened, and what had been so long an open secret to all his little world excepting himself, was known to him.

The immediate consequence of this knowledge was a duel, in which Falkenried's antagonist fell.

Falkenried was sentenced to a long imprisonment, but very soon released, for every one recognized that he had only fought to vindicate his wounded honor.

In the meantime the suit for divorce had been begun, and a decree obtained; Zalika made no contest, nor did she venture to approach her husband again.

Since the last terrible hour when he had called her to account, she trembled at the thought of him. She made desperate efforts however to secure possession of her son, but all in vain.

Hartmut was given to the father unconditionally, and Falkenried barred the mother's every effort with iron inexorableness. Zalika made many attempts to see her son once more, but to no purpose, and fully convinced at last, that she could accomplish nothing, she returned to her own country and her mother's house.

For years her husband had heard nothing from her, until now when she suddenly and unexpectedly appeared in the neighborhood of the German capital, where Major von Falkenried had assumed control of a large military school.

It was the eighth day since Hartmut's arrival at Burgsdorf. Frau von Eschenhagen was in her sitting-room, and opposite her sat the Major, who had arrived but fifteen minutes before.

Her conversation must have been as disagreeable as it was earnest, for Falkenried listened with a face which grew darker at every word, as she went on with her account.

"Hartmut seemed to me greatly altered after the third or fourth day he was here. The first few days nothing could check his overflow of spirits, and indeed one morning I had to threaten to send him home. But, all of a sudden, he became silent and quite downcast. He attempted no more of his mad pranks, spent hours by himself in wandering through our woods, and when he returned from his solitary rambles, just sat and dreamed with open eyes, so that we often had to arouse him as if from a sound slumber. 'He's beginning to think of the future,' Herbert said, but I said: 'There's something more than that wrong; there's something back of all this.' So I took Will to task and questioned him closely; he astonished me with what I extorted from him. He was in the conspiracy. He had surprised the mother and the son one day at their tryst, and Hartmut had pledged him to secrecy, and my boy had really kept silence towards me, me, his own mother! He finally confessed the little he knew, after I had talked to him seriously. Well, it won't happen a second time. I'll look after my Will more sharply for the future."

"And Hartmut, what does he say?" interrupted the father hastily.

"Nothing at all, for I haven't spoken a syllable to him on the subject. He would probably have asked why he had never been allowed to see, or speak to his mother, and that question can only be answered—by his father."

"He has heard it all from the other side, by this time," answered the father bitterly. "Though, of course, he has not heard the truth."

"That is what I feared, so I didn't lose a moment in communicating with you after I discovered the thing. And what will you do?"

"I'll have to think that over," responded the Major with enforced quiet. "I thank you, Regine. I suspected mischief when your letter came urging me to come over at once. Herbert was right, I should not have allowed Hartmut to leave my side for an hour, under any circumstances. But I believed him to be so safe from every approach here at Burgsdorf. And he was so rejoiced at the thought of spending his little vacation here, had so set his heart upon it, that I had not the strength to refuse him;—and then he is seldom happy except when away from me."

A hidden pain lay in the last words, but his listener only shrugged his shoulders.

"That's not altogether the boy's fault," she answered, outspokenly. "I keep my Will under pretty sharp discipline, but he knows well enough, in spite of all that, that he lives in his mother's heart. Hartmut has never learned as much of his father; he only knows his severe, unapproachable side. If he imagined that you almost adored—"'

"He would at once misuse the knowledge and leave me weaponless with his flattery and caresses. He'd rule over me as he does over every one else who comes near him. His comrades follow him blindly, and are as often punished as he for his misdoings. He has your Willibald completely under his control, and his teachers treat him with especial indulgence. I am the only one whom he fears, and, as a natural consequence, the only one whom he respects."

"And you believe fear to be the only weapon to use against him? just now, too, when his mother is, without doubt, overwhelming him with lavish caresses? Do not turn away, old friend, you know I have never mentioned that name before you, but now that it is brought unavoidably to the front again I must speak plainly. I must admit we could expect nothing less from Frau Zalika, than that she would appear again. Nothing would have been gained even if you had not allowed him to leave your side, for you could not guard a lad of seventeen like a little child. The mother would have found some way to see her child, and that is her right—I should do the same."

"Her right?" interrupted the Major violently. "And you say that to me, Regine?"

"I say it, because I know what it is to have an only son. It was right for you to take your child, for such a mother was not fit to educate him; but that you should refuse to let her see her son again, after an absence of twelve years, is a hardness and cruelty which can only be prompted by hate. No matter how great her guilt may have been—the punishment is too hard."

Falkenried looked gloomily on the ground; he knew there was truth in her words; at last he said slowly:

"I should never have believed you would espouse Zalika's cause. Once I injured you deeply for her sake. I tore asunder a bond—"

"Which never had been united," broke in Frau von Eschenhagen, anxious to avoid the subject. "It was only a plan of our parents, nothing more."

"But the thought was a familiar and cherished one in our childhood's years. Do not seek to shield me, Regine, I know only too well how I treated you then—and myself too."

Regine looked straight at him with her clear, gray eyes, but there was something like moisture in them as she answered:

"Well, well, Hartmut, it's all over now, so many years that I do not hesitate to admit that I would have had you then, willingly enough, and perhaps you would have been able to make something more out of me than I have become. I was always a headstrong creature, you know, and not easily ruled, but I should have obeyed you, perhaps you alone, of all the world. But when Willibald Eschenhagen led me to the altar three months after your own marriage, the situation was reversed, and I took the reins in my own hands and began to govern, and have had plenty of practice since then. But let's not talk of that time so long gone by. I never have borne any grudge against you, you know that; we have always been friends in spite of everything, and if you want my assistance or advice now—here I am."

She held out her hand and he placed his own in it.

"I know it, Regine, but in this matter I can only help and advise myself. If you will send Hartmut to me now, I'll speak with him."

Frau von Eschenhagen arose at once to fulfil his wish, but as she left the room she murmured half aloud:

"If it be not already too late. She blinded the father and made him almost insane once; she has surely done as much for the son by this time."

In about ten minutes Hartmut entered; he closed the door behind him, but remained standing near it. Falkenried turned to him. "Come near, Hartmut, I wish to speak with you."

His son obeyed, but reluctantly. He knew already that Willibald had confessed, and that Regine had summoned his father at once, but, united to the shyness with which he always approached his father, there was to-day an obvious defiance, which did not escape the Major. He gave his handsome young son a long, gloomy look.

"My sudden arrival does not appear to surprise you. Perhaps you know why I am come!"

"Yes father, I imagine why!"

"That is well; then we need waste no time with explanatory words. You have learned that your mother still lives, she has seen you and spoken with you. I know that already. When did you see her first?"

"Five days ago."

"And have you seen her daily since then?"

"Yes, at the Burgsdorf fish pond?"

Questions and answers were alike short and precise. Hartmut was accustomed to the abrupt, military manner of his father, for in all his intercourse with him, no superfluous word, no hesitancy or evasion of an answer, was permitted.

To-day Falkenried was especially abrupt, in order that he might conceal his intense excitement from his son's unpracticed eye. But Hartmut saw only the earnest, unmoved countenance, and heard only the cold, severe accents as his father continued:

"I have nothing for which to reprove you, for in this matter I have given you no commands and no word has ever been spoken on the subject between us. But now I am forced to break the silence. You have always believed your mother dead, and I have tacitly encouraged this belief, for I have wished to protect you from recollections which poisoned my life. Your youth at least should be free, I said. But I have not been able to carry out that plan, I see, so now you must learn the truth."

The father paused a moment. To a man of his sensitive feelings it was torture to discuss this subject with his son, but there was no option now, he must speak farther.

"When I was a young man I loved your mother devotedly, and married her against the wishes of my parents, who saw only unhappiness for me in a union with a woman from a foreign land. They were right, the marriage was a most unhappy one, and was finally dissolved by my desire. My son was awarded to me unconditionally, for it was my absolute right. More I will not tell you, for I cannot denounce a mother to her own son, so let that be enough for you."

Short and bitter as this declaration was, it made a singular impression upon Hartmut. His father would not denounce his mother to him, to him, who heard daily the bitterest accusations and invectives against his father from her lips.

Zalika had, as might be supposed, cast all the blame of the separation upon her husband and his countless tyrannies, and her son, who had suffered so much from his father's austerity, gave a willing ear to all her tirades. And yet these few short, earnest words had more effect than all Zalika's passionate outbreaks. Hartmut felt instinctively on which side the truth lay.

"And now, to the main point," Falkenried went on. "What was the tenor of your daily interviews?"

Perhaps Hartmut had not expected this question; a deep red overspread his face, he was silent and cast his eyes on the ground.

"Ah, you do not care to repeat it. I desire to know it. I command you to answer me!"

But Hartmut was still silent; he only pressed his lips closer together, and looked defiantly at his father, who had come close to him now.

"You will not speak? Perhaps a command from the other side keeps you silent? No matter, your silence tells me more than any words. I see how much you are estranged from me already; a little longer with such influences, and you would be lost to me forever. These meetings with your mother are now at an end. I forbid you to see her again. You will go home with me to-day and remain under my protection. Whether that appears cruel to you or not, it must be, and you must obey."

But the Major erred when he believed his son would, as formerly, bow to his stern decree. Hartmut had been for the past few days in a school where all the antagonism of his nature had been aroused against his father.

"Father, you cannot, you dare not order me thus," he cried out now in great excitement. "It is my own mother whom I have found at last, the only one in the whole world who loves me. I will not be separated from her again as I once was. I will not be forced to hate her; threaten, punish me, do what you will with me, but I will not obey this time, I will not obey!"

All the ungovernable passion of his nature broke out in these words; an unearthly fire gleamed in his eyes, and his hands were clenched; every fiber quivered in wild revolt; he was resolved to fight out this battle with his father to the bitter end.

But the burst of anger which he expected did not come. Falkenried looked silently at him, but with a glance of earnest, sad reproof.

"The only one in the whole world who loves you," he repeated slowly. "You seem to forget that you have a father."

"Who has never loved me," cried Hartmut with excessive bitterness. "Since I have found my mother, I have learned for the first time what love is."

"Hartmut!"

The boy seemed almost staggered by this strange tone, vibrating with pain, which he had never heard in all his life before, and the defiance which was about to break forth anew, died on his lips.

"Because I have had no flattering words and caresses for you, because I have been strict and severe in my training, have you doubted my love?" said Falkenried, even in that same strange tone. "Do you know what that severity has cost me against my only, my dearly loved child?"

"Father!" The word had a shy, hesitating sound, but it was not the old shyness and fear; there lay in it a joyful, almost incredulous astonishment, and Hartmut gazed on his father's face as if he could never take his eyes from it. Falkenried put his hand on his son's arm and drew him nearer, while he continued:

"Once I was ambitious, had proud hopes of life, great plans and projects, but I received a blow from which I could never recover. If I strive and struggle now, Hartmut, the only spur I have in life, besides my sense of duty, is you, my son. All my ambitions are centered in you. I strive for nought else on earth but to make your future great and happy; and you can become great my boy, for your talents are unusual, and your mind is as capable for good as for evil. But there is something more, there are dangerous elements in your nature which are less your fault than your fate, and which must be curbed in time, before they obtain a mastery over you, and plunge you into misery. I have been severe with you in order to expel the germs, but it has not been easy for me."

The youth's countenance was in a glow, he hung with bated breath upon his father's every word, and now he said in a whisper, behind which he could scarcely conceal his joy:

"I never dared to think you loved me, you were always so inflexible, so unapproachable—" he broke off and looked up at his father, who put his arm around him and drew him closer to himself. Their eyes met in a long, tender gaze, and the iron man's voice broke as he said softly:

"You are my only child, Hartmut, all that remains to me of a dream of happiness which vanished, leaving only bitterness and disenchantment in its wake. I lost much and bore it;—but if I were to lose you, you,—I could not bear it."

He held his son close in his arms, and the boy threw himself sobbing on his breast, and in this passionate embrace all else seemed to sink from view. They had both forgotten the threatening shadow from the past which was forcing itself between them.

In the meantime Frau von Eschenhagen was harangueing Will in the dining-room. She had already performed that duty once this morning, but she thought the occasion required a second portion. The young heir looked sorely disturbed, he felt himself in a false position both as regarded his mother and his friend, and yet he was quite innocent in the matter. As a dutiful son he listened patiently to the tirade, and only threw a wistful glance now and then toward the table upon which the evening meal was already spread, and of which his mother took not the slightest notice.

"This is what comes of it, when a boy has secrets behind his parents' back," she said in conclusion. "Hartmut will be well watched now, and the

Major won't deal any too gently with him, either, and you, I think, will refrain from assisting in any more plots, if I have anything to say."

"I had nothing to do with it," said Will, defending himself. "I only promised to be silent, and I had to keep my word."

"You should never keep silence toward your mother. She is always and ever an exception," said Frau Regine, decidedly.

"Yes, mamma, that was probably what Hartmut thought; that's how he acted toward his mother," said Willibald, and the remark was so just that nothing could be said in contradiction; it provoked Frau von Jischenhagen none the less, on that account.

"That's something different, something quite different," she answered shortly. But her son asked obstinately:

"Why is it something different here, then?"

"Do not bother me any more with your talk and your questions," his mother went on angrily. "That is a thing which you do not understand, and about which you have no business to trouble your head. It's bad enough that Hartmut has brought you into the affair at all. Now be quiet, and don't trouble me any more about it. Do you understand?"

Will was silent as requested. It was the first time in his life that he had been catechised so sharply and had received so severe a lecture. At this moment his uncle Wallmoden, just back from a walk, entered the room.

"I hear Falkenried has come already?" he said to his sister.

"Yes," she answered. "He came immediately upon receipt of my letter."

"And how did he take the news?"

"Quietly enough, outwardly; but I saw only too well that he was moved to his very soul. He is alone with Hartmut now, and the pent-up storm will burst."

"How unfortunate. But I warned him of all this as soon as I heard of Zalika's return. He should have spoken to his son at once. Now I fear he is adding a second blunder to the first in seeking, with commands and force, to prevent further meetings. That fatal stubbornness of his, which knows no alternative, is terribly out of place now."

"Yes, and their talk has lasted a long time already. I'll just go and see how they're getting on, and whether the Major is too severe or not. You remain here, Herbert. I'll be back immediately."

She left the room, and while Wallmoden paced the floor dejectedly, his nephew sat alone at the supper-table, which no one but himself seemed to notice. He did not venture to eat his supper, for his mother was in anything but a pleasant humor to-day, and he felt no liberties were to be taken. Fortunately she came back in a short time with a gleam of bright sunshine across her face.

"It's all right," she said shortly and concisely. "He has the boy in his arms and Hartmut is clinging to him. They can do as they please now. God be praised! Now you can eat your supper, Will; the confusion that the house has been in all day is over at last."

Will didn't wait to be told twice, but began his meal at the word. Wallmoden shook his head and said half aloud:

"If it only really is over at last!"

Neither Falkenried nor his son perceived that the door had been softly opened and closed again.

Hartmut still clung to his father. He seemed to have lost all shyness and reserve in his newly found happiness. He was so tender, so caressing, that perhaps the Major was not far wrong in saying he would be left defenseless when his son learned of his great love for him. He said little; but pressed his lips again and again to his boy's forehead, and his eyes never left his son's glowing face, which was so near his own. At last Hartmut said softly:

"And my mother?"

A shadow darkened Falkenried's face, but he did not unclasp the arms which held his son.

"Your mother will leave Germany as soon as she learns that she must keep aloof from you," he said, this time without harshness, but most decisively. "You may write her that I will allow you to correspond with her under certain conditions, but I cannot nor dare not allow any personal intercourse."

"Father, consider—"

"I cannot, Hartmut, it is impossible!"

"Do you hate her so much, then?" asked the boy reprovingly. "It was you that sought the divorce, not my mother; she told me so herself."

Falkenried's lips trembled, and bitter words were on them; he felt like telling his son, once for all, that his honor had demanded the separation; but he looked in his child's dark, questioning eyes, and the words died on his lips. He could not betray the mother to her son.

"Let that question rest," he said gloomily. "Perhaps later, you may learn to appreciate my reasons. Now I cannot spare you the bitter alternative; you can only belong to one of us, and must shun the other; you must accept that as your fate."

Hartmut bowed his head; he felt that nothing more was to be said. That all meetings with his mother must cease when he was again under the rigid discipline of the institute, he knew full well; now he was at least permitted to write to her, which was more than he had ventured to hope.

"Well, I will tell my mother," he said, dejectedly. "Now that you know all, you will not oppose my seeing her again?"

The Major was startled; he had not thought of such a possibility.

"When were you to see her again?" he asked.

"To-day, at this hour, at the lake in the wood. She is already waiting for me there."

Falkenried had a fierce battle with himself; a voice within him warned him not to permit this meeting, but he felt that it would seem cruel for him to refuse.

"Will you be back in two hours?" he asked at last.

"Certainly father, or sooner, if you desire it."

"Well, go," said the Major with a deep sigh. It was only his sense of justice which forced the permission from his lips. "As soon as you come back, we will go home. It is nearly the end of your vacation anyway."

Hartmut, who was on the point of starting, turned back suddenly. The words brought forcibly to his mind, what he had forgotten in the last hour, the compulsion and severity of the hated regimen he would again have to endure. He had never ventured openly to avow his aversion for the army, but this hour, which took from him all shyness towards his father, also removed the seal from his lips. After a moment's hesitation he returned to his father, and putting his arm around his neck, said:

"I have a request, a most earnest request to make of you, which I know you will grant, as a proof of your love for me."

The Major's brows contracted as he asked, reprovingly:

"Do you need any proof? Well, let's hear it."

Hartmut clung still closer to him and his voice assumed its sweetest and most flattering tones, and the dark eyes were almost irresistible in their look of entreaty, as he said beseechingly:

"Do not let me become a soldier, father. I do not like the profession you have chosen for me, and I shall never learn to like it. If I have until now, bowed to your will, it has been with repugnance and secret hatred, for I have been wretchedly unhappy; but I have never dared until now, to tell you of it."

The frown on Falkenried's brow deepened, and he unfolded his son's arms from his neck.

"In other words you will not obey," he said in a bitter tone, "and for you obedience is more necessary than anything else."

"I cannot endure force and compulsion," Hartmut broke out passionately. "And the service is nothing else but force and slavery. Always and eternally, obedience; never to have your own way, but ever, day after day, to bow to an iron discipline. Always the same still, cold forms, with your own feelings never allowed to come to the surface—I cannot bear it longer! Everything within me strives for freedom, for light and life. Let me leave it, father; do not confine me longer in such chains. I shall die, I shall suffocate!"

He could not have chosen more ill-advised words with which to plead his cause, to a man who was heart and soul a soldier. They sounded passionate and bitter, yet his arm was still on his father's shoulder; but the Major pushed him back now.

"I had thought the service an honor, and no slavery," he said cuttingly. "It is pretty bad when my own son is the first one to bring it to my notice. Freedom, light and life! Perhaps you think when one reaches his seventeenth year he has acquired the right to plunge into life without any further care or guidance. For you, freedom from restraint would mean destruction."

"And if it did?" cried Hartmut, quite beside himself. "Rather destruction with freedom, than longer life with such restraint. For me the army means bondage and slavery—"

"Silence! Not a word more," ordered Falkenried, so threateningly that the youth, in spite of his fearful passion, was awed. "You have now no choice, and woe to you if you forget your duty. First you must become an officer and do your duty as such to the full, like your comrades; then, if you are still of the same mind and I have no power to prevent it, you can leave, but if I am alive then, I will receive my death blow when my only son—runs away from the service."

"Father, do you take me for a coward?" interrupted Hartmut. "If there were only a war and I could stand in battle—"

"Yes, you would plunge madly and blindly into danger, and, with that very self-will which knows no discipline, rush on to destruction. I know, only too well, this wild, measureless desire for freedom from every restraint, which knows no limits, recognizes no duties; I know from whom you have inherited it, and to what it will eventually lead. But as long as you are under my jurisdiction I will hold you fast to that 'slavery' whether you hate it or not. You shall obey and learn to yield while there is yet time; and you shall learn it. I give you my word for that."

His voice had again the old harsh sound to which his son was so well accustomed, and every vestige of tenderness had died out of his face. Hartmut knew that prayers or defiance were alike useless now. He uttered no syllable, but the old demon-like gleam in his eyes, which robbed him of all his beauty, was again manifest land on the lips so tightly pressed together lay a strange, evil expression as he turned silently to leave the room. His father followed him with his eyes, again he heard the warning voice which came to him as a presentiment of coming evil, and he called his son back.

"Hartmut, you'll be back in two hours? You give me your word for it?"

"Yes, father." The answer sounded angry, but steadfast.

"Very well, then I will treat you as a man. You have pledged your word and may go in peace; be punctual."

The young man had only been gone a few minutes when Wallmoden entered.

"I knew you were alone," he said. "I would not have disturbed you, but I saw Hartmut hasten across the garden just now. Where is he going so late?"

"To his mother, to take leave of her."

The diplomatist looked up startled at this unexpected intelligence.

"With your consent?" he said surprised.

"Certainly, I gave him permission."

"How unwise. I thought you would have seen to it that Zalika did not accomplish her ends; and now, whether it's right or wrong, you are sending your son to her."

"Only for an hour, and only for a farewell, which I could not refuse. What are you afraid of now? Not that there will be any foul play? Hartmut is no baby to be carried off in a carriage in spite of himself."

"But if he were willing it would be a different matter."

"I have his word that he'll be back in a couple of hours," said the Major with emphasis.

Wallmoden shrugged his shoulders: "The word of a boy of seventeen!"

"Who has had a soldier's education and knows the significance of his word of honor. That gives me no anxiety; my fears are in another direction."

"Regine told me you and he understood one another at last," remarked Wallmoden, with a glance at his friend's dark, gloomy face.

"For a few minutes; then I had to be the stern, hard father again, and this last hour has shown me how hard a task it will be to conquer and direct this unruly, undisciplined nature, but for all that, I must and will subdue it."

His friend stepped to the window and looked out upon the garden.

"It is twilight already and the Burgsdorf fish-pond is half an hour's walk from here," he said, half aloud. "You could have this last meeting held in your presence if you saw fit."

"And see Zalika again? Impossible! I could and would not do that."

"If this farewell does not end as you anticipate—if Hartmut does not come back?"

"Then he would be beneath contempt, a liar," said Falkenried, "a deserter too, for he already carries arms at his side. But do not insult me with such thoughts, Herbert. It is my son of whom you speak."

"He is Zalika's son also. But we won't discuss it any more. They are waiting for you in the dining-room; you will not go to-night?"

"Yes, in two hours," answered the Major, steadily and quietly. "Hartmut will be back by then—I'll answer for it."

The gray shadows of evening already lay on field and meadow, and they grew each moment thicker and darker. The short hazy autumn day was at an end, and the clouded sky brought the night down more quickly than usual. A woman's figure could be seen pacing impatiently up and down on the shore of the little lake. She had a dark mantle drawn closely around her shoulders, but she paid little heed to the frosty evening air which was blowing about her; she was feverish with expectation, and her ear was strained to catch the first echo of approaching footsteps.

Since the first day on which Willibald had surprised them both, and they had been forced to take him into their confidence, Zalika had chosen a late hour in the afternoon, and a lonely place in the wood for her meetings with her son. She was accustomed to meet him before the twilight began, in order that he might not attract attention by returning late to Burgsdorf. He had always been punctual, but to-day his mother had waited already an hour, in vain. What accident had detained him, or had their secret been disclosed? Since a third knew it, she was prepared for such a contingency.

All was so silent in the wood that the rustle of her gown and her light footsteps as she walked to and fro, were the only sounds which greeted her ear.

Beneath the tall trees lay long nocturnal shadows; over the pond where there was more light, being free from shade, hung a faint vapory cloud, and over yonder in the meadows, where a pool of water, concealed by the mossy moorland, had formed, the mists had gathered still more thickly and hung like a gray-white veil over all the heath. The air from the meadows was blowing damp and chill.

At last there was a light step, faint and uncertain—then, as it came on quickly in the direction of the pond, firmer and more resolute. Now a slender figure came in view, scarcely recognizable in the gathering darkness, and Zalika flew to meet her son, who, in the next minute lay in her arms.

"What has happened?" she asked amidst the wonted stormy caresses. "Why are you so late? I had begun to despair of seeing you to-day. What detained you?"

"I could not come sooner," Hartmut explained, still breathless, after his long run. "I come from my father."

Zalika drew back.

"From your father? And he knows—?"

"All!"

"So he is at Burgsdorf? Since when? who told him?"

The young man related in a few words all that had happened, but he had not finished when a bitter laugh from his mother interrupted him.

"Of course, they are all in the plot together to keep me from my child. And your father? He has threatened and punished you again as if you were a criminal, because you have been in your mother's arms?"

Hartmut shook his head. The memory of the moment when his father drew him to his breast was yet before him, despite all the bitterness with which the scene had ended.

"No," he said sadly, "but he has forbidden me to see you again, and sternly commanded me to part from you."

"And in spite of all, you are here? O, I knew it!"

Her words had a joyful sound.

"Do not triumph too soon, mamma," her son answered her bitterly. "I only came to say good-bye."

"Hartmut!"

"Father has given me permission to see you this time, and then—"

"Then he will take you away again, and you will be forever lost to me. Is that it?"

Hartmut did not answer, he only threw himself upon his mother's breast with a wild, passionate sob, which had as much anger and bitterness in it, as pain.

It had now grown quite dark and the night was upon them, a cold, misty, autumn night, without moon or starlight, and over in the meadows, where the vapor was so dense, a light rain had just begun to fall, and through the rain and the mist a blue shimmering light appeared, now faint and dull, now with a clear, bright gleam like a flame.

It disappeared, then started forth again a second and a third time—the will-o'-the-wisp had begun its unearthly, spectral dance.

"You are crying!" said Zalika holding her son fast in her arms. "I have long foreseen this day, and if young Eschenhagen had not surprised us the other morning, I should before this have given you the choice between returning to your father and forming some other plan."

"What other plan? What do you mean?" asked Hartmut, perplexed.

Zalika bent over him and although they were alone, her voice sank into a whisper.

"Will you allow this tyranny to go on, will you permit yourself to be separated from your mother and our holy love trodden under foot, without asserting yourself, or protecting our joint right? If you do permit it, you are no son of mine, and my blood does not flow in your veins. He sent you to bid me farewell, and you take his word as final. Do you really come to take leave of me, for long years, in all probability?"

"I must do it," her son broke out despairingly. "You know my father. Against his iron will there is no appeal."

"If you return to him—no! But who will force you to return?"

"Mamma. Do not tempt me, for the love of heaven!" he cried trying to free himself from the arms which held him so fast, but the passionate voice still whispered in his ear:

"What alarms you in the thought? You but go with your mother, who loves you with a boundless love and will live only for you. You have often complained to me that you hate the service into which you are forced. Have you forgotten your longing for freedom? If you go back you have no option, for your father will bind you fast in the chains, and he will but shorten the links, when he sees you are intolerant of them."

She had no need to tell her son this, for he knew it all better than she could tell him. Scarcely an hour since, had he not heard the words: "You shall obey and learn to yield while yet there is time."

His voice was full of bitterness as he replied.

"In any case, I must go back. I have given my word to be at Burgsdorf again in two hours."

"Really?" asked Zalika, sharply and scornfully. "I thought as much. I see he treats you like a child, marks out your every step for you and gives you your allotted time, as if you had no judgment or mind of your own; but the time has gone by to treat you thus, you are old enough to assume the prerogatives of a man. The day has come when you must show that you are a man in action as well as word. A promise wrung from one is valueless; tear asunder this invisible chain by which you are held, and set yourself free."

"No—no," murmured Hartmut, with another effort to free himself, but his mother held him fast in her arms. He turned his face away and looked with hot eyes into the dark night, upon the desolate blackness of the wood and across at the will-o'-the-wisp, still pursuing its erratic course, now rising with convulsive, trembling flame, now sinking into the ground beneath, only to come up again quivering and glimmering. There was something ghostly and horrible, and withal strangely fascinating in the ceaseless dance of this imp of night.

"Come with me, my son," Zalika begged, in those dulcet tones which were hers, as well as her son's. "I have long since prepared all for your coming; I knew of a certainty that this day would surely come. My carriage is waiting a short distance from here. We can soon reach the railway station and will be far on our way before they are any the wiser at Burgsdorf. With me lies freedom, life, happiness! I will take you away and show you the great world, and when you are once in it, you will learn to breathe freely and enjoy life, as one redeemed from slavery. I know what it is to be liberated from slavery. I, too, wore the chains which, in an hour of foolish fascination, I forged for myself, but I should have torn them apart in the first year had it not been for my unborn child. O, freedom is sweet, as you will soon learn."

She knew only too well the words to choose to accomplish her purpose. Freedom, life, happiness. They signified so much. They echoed and re-echoed in the heart of the boy, whose longing for freedom had always been repressed by a powerful hand. Now like a picture from a magician's hand, the fairy-like visions of promised liberty stood before him. He need but stretch out his hand and it was his own.

"My word," he murmured with a last feeble attempt to rescue himself. "My father will despise me—"

"When you have attained to a great, proud future," Zalika interrupted him excitedly, "then go to your father and ask him if he dares to despise you; he would bind you to the earth, but you have wings to fly above it. He does not understand a nature like yours, and never will. Will you destroy yourself for the sake of a mere word and be a slave forever? Come with me, Hartmut, with me to whom you are all the world."

She led him slowly away, and he did not tear himself from her, but, as she caressed him and called him fond names she felt that his going was under protest, and that she had needed all her wiles to accomplish it. A few minutes later the pond was deserted, mother and son had disappeared, and even the sound of their retiring footsteps had died out in the night air. Over the moor moved only that weird, spectral life. The flashing lights appeared and sank again in restless play,—mysterious breaths of flame from the deep.

CHAPTER III

It was autumn again, and the warm, golden light of a September day lay upon the woodland, which stretched away like a green ocean as far as eye could reach.

Hill and valley alternated with each other, all forest clad, and many a mighty and moss-grown trunk in that great wilderness told of the forest primeval which in the early days had covered all this part of South Germany. Elsewhere in the land, railways had been built, until there was scarcely a hamlet whose slumbers were undisturbed by the shrill scream of the locomotive—but "the forest," as the people called it, remained apart, cut off from the world, a vast territory many miles in width, like a great, green island, unmoved by the waves of commotion and progress from without.

Here and there amid the forest green a little village peeped out, or an old castle reared its gray and weather-beaten battlements on high, as if protesting against its impending decay. There was but one building in the whole region which yet stood strong, intact and massive, notwithstanding it was gray with age.

It was called Fürstenstein, and was originally built as a hunting box, for the use of the sovereign. The duke's head forester occupied it all the year round; and during the hunting season some members of the ducal family always held court there for several weeks. It had been built in the early part of the last century, with the lavish waste of room which marked the style of that period. Standing on a high elevation, it commanded a superb view over the surrounding country.

The approach to the castle allowed no view of its proportions, for woods covered the hill upon which it stood, and in places tall fir trees threw their shadows on tower and turret, so that one scarcely realized the immensity of the building until he stood quite at the entrance gate. There were also a number of little structures clustering around the main edifice, which had been added at different periods. Time was not allowed to make inroads here; everything was in perfect order and repair, and the countless rooms on the second floor were always kept ready for the prince, who took possession of them at any time.

The head forester, von Schönau, had occupied the immense ground floor for years, and between filling his house with guests, and making frequent visits to his neighbors, managed to have a very agreeable time, notwithstanding the lonely situation.

He had visitors now; his sister-in-law, Frau Regine von Eschenhagen had arrived yesterday, and her son was expected soon. The two daughters of the Wallmoden family had made good marriages; while the elder married the heir to Burgsdorf, the younger had wedded Herr von Schönau, the son of a wealthy landed gentleman of a noble South German family.

The sisters, in spite of the distance which separated them, had always maintained a close and affectionate intercourse, and since Frau von Schönau's death, which occurred a few years after her marriage, Frau Regine had kept up the intimacy with her brother-in-law.

It was a singular enough friendship which existed between these two, for they always met, armed cap-a-pie, for battle. They were both strong, inconsiderate natures, and every time they saw one another they quarrelled, and as regularly made their peace again, always promising there should be no further strife between them, which promise was kept until their next dispute, for which some opportunity would give rise, sometimes within an hour after their reconciliation, when another pitched battle would begin, as passionate and wordy as the last.

At the present moment there seemed a truce between them as they sat on the terrace in front of the reception room. The head forester, in spite of his advancing years, was an erect, stately man, with strong, sunburnt features; his hair and beard were slightly gray, but still luxuriant. Now he leaned back in his chair listening to his sister-in-law, who generally did most of the talking. Frau Regine was now in her fiftieth year, but the last ten years had not changed her much; her life ran on so smoothly and evenly.

A wrinkle was to be found here and there in her face, and silver threads were weaving their way into her dark hair, but the gray eyes had lost nothing of their clearness and sharpness, the voice was as full and resolute as ever, and her bearing as erect and energetic as formerly.

"Willibald will be here in eight days," she was saying. "The harvesting was not quite done; but everything will be finished within the week, and then he can come to meet his bride. The matter has been settled between us for a long time, but I was resolved to postpone it for some time, for what did a young thing of sixteen or seventeen, with childish notions still in her head know about the orderly direction of a household? Now that Toni is twenty years old, and Will twenty-seven, it is all right. Are you still perfectly satisfied that this betrothal is the best thing for our children's future?"

"Perfectly satisfied," assented the head forester. "I think everything is as it should be. One half my fortune will go, some day, to my son, the other half to my daughter, and I think you may be well content with the portion I have set aside as Toni's wedding gift."

"Yes, you have been very liberal. As to Will, he came into possession of Burgsdorf three years ago; the remainder of the fortune remains, by the will, in my hands, and at my death goes, of course, to him. But I've seen to it that the young people won't suffer. I have made ample provision for them."

"No need for haste. We are only going to celebrate the betrothal now; the marriage won't be until next spring."

And now the first cloud appeared on the clear heaven of their perfect harmony. Frau von Eschenhagen shook her head and said dictatorially:

"We won't postpone it any longer now. The wedding must take place this winter. Willibald has no time to get married in the spring."

"Nonsense, a man always has time to get married," declared Schönau, just as dictatorially.

"Not in the country," asserted Frau Regine. "There something else must be considered; first work, then pleasure. That's always been the rule with us, and that's what I've taught Will."

"I trust he'd make an exception as regards his young wife; otherwise he's little better than a milksop," cried the forester, angrily. "Above all, Regine, you must remember my stipulation. My Toni has not seen your son for two years. If he does not please her—she has free choice, you understand."

His speech touched his sister-in-law on her most sensitive point; her motherly pride was outraged.

"My dear Moritz, I have more confidence than you, apparently, in your daughter's good taste. As for the rest, I hold to the good old custom that children should marry whom their parents select. It was that way in our day, and we have found no cause of complaint. What do young people know of such serious matters any way? But you have let your children have their own way from the very start; any one could soon tell that there was no mother in this house."

"Well, was that my fault?" asked Schönau, incensed. "Perhaps, I ought to have given them a step-mother. I suggested it to you once, but you wouldn't hear of it, Regine."

"No, I had been married once," was the dry answer, and it seemed to increase the head forester's irritation. He shrugged his shoulders spitefully.

"Well, I certainly think you had no cause for complaint against poor Eschenhagen. He, and all his people at Burgsdorf danced when you piped. With me you would not have ordered the regiment about so easily."

"In about four weeks," Frau Regine declared calmly, "you would all have been under my command, Moritz."

"What! You say that to my face? Well, I'd just like to prove it for once," retorted Schönau, full of wrath now.

"Thank you, I shouldn't care to marry a second time, so give yourself no uneasiness."

"I can assure you I didn't mean an offer. I wouldn't think of such a thing for a moment. One refusal was enough for me. So you need not trouble giving me a second one."

With these words the master of the house rose, pushed back his chair noisily, and left his guest abruptly. Frau von Eschenhagen remained quietly sitting alone for some time, then she called out in a friendly tone:

"Moritz."

"What is it?" he growled from the other side of the terrace.

"When are Herbert and his young wife coming?"

"At twelve o'clock," the voice had an ill-tempered ring yet.

"I am so glad. I have not seen him since he was sent to the South German capital, but I have always maintained that Herbert was the pride of our family, and he keeps up enough state for us all. Now you see he is Prussian ambassador at your court, and is 'Your Excellency.'"

"And then he's a young husband of six and fifty, don't forget that," interrupted the forester spitefully.

"Yes, he took his time about marrying, but he made a dazzling match at last. For a man of his years it was no easy matter to win such a wife as Adelheid, young, beautiful, rich—"

"And of common birth," added Schönau.

"Stuff and nonsense! Who asks any questions now-a-days about birth when an immense fortune stands behind it? Herbert can use money now, too; he has been hampered for means his life long, and now, as ambassador, he needs more to keep up the position than he could possibly supply. But my brother need never be ashamed of his father-in-law. Stahlberg was at the head of one of our greatest industries, and a man of honor, through and through. It was a pity he died so soon after his daughter's marriage. At all events they made a very sensible choice."

"So that's what you call a sensible choice, do you, when a girl of eighteen marries a man old enough to be her father?" asked Schönau, who, in the heat of discussion, came back to his sister-in-law again. "To be sure she has a high place in society now, as the wife of His Excellency, the Ambassador, and is a baroness and all that. But to me this beautiful, cool Adelheid, with her 'sensible' ideas, which would do a grandmother credit, is not at all sympathetic. A thoughtless maiden, who falls over head and ears in love, and then declares to her parents, 'This one, or none,' suits me far better."

"Those are fine opinions for the father of a family to express," cried Frau von Eschenhagen, much ruffled. "It's a good thing that Toni inherited my sister's good sense, otherwise she would be coming to you with some such a speech one of these days. But Stahlberg educated his daughter better. I know it from himself. She was trained to follow his wishes, and accepted Herbert at once when he offered himself. But of course you know nothing about educating children; it stands to reason that you should not."

"What? I, a man and a father, and know nothing about educating children?" cried Schönau, red with anger. They were now both on the fair way to have another pitched battle, when they were happily interrupted by the appearance of a young girl, the daughter of the house, who stepped out on the terrace at this moment.

Antonie von Schönau could never be called beautiful, but she had her father's fine figure and a fresh, glowing face, with clear brown eyes. Her nut-brown hair was laid in smooth braids around her head, and her attire, although perfectly suitable for a girl of her station, was yet quite simple. But Antonie was in the first bloom of youth, and that charm outweighed all others. As she stepped out now, looking so fresh and rosy and healthy, she was a daughter after Frau Regine's own heart, and that lady immediately brought the strife to an end and gave her a smiling nod.

"Father, the carriage is on its way back from the station," said the young lady, in very deliberate, almost drawling tones. "It is at the foot of the castle hill already, and Uncle Wallmoden will be here in fifteen minutes."

"Bless me, they have driven quickly!" exclaimed her father, whose face had cleared at the news. "Are the guest chambers in order?"

Toni nodded composedly, as if to say her duties were never neglected; then, as her father left the terrace to watch the approach of the guests, Frau von Eschenhagen, with a glance at the basket which the girl carried on her arm, said:

"Well, Toni, you are always busy."

"I have been in the kitchen-garden, dear auntie. The gardener declared there were no more ripe pears, so I went out to see for myself, and picked a whole basket full."

"That's right, my child," said her future mother-in-law, highly pleased, "you must keep an eye on the servants and use your hands, too, occasionally, if you want to get on in this world. You'll make a fine housekeeper. But come, now, we must go to meet your uncle, too."

Herr von Schönau was already far across the terrace, and was just starting down the broad flight of stone steps which led from the castle court, when a man stepped out from one of the side buildings, and stood, respectful and silent, with his hat off.

"Well, Stadinger, is that you? What's brought you to Fürstenstein?" the head forester called out. "Come here!"

Stadinger approached as commanded; in spite of his snow-white hair he came forward with a firm, erect step, while a pair of sharp, dark eyes peered out from his brown, weather-beaten face.

"I was with the castellan, Herr von Schönau," he explained, "and have been asking him to lend us a few of his servants to help us, for we're busy up to our eyes at Rodeck, and have not people enough for all the work."

"Ah, yes, Prince Egon is back from his Oriental tour. I heard that before," said Schönau. "But how does it happen that he's come to such a small place as Rodeck, with little room and less comfort?"

Stadinger shrugged his shoulders. "Heaven knows! But our young prince follows his own sweet will, and no one dare ask why. One morning the news came, and the castle people hardly know whether they are standing on their heads or their heels. I had enough trouble to get the place ready in two days."

"I can believe that; no one has visited Rodeck for years, but the prince's visit will put some life in the old walls, at any rate."

"Well, it turns everything topsy-turvy," growled the castle steward. "If you only knew how we have been upset, Herr Schönau. The hunting-room is crammed full of lion and tiger skins, and all sorts of stuffed animals, and monkeys and parrots are sitting around in all the rooms. The whole place is in such an uproar from them that one can't hear one's self speak. And now his highness has just announced to me that there are a troop of elephants and a great sea-serpent on the way. I think I struck a blow at them, though."

"What is on the way?" inquired the head forester, who did not believe he had heard aright.

"A sea-serpent and a dozen elephants. I have fought against them with all my might. 'Your highness,' I said, 'we cannot accommodate any more animals, and as to the sea-serpent, such a beast will need water and we have no pond at Rodeck. And if the elephants do come we'll have to chain them to trees in the forest, I know no other way.'"

"'That's just the thing' his highness answered, 'just chain them to the trees, that'll be very wild and picturesque, and we'll send the sea-serpent to board at Fürstenstein; the castle fish-pond is big enough.' Herr Schönau, he will people the whole neighborhood with these monsters, I believe."

The head forester laughed aloud, and gave the steward, who seemed to enjoy his special favor, a hearty slap on the shoulder.

"But, Stadinger, have you really taken all this in earnest? You ought to know the prince better. He certainly does not seem to come back any steadier than he went away."

"No indeed, he does not," sighed Stadinger. "And what his highness does not devise for himself, Herr Rojanow hatches for him. He is the worst of the two. It's hard lines that such a dare-devil should be quartered on us."

"Rojanow? Who is he?" asked Schönau, all attention now.

"I hardly know, but he's come with the prince, who cannot live without him. He met this friend in some heathen country. Maybe he is a half-heathen, or Turk; he looks enough like one, with his dark face and strange eyes. And the fellow, with his airs and orders acts as if he were the lord and master of Rodeck. But he's as handsome as a picture, handsomer even than our prince, who, by the way has given orders that Herr Rojanow is to be obeyed in all things just like himself."

"More than probable it's an adventurer with whom the prince is amusing himself," murmured Schönau, and aloud he said: "Well good-bye, Stadinger, I must meet my brother-in-law now, and don't lose any sleep over the sea-serpent. When his highness threatens you with it again, tell him I will gladly keep it for him in our fish-pond, but I must see it alive first."

He nodded laughingly to the old steward and stepped down to the entrance gateway. Frau von Eschenhagen and her niece were already there, and a minute after he joined them, the carriage turned into the broad, smooth road and was driven rapidly up to the great entrance.

Regine was the first to greet the travelers. She pressed her brother's hand so heartily that he was forced to draw it back. The head forester was somewhat diffident; he had a certain feeling of shyness in the presence of his diplomatic brother-in-law, whose sarcastic tongue he secretly feared.

But Toni did not allow "his excellency" her uncle, or his wife, either, to ruffle her wonted composure.

The years had not treated Herbert von Wallmoden so gently as they had his sister. He had aged perceptibly; his hair was grey now, and the sarcastic lines around his mouth had deepened. But he was the same cold aristocrat as ever, perhaps even a shade colder and more distant. With the exalted position to which he had attained, the feeling of superiority, which had ever been his chief characteristic, seemed to strengthen.

The young wife by his side was always taken by strangers to be his daughter. Unquestionably the ambassador's choice had proved his good taste. Adelheid von Wallmoden was indeed lovely, but her beauty was of that chill, statuesque type which awakens only cold admiration, and she seemed to have been born to occupy the position in the world to which her marriage had raised her. The young bride, not quite nineteen, and only six months a wife, exhibited a coolness of behavior and as complete a knowledge of all the forms and obligations of her social position, as if she had been at the side of her elderly husband for half a lifetime.

Wallmoden was politeness and attentiveness itself to her. He offered her his arm now, after the first greetings were over, to conduct her to her own apartments, and a few minutes later returned alone to the terrace to have a talk with his sister.

The intercourse between this brother and sister was in many respects very singular.

Regine was as uncouth in outward appearance as she was rugged in character, and the direct opposite of her courtly brother in every particular; but still, as they sat side by side now, after their long separation, there was a look on both faces which told that the mysterious bond of kinship was much to them both, despite the antagonism which so often came to the fore.

Herbert was made rather nervous during their conversation, for Regine did not think it necessary to refrain from brusque questioning or candid comment, and her brother was frequently embarrassed and annoyed by both, but he had learned from experience the uselessness of striving to check her open speech, so gave himself up to the inevitable with a sigh. Of course, among other things, she spoke of Willibald's and Toni's betrothal, of which Wallmoden fully approved.

The subject had been worn threadbare long years ago, so there was little really to be said. And now Frau von Eschenhagen branched off on another theme.

"Well, Herbert, how do you feel now you're a married man?" asked his sister. "You certainly were long enough about making up your mind, but better late than never, and I must admit that for an old gray-head like you, you have made a very good selection."

This frank reference to his age did not seem to please the ambassador; he pressed his lips tightly together for a moment, and then answered his sister sharply:

"My dear Regine, you should strive to use a little tact in your conversation. I know my age well enough, but the position which I occupy, and to which I elevated Adelheid by marriage, more than compensates for the difference in our ages."

"Well, that's true enough, and the marriage portion she brought you is not to be despised," assented Regine, quite unmoved by his sharp tones. "Have you presented your wife at Court yet?"

"Yes, two weeks ago, at the summer Capitol. My father-in-law's death prevented my doing so before. But this winter we must keep open house, as my position demands it. I was greatly surprised and pleased at Adelheid's behavior at Court. She acted with a calmness and proud security, upon this entirely strange ground, which was worthy of all praise. I was all the more convinced how wise my choice had been in every respect. Well now, about home matters; before everything else, tell me about Falkenried?"

"Well, what is there for me to tell? Don't you write one another regularly?"

"Yes, but his letters are always short and monosyllabic. I wrote him of my marriage, but his congratulations were very laconic. You must see him frequently, since he has been made minister of war, as you are so near the city."

A shadow darkened Regine's clear eyes, and she shook her head sadly. "You are mistaken, the colonel scarcely ever comes to Burgsdorf. He grows more reserved and unapproachable each year."

"I am sorry to hear it; he has always made an exception of you, and I hoped you could use your influence to bring him often to Burgsdorf. Have you made no attempt to renew the old intimacy?"

"I did at first, but I have finally given it up as hopeless, for I saw that I was only annoying him. There is nothing to be done, Herbert. Since that unfortunate catastrophe he has been turned to stone. You have seen him several times yourself, since then, and know he lives bereft of hope."

Wallmoden's face clouded darkly, and his voice was very bitter as he replied: "Yes, that boy Hartmut has done for him, that's certain. It's over ten years ago now, however, and I did hope Falkenried would take some interest in life again by this time."

"I never hoped that," said Frau von Eschenhagen, earnestly. "The life has all gone from the roots. I shall never forget, as long as I live, how he looked on that fateful evening, when we waited and waited, first with uneasiness and apprehension, then with deadly anxiety. You grasped the truth at once, but I would not let you say a word while there was a chance. I can see him now as he stood at the window staring out into the night, with drawn features and face like death, and to every word of ours only the one answer. 'He will come! He must come! I have his word.' And when in spite of all, Hartmut did not come, and we repaired to the railway station at daybreak, only to learn that they two, mother and son, had taken the express train hours before. God preserve us, may I never see such a look on a man's face again. I made you promise to stay by him, for I thought he would put a bullet through his heart before the day was over."

"You were wrong there," said Wallmoden with decision. "A man of Falkenried's temperament would consider it cowardice to commit suicide, even though the days of his life were one continued torture. I do not venture to think what would have happened though, had he been allowed to carry out his intention at that time."

"I know," interrupted his sister, "that he asked for his discharge, because, with his keen sense of honor, he could not bear to serve longer, after his son had become a deserter. It was a step prompted by despair."

"Yes, and it was his only salvation, that he, with his military knowledge and skill, was not allowed to sink into oblivion. The chief of the General's staff took up the matter and brought it before the King, and they decided that the father should not be allowed to sacrifice himself for a boy's rash action, and that the service could not lose such a highly esteemed officer. So they would not accept his resignation, but permitted him to go to a distant garrison, where the matter was never mentioned in his presence. Now, after ten years, it's buried and forgotten by the whole world."

"With one exception," said Regine sorrowfully. "My heart aches whenever I think of what Falkenried once was, and what he is now. The bitter experience of his marriage made him gloomy and unsocial, but in good time he recovered himself a little, and his whole soul turned to his boy and his boy's advancement. Now everything is lost and the rigid, stark fulfilment of duty is all that remains; all else is dead within him, and as a sequence, all his old friendships have become painful to him—we must let him go his own way."

She broke off with a sigh, as the face of her girlhood's friend came before her mind's eye. Then laying her hand on her brother's arm, she said in conclusion:

"Perhaps you are right, Herbert, when you say that a man chooses more wisely when he has come to years of discretion. You need not fear Falkenried's fate; your wife has good blood in her veins. I knew Herr Stahlberg well; he worked earnestly and with capability, too, or he would never have succeeded as he did in life. And he was ever an honest man, even after he became a millionaire, and Adelheid is her father's daughter, bone and sinew. You have chosen well for yourself, and I rejoice with you from the bottom of my heart."

The little hunting castle of Rodeck which belonged to the princely house of Adelsberg, lay but a few miles distant from "Fürstenstein," in the midst of the deep forest. The small, plain building containing at most but a dozen rooms, had been hastily prepared for the unexpected coming of the prince. It had not been used for years, and had a neglected appearance. But as one stepped out from the dark, gloomy forest upon the light greensward, and saw the old building with its high, pointed roof, and its four little towers guarding the corners, it seemed very picturesque in its loneliness.

The Adelsbergs were old-time princes of the German empire who had long since lost their sovereignty, but who still retained their princely title, together with an immense fortune which included very great landed possessions. The family had dwindled in number so that there were but few representatives left, and only one in the direct line, Prince Egon, and he as owner of the family estates and through kinship on his dead mother's side with the reigning house, played a conspicuous part among the nobility of the country.

The young prince was understood to be very wild and erratic, and a man who was always forming eccentric attachments. He cared little for princely etiquette, and followed the whim of the moment. The old prince had held the reins with a tight hand, but at his death Egon von Adelsberg became his own master, and since that time, had followed his own free course without check or restraint.

He had just now returned from a two years' tour in the East, and instead of going to his palace in the capital, or to one of his magnificently appointed castles, always in readiness to receive him, no matter what the season, he had, on the spur of the moment, decided upon this little hunting castle of Rodeck, where he could not be comfortably housed, and where the few retainers who took charge of the place, were ill-prepared for such an honor. But as old Stadinger had said, no one dare ask why of the prince; he did as the humor of the hour pleased him.

It was the morning of a sunny autumn day. Upon the broad velvety lawn, two men attired in hunting costume, were standing talking to the steward, while in the broad court a few yards beyond, stood a light, open carriage, awaiting its owner's pleasure. The two young men seemed, at a first glance, to resemble one another. Both had tall, slender figures, deeply browned faces, and eyes in which the fiery arrogance of youth burned fiercely; but a nearer view showed how totally dissimilar they were, after all.

It was evident that the younger man, who was about twenty-four years old, owed his dark complexion to his long residence beneath a fierce sun, for his light, curly hair and blue eyes were not the fitting accompaniments for such a browned skin, but were unquestionably German. He had a blonde beard, curly like the hair which surrounded his handsome, open countenance, but the face hardly coincided with one's ideas of perfect beauty. The forehead was somewhat too narrow and the features were not regular, but something in his expression reminded one of clear sunshine, it was so good-natured and so winning.

His companion, who was a few years his senior, had nothing of this sunlight in his face, although his appearance was undoubtedly the more distinguished of the two. Slender, like his companion, he was much the taller, and his dark skin was not the legacy of an eastern sun. It was of that faint brown which makes the freshest face look pale, and the blue-black hair, which fell in heavy locks on his high forehead, only served to heighten this appearance of pallor. It was a beautiful face, with its noble, proud lines so marked and expressive, but there were deep shadows on it, too, on the brow and across the eyes, shadows found but seldom in so youthful a countenance. The great, dark eyes in which a shade of melancholy always lay, spoke of hot, unrestrained passion, and the fire which blazed within them had a mysterious, unearthly fascination. One felt that these orbs possessed some uncanny power, but they were in accord with the man's whole personality, which had about it something of this same strange witchery.

"Well, I cannot help you, Stadinger," said the younger of the men. "The new cases must be unpacked and places found for the things. Where—that is your business."

"But, your highness, it is absolutely impossible!" remonstrated Stadinger, in a tone which showed that he was on a pretty sure footing with his young master. "There's not an empty corner in all Rodeck. I have had the greatest trouble already to house all the people your highness brought with you, and every day chests bigger than a house are arriving, and ever the same cry: 'Unpack that, Stadinger! Make a place for this, Stadinger.' And hundreds of rooms empty in the other castles."

"Stop grumbling, you old ghost of the woods, and make places," interrupted the prince. "The chests that have come must be unpacked in Rodeck for the time being at least, and if the worst comes to the worst, you must find room in your own house for them."

"Yes, indeed, Stadinger has room and to spare in his own house for them," it was the tall, dark man who spoke now. "And I'll superintend the unpacking myself."

"That's a good plan," said the prince, heartily, "and Zena can assist him; she is at home yet, I suppose?"

"No, your highness, she has gone away."

"Away!" cried prince Egon. "And where has she gone?"

"To the city," was the laconic answer.

"That won't do. You should keep your grandchild with you here at Rodeck all winter."

"That matter seems to have arranged itself," answered the steward with quiet dignity. "Just now my old sister, Rosa, is at home with me. If you should come to my humble dwelling, Herr Rojanow, she would feel greatly honored."

Rojanow gave him a glance which was anything but friendly, and the young prince said sharply:

"Look here, Stadinger, you are treating us after a most unwarrantable fashion. You send Zena away, for no reason in the world, and she's the only one worth seeing about the whole place. There's not a woman in Rodeck who isn't past sixty and whose head doesn't wobble from side to side, and as to the belles of the kitchen whom you brought from Fürstenstein to help us out, they're worse looking than our own people."

"Your highness need not look at them," suggested the steward. "I gave strict orders that none of the maids were to come into the castle, but if your highness goes to the kitchen, as you did the day before yesterday—"

"Well, I must inspect my domestic arrangements once in a while. But I won't go near the kitchen a second time, I promise you that. But I'm provoked enough at you for having gathered together all the repulsive looking creatures in the neighborhood as soon as you knew I was coming. You should be ashamed of yourself, Stadinger."

The old man looked his young master full in the face, and his voice had an impressive sound, as he answered: "I am not at all ashamed, your highness. When that prince of blessed memory, your father, assigned me to this peaceful post, he said to me: 'Keep everything quiet and orderly at Rodeck, Stadinger; remember, I depend upon you.' Well, I have kept everything in order around this castle for twelve years, and more especially have I guarded those of my own household, and I mean to do so for the future, too. Has your highness any other orders for me?"

"No, you old boor!" cried the prince, half amused, half angry. "Go on, now; we don't need any sermon on morals."

Stadinger obeyed, he bowed low and marched off. Rojanow glanced after him and shrugged his shoulders with a sneer.

"I admire your forbearance, Egon; you certainly permit your servants to speak very freely—"

"Oh, Stadinger is an exception," declared Egon. "Of late days he has allowed himself great latitude, but as to his sending Zena away he wasn't far wrong. I'd have done the same thing in his place."

"It isn't the first time the old fellow has made so bold as to call us both to account. If I were his master—he'd get his dismissal in this same hour."

"I'm afraid if I attempted that, it would be all the worse for me," laughed the prince. "Such an old heir-loom, who has served three generations already, and trotted me on his knee as a baby, deserves to be treated with respect. I would gain nothing by commanding and calling him to account. Peter Stadinger does what he pleases, and whenever it suits him, reads me a little text into the bargain."

"How you can permit such liberties is incomprehensible."

"It is natural that you should not understand it, Hartmut," said his friend, earnestly. "You only know the submissiveness of Sclavish servants in your own home, and in the Orient. They kneel and prostrate themselves whenever opportunity offers, and betray their masters at every turn, when it can be done with safety. Stadinger is a man with no civility in him. It doesn't make the least difference to him that I am 'your highness.' He is no respecter of persons, and has often said the most insulting things to my face, but I could leave hundreds of thousands in his hands, and he would guard every pfennig, and if Rodeck were in a blaze, and I within it, his seventy years would not prevent him plunging into the flames to rescue me—that's how it is with us in Germany."

"Yes, with you in Germany," Hartmut repeated slowly, as he fixed his eyes dreamily on the forest shadows.

"Are you as much prejudiced against us as ever?" asked Egon. "I had to beg you hard enough to get you to come with me, for you seemed resolved never to put foot on German soil again."

"I would I had not done so," said Rojanow, darkly. "You know—"

"That you associate bitter memories with my country—yes. You told me that much, but you must have been a boy at the time. You should have outgrown your dislike by now. You are, on this point, so obstinately reserved, that to this day I have never learned what it is that you—"

"Egon, I beg you, drop the subject," said Hartmut, almost rudely. "I have declared to you more than once, that I will not and cannot speak on the subject of my early life. If you are suspicious of me, let me go; I have not forced myself upon you, you know that, but I will not endure this questioning."

The hard, proud tone which he used toward his princely friend, seemed not unknown to the latter, who only shrugged his shoulders and said appeasingly:

"How excited you get in a moment; I believe you are right when you maintain that the air of Germany makes you nervous. You certainly have changed since you set foot in the country."

"Possibly; I feel it myself, and I know I annoy you with my queer tempers lately, so you'd better let me go, Egon."

"I will guard you well, instead. I did not catch you so easily that I can let you fly again after all my trouble. So remember that, Hartmut, for I won't let you go free at any price."

The words had a joking sound, but Rojanow seemed to resent them. His eyes were dark, almost threatening, as he replied:

"But what if I will go?"

"But you won't, for I will hold you closer than ever." Egon laid his arm affectionately on his friend's shoulder. "I wonder how this bad, obstinate Hartmut can answer to his conscience for even thinking of leaving me alone. Have we not lived together for nearly two years, and shared the same dangers and pleasures like brothers? And now you talk about deserting me, without even a question as to how I'll get along without you. Do you think I value your friendship so little, dear old fellow?"

The words were so warm and sincere that Rojanow's ill-temper was conquered. His eyes lighted up at the mention of their long and close friendship, and he answered in a voice which bespoke a sincere affection for his friend:

"Do you think that any one but you could have drawn me to Germany at all?" he said, softly. "Forgive me, Egon. I am an unstable nature and have always been a rover since—since my boyhood."

"Well, learn to settle yourself here—here in my home," exclaimed Egon. "I only stay at Rodeck that you may see its many and varied beauties. This old building, hidden away in the midst of the forest, is a veritable production of fairy-land, a woodland poem, such as you will not find at any of my other castles. The others suit me better, though I know this is to your taste. But now I must really go. You won't ride?"

"No, I will enjoy the much-praised poetry of these woods, which seem to weary you so soon. You can make your visit alone."

"I'll admit I'm not a poet like you, who can muse and dream all day long," said Egon laughing. "For a full week we have led hermits' lives, but I cannot live on sunshine, woody odors and Stadinger's sermons any longer. I must see my fellow-men, and the head forester is the only gentleman in the neighborhood; and besides, Herr von Schönau is a splendid, jolly fellow. You will like him when you meet him."

He jumped into the carriage, waved a parting greeting to his friend, and was off. Rojanow looked after him until the vehicle had disappeared behind the trees, then he turned and struck into a path which led into the forest.

He carried a gun over his shoulder, but his thoughts were not bent on sport. He went on heedlessly, with no idea of direction, and with no thought of the distance which he was putting between himself and Rodeck, which was each moment becoming greater.

Prince Adelsberg was right when he said he knew this wild, mountain scenery was to his friend's taste. The very air had for him a certain sorcery. He stood still at last and took some long, deep breaths, but the cloud on his brow had not yet disappeared; it grew darker instead, as he leaned against a tree and cast his eyes around him.

The beauty of the sunny, autumn day, the picturesqueness of the grand old wood, could not bring to this handsome, joyless face one expression of peace or content.

He saw this country for the first time; his boyhood's home lay far to the north, and yet this place, so different from his father's birthplace and his own, brought back the past with all its painful recollections, and awakened anew within him feelings he had thought long dead and buried. Feelings and thoughts which had never troubled him during the long years in which by land or sea, he had drunk of that freedom for which he had sacrificed so much.

The old German woods! They whispered here in the South, just as they had done in the North; the same wind moved the branches of the fir and the oak, and whistled through the tops of the distant pine trees. Yes, these were the self-same voices which had once told all their secrets to the willful boy lying on the mossy bank of the Burgsdorf fish pond.

There was a stir and sound as of some one moving between the trees. Hartmut looked up indifferently, expecting to see an animal of some kind spring out, but he saw instead the fluttering of a light gown between the low bushes, and from a little side path, which he had not before noticed, a young lady stepped out, almost in front of him, and stood hesitatingly, evidently uncertain what direction to take.

Rojanow was roused from his dreaming by this unexpected apparition, and the stranger caught sight of him at once. She appeared surprised, too, but only for a second, then she stepped forward, and said, with a slight bow:

"May I beg you, sir, to show me the way to Fürstenstein? I am a stranger here and have lost my way, and am, I fear, far from the place I seek."

Hartmut had taken in at a glance the young lady's appearance; and resolved immediately to become her guide. He did not know the way for which she inquired, and only had a vague idea of the direction in which the castle lay, but that troubled him little. He bowed gracefully as he said:

"I place myself quite at your disposal, Fräulein. Fürstenstein is some distance from here, and it would be impossible for you to find the way alone. I must, therefore, beg you to allow me to accompany you."

The lady had expected nothing more than that the way would be pointed out to her; this stranger's offer was not altogether agreeable, but she feared she might lose her way a second time, and the perfect politeness with which the offer was made, scarcely left her any choice. After a moment's hesitation she bowed slightly and said:

"I thank you. Pray let us lose no time, then."

CHAPTER IV

Rojanow fastened the strap which held his gun a little more securely, and turned at once into a narrow, half overgrown path, which lay unquestionably in the direction of Fürstenstein.

Without further parley he assumed the role of guide, and the adventure began to have charms for him.

The stranger was certainly lovely enough to inspire him with zeal in her service. The clear, delicate oval of her face, the high, smooth forehead, with its heavy crown of blonde hair, the regular features, were all in perfect harmony. The beauty of the countenance was faultless, though cold and symmetrical, with an expression which betokened energy of character and great strength of purpose. The girl was at most only eighteen or nineteen years old, but oddly enough, she possessed none of that indescribable attractiveness which seems the natural accompaniment of girlhood, nothing of the hilarity and naiveté of youth. The great blue eyes gazed at you earnestly but coldly, and you felt instinctively that the soul which looked out through them never lost itself in girlish dreams of brave heroes and suppliant lovers. The bearing and appearance was haughty and reserved, yet in form and gesture she was gracefulness itself.

Rojanow had time and leisure to notice all this as he directed her course, sometimes behind her, sometimes in front, now holding back the low, overhanging branches, and a second later warning her of some sudden irregularity in the ground. The narrow forest footpath was anything but a pleasant road for a ramble, and was an especially trying passage for the woman. Her dress caught frequently on thorn and branch, and her long gauze veil had to be loosened from more than one bramble, while her feet sank, time and again, in the soft, moist, moss-covered earth. It could not be helped, and yet Hartmut felt in his self assumed position as guide, that he was not covering himself with as much glory as be could have wished.

"I regret extremely, Fräulein, that you are obliged to take so uncomfortable a path," he said politely. "I fear you will be exhausted, but we are in the thickest part of the forest and have consequently no choice."

"I do not become exhausted so easily," was the answer. "I care little about the disagreeable features of the way, if it will but lead me to the goal."

The remark had a somewhat unusual sound coming as it did from the mouth of a young girl; Rojanow thought so, at any rate, and he gave a slight mocking smile as he repeated:

"If it lead to the goal! You are quite right, that is my idea too; but ladies generally cherish other opinions. They prefer to be carried quietly over all the rough places."

"Not all! You err there; many women much prefer going alone, without submitting to watch and ward, as though they were children."

"Well, perhaps there are exceptions. I prize the accident which has afforded me the opportunity of seeing so charming—"

Hartmut, who was on the point of uttering a very florid compliment, stopped suddenly, for the cold blue eyes met his with such a look of surprise and hauteur that the words died on his lips.

At this moment the lady's veil caught once more in the branch of an overhanging thorn, which held it fast. She stopped, and her attentive companion reached out his hand to free the delicate tissue, when she suddenly tore it from her hat, with a quick motion, and left it fluttering on the branch.

Rojanow bit his lips in vexation; the adventure was not at all what he had expected. He had thought to find this young woman a dependent, timid creature, who would be very grateful and would turn to him for protection, just like many another with whom he had come in contact in his rovings; but this pale girl made it very clear to him by a glance, that he was nothing but a guide and must conduct himself as such. Who, and what was she? Still in her teens, and yet acting with all the reserve and self-possession of a great lady, knowing full well how to make herself unapproachable. He resolved to enlighten himself on this matter.

Now the narrow path ended and they stepped out into a small clearing in the forest, with thick woods again to the left. It was not an easy thing just here for a man who knew nothing of the region to decide which direction to take. But Hartmut was not to be daunted, neither did he intend to exhibit any irresolution, so with apparent security he went on in the same direction they had followed from the beginning, and fortunately enough soon struck into a broad wagon road which crossed that part of the forest. Before long, thought Hartmut, they must surely come to some place where they could obtain a view of the surrounding country and get their bearings.

The wider road enabled him to walk beside his companion, and he resolved to enter upon a conversation which the many obstacles in their path had made, until now, almost an impossibility.

"I have hesitated about presuming to present myself to you, Fräulein," he began. "My name is Rojanow, and I am, for the time being, at Rodeck, a guest of Prince Adelsberg, who, if you reside at Fürstenstein, has the advantage of being your neighbor."

"No, I do not belong to Fürstenstein. I am, also, only a guest," replied the lady. The princely neighbor and name of her companion, appeared to be alike matters of indifference to her; neither did she deem it necessary to give her own name in return. She merely bowed slightly as she spoke.

"Ah, then you probably live in the capital, and are only here to enjoy a few weeks of the fine autumn weather?" continued Rojanow.

"Yes."

The monosyllable had a very cold, reserved sound, but Hartmut was not the man to be turned from his course by a rebuff. He was accustomed to overcome all restraints and obstructions by the power of his fascinations, and that one of the sex from which he had never received anything but adulation, should refuse to succumb, was little less than an insult. There lay a charm, too, in the thought that he would force this lovely creature into conversation with him, notwithstanding her reserve.

"Are you pleased with Fürstenstein?" he asked. "I have never been near the castle, and have only seen it in the distance, but it seems to overawe the whole region with its magnificence. A singular taste indeed to find anything lovely in this landscape, and erect a palace here."

"Evidently not your taste, at least."

"I am not specially fond of uniformity, and here there is nothing but sameness. Woods and woods, and nothing but woods—at times one is almost driven to despair."

There was a hidden rancour in these words, as if the poor German forest, with its whispers and its winds was to blame for all the bitterness which lay in the soul of this returned wanderer; it almost seemed as if he must flee from them, for he could hardly endure the simple, earnest song of olden times which fluttered down to him from the tall fir trees. But his companion only heard the slighting tone.

"Are you a foreigner, Herr Rojanow?" she asked.

A black shadow crossed Hartmut's brow, and he hesitated for a moment before he answered, coldly:

"Yes, Fräulein."

"I thought as much from your name and appearance, and from the peculiar opinions which you express, as well."

"At any rate, they are unbiased and candid," answered Hartmut, nettled by the reproof which lay in the last words. "I have been pretty much all over the world, and am just back now from the Orient. To him who knows the ocean with its radiant, transparent blue, or its terrible, deadly storms, to one who has basked in the witcheries of the warmth and light of the tropics, everything here seems cold and colorless; these eternal green forests are, in fact, the only features of a German landscape."

The compassionate shrug of the shoulders with which he concluded, appeared to rouse his companion from her imperturbability. An expression of displeasure crossed her face, and her voice had in it a tone of resentment, as she answered:

"That is altogether a matter of taste. I know, if not the Orient, at least Southern Europe very well; those sunny, glowing landscapes, with their vivid colorings attract one in the beginning—that is true enough—but soon, too soon, exhaust one. You lose all strength and vitality; you can stagnate and dream, but you can never live and work. But why discuss it? Naturally you know nothing of our great forests, or our people either, I presume."

Hartmut smiled with an unmistakable satisfaction. He had succeeded in breaking through this icy reserve. All his arts and blandishments had been exercised in vain, but he now saw that the momentary resentment had added the charm which was needed to her lovely, cold features, so he determined to arouse her still further.

If he felt aggrieved he would also find pleasure in exciting her.

"That sounds like a reproof which I shall have to bear," he said derisively. "Possibly I don't view the affairs of life as you do. I am accustomed to use other scales of measurement for nature, and for mortals as well. 'Live and work!' The whole question hinges upon the definition of these words. I have lived, years at a time, in Paris, that great central point of all civilization, where life ebbs and flows in a thousand streams. He who has been wont to stem the tide in these great, almost overwhelming waters, can nevermore find a place in the little relations, in the narrow judgments and pedantries, in all this marasmus which the noble Germans call life."

The insulting expression which he laid upon the last words, obtained for him his desire. His companion suddenly stood still and measured him from head to foot, while a flash of anger shot from her cold blue eyes. She seemed for the minute to have an angry answer at her tongue's end, but she forced it back, and drawing herself up to her full height, said in a tone of contempt and disdain:

"You forget, sir, that you are speaking to a German—I now remind you of that fact."

Hartmut colored to the roots of his hair at this merited reproof given to a stranger, a foreigner, as she supposed, who had forgotten himself. What if this girl knew to whom she was talking, what if she ever learned —a feeling of shame overcame him for the second, but he was a man of the world and controlled himself once more.

"I beg your pardon," he said, with a slight, half-mocking bow. "I was under the impression that we were merely exchanging impersonal opinions. I sincerely regret having annoyed you, Fräulein."

A scarcely perceptible movement of her head, and a slight shrug of the shoulders showed him that he had no power to really annoy her.

"I could certainly not think of influencing your judgments, but as our ideas are so radically opposed, I think it would be better to drop the conversation altogether."

Rajanow showed no disposition to continue it. Now he knew for a surety that the cold eyes could sparkle and blaze with anger, he had forced them to do it, but the thing had ended otherwise than he had expected. He gave the slight figure at his side a half-inimical glance, and then his eyes lost themselves again in the dense green of the forest.

There was something captivating after all about this forest loneliness under the first light breath of autumn, a breath which touched the leaves tenderly and laid such delicate tints upon them, brightening the lovely landscape with its vivid reds and varied browns, with its glimpses here and there of bright gold where the sunlight pierced the woodland shade. The branches of the tall trees, centuries old, swayed gently to and fro, and threw long, cool shadows across the occasional open spaces, where the wild forest flowers rested on the breast of the moss-covered earth. An occasional pool of water, lying silent and placid, mirrored the clear, blue sky with its fleecy clouds, which seemed to intermingle with the tall green branches, as both cast their reflection in the water beneath. Only the soft rustling of the leaves, and the hum of thousands of insects as they sang together a sweet, dreamy forest song was to be heard. The very sunbeams seemed to echo this melody as they followed closely the two wanderers, as if this man and woman had come beneath their ban and would have some penalty to pay for crossing their shining path so carelessly. Suddenly an unexpected barrier stood in their way. From a thickly wooded elevation, a broad mountain stream came rushing down, seeking its way between bushes and rocks. Rojanow halted abruptly and cast a quick glance up and down, to see if any means of crossing were to be found, but his eyes could discover nothing, and turning to his companion, he said:

"I fear we are in an unpleasant situation here. This stream barricades our path completely. Usually it is no hard matter to cross it, for those mossy stones make a good enough bridge, but yesterday's heavy rain has misplaced them or covered them completely."

The young lady had stopped, too, and was looking up and down the stream also, for some crossing.

"Could we not cross farther up?" she asked, indicating a certain spot above them.

"No, because the water is swifter and deeper in that direction. This is the best place to get across. There is nothing to be done but to carry you over, and that, with your permission, I will do."

The offer was made most courteously, almost hesitatingly, but there was a gleam of triumph in Hartmut's eye, notwithstanding his modest demeanor. This time she must accept his assistance, even if she had left the veil hanging in the thorns rather than do so. There was no choice now, she must trust herself in his arms in order to reach the opposite shore. He came up to her now as if he took her consent for granted, but she drew back.

"I thank you, Herr Rojanow." Hartmut smiled with an irony which he made no attempt to conceal. He was master of the situation now, and thought to remain so.

"Would you rather go around?" he asked. "It will take us more than an hour and here we will be across in a minute or two. You need not doubt the strength of my arms, and I am sure footed; it is not at all a dangerous place to cross."

"I agree with you," was the quiet answer, "and for that reason I will essay to cross it alone."

"Alone? That is impossible, Fräulein."

"To step through a forest brook? I do not consider that an especially difficult achievement."

"But the water is deeper than you believe. You will be wet through and through, and besides—it is really impossible."

"A wetting will do me no harm, for I do not take cold easily. Pray lead the way and I will follow."

That was clear enough and sounded so peremptory that further remonstrance was impossible. Hartmut bowed without speaking, and stepped at once into the water, his high hunting boots serving him good purpose.

He was right enough, the water was deep and swift, and the stones were so slippery that he found it difficult enough to set his foot firmly on them. He had a slight sneer on his lips as he stepped upon the opposite bank and turned to wait for the girl whom he was so anxious to protect, but who rejected all his advances so proudly. Would she venture or would the first step terrify her and force her to call him back? No, she had gathered up her skirts and followed without hesitation, notwithstanding the fact that her silk stockings and thin low shoes afforded no protection whatever. She stepped slowly and carefully on the stones over which he had just gone, until she came to the middle of the stream. Here, while the strong man's foot had been able to find a safe resting place, the woman's smaller one sought in vain for a secure support on the slimy stones. Her high heels were as much in her way as her gown, the edges of which were already thoroughly drenched. Her courage forsook her for the moment, she made several false steps, then stood perfectly quiet and cast an involuntary glance toward the opposite bank, where Hartmut stood watching her in silence, resolved to raise no hand toward her assistance until requested to do so. Perhaps she read this in his eyes and it gave her back her strength. With a look of decision on her face she gave up all further search for a secure stepping stone, and planted her foot firmly on the pebbly bottom of the stream, and a second later, thoroughly wet now, she clutched the low bough of a tree in preference to Hartmut's outstretched hand, and drew herself up on the further bank. Then turning with dripping garments, to her guide, said:

"We will go on, if you please. We cannot be very far from Fürstenstein."

Hartmut gave no syllable of reply, but a feeling akin to hate rose within him as he looked at this woman who preferred such great discomfort rather than come into closer contact with him even for a moment.

This proud, spoiled man whose dazzling personality won all hearts, felt the humiliation which had been forced upon him most keenly, and execrated within himself the chance which had brought about this meeting.

They went on as rapidly as possible now, and Hartmut cast a glance, from time to time, at the slender, silent figure with its heavy bedraggled skirts, the drippings from which marked their course by a long line of moisture. He kept an attentive eye on the woods on either side; this dark forest road must come to an end some time.

His course had been the right one after all, which at least was some slight satisfaction to him. After a few minutes he came to an elevation which afforded him a view of the region round about. Yonder, across a sea of forest trees, rose the towers of Fürstenstein, and at the foot of the hill on which he stood a broad carriage road was plainly visible, and this road, winding through a part of the forest, led directly to the foot of the castle hill.

"Yonder is Fürstenstein," said he, as he turned and spoke to the young girl for the first time since they had left the stream. "It is about half an hour's walk from here, though."

"O, that is nothing. I am grateful to you for guiding me so successfully, but the way is very plain now, and I will trouble you no longer."

"I am subject to your orders," said Hartmut coldly. "If you desire to dismiss your guide so summarily, he will no longer force himself upon you."

The lady felt the reproof implied in his words. After a man had spent a couple of hours in her service, he did deserve something more than a contemptuous dismissal, even though she had found it necessary to keep him at a distance.

"I have taken too much of your time already," she said, unbending a little. "You have introduced yourself to me, Herr Rojanow, and I must, in return, tell you my name before I say good morning—Adelheid von Wallmoden." Hartmut drew a short breath, and a fleeting red colored his face as he repeated, slowly:

"Wallmoden!"

"Are you familiar with the name?"

"I have heard it, but not here, in—in North Germany."

"Very probable; that is my husband's home, and mine, too."

Rojanow's face showed extreme surprise as he heard this young girl, whom he had taken as a matter of course, for unmarried, speak in so matter-of-fact a tone about her husband, but he bowed, and said most courteously:

"I beg your pardon, my dear madame, for mistaking you for a girl, but I could not know you were married. And I now know that I have never had the honor of meeting your husband. The only one of the name with whom I was ever familiar, was a gentleman now past middle life. He belonged to the diplomatic service, and his name, if I do not mistake, was Herbert von Wallmoden."

"That is my husband, and he is at present ambassador to this country. He will be looking anxiously for me now, so I must not linger a moment longer. Again let me thank you, Herr Rojanow." And with a bow of adieu, the lady hurried down the hill toward the carriage road.

Hartmut stood looking after her, like one in a maze; heavy beads of perspiration stood out on his forehead. So soon? He had scarcely set foot on German soil, and here he was met at once by the old names and all the painful memories which their mention entailed.

Herbert von Wallmoden, Frau von Eschenhagen's brother, Willibald's guardian and his own boyhood's friend. Rojanow felt a sharp cut like a dagger thrust through his breast. He drew himself up and threw his shoulders back, as though he would throw from him some overwhelming burden, and the old bitter, mocking smile came to his lips again, as he said, half aloud:

"Uncle Wallmoden hasn't wasted any of his opportunities, that's evident. His hair's gray by this time, but it hasn't prevented him winning a lovely young wife. To be sure, an ambassador is a fine match, and it is evident that Adelheid von Wallmoden was born to marry such a man. She has all the aristocratic airs and manners which are the one thing needful in the diplomatic circle. Doubtless he's had her well trained to take her place in the diplomatic school. Well, he's fared well in this world, there's no doubt of that."

His eyes followed the young wife, who had just reached the foot of the hill, and a deep scowl settled on his brow.

"If I meet Wallmoden here, and perhaps I won't be able to avoid it, he'll recognize me without a doubt. Then he'll tell her all about it, and if she ever sees me again, and gives me one of her contemptuous glances, I'll—" He stamped his foot on the ground with fury at the thought, and then gave a bitter laugh.

"Pah! What need I care? What does this pale, blue-eyed creature, with her cold blood, know of freedom, of the throes of passion, of the storms which come to some lives? Let her pronounce sentence on me. Why should I shun a meeting? I will face her and bid her beware."

And with a haughty movement of his head he turned his back on the slender figure, and strode back again into the woods.

CHAPTER V

The betrothal festivities to which Baron von Wallmoden and his wife had been bidden were carried out to the letter. Antonie von Schönau plighted her troth to her cousin, the heir of Burgsdorf.

The young people had known their parents' plan for years, and were fully agreed as to its accomplishment. Willibald subscribed like a dutiful son, to his mother's opinion that she was the suitable person to choose his life's companion for him, and he had waited patiently her pleasure as to the time when his betrothal should become an accomplished fact; the thought of having his little cousin Toni for a wife was very pleasant to him. He had known her since childhood, and she suited him exactly. She was a girl absolutely bereft of romance, and Willibald knew she would make no sentimental demands upon him, to which he, with the best will in the world, had not the temperament to respond. Toni, for her part, possessed that good taste for which Frau Regine had given her credit. Will pleased her very well, and the prospect of being mistress of Burgsdorf pleased her still better—in short, everything was as it should be.

The newly betrothed pair were at the piano in the drawing-room, and Toni was entertaining her lover with music, not voluntarily, however, but at her father's request, for she herself considered music a wearisome and superfluous accomplishment. But the head forester had insisted that his daughter should show she was not educated in housewifery alone, but had learned something at boarding-school as well. He was walking to and fro on the terrace with his sister-in-law now; they had come there to listen to the music, and discuss for the hundredth time the happiness and prospects of their children. They had, as usual, soon drifted away from pleasant topics and their contention was growing fiercer each moment.

"I really don't know what to think of you, Moritz," said Frau von Eschenhagen, very red in the face. "You don't seem to comprehend the impropriety of permitting such an intimacy. When I ask you who is the school-girl friend of Toni's who is expected at Waldhofen, you answer me coolly and complacently, that she is a singer who has been on the stage of the Court theatre for some time. An actress, a theatrical star. One of those wretched, frivolous creatures who—"

"But, Regine, don't fly into such a passion," interrupted her host angrily. "You speak as though the poor soul had lost her character just because she went on the stage."

"So she has, so she has!" Regine answered excitedly. "Who ever enters that Sodom and Gomorrah goes down to the bottom at once and can never rise again."

"That's flattering to the Court theatre company, at least," said Schönau dryly. "But we go to see them just the same."

"As spectators! That's quite a different thing, though, for my part, I'm opposed to encouraging such people at all. Will goes to the theatre very little, and never without me. But while I, in the performance of my duty as a mother, have guarded him from any intercourse whatever with such people, you permit his future wife to come within their poisonous influence. It's enough to make the heavens cry out!"

She had raised her voice almost to a shriek at the last, partly from excitement, and partly to be heard by her brother-in-law, for the musical production was noisy now, and sent forth loud, discordant sounds through the open glass door. Toni had good strong wrists, and her touch on the piano reminded one of the stroke of an axe on hard wood. Her three listeners had strong nerves, but low speech was certainly an impossibility.

"Let me explain the matter to you," said the forester appeasingly. "I have told you already that this was an exceptional case."

"Marietta Volkmar is the grandchild of our good old doctor at Waldhofen. His son died while still in the flower of youth. The young widow followed her husband the very next year, and the poor little orphan came to her grandfather. That was ten years ago, just after I had been assigned to Fürstenstein. Doctor Volkmar became our family physician, and his grandchild the playfellow of my children. As the school in Waldhofen was a miserable affair, I begged the doctor to permit his little one to come here and share the childrens' instruction. Then while Toni was at boarding-school for two years, Marietta was in the city pursuing her musical education, and, as a matter of course, their daily intercourse ceased. Marietta, however, has always visited us regularly during her vacations, when she came home to her grandfather, and I do not see why I should forbid her doing so as long as she remains respectable and honest."

Frau von Eschenhagen had listened to this reasonable explanation without unbending in the least. She now said spitefully:

"Respectable and honest in a theatre! Every one knows well enough what goes on in such iniquitous places; but you seem to take it as lightly as does Dr. Volkmar, who for that matter looks honest and venerable enough with his open face and long white hair. How he can send a soul entrusted to his care, his own flesh and blood at that, on to certain destruction, is beyond my comprehension."

"Regine, I always thought you a most rational woman, but in this matter you have no sense at all. The theatre and every one connected with it has always been proscribed by you, and yet you know absolutely nothing about it. It was no easy matter for the doctor to allow Marietta to go on the stage. That I know, for we talked it over frequently. It is not for us who sit in warm nests and can provide lavishly for our children, to sit in judgment upon other parents who earn their daily food with labor and bitter care. Volkmar, though seventy years of age, works day and night, but his practice brings him in little, for this is a poor, sparsely settled neighborhood, and after his death Marietta will have nothing."

"Then he should have made a teacher or a companion of her; that is a decent way to earn one's bread."

"God preserve me from bread so earned. No one knows how the poor thing would be used and ill treated. If I had a child who was dearer to me than life, whose fate it was to earn her own living, and I was told that she would have a brilliant future, and put money in her purse if she went on the stage, I would say 'go!' you may depend upon it."

This avowal seemed to take the ground from under Regine's feet. She stood for a moment gazing at him with frightened face. Then she said, solemnly:

"Moritz—it makes me shudder to hear you."

"Well, if it gives you pleasure to shudder, don't stop on my account. But when Marietta comes as usual to Fürstenstein, I will not send her back, neither shall I raise any objection if Toni goes to her at Waldhofen. So we need say nothing more about it."

Then Herr von Schönau cried out to his daughter, who was still pounding away, that the window-panes were rattling and the strings of the piano would be ruined. He did not really care a particle how much noise she made, neither did her aunt, who answered him now, promptly and sharply:

"Well, there's one comfort at least, Toni will soon be married. Then this friendship with the theatrical prodigy will be at an end. I give you my word for it, that no such guests will be allowed within the walls of Burgsdorf, and Willibald will not permit his young wife to keep up any correspondence either."

"That means that you will not permit it," sneered the head forester. "There are no yeas or nays in poor Will's life, he is only the obedient servant of his dear mother. It is really remarkable how you can keep the fellow, a man grown and soon to be a husband, so cowed down and under the lash."

Frau von Eschenhagen threw her head back, more insulted than ever now.

"I believe I understand my responsibilities better than you. Perhaps you would like to reprove me for educating my son to honor and love his parents?"

"Ah, but there's a point where love leaves off and tyranny begins. You have made Will quite stupid under your eternal tutelage. You couldn't let him make his own offer of marriage even. The matter was an old story to you, so you interfered as usual, without giving the poor boy a chance. 'The affair is all arranged for you, children. Your parents have settled it all for you. You are to marry one another. I give you my blessing; now kiss one another, for you are betrothed.' That's the kind of a stand you took. I, also, was taught to love and honor my parents, but if they had attempted to woo my bride for me, they'd have heard me sing another tune. And that boy of yours took it as quietly as possible; I really believe he was rejoiced that he did not have to propose for himself."

The excitement of the two had by this time reached fever heat, and it was a fortunate thing that the noise from the piano drowned all further conversation. Fräulein Antonie had great strength in her hands, and her only idea of music was to make all the noise she could; one would have thought a regiment of soldiers was storming a fort. Just now the noise irritated her father, who wanted to hear himself speak.

"Toni, Toni, don't break the new piano in two with your thumping," he shouted crossly. "What is it you are playing, anyway?"

Toni was working away bravely, notwithstanding the perspiration was running down her face. Near her sat her lover on a little sofa, his eyes shaded by his arm as he leaned back, his very soul steeped, as it were, in the music. At her father's question the fair musician turned slowly on her stool and answered in a half-sleepy tone:

"That is the 'Janizary March,' papa. I thought it would please Will, as he is a soldier, you know."

"Yes; a dragoon by accident," muttered her father, as he stepped over to his future son-in-law, who hardly seemed to appreciate the delicate attentions of his fiancée.

"Well Will, what do you say to all this fine music?—Will, don't you hear me? I believe upon my life he's sound asleep."

The young heir, aroused now by the scolding voices on all sides, rubbed his eyes and looked at them with a dazed, drowsy air.

"What—what is the matter? Yes, it was very beautiful, dear Toni."

"Yes, to be sure it was," cried the head forester with an angry flash of his eye. "You need never trouble yourself to play for him again, my child. But come, let us leave this ardent lover to finish his nap in peace. He has good strong nerves, I must say that for him."

With these words the irate father gave Antonie his arm and led her from the room. But Frau von Eschenhagen, already highly incensed, felt that her son's inattention to his sweetheart was an additional insult, and now turned upon poor Willibald in a fury.

"Well, you have overstepped the limits of common decency, this time!" she cried in a rage. "Your blessed father wasn't much of a carpet knight in his day. He was engaged to me just twenty-four hours when he fell asleep, too, while I played for him; but I waked him up after such a fashion he never did it a second time I can assure you. Now go after Toni this minute and say what you can to excuse yourself; she has reason to be sorely vexed with you."

Regine took him by the shoulder and pushed him out of the door, as she ended her tirade.

Will took all she said quietly enough, and went at once to make his peace with his cousin. He felt really frightened over his ill-timed slumber, but he had been tired, and the music wearied him greatly.

So he was very contrite as he entered the room in which his cousin was standing at the window.

"Dearest Toni, do not be angry with me," he began, apologetically. "It was so hot, and your beautiful music had something so soothing in it that—"

Toni turned to him. It was certainly the first time that the Janizary March had ever been called a soothing composition; but the crushed, penitent look of her lover, who stood like a sinner awaiting condemnation, restored her to good humor, and she held out her hand to him, as she said heartily:

"No, I am not in the least angry with you, Will. I never cared about the stupid music, myself. We'll find something more sensible than that to do when we get to Burgsdorf."

"Yes, that we will," answered Will, cordially, as he pressed the outstretched hand warmly. He would never have thought of kissing it. "You are so good, Toni."

When Frau von Eschenhagen came upon the lovers a few minutes later, she found them absorbed in the milk and cream question. The mode of conducting a dairy in South Germany differed from that common in the North. It was a subject of which Will never tired, and his mother felt grateful in her heart for a daughter-in-law who had no uncomfortable sensitiveness.

A little later, Will found an opportunity to win complete forgiveness. Toni was anxious to get the evening post as soon as it arrived. She complained, also, that something which had been ordered for supper had not been sent from Waldhofen, and that a message which had been entrusted to a groom, had not, she feared, been properly delivered. So Willibald offered to go at once, and set all these vexatious trifles to rights, and his offer was graciously accepted.

Waldhofen was a place of great importance to the mountaineers, though in itself it was but a small town. It was about thirty minutes' walk from Fürstenstein, and was an important centre for all the little villages and hamlets scattered through the forest.

There was seldom a soul to be seen on the streets during the afternoon hours, and it seemed a deserted, desolate place to Herr von Eschenhagen, as he crossed the dreary market-place on his way from the post-office.

He had attended to the other errands first, and delivered the message, which concerned the sending of a chest to Fürstenstein. As the streets were of no interest to him, he turned now into a side road, where there were neat little houses, with fresh, green little lawns in front. The road was uneven and muddy after yesterday's heavy rain, but Willibald was a countryman himself, and paid no heed to bad roads, so he walked on now without a murmur.

He was in a very contented frame of mind, both as regarded himself and the world at large. Here he was, a strong, healthy young man, with a generous share of this world's goods, and the pleasurable thought that he was engaged to be married to a girl who suited him, and who would, he knew, make him a good wife.

A heavy, lumbering carriage came up the narrow, uneven road, along which he was trudging. There was a large trunk strapped on the back, and various bundles and boxes covered the seats within. Willibald wondered to himself why any one had chosen such a miserable little lane, which the recent rains had made totally unfit for vehicles, instead of taking the wide, decently paved street. The coachman seemed to be in anything but a happy frame of mind. He turned now in his seat, and said to the traveler, of whom Willibald had not caught a glimpse:

"Now really Fräulein, we can go no farther. I told you before that we couldn't get through here, and now you see for yourself how the wheels stick in the mud—its a pretty piece of business."

"It is not very far," sounded a clear young voice from the depths of the carriage. "Only a few hundred steps, farther. So please go on no matter how slowly."

"What can't be done, can't be done!" announced the driver in a philosophic tone. "I cannot go forward through this mire, and I won't. We must turn back."

"I will not ride through the town." The clear voice had a decided, defiant tone this time. "If you won't go through this lane, stop, and I'll get out here."

The driver stopped at once, clambered down from his seat and opened the heavy door, and a second later a slender girl jumped from the carriage; jumped skillfully, too, for she landed on a dry place without coming in contact with the mud and mire which surrounded her on all sides. Then she took a view of her surroundings. But just before her the road had an abrupt turn, so she could not see very far.

The young lady was evidently annoyed to find herself farther from her destination than she had supposed. Then her glance fell on Herr von Eschenhagen, who, coming from the other direction, had just reached the bend in the road.

"I beg pardon, sir, but is the road passable?"

He did not answer at once for he was dumb with admiration at the wonderful and graceful leap which she had just made. She had gone through the air like a feather, and landed on the only dry spot on the whole road.

"Don't you hear me?" she repeated, impatiently. "Do you know whether the road is passable or not?"

"I—I am on the road now," he answered, rather staggered by the sharp, dictatorial tone.

"I can see that for myself. But I have no high boots like you. What I want to know is whether the road is as muddy as this all the way or not? Are there any dry places? Great heavens! can't you answer?"

"I—I believe you will find it dry after you get past this bend here."

"Very well, then, I will venture. So you can turn back, driver, and leave my luggage at the post-office opposite the market-place, and I'll send for it. Wait. Hand me down that black satchel, and I'll take it with me."

"But it's too heavy for you to carry, Fräulein, and I can't leave my horses to take it for you," objected the coachman.

"Well, then, give it to that gentleman yonder. It's not very far to our garden gate. Will you please take that black leather satchel, sir—the one on the back seat with the heavy straps. Can't you hurry?"

The little foot stamped impatiently on the ground, for the master of Burgsdorf stood and stared at her with open mouth. It was something new to him to be commanded and disposed of in this way by a young woman; but at the last imperious words he came bashfully forward and took the satchel from the driver's hand. The young lady evidently thought it the most natural thing in the world to ask his assistance.

"There," she said, shortly. "Now, driver, go back to the post-office, and I'll pick my way through the Waldhofen mud."

She gathered her gray traveling cloak and frock around her and stepped along quickly, picking her way carefully as she went, and keeping as close as possible to the low hedge which bordered the road, while Willibald, of whom she took no notice, trotted on behind with her belongings. He thought he had never seen anything half so lovely as this graceful, slender creature, who scarcely reached up to his shoulder, and he feasted his eyes on the little figure as he followed after.

There was something more than ordinarily gracious and pleasing in the young girl's movements, and in her whole appearance, and she carried her little head with its mass of curly dark hair which no hat could keep concealed, with a jaunty air. Her features were irregular, but they wore an expression of saucy defiance, which with her large, dark eyes and rosy mouth, and the little dimple in the chin, made up for all imperfections of contour. The gray traveling costume, while simple in the extreme, was well and tastefully made, and told that its fair wearer was of another world than that of Waldhofen.

The road, after they had rounded the bend, was, as Willibald said, much drier, though they still had to keep close to the low, hedge-hidden wall, and take very careful steps to avoid the wet, muddy hollows. There was no conversation between the two. Will would never have thought of speaking, so he trudged on patiently, while his guide hurried forward as rapidly as the way would permit, and apparently never troubling herself about the meek burden-bearer in the rear.

In about ten minutes they reached a low garden gate at which the girl stopped abruptly. She leaned over, and pulling out a little wooden bar, opened it. Then she turned to her escort, if such he could be called, and said:

"I thank you, sir. Please give me my satchel now."

The satchel, in spite of its small size, was much too heavy for her little hands to hold. Willibald was, for the first time in his life, seized with a knightly impulse, and declared the satchel was much too heavy for her, and that he would carry it to the house for her. She accepted his courtesy with a careless nod of approval, and turning hastily, went through the small, well-kept garden to the back door of the little old-fashioned house, on which the long afternoon shadows were lingering. Now for the first time, the newcomer was seen from within, and an elderly woman started out from the little kitchen, crying:

"Fräulein! Fräulein Marietta, you have come to-day. Ah, what joy, what—"

Marietta flew toward her and put her hand over her mouth.

"Hush! hush! Babette. Speak softly, I want to surprise grandpapa. Is he at home?"

"Yes, the Herr Doctor is at home and is in his study. Will you go right in, Fräulein?"

"No, I'll go into the front room and play a soft accompaniment, and sing him his favorite song! Be careful, Babette, he must not hear us."

She went in on tiptoe, as noiselessly as an elf, across the old hall, and softly opened the door of a little, low-ceilinged corner room; Babette, who, overcome by joy and surprise, had not noticed the stranger standing in the shadow, followed her dear Fräulein. The door was left open, and Willibald could hear a cover laid back cautiously and a chair pushed gently in place. Then she began a low prelude. The sounds which the old worn out spinet gave forth were tremulous and thin, and made one think of an ancient harp; but the maiden's voice recalled the lark's song of rejoicing.

The singing was not long continued, for a door opposite was opened hastily, and an old man with white hair appeared upon the threshold.

"Marietta! my Marietta, is it really you?"

"Grandpapa!" cried the young girl exultantly, as she ceased her song and rushed forward to throw herself in the old man's arms.

"You bad child. Why did you frighten me so?" he said, tenderly. "I did not expect you until day after to-morrow, and intended going to the railway station to meet you. When I heard your voice so suddenly just now, I believed my ears had deceived me."

The girl laughed out gaily like an excited child.

"Ah, I have succeeded in surprising you, grandpapa, haven't I? I came up the back road, but the wheels stuck so in the mud that I had to get out and walk part of the way. I came in through the garden and by the back door—well, Babette, what is it?"

"Fräulein, the carrier is still waiting with the satchel," Babette had just discovered that a stranger was on the premises. "Shall I give him money for a drink and let him go?"

The young man, thus designated as the carrier, still stood, satchel in hand, awaiting Marietta's pleasure. Dr. Volkmar turned at once, and recognizing who it was, cried in a frightened tone:

"Good heavens—Herr von Eschenhagen!"

"Do you know the gentleman?" asked Marietta, without any especial interest or surprise, for her grandfather, being the only physician in the region, of course knew every one.

"To be sure I know him. Babette, take the valise at once. I beg your pardon, sir. I did not know that you were acquainted with my granddaughter."

"Why, we never saw each other before to-day," explained Marietta. "But, grandpapa, will you not introduce me to this gentleman?"

"Certainly, my child. Herr Willibald von Eschenhagen of Burgsdorf—"

"Toni's betrothed!" interrupted Marietta delighted. "O, how comical that we should meet each other for the first time in the mud. If I had known who it was I would not have treated you so cavalierly, Herr von Eschenhagen. I let you walk behind me as though you were a veritable porter. But why didn't you speak?"

Willibald didn't speak now, but looked stupidly at the little hand which was extended to him. He felt he must do or say something, and as it was an impossibility for him to speak, he grasped the little hand in his great, brawny palm and pressed and shook it vigorously.

"Oh!" cried Marietta as she drew back hastily. "You have a terrible grip, Herr von Eschenhagen. I believe you have broken my finger."

Willibald, glowing from embarrassment and mortification, was about to stammer an apology, when the doctor came to his rescue by inviting him to come in. This invitation he accepted without speaking, and followed his host into the house. Marietta took the principal part in the conversation. She gave a very amusing account of her meeting with Willibald. Now that she knew he was her dear Toni's lover, she treated him with all the familiarity and freedom of an old friend. She asked question after question about Toni and the head forester, and her tongue went on without rest or intermission.

To the young man who sat so silent and listened so eagerly, the girl's pleasant, bird-like chatter was quite bewildering. He had met the doctor on the previous day at Fürstenstein and had heard some talk of a certain Marietta who was a friend of his fiancée. Who or what she was, or from whence she came, he did not know, for Toni had not been very communicative on that occasion.

"And to think of this excited child leaving you standing at the back door, while she came in to play and sing to decoy me from my study," said Dr. Volkmar shaking his head. "That was very impolite, Marietta, very impolite indeed."

The young girl laughed merrily, and shook her short, curly hair.

"O, Herr von Eschenhagen has not taken it amiss. But as he only heard a bar or two of your favorite song, I think the least I can do is to sing it all for him now."

And without waiting for an answer, she seated herself at the piano, and again the clear, silvery voice with its bird-like notes, broke forth on the evening air. She sang an old, simple ballad, but with such expression, such pathos and sweetness, that a bright spring sunlight seemed to enter and flood the little rooms of the old house. But no sunshine was half so bright as the joy which lit up the face of the old white-headed man, upon whose forehead lay the shadows of years and sorrow, and on whose cheeks care had pressed deep furrows. With a half-pathetic, happy smile he listened to the old familiar melody, which spoke to his heart like a voice from his own lost youth.

But he was not the only attentive listener. The master of Burgsdorf, who had fallen asleep amid the thunders of a military march, and who had felt himself entirely in accord with Tom when she declared music to be stupid, listened almost breathlessly to the enchanting strains. Such music was a revelation to him. He sat, leaning forward in his chair, as if fearful of losing a single note, with his eyes fastened upon the pretty maiden, who, singing with all her soul, moved her little head backward and forward with a graceful movement as she warbled forth her sweet song. When it was ended Willibald leaned back in his chair with a heavy sigh, and drew his hand across his eyes.

"My little singing bird," said Dr. Volkmar tenderly, as he rose and leaned over his grandchild and kissed her forehead.

"Well, grandpapa," she said teasingly, "has my voice lost anything within the last few months? But I fear it does not please Herr von Eschenhagen. He has no word of commendation for me."

She turned to Willibald with the assumed sulky look of a spoiled child. He rose now and came over to her.

A slight flush diffused his face, and in his eyes, usually so expressionless, shone a new light.

"Oh, it was very beautiful!"

The young singer might be forgiven for having expected something more then these few embarrassed words; but she felt the deep, honest admiration which they conveyed, and understood at once that her song had deeply impressed the taciturn stranger. She smiled pleasantly as she replied:

"Yes, it is a sweet song. I have scored more than one triumph singing it as an encore."

"As an encore?" repeated Will, with no idea of what she meant.

"Yes, at the theatre, which I have just left to visit grandpapa. I was such a success, grandpapa, and the director wanted me to give up all my vacation, but I had surrendered so much of it already to suit him that I declared I would have these few weeks with you."

Willibald listened to all this with increasing astonishment. Theatre, vacation, director, what did it all mean? The doctor noticed his astonishment.

"Herr von Eschenhagen does not know what you are, my child," he said quietly. "My granddaughter has been educated for an opera singer."

"How soberly you say it, grandpapa," cried Marietta, springing up and drawing her little slender figure to its full height, as she said, with an assumption of great dignity:

"For the past five months a member of the renowned and worshipful Ducal Court theatre, a person in a responsible position and worthy of all honor. Hats off, gentlemen!"

A member of the Court theatre company! Willibald drew himself together, as it were, when he heard the fatal words. The well trained son of his mother, he had a great abhorrence for all actors and actresses. He stepped unwittingly, three steps back, and stared in amazement at the young lady who had just made so startling and so frightful an announcement. She laughed out loud as he did so.

"Oh, you need not manifest so much respect for me, Herr von Eschenhagen, I will permit you to stand by the piano. Has Toni never told you that I belong to the theatre?"

"Toni? No!" stammered Willibald, greatly disconcerted. "But she is waiting for me. I must go to Fürstenstein. I have stayed here much too long already."

"How extremely polite," laughed the girl, with a good-natured sneer. "It is not very polite to us, but where your bride is, there should you be also."

"Yes, and with my mother, too," said Will, who had a feeling that something dreadful was threatening him, and to whom his mother seemed a protecting angel. "I beg your pardon, but I have been here much too long already."

He stopped abruptly, remembering that he had said these words once before, but as none better offered themselves to his disturbed brain he repeated them for the third time.

Marietta was half dead from suppressed laughter. Dr. Volkmar declared, most courteously, that he would not think of detaining his guest a second longer, and begged him to give his compliments to the head forester and to Fräulein von Schönau.

The young man scarcely heard him; he reached for his hat, muttering some word of farewell, and was off without delay. He had but one thought, and that was to get away as quickly as possible. The good-natured, scarcely restrained laughter confused him greatly.

When the doctor returned, after having accompanied Willibald to the door, he found his grandchild half suffocated with laughter, while the tears were rolling down her cheeks.

"I don't believe that lover of Toni's is quite right here," she said, as she tapped her forehead with her finger. "First, he carried my satchel and was as dumb as a fish; then he thawed out a little when I sang, and now he is off on a run to Fürstenstein and his mother, before I have a chance even to send Toni a message"

The doctor smiled, but it was a pained smile. He had observed this stranger more closely than Marietta, and knew only too well what caused the sudden and great anxiety to get away from the house.

"Evidently the young man is not much accustomed to ladies' society," he answered evasively; "he's under his mother's thumb apparently, but he seems to please his sweetheart, and that's the main thing."

"He's a handsome man," mused Marietta, "a very handsome man. But, grandpapa, I believe he's also a very stupid one."

Willibald in the meantime had gone, almost on a run, to the nearest street corner, and there he halted and tried to overcome his bewilderment and collect his thoughts. It was some time before he started slowly on his homeward way, and while standing dazed and stupid in the little country road, he threw more than one glance back at the doctor's house.

What would his mother say? She, who all her life had spurned the play-actor as she would a reptile. And she was right, Will saw that clearly; there was a sorcery about such people against which one needed protection.

But if this Marietta Volkmar should see fit to go to Fürstenstein to visit her girlhood's friend! The young heir was horrified at the thought, and assured himself that he was horrified, but there was a new light in his eyes all the while. He saw suddenly, in his mind's eye, the reception room at Fürstenstein, and the piano at which his betrothed had sat so long that day, but in her place was a dainty little figure, with a perfect glory of curly brown hair around her head; and the heavy notes of the "Janizary March" changed into the soft, pleading tones of the old-time ballad, and in the midst of it all, broke out the clear, bubbling laugh which sounded like music, too.

And all this sweetness was lost forever, both in this world and in the next, because it had been seen and heard on the stage. Frau von Eschenhagen had often expressed her views on that subject, and her son, a good, obedient son always, looked upon her as an oracle. But now he heaved a deep sigh, as he said half aloud:

"What a shame! What a lamentable shame!"

CHAPTER VI

The little mountain of Hochberg rose about half way between Fürstenstein and Rodeck. It was celebrated, and justly, for the fine and extensive view which could be obtained from its highest point. An ancient stone tower, all that now remained of a castle long since fallen into decay, stood upon the extreme summit.

A few peasants, more zealous than their neighbors, had built a little inn or house of rest and refreshment at its base. They made a pretense of keeping the mountain roads in order, and demanded a fair toll from the stray tourist who came to climb the winding tower stairs.

Strangers came but seldom, however, into this wild, unknown mountain region. In the autumn especially, visitors were few and far between. This bright, warm September day had, however, proved seductive. Two gentlemen on horseback, attended by a groom, had dismounted at the door and gone up into the little tower, and they had been followed, a half hour later, by some guests from the neighborhood, who had driven up the mountain-side in a light carriage.

The gentlemen were now standing on a little stone platform of the tower, and one of them was talking eagerly and excitedly as he called his companion's attention to certain newly-discovered beauties in the landscape. "Yes, our Hochberg is celebrated, there's no doubt of that," he said finally. "I felt I must show it to you, Hartmut. Do you not think the view across this far green ocean of forest is unparalleled?"

Hartmut did not answer. He seemed to be searching for some particular place through his field glass.

"In which direction does Fürstenstein lie? Ah, I see, over yonder. It seems to be an immense old building."

"Yes, the castle is well worth seeing," said Prince Adelsberg. "You were quite right, though, day before yesterday, to refuse to accompany me there. The visit worried me to death."

"Indeed! You spoke very enthusiastically of the head forester to me."

"Yes, I always enjoy a chat with him, but he had gone driving, worse luck, and only returned just as I was leaving. His son is not at Fürstenstein either, he's at college studying forestry, and so I was entertained by the daughter of the house, Fräulein Antonie von Schönau. I had a weary hour, I can assure you. A word every five minutes, and a minute getting that one out. She's a fine housewife, I fancy, with no brains for anything beyond. It was up hill work talking to her, and no mistake; then I had the honor of meeting her lover. A genuine, unsophisticated country squire, with a very energetic mother, who evidently has both him and her future daughter-in-law well under her control. Oh, we had a highly intellectual conversation, which ended in their asking my advice about the culture of turnips—I'm so well up in turnips, you know. Just then, happily, the head forester and his brother-in-law, Baron Wallmoden, returned."

Rojanow still held the field glass to his eyes, and was seemingly indifferent to his friend's gossip. Now he said in a questioning tone, "Wallmoden?"

"The new Prussian ambassador to our court. A genuine diplomatist, too, if I may judge from appearances; aristocratic, cold, dignified and reserved to the last degree, but good form, very good form. His wife, the baroness, was not visible, but I bore her absence with resignation, for he's a white-haired elderly man, and I doubt not his wife's of the same stripe."

Hartmut's lip curled as he took the glass down from his eyes. He had not mentioned his meeting with Frau von Wallmoden. Why not forget the very name as soon as possible?

"Our romantic loneliness will soon end, Herr von Schönau tells me," continued Egon. "The whole court is coming to Fürstenstein for the hunting season, and I can count on a visit from the duke. He'll come over to Rodeck as soon as he arrives. I'm not overjoyed, I can tell you, for my respected uncle will preach at me about my morals in a way poor Stadinger never thought of doing, and I'll have to stand it, too. At any rate Hartmut, I can take this opportunity to present you."

"If you think it necessary, and the etiquette of the court permits."

"Bah! The etiquette won't be so strictly observed here, and besides the Rojanows belong to one of the Bojarin families of your country."

"Certainly."

"Well then, there's nothing to prevent your being presented. I am very anxious to have the duke meet you, then I'll tell him about your 'Arivana,' and as soon as he hears your play, he'll have it put on the court stage. I've no question of it."

The words conveyed the deep, almost passionate admiration which the prince had for his friend. The latter only shrugged his shoulders as he replied carelessly:

"That is possible, if you intercede for me, but I do not want to owe my success to any man's efforts in my behalf. I am no poet of repute; I scarcely know whether I am a poet at all or not, and if my work cannot make its own way I shall not force it on the world."

"You'll be obstinate enough to let a fine opportunity slip, that's like you. Have you no ambition?"

"Only too much, I fear; perhaps that's the origin of what you call my obstinacy. I have never been able to subordinate myself and conform to the rules of every day life, and as to the restrictions and trammels of your German courts, I could not adjust myself to them."

"Who told you you would have to adjust yourself to them?" questioned Egon laughingly. "You will be flattered and spoiled there, as everywhere else, for you will appear in the heavens like a meteor and no one ever requires stars of that nature to follow a prescribed orbit. Moreover you will be both a guest and a foreigner; and as such will occupy an exceptional position. When in addition to that, the poet's halo shines round your head—"

"You will have found means to bind me to your country, you think?" interjected Hartmut.

"Well yes, I certainly have not supposed that I, myself, possessed the power to attach to us permanently so wild and restless a spirit. But the rising fame of a poet is a bond which is not so easily broken. This very morning I took an oath to keep you here at any cost."

Rojanow gave him a surprised, searching look. "Why this morning?"

"Ah, that's my secret," said Egon mischievously. "But here comes some one to join us. I hear steps on the stairs."

Yes, there were steps coming up the old stone stairway, and a second later the bearded face of the old watchman peered out at the men on the platform.

"Please be careful, my lady," he was saying. "The last few steps are very steep; now here we are on the platform." He held out his hand to assist the lady, who was following him closely, but she paid no heed to his offer and stepped lightly out on the little stone balcony.

"What a lovely girl," whispered Prince Adelsberg to his friend; but Hartmut, instead of answering, was making a deep and formal bow to the lady, who could not conceal a look of surprise when she saw him.

"Ah, Herr Rojanow, you here?"

"I am admiring the fine views from Hochberg of which you, madame, have heard also, apparently."

The prince's face bore a surprised look when he heard Hartmut address this lovely girl as madame, and saw that she knew him. He came forward immediately, in order that he might share his friend's acquaintance, so Hartmut was constrained to introduce Prince Adelsberg to the Baroness von Wallmoden; he made a passing allusion to the meeting in the wood, for the young wife was wrapped in her mantle of icy indifference. It was scarcely necessary to-day, for Rojanow was as fully determined as she, to consider their acquaintance as of the slightest.

Egon cast a reproving glance toward his friend, for he could not comprehend how any one could keep silence about such a happy accident as that of piloting so lovely a woman through the wood. He entered at once, and with animation, into a conversation with the baroness. He spoke of himself as a neighbor, and of his recent visit to Fürstenstein, and his regret, great regret, at not meeting her on that occasion. But with all his chatter, the prince kept himself well within bounds, and was the polite and agreeable courtier. He knew full well that the wife of the Prussian ambassador, no matter how young and beautiful, was not to be approached with vapid, idle compliments. Hartmut had made that error in addressing the unknown girl in the wood, but Egon had the advantage of knowing to whom he spoke, and succeeded at last in thawing the beautiful baroness by his gracious, suave manner. Finally he showed her the landscape, and pointed out and explained the especial objects of interest.

Hartmut did not enter into the conversation at all, but after handing the field glass to his friend, excused himself on the plea of searching for a lost pocket-book. The watchman of the tower volunteered to go in search of it for him, but Rojanow declared he would go and look for it himself. He remembered the exact place, where, as he mounted the stairs, he had heard something drop, but had paid no attention to it at the time. He would go and find it, and then return to the platform. And with a bow he left them.

Egon, under other circumstances, would have expressed his surprise that Hartmut did not accept the old watchman's offer, instead of going himself. But now he saw his friend depart without protest; he was not unwilling to have the field to himself. The baroness had already raised the glass to her eyes, and was following attentively his explanations and comments on the surrounding country.

"And over yonder, behind that mountain of forest, lies Rodeck," he said at last. "The little hunting lodge where we two misanthropes live like hermits, cut off from all the world beside, save the apes and parrots which we brought from the East, and they, by the way, are growing very melancholy in their new home."

"One would never take your highness for a misanthrope," said Frau von Wallmoden with a fleeting smile.

"I confess I haven't much taste for it, myself, but once in a while Hartmut has a touch of the disease, and it is for his sake that I have buried myself in this solitude."

"Hartmut? That is a Hungarian name! It's very surprising that Herr Rojanow speaks such pure German without the slightest accent. And yet he told me he was a foreigner."

"Yes, he is from Roumania, but he was educated, partially at least, by kinsfolk in Germany, from whom he also got his Christian name." The young prince explained so unconcernedly that it was evident he knew as little about his friend's family as did his listener.

"You seem to be very partial to him." There was a slighting tone in her voice.

"Yes, I am indeed," exclaimed Egon, roused in an instant. "And not I, alone. Hartmut has one of those attractive, genial natures, which wins upon all who know him. But the stranger who does not see him unrestrained and at his best, can form no judgment of what he is. Then a flame of fire bursts from his soul, and touches all those with whom he comes in contact. He exercises a charm which none can resist, and where he leads all must follow."

This glowing eulogy was listened to with cool indifference by the young woman, whose whole attention seemed to be centered in the landscape, as she answered:

"You are right, doubtless. Herr Rojanow's eyes indicate an unusually fiery temperament, but their expression is uncanny and surely not sympathetic."

"Perhaps because they have that peculiar and demoniacal expression which is always the indication of genius. Hartmut has great talent; he sometimes frightens me with it, and yet it attracts me irresistibly. I really do not know how I could live without him, now. I shall do everything in my power to make him remain with me."

"In Germany? Your highness sets yourself a hard task. Herr Rojanow has a very contemptuous opinion of our country, I can assure you. He expressed himself most forcibly to that effect, the other day in the wood."

The prince listened attentively. These words explained to him what he had at first thought so singular; why Hartmut had not mentioned to him the meeting with the baroness. He smiled as he said: "Ah, that's why he never mentioned meeting you to me. You probably showed him you did not approve of his candid avowal concerning Germany; you served him just right, for there's no sense in his lying so persistently. He has often angered me with his harangues against my country, all of which I thought he meant, at the time, but now I know better."

"You do not believe, then?" Adelheid turned suddenly and faced the speaker.

"No, I have the proof of it in my hand. He fairly revels in our German scenery. Your ladyship looks at me incredulously; may I tell you a secret?"

"Well?"

"I went to Hartmut's room, this morning, to look for him," began the prince, "and he was not there; but I found on his desk what was better than finding him—a poem which he had evidently forgotten to lock up, for he never intended it for my eyes, that's certain. No pricks of conscience prevented my stealing it, and I have it with me this minute. If you would care to glance at it—"

"I do not understand the Roumanian tongue," responded Frau von Wallmoden, with a slight sneer; "and I imagine Herr Rojanow has not condescended to write in German."

For answer Egon drew a paper from his pocket, and unfolded it. "You are prejudiced against my friend, I see, but I do not want to leave him in the false light in which he has placed himself in your eyes. May I not read this to you, and let his own words be his justification?"

"If you desire."

The words were spoken indifferently, but Adelheid's eyes sought the paper with an expression of keen interest. A few verses, written in a careless, hasty hand, covered the white page. Egon began to read. They were indeed German verses, but in them was a pureness and euphony which told that they could only have been written by a master of that tongue, and the description which they gave was one well known to both listeners. Deep, sad, woodland loneliness, pervaded by the first breath of autumn; endless green depths which swayed and beckoned with their gloomy shadows; fragrant meadows flooded with the golden sunlight; silent stretches of water in the far distance, and the noisy murmur of the mountain brook, as it rushed down from some nearer height. This picture had life and speech in it, too, and had its echoes of an old-time woodland song; the rustle and whisper of the swaying branches sounded to the ear like a soft, low melody, and above all and through all, was the deep, pent-up longing for that peace which was the background of the whole scene.

The prince had begun with fervor, and entering into the spirit of the poem, read clearly and intelligently. As he finished, he turned to the baroness with a triumphant, "What do you say to that?"

Frau von Wallmoden had not lost a word; she had not looked at the reader, though, but had gazed across the distant hills. Now, at the prince's question, she turned slowly. "Is this the language of one who despises our country?" he continued, confident he had the best of the argument. And as he looked closely at her, while demanding justice for his friend, he realized for the first time, just how lovely this Frau von Wallmoden was. The rosy tints of the setting sun softened the look in the lovely eyes, and added beauty to the tender oval of her face; but there was no softness in the cold, deliberate answer: "It is really quite surprising that a foreigner should understand our language so well."

Egon stared at her. Was this all she had to say? He had expected something quite different. "And what do you think of the poem itself?" he asked.

"Very full of sentiment. Herr Rojanow seems to possess a great deal of poetical talent. Many thanks for your field glass, and now I must go down to my husband. I fear he is tired already, waiting for me."

Egon folded his paper without a word and returned it to his pocket. He had been very enthusiastic over his friend's production, and this young woman, colder and more frozen than ever now, chilled him to the bone.

"I have had the honor of meeting his excellency, and will accompany you down, with your permission," he said, courteously.

She gave a slight bow of acknowledgment and left the platform, followed by the Prince, who had grown suddenly very taciturn. He felt annoyed on his friend's account, and regretted now that he had read, what to him seemed such a wonderful poem, to a woman who evidently knew nothing whatever of poesy.

Hartmut had, in the meantime, after leaving the platform, descended the winding stairs slowly. The lost purse was a mere subterfuge, for it lay in its accustomed place in an inner pocket.

Adelheid von Wallmoden had mentioned to the prince, soon after she joined them on the platform, that her husband was awaiting her in the little inn, but that he had not cared to climb the steep, dark stairs. Hartmut knew he could not avoid a meeting, but he would at least brave it without witnesses.

If Wallmoden saw his old friend's son and recognized him, he might not be able, for the moment, to master his surprise.

Hartmut did not fear this meeting, though he knew it would be both painful and uncomfortable. There was but one in the whole world whom he feared; but one pair of eyes under whose gaze he would lack courage to lift his own, and in all probability he would never meet that one.

He could face all others with a proud defiance; he had but exercised his right in abandoning a hated career. He was decided that there should be no questioning or reproving; if he were recognized, he should request the ambassador in a most decided manner, to make no reference whatever to a past with which he was done forever.

Upon the little veranda of the summer inn, Herbert von Wallmoden sat with his sister. The impending arrival of the duke and his court for the autumn hunting had detained the head forester at home, where he was in great demand. The betrothed pair stayed at Fürstenstein, also, and as nothing better offered itself for the day, the three guests decided to come to Hochberg.

The view was especially fine this afternoon and the air was like summer. "This Hochberg is really worth seeing," said Frau von Eschenhagen, as her eyes went searchingly over the landscape. "But we have nearly as good a view here as up above. I certainly will never climb up those dark stairs, and lose my breath to see any more. No, I thank you."

"Adelheid was of a different opinion," responded her brother, as he gave a fleeting glance up the tower. "She suffers neither from fatigue nor heat."

"Or cold either. That was proven the day she was drenched to the skin. She hasn't even a sniffle from it."

"I have requested her to take a servant with her in future when she goes upon her rambles," said Herbert quietly. "To be lost in the forest and have to wade through a brook and then finally be forced to call to her aid a stray huntsman, are things that I do not care to have repeated. Adelheid saw that as clearly as I, and will not go unattended for the future."

"Ah, she's an excellent, sensible wife, a healthy nature through and through, with a proper aversion for adventure and romance," said Regine warmly. "Ah, there are other visitors on the tower. I thought we would be the only guests to-day."

Wallmoden glanced indifferently toward the tall, aristocratic young man who had just emerged from the tower door and was coming toward them; Frau von Eschenhagen's glance was careless, too, but her look changed to one both sharp and intense, and she cried out:

"Herbert, look!"

"At what?"

"At that stranger. What a strange resemblance."

"To whom?" asked Herbert, looking searchingly, too, into the face of the stranger, who was nearer them now.

"It's impossible! That is no passing resemblance. It is he, himself," cried his sister.

She sprang up pale with excitement, with her eyes fixed and staring at the young stranger, who was just putting his foot on the first step of the shaded veranda. Now his eyes met hers, his large, dark, flaming eyes which had so often looked into her own and pleaded for him in his childhood, and all doubts vanished.

"Hartmut, Hartmut Falkenried! You!"

She stopped suddenly, for Wallmoden laid his hand heavily, very heavily, on her arm, and said sharply: "You are in error, Regine, we do not know this gentleman."

Hartmut was startled, when, upon reaching the top step, he recognized Frau von Eschenhagen. The lattice-work had prevented his recognizing her, and for her presence he was not prepared. But at the very moment when he realized who it was, the ambassador's words sounded in his ears. He understood only too well what the tone and words implied and the blood rushed to his temples.

"Hartmut!" Frau Regine called again, looking uncertainly at her brother, who still held her arm fast.

"We do not know him," he repeated in the same tone. "Must I repeat it to you again, Regine?"

She understood his meaning now, and turned with a half-threatening, half-pained glance from the son of her old-time friend, as she said bitterly: "You are right. I was mistaken."

Hartmut drew himself to his full height, and an angry look flashed across his face as he drew a step nearer.

"Herr von Wallmoden!"

"What is it?" answered the other in a sharp, but contemptuous tone.

"Your excellency has but forestalled me," said Hartmut, forcing himself by mighty effort to speak quietly. "I came to request you not to know me. We are strangers to one another."

Then he turned with a haughty, defiant air, and disappeared within the little inn.

Wallmoden looked after him with knitted brow, and then turned to his sister. "Could you not have restrained yourself, Regine? Why make a scene? This Hartmut exists no more for us."

Regine's face showed clearly her intense excitement, and her lips trembled as she answered:

"I am no such staid diplomat as you, Herbert. I have not yet learned to be calm and indifferent when one whom I have for years imagined dead, or gone to ruin, suddenly springs up before me."

"Dead? He was too young to make that a probability. Gone to ruin? That is indeed possible, judging from his life lately."

"What do you mean?" asked his sister excitedly. "What do you know of his life?"

"I know something of it. Falkenried is too dear to me to make me lose sight altogether of his son. I have never mentioned what I knew to either of you. But as soon as I returned to my post, ten years ago, I used my diplomatic position to ascertain what I could concerning them."

"And what did you learn?"

"At first, only what we already knew, that Zalika had taken her son to Roumania. You knew that her step-father, our cousin Wallmoden, had died some time before, and after her divorce from Falkenried she always lived with her mother. From that time we heard nothing of her until she came to Germany to capture her son, but just before she came, as I learned, she inherited a large fortune by the death of her brother."

"Her brother? I never knew she had one."

"Yes, he was ten years her senior, and on attaining his majority had become master of a large estate. His mother's second marriage was childless and he never married. When he met with a sudden death while hunting, Zalika, being next of kin, fell heir to his large possessions. As soon as she entered into possession, she began at once to plan how she could get her son. You know that part of the story. Then they passed a few years in a wild, erratic life upon her Roumania estate, and they fairly flung money away in their extravagance. After that they became bankrupt, and mother and son went out into the world like gypsies."

Wallmoden told all this in the same cold, contemptuous tone as that in which he had spoken to Hartmut and in Regine's face, too, was a look of abhorrence for the wife and mother who had fulfilled so ill the duties of her station. But she could not restrain the anxiety she felt for the son, as she asked:

"And since then? Have you heard nothing further?"

"Yes, on several occasions. Once when I was with the embassy at Florence, I heard her name mentioned incidentally. She was at Rome; then a year after that she was back in Paris again; and sometime later I heard that Frau Zalika Rojanow was dead."

"So she is dead," said Regine, softly. "How did they live all these years?"

Wallmoden shrugged his shoulders. "How do all adventurers live? Perhaps they had saved something from the shipwreck, perhaps they hadn't. At any rate she was to be found in the saloons of Rome and Paris. A woman like Zalika could always find assistance and protection. As a Bojar's daughter she had her title of nobility, and even the forced sale of her Roumanian estate, about which many knew, may have aided her to play her *rôle*. Society opens its arms only too willingly to such as she, especially when they have talent, and that Zalika undoubtedly had. By what means she lived is another question."

"But Hartmut, upon whom she forced such a life, what of him?"

"He's an adventurer. What else could you expect?" said the ambassador in his curtest tone. "He inherited her temperament, and his life with her has developed the dormant tendency. Since his mother's death, three years ago, I have heard nothing of him."

"And why did you keep all this from me?" said Regine, reprovingly.

"I wanted to spare you all I could. You had always given the boy too warm a place in your heart, and I thought it better to let you imagine him dead. Have you ever told Falkenried any of your idle speculations concerning him?"

"Once I ventured to speak of the past to him. I hoped to break through the icy reserve which he always maintains towards me now. He looked at me, I will not soon forget his eyes, and said with fearful impressiveness: 'My son is dead. You know that, Regine. We will let the dead rest in peace.' I have never mentioned Hartmut's name since then."

"I suppose I hardly need counsel you to be silent when we return home," continued her brother. "On no account let Willibald hear of this meeting, for he's so good-natured that he'd be off at once if he heard his boyhood's friend was in the neighborhood. It's much better he should know nothing about it. If there should be a second meeting I will just ignore the fellow. Adelheid does not know him; in fact she doesn't even know that Falkenried had a son."

He broke off suddenly and arose, for his young wife and her escort emerged at that moment from the tower door. The prince greeted the ambassador and his sister, whom he had met a day or two before, and asked quite innocently whether they had seen his friend Rojanow, who had disappeared from the tower a few moments before.

Wallmoden threw a warning glance toward his sister, who stared at the prince in surprise, and answered promptly and politely that he had seen no gentleman, and added that he was just on the point of going in search of his wife, as it was quite time they should return home. The order to the groom was given at once, and a minute later the prince was bowing low to the fair woman and her husband, whom he had accompanied to the carriage. He stood a full minute looking after them when the carriage rolled away.

Hartmut stood at the window of the little public room looking at the trio in the carriage, also.

On his face lay the same deadly pallor as when the name of Wallmoden was mentioned two days before, but to-day it was the pallor of a wild, intense anger. He had steeled himself against question or reproof; these he would have met with supercilious arrogance, but the contemptuous manner in which he had been set aside struck him to his heart's core. Wallmoden's words to his sister, "We do not know him. Must I repeat that again?" incited his whole being to revolt. He felt keenly the sentence which lay in them. And Aunt Regine, too, the woman who had once shown an almost motherly affection for him, she turned her back on him as if ashamed of her first impulse to speak to him. That was too much!

"Oh, here you are at last," sounded Egon's voice from the door. "You disappeared most mysteriously. Well, did you find your pocket-book?"

Hartmut turned toward his friend; he felt he must be on his guard.

"Yes," he said absently. "I found it on the stair, as I expected."

"You might as well have let the watchman get it for you. But why didn't you come back? 'Twas very shabby of you to desert Frau von Wallmoden and me. You have not, I fear, won the lovely lady's favor. You were most ungracious."

"I shall have to endure my misfortune as best I can," said Hartmut with a shrug.

The young prince came nearer, and laid his hand affectionately on his shoulder.

"Or perhaps you incurred her displeasure day before yesterday? It is not your wont to go off on a tangent when you are conversing with a charming woman. O, I know all about it; the baroness thought fit to reprove you for your attack on Germany, and you resented it. Now, a man should agree to everything which comes from such lips."

"You seem to be quite excited," sneered Hartmut. "Better look to it that the gray-haired husband does not grow jealous, in spite of his years."

"Yes, they're a singular couple," said Egon, half aloud, as if lost in thought. "This old diplomat, with his gray hair and his keen, immobile face, and the young wife with her dazzling beauty like a—like a—"

"Northern light, above a sea of ice. It is a question which of the two is farthest below freezing point."

Prince Egon laughed out at the comparison. "Very poetical and very malicious. But you are right enough. I felt the icy breath of this polar star several times myself. It's just as well I did, for it is all that saved me from falling head over heels in love with her. But I think we'd better be starting now, don't you?" He turned to the door to order the groom to bring around the horses.

Hartmut, on the point of following him, turned once more to glance from the window at the carriage, which could be seen through an opening in the trees. He clenched his fist as he muttered:

"We will speak yet, Herr von Wallmoden. I will remain now. He shall not imagine that I am a coward and flee from him. Egon shall bring my work to the notice of the court. We shall see then whether he will dare to treat me like an adventurer. He shall pay yet for that glance and tone."

CHAPTER VII

At Fürstenstein everything was in readiness for the reception of the Court. The ducal party was coming this autumn for the entire hunting season, which lasted for several weeks, and the duchess was expected as well. The second floor of the castle, with its countless rooms, was prepared for the illustrious guests, and some of the officials and servants had already arrived. The little town of Waldhofen, through which the duke would pass, was in a state of excitement, too, as the townspeople made their modest preparations to do the great man honor. The Wallmodens had come for a short visit, but under existing circumstances, decided to prolong it; in fact the duke himself, learning of their whereabouts, and desirous of showing the ambassador and his wife some especial mark of his favor, had expressed a desire to meet them at Fürstenstein. This amounted to an invitation which it would have been unwise to refuse.

Frau von Eschenhagen and her son were to remain also, to have an opportunity of "viewing these Court people close at hand." The head forester, in view of the prospective hunting which was his especial care, had daily interviews with the under foresters and their subordinates, and kept them all pretty well on their legs, that nothing might be neglected. Life at the castle just at present was anything but monotonous. In Fräulein von Schönau's room, this bright morning, there were sounds of gay chatter, and many a clear, good-natured laugh. Marietta Volkmar had come for a little gossip with her old friend, and as usual during such visits, the laughter and the babble knew no end. Toni sat in the window-seat, and near her stood Willibald, who, by his mother's special orders, was to play the *rôle* of sentinel.

Frau von Eschenhagen had not yet been able to accomplish her purpose concerning the opera singer. Her brother-in-law had remained obdurate, and even from her future daughter, whom she imagined so pliant, she had met with decided resistance when she demanded that all intercourse should be broken off between the two. "I cannot do that, dear auntie. You ask too much," Toni had answered. "Marietta is so noble and good. I could not wound her so deeply."

"Noble and good!" Frau Regine shrugged her shoulders over the inexperience of this girl whose eyes she might not open; but she was diplomatic enough to let the subject drop for the present and bide her time. Willibald, accustomed to confide in his mother, had told her of his meeting with Fräulein Volkmar, and how he had enacted the part of porter at her suggestion. Frau von Eschenhagen was, naturally enough, incensed at the thought that her son, the heir of Burgsdorf, should act as lackey for a "theatrical hussy." She drew, for his benefit, a picture of this child of the devil, and explained how it would be an impossibility for her to follow such a shameless life without being thoroughly bad. Willibald, of course, was horror stricken at what he heard, and agreed fully with his mother that his future wife must be protected from so contaminating an influence.

He received orders never to let the young girls be alone, and to watch carefully how this Marietta behaved. At the very first intimation of a disgraceful word or action, Regine would go to her brother-in-law and demand that he should no longer permit his daughter to associate with such an one; then she would call her son as witness, and the incubus would be expelled at once and forever from their presence. Willibald had been on guard when Marietta paid her first visit to Fürstenstein, had accompanied Toni to Waldhofen when she went to the old doctor's to see her friend, and he was now at his post again, to-day, in Antonie's boudoir.

Antonie and Marietta were chatting over the approaching arrival of the Court at Fürstenstein, and the former, who possessed little taste in the matter of dress, was asking her friend's advice about some details of the toilette, and Marietta was giving it eagerly.

"What are you going to wear with this gown?" asked Marietta. "Roses of course, white or very delicate ones. They will suit admirably with this faint blue."

"No, I can't get roses," Toni declared. "I shall wear china asters."

"Better wear sunflowers. Why should you, a young girl, just affianced, too, wear such autumnal flowers? I do love roses so, and wear them whenever opportunity offers. I was so disappointed that I couldn't have one for my hair for the burgermeister's party to-night, but there isn't one to be had in Waldhofen. It is getting late in the year for them."

"The castle gardener has a rose tree in bloom in one of the hot-houses," said Antonie in her sleepy manner, which formed so decided a contrast to her friend's sharp, decisive tones.

Marietta shook her head with a laugh. "They're for the duchess without doubt, so we cannot beg for them, and must think of something in their stead. And now that we are entering upon the toilet question, your presence, Herr von Eschenhagen, is quite unnecessary. You don't know anything about such matters, and our chatter must weary you greatly. But in spite of all, you don't desert us, and what have I done so very remarkable, pray, that you stare at me all the time?"

The words sounded very ungracious. Will was startled, for the last question was only too true. He had just been thinking how well a fresh, half-blown rose would look peeping from those dark, curly locks. Toni, who had not observed how attentively he was gazing at her friend, now said good-naturedly:

"Yes, Will, do go. You'll be wearied to death with our gossip, and I'm not half through yet—I have a great deal to tell Marietta."

"As you will, dear Toni," answered her lover, hesitatingly. "But I may come back again?"

"Of course, whenever you wish."

Willibald went. It did not annoy him in the least, this having to desert his post of observation. He was thinking of something quite different as he stood for a moment alone in a little ante-room. The result of his thoughts was that he left the castle a few minutes later, and directed his steps toward the head gardener's quarters.

Scarcely had he left the room when Marietta sprang up exclaiming:

"Heavens, but you're a pokey pair of lovers!"

"But, Marietta," said Toni, vexed.

"Yes, whether you are vexed with me or not, I must say it. I had expected such a jolly time when I heard you were engaged. You never were particularly lively, but as for this fiancé of yours he don't seem to know how to talk at all. What in the world did he say when he proposed to you? Or did his mother do it for him?"

"Don't jest all the time," said Toni, really angry now. "It's only in your presence he's so silent; when we're alone he can talk glibly enough."

"Yes, over the new threshing-machine which he has invented himself. I heard him talking about it just as I came in, and you were listening all ears. Oh, you'll be a pattern man and wife, and rule Burgsdorf in a most exemplary manner, but heaven protect me from such a happy marriage."

"Marietta, you are very rude," said the young girl, highly incensed now. In the same moment her friend had thrown her arms around her neck, and said coaxingly: "Do not be angry, Toni. I did not mean to be disagreeable, and do indeed rejoice in my heart if you are happy; only you see—every one to his taste; my husband must be different from yours."

"Well, what must he be, pray?" asked Toni, resentful yet, but mollified by her friend's coaxing tone.

"In the first place he must be under my rule and not under his mother's; second, he must be an honest, upright man, of whose protection I can feel assured—that's not inconsistent with petticoat government, so long as I do the governing. He need not be much of a talker. I'll attend to that part myself. But he must love me, love me better than father and mother or houses or lands, better than his threshing-machine, even—I must be first in his thoughts, ever and always."

Toni shrugged her shoulders contemptuously. "You have very childish ideas at times, Marietta; but let us decide about the gowns."

"Yes, we'd better do that at once, for your dearly beloved will come back soon and plant himself down like a sentinel between us. He certainly has a talent for standing sentry. Now as to this blue silk—"

Even now the pros and cons of dress could not go on smoothly, for Frau von Eschenhagen opened the door at this moment, and called Toni to give her advice concerning some household matter. Toni rose at once and left the room, but, instead of following her, her aunt remained and sank down in a chair by the window. Frau von Eschenhagen wished to see for herself. Will had not satisfied her; he had grown red and embarrassed when called upon to repeat the girlish gossip which had taken place between the two maidens, and his mother, who believed all this light chatter but a cloak for something worse, determined to take the matter into her own hands.

Marietta had risen respectfully at the entrance of the elder woman, whom she had met but once before, and whose inimical bearing toward herself she had not perceived in the joy of her first meeting again with her friends. She only noticed that Toni's future mother-in-law was not a cordial woman. This morning Frau Regine looked her over from head to foot with a critical eye. Marietta seemed to her like all other girls, but she was pretty, very pretty—and that was bad. She had short curly hair all over her head—and that was worse.

There was no mistaking Frau Regine's attitude toward the young singer, whom she now begun to question. "You are a friend of my son's betrothed, I believe?"

"Yes, my lady," was the unconcerned reply.

"A friend since childhood, I understand. You were brought up and educated by Dr Volkmar?"

"Yes, I lost my parents when I was very young."

"So my brother-in-law was telling me. And what was your father's calling?"

"He was a physician, the same as grandfather," answered Marietta, more amused than annoyed by this examination, the object of which she did not suspect. "And my mother was a physician's daughter, so we might well be called a medical family, might we not? I'm the only one who has branched off into another profession."

"Ah—what a pity," said Frau von Eschenhagen, impressively. The young girl looked at her puzzled. Was she joking? No, there was no expression of pleasantry on the lady's face as she continued: "You will agree with me, my child, that the descendant of an honorable and respected race should show herself worthy of her family. And you should have thought of that in choosing your vocation."

"Good heavens, but I couldn't study medicine like my father and grandfather," cried Marietta, laughing outright. The matter seemed a joke to her, but her merriment displeased her severe questioner, who said, sharply:

"There are, thank God, plenty of honorable positions for young girls. You are a singer?"

"Yes, madame, at the Court theatre."

"I know it, I know it! Do you feel inclined to resign your position there?"

The question was put so suddenly and in such a domineering tone, that Marietta involuntarily drew back. Since her first meeting with the son, when he had seemed so stupid and silent, and had run off so precipitately, she had decided within herself that he was not of sound mind. Now the thought came to her that his weakness was an inherited disease from his mother; for certainly this woman could not be in her right mind.

"To resign my position?" she repeated. "And why?"

"Upon moral grounds, altogether. I am ready to offer you a helping hand. If you will turn your back upon those paths of frivolity and vice, I pledge myself to obtain for you a respectable position as governess or companion."

The young singer understood at last why the matron had been so concerned; she threw her head back with an angry, half spiteful movement. "I thank you very much. I love my profession dearly, and have no thought of exchanging it for any dependent position. Besides, I fear my education has not fitted me to make an efficient upper housemaid."

"I expected some such answer," Frau von Eschenhagen replied, nodding her head darkly, "but I felt it my duty to make at least one appeal to your conscience. You are very young, and, consequently, are not altogether responsible; the heavier blame falls upon Dr. Volkmar for allowing his son's child to enter such a vicious career."

"My dear madame, I must request you to leave my grandfather out of the play altogether," Marietta spoke excitedly now. "You are Toni's future mother-in-law, otherwise I would not have allowed this questioning. But an insult to my grandfather I will not permit from any human being."

The two excited women had not heard a distant door open, and did not know that Willibald had entered. He seemed frightened when he saw his mother, and slipped something which he carried carefully wrapped in paper, into his coat-pocket, but he kept his place by the door.

"I have no intention of quarreling with you, my child," said Frau Regine in an arrogant tone. "But I am, as you say, Toni's future mother-in-law, and as such deem it my duty to protect her from all improper intercourse. I beg you will not misunderstand me. I am not proud, and the grandchild of Dr. Volkmar is, in my eyes, a fit companion for my niece; but a lady of the theatre will, rightly enough, seek her companions among the theatrical circle, but here at Fürstenstein—you understand me, I hope?"

"Oh, yes, I understand you, my dear madame," cried Marietta, her whole face aflame now. "You need say nothing further; I have but one word to ask. Do Herr von Schönau and Antonie agree with you in what you have just said?"

"As regards the root of the matter, certainly. But I would not have you think for a moment that they would refuse to—" a very expressive shrug of the shoulders concluded this sentence. The upright and truth-loving woman did not for a moment imagine she was guilty of an untruth; her prejudices were deeply rooted, and she could not imagine the head forester not agreeing with her at bottom, notwithstanding his contradictory nature prevented him admitting it frankly; as for Antonie, she was a good-natured little thing, but she lacked the stamina required to end such an intimacy, and her aunt, in consequence, was resolved to end it for her. But at this critical moment something unexpected happened. Willibald stepped forward and said, half reproachfully:

"But, mother—"

"Is it you, Will? What are you doing here?" asked his mother, to whom this interruption was anything but pleasant.

Willibald understood full well that his mother had been ungracious, and he usually retreated as quickly as possible when he found her in a bad humor. To-day he took his stand with unwonted bravery. He came a step nearer and repeated: "But, mother, you must have misunderstood them. Toni never thought of such a thing, Fräulein Volkmar."

"What do you know about it? Do you mean to accuse me of falsehood?" his enraged mother turned on him. "What business is it of yours what I discuss with Fräulein Volkmar? Your bride's not here, you can see that for yourself, so you may go, also, and at once!"

The young heir had flushed deeply at this tone, to which he was well accustomed; but before this girl it seemed to shame him, and he looked as though he would resist his mother's authority for once. His face assumed a defiant expression, but a threatening, "Well, don't you hear me?" conquered him as usual. He turned hesitatingly, and left the room, but the door behind him remained half open.

Marietta glanced after him with a contemptuous curl of the lip and then turned back to her adversary. "You need give yourself no further uneasiness, my dear madame. I have come to Fürstenstein for the last time. As the head forester had received me with his old-time cordiality, and as Antonie was as affectionate toward me as ever, I could not know that they felt that there was a stain upon me on account of the profession which I follow. Had I suspected such a thing I surely would not have inflicted myself upon them. It will not happen in the future, never again."

Her voice failed her, and her face bore a new, pained expression, while it was with difficulty she restrained the tears. Frau von Eschenhagen felt she had gone too far in her candid statement.

"I do not want to annoy you, my child," she said, unbending a little. "I only wanted to make it clear to you that—"

"Not want to annoy me when you say such things to me?" interrupted the girl with flashing eyes. "You treat me like an outcast, not fit any longer for association with decent people, and why? Because I earn my bread with the talent which God has given me, and give pleasure to mankind at the same time. You traduce my old grandfather who made great sacrifices to have me well educated, and who saw me go out into the world with a heavy heart. The bitter tears stood in his eyes as he clasped me in his arms, and said, as he bade me good-bye: 'Be honest and true, my Marietta. One can be that always, no matter what their road in life. When I close my eyes on this world I shall have nothing to leave you. You will have to fight your own battle. Well, I have remained honest and true, and shall remain so, even though everything is not as easy for me as for Toni, the daughter of a rich father, who only leaves her parent's home to go into her husband's. But I don't envy her the happiness of calling you mother."

"Fräulein Volkmar, you forget yourself," said the insulted mother drawing herself to her full height. But Marietta wasn't going to be silenced now, she was too excited.

"O, no, it is not I who forget myself. It was you who insulted me without cause, and the head forester and Antonie must be well under your influence to turn away from me. But no matter. I do not desire the friendship of any girl who will allow herself to be bullied and brow-beaten by a mother-in-law. I am done, once for all. Tell Toni I say that, Frau von Eschenhagen."

She turned away with a passionate motion and left the room. In the front one, however, she could retain her composure no longer, and the hot tears, kept back so bravely until now, forced themselves from her eyes. With a passionate sob the young girl leaned her head against the wall and wept bitterly. She heard her name called in a low, trembling tone, and turning, she saw Willibald von Eschenhagen, in his hand the very paper which he had so hastily concealed in his pocket. It was crumpled now, but within, as he unfolded the paper, lay a delicate spray of leaves with two fragrant half-blown roses.

"Fräulein Volkmar," he stammered again. "You wished for a rose, please accept—" In his eyes and in his whole bearing one could read plainly that he deplored his mother's ruthless candor. Marietta repressed her sobs, the tears were still glistening in her eyes, as she looked up at him with an expression of disdain and contempt.

"I thank you, Herr von Eschenhagen," she said with acerbity. "You heard distinctly the words which your mother spoke to me, and whatever else they may have meant, they most certainly meant that I was to be shunned. Why do you not obey them?"

"My mother has done you an injustice," said Willibald, half-aloud. "And she did not speak in the name of the others. Toni knew nothing about it, believe me. She—"

"Then why didn't you speak out and say so?" interrupted the girl with growing anger. "There you stood, listening to a shameful, insulting attack upon a young, defenseless girl, and hadn't enough manhood to come forward and take her part. True enough, you did attempt something of the kind, but you were well scolded, and sent off like a school-boy, and you went without a word, too."

Willibald stood like one in whose ears heavy thunder is echoing. He had felt most keenly the injustice of his mother's scathing remarks, and was trying in his timid way, to do what he could to make amends and show his good will, and here he was being soundly rated for his pains. He stood and stared at her without speaking, and his silence incensed the girl still more.

"And now you come and bring me flowers," she continued with growing excitement. "Secretly, behind your mother's back, and do you think I would accept such an insult? First learn how a man should behave when he witnesses such an iniquity, then pay attention to trifling courtesies afterwards. Now—now, I will show you what I think of you and your present." She tore the paper from his hand, rolled it like a ball and threw it upon the floor, where she stamped on it passionately with her little foot.

"But Fräulein—" Willibald, vacillating between shame and anger, would have interfered to save his roses, but the dangerous look in the dark eyes warned him to keep back.

"Now we are quits. If Toni knows nothing about all this I am sorry, but I shall stay away for the future rather than expose myself to fresh insults. I pray she may be happy, though I should certainly not be so in her place. I am only a poor girl, but I would never marry a man who was afraid to speak without his mother's permission. No, not if he were heir to Burgsdorf ten times over."

With this she turned her back upon the heir, and a second later left the room.

"Will, what does this mean?" sounded the voice of Frau von Eschenhagen, who stood in the half-open door. As she received no answer, she crossed the room to her son's side with a step and manner which prophesied no good for that young man.

"That was a most remarkable scene which I have just witnessed. Will you be good enough to explain to me what it signifies? That little insignificant thing, bubbling over with passion and anger, telling you the most disgraceful things to your very face, and you standing there like a sheep, taking them all."

"Because she had the right to say them," said Will, still looking down at the scattered rose leaves.

"She had what?" asked the mother, who could not believe she heard aright.

The young heir raised his head and looked at her; his face wore a new and singular expression.

"She had the right of it, mother. It is true you have always treated me like a school-boy, so how could I defend myself against such an accusation?"

"Boy, I believe you have lost your senses," said Frau Regine.

Willibald was roused now. He continued: "I am no boy, I am the heir of Burgsdorf, and twenty-seven years old. You have always forgotten that, mother, and so have I, for that matter, but I remember it to-day."

Frau von Eschenhagen gazed astonished at her son, so tractable all his life until this moment. "I verily believe you are becoming refractory. Let us have no more of it, for you know I would never permit such a thing. What has come over you that you make such reckless assertions? Because I have seen fit to bring this very unsuitable intercourse to an end, and dismiss this Marietta, do you take it upon yourself, as soon as my back is turned, to make formal apologies and present her with roses which you have just plucked for your bride? I don't know what's come over you. It's the first time in your life you ever acted so. Toni will be very much displeased when she learns what has become of her roses. It served you just right to have the little vixen trample them under foot. You won't be guilty of such idiotic folly soon again, I fancy."

"I did not pluck the roses for Toni, but for Fräulein Volkmar," Will explained, defiantly.

"For—?" the name stuck in the excited woman's throat.

"For Fräulein Volkmar! She was wishing she had a rose to wear in her hair this evening, and said she could not get any in Waldhofen. So I went to the gardener and got them for her—now you know all about it, mother."

Frau von Eschenhagen stood like the pillar of salt; she had become deadly pale and for a moment the light seemed to go out; she saw such fearful possibilities that she lost all power of speech and motion. Then suddenly she regained all her old strength. She grasped her son's arm impressively, as if to make sure of him under all circumstances, and said curtly:

"Will—we will start to-morrow."

"Start where?"

"For home. We will start early, at eight o'clock, in order to catch the afternoon express, and reach Burgsdorf the day following. So go at once to your room and do your packing."

The commanding tone did not this time make the slightest impression on her son. "I do not intend to pack," he declared, doggedly.

"You will pack at once, I tell you!"

"No," said the son. "If you wish to go, mother, then go—I remain here."

This was rebellion, and it removed the last doubt in the mother's mind that there was something at the bottom of all her son's assertiveness. She said now in her hardest tone: "Boy, wake up, be yourself again! I really don't believe you know what has come over you. But I will tell you. You are in love—in love with Marietta Volkmar."

She brought out the last words in a towering rage, but Will was not overwhelmed by them. He stood for a moment staring in surprise, as if wondering if it was really that which had overtaken him, then a light seemed to dawn upon him.

"O!" he said, drawing a deep breath, and a slight smile flitted across his face.

"O! is that your only answer?" broke forth the furious mother, who, in spite of everything, still hoped for a contradiction. "You do not even deny it. And this is what I must live to see in my own son, whom I educated so carefully and never allowed to leave my side. While I was having you watch and protect your betrothed from this infamous woman, you were acting a hypocrite. And she playing the virtuous, deeply injured part before me, that creature—"

"Mother, be silent! I will not allow that," interrupted Willibald, angry too, now.

"You will not allow it—what does that mean?"

Frau von Eschenhagen stopped suddenly and listened.

"There comes Toni, your betrothed bride, to whom you have pledged your word, who wears your ring. How do you purpose treating her?" She had at last found the right means to conquer her son, who now hung his head despondently as Antonie entered the room.

"You're here already, are you, Will?" she asked. "I thought—but what is the matter? Has anything happened?"

"Yes," said Regine, who, as usual seized the reins without fear. "We have just received a telegram from Burgsdorf which will compel us to start for home to-morrow morning. You need not be alarmed, my dear child, it is nothing serious, only a piece of stupidity,"—she laid a sharp accent upon the last words,—"a piece of stupidity which will soon right itself, and the sooner its checked, the sooner the matter'll be ended. I'll explain it all to you later, but we must go now; it can't be helped."

Antonie listened attentively, but it required more than such an announcement to stir her from her wonted repose, and the declaration that it was nothing of moment, satisfied her. "But will Willibald have to go, too?" she asked, without any special eagerness. "Can not he remain?"

"Well, Will, can't you answer your sweetheart?" said his mother, fastening her sharp gray eyes on her son. "You know best all the circumstances. Do you think you can afford to remain here?"

There followed a short pause. Willibald's glance met his mother's; then he turned toward Toni and said, in a half-depressed tone:

"No, Toni, I must go home—there is nothing else for it."

Toni took this news, which another girl would have seriously deplored, very calmly, and began to plan where they had better dine on the morrow, for they had a long distance to go by carriage before they would meet the express train. This troubled her much more than the parting, and she finally decided that she would prepare a luncheon for them, so that they need have no care concerning their midday meal.

Frau von Eschenhagen triumphed in her heart as she went to announce their departure to her brother-in-law. She had already decided upon the reason which she would give him for their abrupt departure. Of course a great many things could happen on a large estate like Burgsdorf, which would demand the master's presence at a moment's notice. So the head forester knew no more than his daughter, although he, in his blindness, had been the cause of it all.

As for the rest, Frau Regine did not doubt her powers as soon as she should get her son away from the influence of this witch. He had shown himself amenable to reason at the last moment. She would say nothing more to him now, save to point out what his betrothal to Toni demanded from him as a man of honor, and what a fatal error it had been to allow another to influence him even for an hour.

"Wait, my son," she said grimly, to herself, after conning over the whole thing for the twentieth time, "wait. I will teach you to harbor such sentiments, and revolt against your mother. Only wait until I get you to Burgsdorf, then God have mercy on you, if you evince any signs of obstinacy!"

CHAPTER VIII

There was life and animation and excitement upon that momentous day when the duke and duchess, with their numerous retinue, were expected at Fürstenstein; even the old forest, which had been witness to so many magnificent hunts in its time, put on its warmest colors, and showed in the clear sunlight its deepest reds and most vivid greens.

The reigning duke was, above all things, an ardent and keen sportsman, and he rarely missed a few days of sport at this season. Now when he was coming for several weeks, and was bringing with him such a large suite, it was found that Fürstenstein, notwithstanding its size, could not accommodate them all. Suitable quarters had to be found in Waldhofen, and that little town was in a state of pleasurable excitement in consequence.

Prince Adelsberg, besides being the owner of the adjoining estate and castle, was also connected in some way with nearly all the families forming the ducal suite, and could not of course neglect them. Some of the men had been invited to take up their quarters at his little hunting lodge, so that the life and bustle which centered at Fürstenstein, extended to the woodland loneliness of Rodeck.

To-night the castle was brilliantly illuminated, and the colored lights which gleamed from its many windows, threw a rosy glow over wall and tower. It was the first large gathering since the arrival of the Court, and every one in the whole neighborhood who laid any claims whatever to social rank, had been invited. The interior of the castle had been gorgeously decorated, and the spacious rooms with their lights and music, and throngs of elegantly attired woman, together with the glittering appearance of the men in their court costumes, formed a scene not soon forgotten.

Prominent among the many grand ladies of the little court was the wife of the Prussian ambassador. It was her first appearance among them, her father's death, following immediately upon her marriage, having secluded her, and now, in the little circle where her husband's position gave her much prominence, she was the cynosure of all eyes. The duke, too, and his duchess, to whom she had been presented a few weeks previous, treated the ambassador's wife with special deference.

The court ladies, however, looked upon the appearance of this new star with anything but satisfaction. They all discovered soon enough, that Frau von Wallmoden, with her cold and haughty manner, was a very proud woman, and certainly she had no reason to be so; they knew only too well who she was: only a burger's daughter, who had no right to be in their charmed circle at all; her father's great wealth, and a certain prominence to which he had attained by success in his manufacturing interests, were all she could lay claim to at best. But she certainly carried herself with remarkable security; they all admitted that it was evident her husband had schooled her carefully for her first appearance, for she made no mistakes.

The men were of another opinion. They found that the ambassador had proven himself a profound diplomatist in this, as in other things. He, standing on the threshold of old age, had married a beautiful young girl with a fortune, which fortune, if report did not err, had been greatly augmented since their marriage, and was still on the increase. Such a condition of affairs was to be envied. Wallmoden was not the least surprised at the impression which his wife's beauty and manners made upon them all, and he took it, as the true diplomatist takes all things, as a matter of course. He had expected nothing else, and would on the contrary have been surprised if she had not created a sensation.

He stood for one moment now, in a window recess with his brother-in-law, the head forester, and asked casually, while he glanced indifferently over the heads of the guests:

"Who is it Prince Adelsberg has with him? Do you know?"

"You mean the young Roumanian? No. I see him to-day for the first time; but I have heard about him before. He is Prince Egon's bosom friend, and accompanied him on his oriental tour. He's as handsome as a picture, and how the fire does flash in his eyes."

"He looks to me like an adventurer," said Wallmoden, coldly. "How did he come to be invited here? Has he been presented to the duke?"

"Yes, at Rodeck, so I heard. The duke went over there the first thing. Once in a while Prince Adelsberg succumbs to the, rules of etiquette. But as to this invitation, it signifies nothing; every one is invited here to-day."

The ambassador shrugged his shoulders.

"It is hardly wise to invite persons about whom you know absolutely nothing into your midst."

"You diplomatists want all the credentials sealed and delivered," laughed his brother-in-law. "There's something aristocratic looking about this Rojanow, too, which one does not expect to see in a foreigner. But I'm glad enough to invite any one out of the common for his grace. He must be wearied with this endless court etiquette and court gossip, year in and year out. The duke, by the way, seems to have taken a great fancy to this young Roumanian already."

"Yes, so it seems," said Wallmoden, a cloud gathering on his brow.

"As for the man's history, if he has any, what does it matter to us? Well, I must look after Toni, and see how she's getting along without that lover of hers. That was a queer freak of Regine's. As soon as anything concerning her beloved Burgsdorf comes on the tapis, nothing will keep her. And she raises such a racket with her son, too. She might as well have left Will here. No one knows why she dragged him away; just before the duke came, too.—I'm sure I'll never understand your sister."

"It's a good thing she did," muttered Wallmoden, as he separated from von Schönau. "If Willibald had seen his boyhood's friend here, there would have been another scene, doubtless. Who would have thought that Hartmut would carry his defiance so far as to go to a house where he must have known he would meet the ambassador."

Prince Adelsberg, who, through his name and wealth, and his near kinship to the reigning house, took a first position in the brilliant little circle, had made a point of introducing his dearest friend to the duke, at Rodeck, and the stranger had impressed the duke so favorably that he had made special comment of him to the duchess.

This Rojanow, with his charming personality and the air of mystery which surrounded him, had only to exert himself to receive due attention on all sides.

And to-day he exercised all those fascinating qualities which he possessed in fullest measure. His conversation sparkled with wit and animation, and his ardent temperament imparted to everything he said the stamp of originality, while united with this he showed himself a master of social courtesies.

It was no difficult matter for the ambassador to avoid the Roumanian; in a large house filled with guests, such avoidance is an easy matter, and neither of these two were anxious for a meeting. Wallmoden turned now into an adjoining room, where the duke's sister, the Princess Sophie, was holding a little court. The princess had married the younger son of a princely house, but had been a widow now for years, and had lived since her widowhood at her brother's court, where she was by no means a favorite. The duchess was beloved for her gentleness and kind heartedness, by all who came in her way, but her elderly sister-in-law was disliked heartily for her arrogance and acerbity. They all feared her sharp tongue, which never failed to bring to light disagreeable features or fancies, as the case might be, concerning those with whom she had to do.

Herr von Wallmoden did not escape this fate; he was received most graciously and congratulated at once upon the great beauty of his wife, about which there could be no dispute.

"Your excellency has indeed my warmest congratulations. I was quite surprised when your young wife was presented to me. I had, as a matter of course, expected to meet a much older woman."

The "matter of course" had a malicious sound, for the princess had known for the past six months that the elderly ambassador was married to a girl of nineteen; he smiled in a perfectly placid manner, as he answered:

"Your highness is very good. I cannot be too thankful if my wife has made a favorable impression upon yourself and your family."

"O, you need not doubt that the duke and duchess are quite of my opinion. Frau von Wallmoden is really a beauty—Prince Adelsberg seems to think so also. Perhaps you have not noticed how greatly he admires her?"

"Yes, your highness, I have noticed it."

"Really? And what do you say to it?"

"I?" asked Wallmoden, composedly. "Whether or no she cares to accept the prince's homage is wholly and solely my wife's affair. If she finds any pleasure in it—I certainly will lay no commands upon her."

"Your enviable confidence in your wife should be an example to younger husbands," replied the princess, angry that her arrow had missed its aim. "It is very pleasant, at least for a young wife, to feel that her husband is not jealous. Ah, here comes Frau von Wallmoden herself, with her knight by her side. My dear baroness, we were just speaking of you."

Adelheid von Wallmoden, who with Prince Adelsberg, had just entered the room, made a courtesy to the princess. She was indeed dazzling in her beauty to-day, for her rich Court toilette so well chosen, suited her most admirably. The costly white brocade, with its long, heavy folds, set off her slender figure to advantage, the pearls which encircled her neck, and the diamonds which glistened in her light blonde hair, were jewels well worth the notice of connoisseurs; but that which was most worthy of attention was the singular coldness and earnestness of this young wife's face and bearing. She bore no resemblance whatever to others of her own age in this brilliant assemblage, who were for the most part married also, and who were decked out in all the witcheries of lace and flowers. They possessed nothing of her stateliness, but she in turn had none of their sweetness or assumed gentleness; none of that premeditated amiability which society women assume under the public gaze. The severe rigidity of that lovely face was a heritage from her father, whose stern, austere nature had left its impress upon her soul as well.

Egon kissed the hand of his illustrious aunt, and murmured a few polite words of greeting, but the amiable attention of her highness was directed toward the beautiful woman who had just joined them.

"I was just saying to his excellency, that you found yourself at home very readily in our little Court circle, my dear baroness. You are entering our little society for the first time to-day, and have lived, no doubt, in a very different atmosphere until now. Your name was—?"

"Stahlberg, your highness," was the quiet reply.

"Oh, yes, I remember it now. I have heard the name often enough. It was well known, I believe—in mercantile circles."

"My dearest aunt, you must permit me to set you right in this matter," interrupted Prince Egon, not wishing to lose an opportunity to anger his aunt. "The Stahlberg manufactures have a worldwide reputation, and are as celebrated across the ocean as here. I had an opportunity, when I was in North Germany, to learn something about them, and can assure you that these works, with their iron foundries and enormous factories, their colony of officers and army of workmen, could absorb many a little principality, whose rulers have no such unlimited power as had the baroness' father."

The lady threw her princely nephew anything but a friendly glance; his interference was to her mind most uncalled for.

"Indeed! I had no conception of such greatness," said she innocently. "I shall have to greet your excellency from this time forth as a great ruler."

"Only as a regent of the empire, your highness," answered the ambassador, seconding, a little apparently harmless joke. "I am only my father-in-law's executor, and guardian of my wife's younger brother, who will assume the entire management of the works as soon as he reaches his majority."

"Ah, indeed. The son will have to learn to keep a watchful eye over his inheritance. It is really astonishing to me to see what in these days can be accomplished by the energy of a single man. It is all the more creditable, too, when he, like the father of our dear baroness here, springs from the people. I think I heard that, but I may be mistaken!"

Princess Sophie knew well that the ambassador, with his old Prussian noble ancestry would find this rehearsal of his father-in-law's station in life anything but pleasant, and it gave her great satisfaction to note that none of the little group who surrounded her, lost a word of the conversation, which was meant to humiliate the lovely new comer. Baroness von Wallmoden drew herself up proudly as she replied:

"Your highness has been correctly informed. My father was of the people, and entered the capital a poor boy with no means whatever at his command. He had many and great struggles, and worked for years as a simple artisan, before he could lay even the foundations for his great undertaking."

"How proudly Frau von Wallmoden says that," cried the princess laughing. "O I love such childlike attachment, above everything. And Herr Stahlberg—or was it von Stahlberg? The great industrial heads often get titles of nobility."

"My father took no such title, your highness," said Adelheid, meeting the other's glance quietly but directly. "It was offered to him but he refused it."

The ambassador pressed his lips tightly together; he could not forbear thinking this last utterance of his wife very undiplomatic. The countenance of the princess assumed at once an irritated expression, and she answered, with an unconcealed sneer:

"Well, it is at least fortunate that this aversion was not inherited by the daughter. Your excellency will know how to appreciate it. Please give me your arm, Egon. I want to find my brother."

She bowed coldly to those around her as she took the arm of her nephew, in whose face was plainly written:

"Now it is my turn."

He did not deceive himself, his aunt had no intention of seeking the duke; she turned into an adjoining room with her young kinsman that she might have him under her eyes without interruption for a little time. At first she expended her anger against this unbearable, arrogant Frau von Wallmoden, who boasted of the vulgar pride of her father, while she herself married a baron for his title, for, of course, she could feel no love for a man who was old enough to be her father. Egon was silent for he had speculated on that matter himself. How had so unequal a marriage ever come about? But his silence just now was resented by his incensed aunt.

"Well, Egon, why don't you say something? Really it does seem as if you were this woman's sworn knight, you are by her side continually."

"I always do homage to beauty, when it comes in my way, you certainly know that, my dear aunt," explained the prince, striving to shield himself, but he only brought down a fresh storm on his head.

"Yes, I know that—I'm sorry to say. You have in this particular always exhibited great folly. You do not seem to remember all my warnings and admonitions before you started for the Orient."

"O, yes, I do," sighed Egon, to whom the very memory of those endless lectures was an oppression.

"Really! But you have not returned more sensible or settled. I have heard things—Egon, there's only one salvation for you—you must marry!"

"For heaven's sake! Anything but that!" exclaimed Egon, in such a voice of affright that the princess shut her fan with an angry snap, as she said in a sharp tone:

"What do you mean by that?"

"O, nothing but my own unworthiness to enter into such a holy state. You yourself, your highness, have often assured me that I was specially created to make a wife unhappy."

"If the wife does not succeed in making you better. But you are a hopeless case. At any rate this is neither the time nor the place to discuss so serious a matter. The duchess is planning a visit to Rodeck, and I am thinking of accompanying her."

"What a charming idea," said Egon, to whom the thought of an invasion by his noble kinsfolk was even more terrifying than the marriage plan. "I am rejoiced that Rodeck, notwithstanding its isolated situation, contains something worthy of notice just at present. I brought a good many curiosities home with me from my journey, among other things a lion, two young tigers, and some very rare snakes."

"But not alive?" interrupted his aunt.

"Of course, your highness."

"The Lord preserve us! Your life is not safe."

"Oh, they're not so dangerous after all. Only a few of the beasts have broken away; the people are so afraid of feeding them—but they were caught again and have not done any harm up to this time."

"Up to this time! A nice condition of affairs, I must say," exclaimed the princess angrily, "to keep every one in the region in constant danger of their lives. The duke ought to forbid you such diabolical amusement."

"Oh, I trust not, for I'm just trying to tame them. But I have some domesticated creatures to show, as well. Among my servants are several lovely girls who are well worth looking at in their picturesque national costumes."

Egon thought with a shudder, as he made this assertion, of the wretched old woman for whose appearance he had to thank the ever-watchful Stadinger, but he had not miscalculated the effect of his announcement. His amiable aunt drew herself up with an angry snort, and measured him with no conciliatory glance.

"Oh, you have them at Rodeck also?"

"Yes, indeed; and little Zena, the granddaughter of my old steward, is a lovely little thing, and if you do me the honor of visiting me, dear aunt, I'll—"

"I will not go near the place," his aunt interrupted sharply. "There must be nice goings on at Rodeck anyway, which keep you there with that young foreigner who is another of the curiosities you brought from the Orient. He looks like an out and out brigand."

"My friend Rojanow? He longs for the honor of being presented to you above all things. I may introduce him now, may I not?" and without waiting an answer, he hurried away to fetch Hartmut.

"Now its your turn, my boy," he said, seizing his friend by the arm. "I have been the sacrificial lamb long enough, and now my angelic aunt must have some one else to turn on the spit. She wants to marry me off at once, and she thinks you're a veritable brigand, but, God be praised, she won't come to Rodeck. I've made that my special care."

The next moment the two friends were standing before the princess, and Egon presented the latest victim with an amiable smile.

After the princess's abrupt departure, Herr von Wallmoden remained for a few minutes chatting with the little group which the irate lady had deserted. Then, offering his wife his arm, he walked slowly through the long salons, greeting an acquaintance here, or saying a word to a friend there, until they had reached the last of the gaily decked suite which happened to be empty. The tower-room was used generally only as a resting place and a point of observation, from which a very good view of the forest heights could be obtained, but to-day it was richly carpeted and the walls were hung with heavy tapestries, while choice plants were scattered about in artistic groupings and designs, so that the little room was as shaded and picturesque as could be desired, and a rest to both eye and brain, after the glitter and noise and light of the larger ones. The ambassador had judged aright in thinking he would have an uninterrupted moment with his wife, for whom he now drew forward a low chair.

"I must call your attention to the fact, Adelheid," he began in a low, condemnatory tone, "that you were guilty of great imprudence, just now. Your speech to the princess—"

"Was in self-defence," the young wife broke in. "You understood, as well as I, the object of the whole conversation."

"That's as it may be. You have, on your first entrance into society, made an enemy who will make both you and me feel her animosity very keenly as time goes on."

"You!" Adelheid looked at him in surprise. "Will you, the ambassador of a great nation, have anything to fear from a malicious woman, who happens to be related to the ducal house?"

"My child, you do not comprehend," responded her husband, coolly. "An evil-tongued woman can be more dangerous than any political opponent, and Princess Sophie is famed in this respect; even the duchess herself fears her slanderous tongue."

"In that the duchess and I differ—I do not fear her."

"My dear Adelheid," said the ambassador with a superior smile, "that proud movement of the head does you great credit. But at Court, you must learn to do as others do. One cannot give royalty a lesson before too many witnesses, and that is what you did when you spoke of your father's declination of a title of nobility. It was not necessary for you to be so explicit concerning your father's origin."

"Should I have falsified?"

"No, but it was a well known fact—"

"Of which I am proud, as was my father before me."

"You are no longer Adelheid Stahlberg, but the Baroness Wallmoden"— the baron's voice had assumed a sudden sharpness. "And you, yourself, will be forced to admit that when a woman has married into a family of the old nobility, it is hardly fitting for her to sneer at the nobles."

The young wife's lips were drawn in with a bitter expression. Although she had been speaking in a subdued tone, she dropped her voice still lower, as she said now: "Have you forgotten, Herbert, why I gave you my hand?"

"Perhaps you have had cause to regret it?" he said, questioning instead of answering.

"No," said Adelheid with a deep breath.

"I thought you were perfectly contented with the position to which you had attained by marrying me. As for the rest you know I exercised no control over you. I left it to your own free will."

His wife was silent, but the bitter expression was yet on her lips. Wallmoden rose and offered her his arm.

"You must permit me, my child, to help you at times, for you are inexperienced," he said in his wonted polite tone. "I have had every reason to be contented with your tact and discretion, but to-day I thought it necessary to give you a hint. Will you take my arm?"

"I will remain here a few minutes if you please," said Adelheid. "It is so stifling in the saloon."

"As you please. But I must beg you to come back soon, otherwise your absence will be noticed."

He saw that she was vexed and disturbed, but he thought best to take no notice of it. He knew well what was expected from them both in their little world, and felt for both their sakes it was better to educate his wife from the start in those matters which she did not seem to grasp fully.

He left her now, and Adelheid leaned back in her chair and gazed fixedly at the flowering plants which were grouped by her side, but under her breath she whispered with a gasp:

"*My own free will. O my God!*"

Prince Adelsberg and his friend had, in the meantime, been dismissed, and had made profound bows before the princess as she rose to leave the room. The sharp features of her highness wore an unusually mild expression, and Rojanow was favored with a very gracious smile as she departed.

"Hartmut, I believe you are a witch," said Egon, half aloud. "I have had proof many times that you are irresistible, but this last effort of yours throws all others in shadow. For my gracious aunt to have so prolonged an attack of amiability is unknown in the annals of the family."

"Well, my reception was ungracious enough. Your aunt seemed to think at first that I was a full-fledged brigand."

"But it only took ten minutes to win her smiles and make you a declared favorite. What is it you have about you, old fellow, which wins on every one? It makes one believe in the old fable of the rat-catcher."

The old scornful expression, which effaced all his beauty, swept across Hartmut's face now, as he said contemptuously:

"I understand how to sing to tickle the ears of my hearers. You have to strike the chords according to the taste of your listener, but after you have learned that secret no one can withstand you."

"No one?" repeated Egon, as his eye glanced over the room.

"No, not a single soul, I assure you."

"Oh, you're a pessimist with all your inferences. I only wish I knew where Frau von Wallmoden was, but I don't see her in any place."

"His excellency was reading her a little sermon on her undiplomatic utterances in the other room a short time ago."

"Why, did you hear what she said?" asked Egon, surprised.

"Certainly, I was standing by the door."

"Well, I'm glad enough my worshipful aunt was given a snub, and wasn't she furious over it, though; but do you believe that the ambassador would take his wife to task for—hush, here he is himself."

Yes, there was Baron von Wallmoden himself, true enough, and just in front of them as they came from an adjoining room.

It was impossible to avoid a meeting now, and the young prince, who had no premonition that any secret relations existed between the two, hastened to present them.

"Permit me, your excellency, to atone for the neglect of which I was guilty on the mountain the other day, but my friend had disappeared for the moment when we came down from the Tower. Herr Hartmut Rojanow—Baron von Wallmoden."

The eyes of the two men met, the one with a sharp, contemptuous gaze, the other, equally sharp, but haughty and defiant. The ambassador was too much of a diplomat, however, to be other than the courteous gentleman.

His greeting, though cold, was polite, but he turned at once to the prince to speak, and chatted to that gentleman alone for the minute or two that they stood together.

"His excellency is more of a ramrod than ever to-day," said Egon to his friend as they went on. "Whenever that cold, calculating countenance comes near me I feel frost-bitten and long to fly to the torrid zones."

"I suppose that's why you seek to bask in the rays of that glittering northern light, his wife," said Hartmut with a sneer. "Can you tell me for whom we are searching, in this weary pushing and crowding through these heated rooms?"

"I want to find the head forester," said the prince, irritated at his friend. "I want you to meet him, but you are in one of your bad humors to-day. Perhaps I'll find Schönau in the arrow-room. I'll go and look at any rate."

He left his friend abruptly, and did indeed set out for the arrow-saloon, where the duke and duchess were, and where he hoped to find Adelheid von Wallmoden. Unhappily for him, just at the entrance of the room, he was once more entrapped by his aunt, who pointed imperiously to a chair by her side. She wanted to hear all there was to be told about the handsome and interesting young Roumanian, who had quite won her heart, she said, and her uneasy nephew was obliged to possess his soul in patience as he answered her many questions.

The noise and the merriment were at their height, as Hartmut now threaded his way alone among the throng. He also sought someone, but he was more fortunate than Prince Egon; casting a fleeting glance into the tower-room, the entrance to which was almost hidden by portieres and exotics, he saw the edge of a white satin train which swept the floor, and in the next second he stood upon the threshold.

Adelheid von Wallmoden still sat on the same spot where her husband had left her. She turned her head slowly now as some one entered.

Suddenly she sat erect, and then returned the young man's deep obeisance with her accustomed icy bow.

"Have I disturbed you, baroness?" he asked. "I fear you sought this room for quiet, and my intrusion was unintentional, I assure you."

"I only sought a cool place; the heat of the larger rooms seems almost suffocating."

"I came for a like reason, but as I have not had an opportunity to greet you before to-day, my dear madame, permit me to do so now." The words sounded very formal. Rojanow had come a step nearer as he spoke, but he still remained at a respectful distance. No movement of hers since he entered had escaped him, and a singular smile lay in his eyes as he looked steadily at the young wife.

She had made a motion as if to rise and depart, but the thought that such a sudden course could only be constructed into flight, restrained her in time. So she leaned back in her chair again and bent over a branch of great purple-red camelias.

As she plucked a blossom, she answered his question carelessly enough, but her face had assumed the same look of determination and force which it wore the morning on which she stood for a second in the middle of the forest brook. Then she had stepped knee deep into the water rather than accept his services. Here in the castle, with noise and motion on all sides, there were no such obstacles to be overcome, and now the same man, with his dark glance, stood opposite her, and never took his eyes off her face.

"Will you remain much longer at Rodeck?" she asked, with the conventional tone and manner usually accorded a chance acquaintance.

"Probably for a few weeks yet. As long as the duke is at Fürstenstein, Prince Adelsberg will not be apt to desert his hunting lodge. Later I intend accompanying him to the capital."

"And there we shall hear of you as a poet, I presume?"

"Of me, my dear baroness?"

"I heard so at least, from the prince."

"O, that is only one of Egon's ideas," said Hartmut, lightly. "He has taken it into his head to have my 'Arivana' brought out on the stage."

"'Arivana?' A singular title."

"It is an oriental name taken from an Indian legend, but its poetical witchery made such an impression upon me that I could not resist the temptation to create a drama from it."

"And the heroine of this drama, is she called 'Arivana?'" asked the baroness.

"No, that is only the name of a sacred place of refuge during the middle ages, upon which the scene of the drama was laid. The heroine's name is—Ada."

Rojanow spoke the name half-aloud, with a certain hesitation, and gave her a triumphant glance as he saw the same lowering of the head over the flowers as when he first spoke; he came a few steps nearer now while he continued:

"I heard the name for the first time on Indian ground, and it had for me a strangely sweet sound, so I adopted it for my character, and now I learn here that it is, in this country, but the abbreviation of a German name."

"Of Adelheid—yes. I was always called Ada in my father's house. But it is not at all remarkable that the same sounds are repeated in different languages."

The words were spoken coldly, but the speaker did not raise her eyes from the flowers with which her hand played.

"Not at all," agreed Hartmut. "It has often been a surprise to me to hear the same fable repeated in different countries over and over again. The coloring is different, to be sure, but the passion, the woe, the happiness of our human race is alike in them all."

Adelheid shrugged her shoulders.

"I won't dispute over the matter with a poet, but doubt it, notwithstanding. I think our German legends wear a different countenance from the dreamy tales of India."

"Perhaps, but when you study them deeply, you will discover the same features in both. These common features are manifest in the legend of 'Arivana,' at least. The principal character is that of a young priest who has consecrated himself, body and soul, to the service of his divinity, to the holy fire, but in time he is mastered by an earthly love with all its glow and passion, till his priestly vows dissolve in its consuming flame."

He stood opposite her, quietly and respectfully, but his voice had an odd, covert sound, as if something of deeper significance were hidden beneath this story. Frau von Wallmoden looked up at him suddenly, and said, gazing earnestly into his face:

"And—the end?"

"The end is death, as in all these legends. The knowledge of the broken vows comes to light and the guilty ones are offered as a sacrifice to an enraged deity—the priest perishes in the flames with the woman whom he loves."

There was a second's pause after the last words were spoken, then Adelheid rose abruptly; she would end this conversation at once.

"You are right; no doubt the legends do resemble ours; it is only the old story of sin and atonement."

"Do you call that sin, my dear lady?" Hartmut dropped suddenly the more formal madame or baroness. "Men call it sin and punish it accordingly, without any premonition that such a punishment will lead to perfect happiness. To pass away in a flame of fire after one has enjoyed the highest earthly joys, and is yet surrounded by them in death. Ah! that is to die like a god—far better such a death than a long, stupid, humdrum existence. Eternal, undying love rises like a flaming brand to the heavens above, in defiance of mankind's sentence—do you not think such an ending is enviable?"

Adelheid's face was pale, but her voice was as steady and cool as ever, as she answered:

"No, nothing is enviable but death for a high and holy duty. One can forgive sin, but can never admire it."

Hartmut bit his lips and gave the slender, white robed figure who stood near him a threatening glance.

"Ah, what a hard sentence to meet my drama at the outset, for I have expended all my strength in transfiguring just such love and death. What if the world's judgment is like yours—I beg your pardon, madame."

He crossed to the divan upon which she had been sitting, where her fan and the camelia blossom yet lay.

"I thank you," said Adelheid, extending her hand for them, but he only handed her the fan.

"I beg your pardon—I wrote my 'Arivana' upon the veranda of a little Indian house where these lovely flowers were gleaming through the dark foliage on all sides, and to-day they greet me here again in the cold north. May I not keep this blossom?"

Adelheid made a little impatient motion.

"No; for what reason?"

"For what reason? As a reminder of the harsh sentence which my poem has received from the lips of a woman who bears the same name as my heroine. There were many white blossoms, baroness, but you broke off unconsciously the deep purple-red. Poets are superstitious above all things. Let me keep this as a token that my work may yet find favor in your eyes, when you learn to know it. You do not know how much it contains."

"Herr Rojanow, I—"

It was apparent to him, both from her voice and manner, that she meant to refuse his petition, so he interrupted her in a subdued, but passionate tone:

"What is a single blossom to you which you plucked heedlessly and cast aside so carelessly? To me—baroness, as a favor—I beg you, baroness."

He stood close by her side. The witchery of voice and eye which had so often overcome all obstacles in his boyhood's days, and which had then been exercised, unconsciously, had become a great power in these later years, and one which he knew how to use only too well.

His voice had again that soft, persuasive tone which fell on her ear like music, and his eyes, those dark, fathomless eyes, were fixed on the young wife with a half melancholy, half pleading expression. Adelheid's face had grown very white now, but she did not answer.

"Please," he repeated, in a lower, more pleading tone, as he pressed his lips to the purple-red blossom; but this last motion seemed to break the spell. Adelheid reached her hand out suddenly.

"I must insist upon your giving me my flower, Herr Rojanow. It is for my husband."

"Indeed, then, I beg your pardon, madame."

He held out the flower to her with a profound bow, and she took it with a scarcely perceptible motion of the head, then the heavy white train of her robe rustled past him—he was alone.

All in vain! Nothing affected this icy nature. Hartmut stamped his foot in a fury. Scarcely fifteen minutes ago he had asserted to Prince Egon that he could sing to please the ear of any woman. Now he had sung again that song which never before had failed him, and all to no purpose. But this proud, arrogant man could not believe that the game which he so often won had been lost this time, and in this knowledge lay his determination to win yet at all hazards.

And should it only remain a game? He had not called himself to account as yet, but in the intense interest which this beautiful woman excited within him, there was a strong mixture of hate. There had been an antagonistic feeling on that first day in the wood, and since then he had been repelled and attracted by turns; it was just that which spurred him on.

Love, the holy, pure significance of that word, was a stranger to the heart of Zalika's son. He had learned much that was harmful at the side of his mother, who had made such a shameless spectacle of her own husband's love; and the many women who were her companions and associates in her Roumanian home, but echoed her sentiments concerning love and fidelity. Their later life, unstable and adventurous, with no ground under their feet, had ruined altogether all ideals of happiness and love in the young man's breast; he learned contempt before he learned love, and now he received his well-deserved humiliation as an insult.

"You keep me at bay now," he murmured. "You are battling against yourself. I have felt it and seen it, but in such a battle the man is always victor."

A slight rustle of a curtain made him turn round. It was the ambassador in search of his wife, whom he thought still here; he stood on the threshold and threw a hasty glance around the room, when he caught sight of Hartmut. He stopped and hesitated for a moment, then he said half aloud:

"Herr Rojanow—"

"Your Excellency!"

"I would like to speak to you alone for a few minutes."

"I am at your service."

Wallmoden stepped forward into the room now, but he took up his position so that he could keep his eye on the entrance.

It was scarcely necessary, for the doors into the dining-hall were just opened, and the room adjoining the tower-chamber was deserted.

"I am surprised to see you here," began the ambassador, in the subdued, but severely cold tone which he had used the day of their first meeting at Hochberg, and it brought the blood to the younger man's brow to-day, as it had done then. He straightened himself proudly as he answered:

"And why, your Excellency?"

"That question is superfluous; in any case I did not imagine that I should be forced into the position of being presented to you by Prince Adelsberg."

"It was I who was forced," answered Hartmut, sharply and promptly. "I do not suppose you consider me an intruder? You know full well that I have a right to be here."

"Hartmut von Falkenried certainly had a right—but all that is changed."

"Herr von Wallmoden!"

"Pardon me, but not so loud," interrupted the ambassador. "We can be heard here easily, and you would certainly not like strange ears to hear the name which I have just spoken."

"I am bearing my mother's name at present, to which I have certainly a right. When I laid aside the other, it was out of respect—"

"To your father," interrupted Wallmoden, impressively.

That was an admonition which Hartmut found hard to bear. "Yes," he answered curtly, "and I confess it would be painful to me if I should be forced to mention—"

"And with reason; your *rôle* here would, in that event, be played to the end."

Rojanow stepped close to the ambassador with an angry movement, as he retorted:

"You are the friend of my father's youth, Herr von Wallmoden, and I, in my boyhood days, called you uncle. But you forget that I am no longer the boy whom you could order about and censure at pleasure. The man looks on all that as an insult."

"I purpose neither to insult you, nor to make mention of former associations which have no longer any existence for either of us," said the ambassador. "I sought this interview in order that I might explain to you that it is not possible for me, in my official position, to see you in constant intercourse with the Court and keep silence. It will be my duty to explain all to the duke."

"Explain all? All what?"

"Many things about which none of the people here, not even your friend Prince Adelsberg, know. Listen to me, Herr Rojanow. I will not do this except it is forced upon me, for I have an old and dear friend to spare. I know how a certain occurrence struck him down ten years ago, an occurrence which is buried and forgotten these many years in our country now; but if all this was brought up and gossiped over again—Colonel Falkenried would die."

Hartmut paled perceptibly, and the scornful expression faded from his lips.

"He would die!" the words rang in his ears. He knew only too well how true they were, and for the moment all defiance died within him.

"It is to my father that I am answerable, at any rate," he responded, controlling his voice with an effort. "To him alone and to no other."

"He will scarcely call you to account—his son is dead to him. But we can let that rest. I speak especially of those later years which your mother and you spent in Rome and Paris, where you lived at a glittering pace, in spite of the fact that the Roumanian estate had been sold under the hammer."

"You seem to know all the particulars," retorted Rojanow, highly indignant now. "We were not aware that we were under such vigilant inspection. As to our manner of life, we lived as best pleased ourselves, upon the remnant of the fortune which was saved from the wreck."

"There was nothing saved, the whole fortune was squandered, even to the last heller."

"That is not true," interrupted Hartmut stormily.

"It is true. Don't you think I know more about it than you?" The ambassador's voice was sharp and sneering now. "It is very possible that Frau Rojanow did not consider it necessary to explain to her son the means by which she obtained her gold; better to leave him in ignorance. I know from whence the money came—if she did not tell you, so much the better for you."

"Have a care, sir, about insulting my mother," the young man was beside himself now, "or I may forget your gray hairs, and demand satisfaction."

"For what? For an assertion which I can back with indisputable proof at any moment? Let us put aside all such mad folly and say no more on that subject. She was your mother and she is dead, so her past shall be a dead letter to us. I have only this one question to put to you, whether you will, after this conversation, remain here and become one of the circle which Prince Adelsberg has opened for you?"

Hartmut had become deadly pale at the allusion made to his mother, and the source from which she had obtained money, and the first stare with which he gazed at the speaker showed only too clearly that he had no knowledge of anything disreputable, but at the last question he began to recover himself. He cast an almost insane glance at his enemy, and a wild determination sounded in his voice as he answered:

"Yes, Herr Wallmoden, I shall remain."

The ambassador had not expected this answer; he had thought after his conversation the matter would be ended.

He evinced no surprise, however, and said:

"Really? So you decide to remain? You are accustomed to play high, and expect to do it here? We will have to interfere with that, I fear. Better think it well over before you decide finally."

With that he turned quickly on his heel and left the room, just in time to meet the head forester at its entrance.

"Where have you been hiding yourself, Herbert?" Schönau asked impatiently. "I have been searching the whole place for you."

"I went to the tower-chamber in search of my wife."

"She's in the dining-room with all the rest of the world, but you have been missed already. Come, it is time that we got something to eat."

With which the head forester took hold of his brother-in-law's arm and led him away, after his usual jolly manner.

Hartmut stood where von Wallmoden had left him. His breath came fast and thick, and he was almost stifled with the feelings of shame, and hate, and revolt, which surged within him. The ambassador's significant speeches had crushed him utterly, although he had hardly grasped their full meaning. They tore aside the veil with which he, half unconsciously, half purposely, had enveloped himself. He had believed implicitly what his mother told him concerning the portion of their fortune which was saved to them, and which enabled them to live and travel. But there were times when he had chosen to close his eyes rather than enter into investigations.

When his mother's hand had torn him so suddenly from his father's side, when after the hard discipline of obedience and duty, he had been plunged into a life of boundless freedom, he had allowed himself an unchecked rein, having no one to whom to account for his actions. He was too young for reflection or judgment, and later—but it was too late for him then, and habit had woven a net about him which could not be destroyed. Now for the first time it was shown him clearly and definitely what that life was which he had led so long; the life of an adventurer, and as an adventurer he was to be expelled from society.

But above all the shame was the sense of ignominy and defeat, the feeling of intense hatred toward the man who had told him the truth. That unholy heritage from his mother, the hot, wild, passionate blood, which had proven so fatal to the boy, welled up like a stream of fire in the man's breast and extinguished all feeling but that of revenge. Hartmut's handsome features were still disfigured with passion and anger, when, with compressed lips, he finally left the tower room.

He knew and felt but one thing, that he must have revenge, revenge at any price.

It was late when the guests arose from the table. The duke and duchess retired soon after, and carriage after carriage ascended the castle hill, and descended soon after with its full complement of departing guests; lights were extinguished, and bolts and bars were drawn, and Fürstenstein was soon enveloped in silence and darkness.

From the rooms occupied by Baron von Wallmoden and his wife lights were still shining. Adelheid stood at the window peering into the darkness. She yet wore her rich court gown, and as she leaned her head against the pane, lost in thought, her attitude was one of weariness and languor.

Wallmoden sat at his writing table, reading hastily the dispatches and letters which had arrived during the day. One or two seemed to contain matter of importance, for he did not place them with the pile which were to be answered or destroyed early in the morning, but took up his pen and made a check across them in red ink; then he arose and crossed the room to his wife.

"This comes unexpectedly," he said. "I'll have to go to Berlin at once."

Adelheid turned round surprised.

"This is very sudden."

"Yes, I had hoped to settle the matter by letter, but the minister desires a personal conference. I must take my leave of the duke early in the morning, and set off at once. I'll be away about eight days, I presume."

In the shadow of the curtain Adelheid's face could not be seen clearly, but one could fancy a sigh of relief escaped her, as if her heart was to be lightened of a burden.

"At what hour do we start?" she asked quickly. "I must give my maid her orders at once."

"We? It's a purely business affair, and I am going alone."

"But that won't prevent my accompanying you!"

"There would be no object in that. I'll only be away a week or two."

"But I—I'd like to see Berlin again."

"What a whim!" her husband answered, shrugging his shoulders. "I'll have so many claims upon my time that I could not have you with me."

The young wife had stepped to the table, and stood in the glare of the lamp. She was very pale now, and her voice had a pleading sound as she said:

"Very well, then, I will go home. But it is not possible for me to remain at Fürstenstein alone, without you."

"Alone!" The ambassador gave her a puzzled look. "You remain with our kinsfolk whose guests we are. Since when have you become so anxious for protection? That is a peculiarity which I had never observed in you until now. I don't understand you, Adelheid; it's a most singular caprice which you have taken into your head, this desire to accompany me."

"Well, call it a caprice. But let me go with you, Herbert—please let me go."

She laid her hand beseechingly on his arm, and her eyes had an intense and anxious expression, as she looked at her husband. There was a superior, almost sneering smile on his lips, as he answered her:

"Now I understand it. The scene with the princess was so unpleasant to you that you dread other skirmishes of a like nature. You must steel yourself against such sensitiveness, my child; you should see that for this very reason, it is imperative for you to remain. At court every word, every glance signifies, and your sudden departure might give rise to any kind of a report. You must hold your ground from the very start at court, or you will find your difficulties increase rather than diminish."

The wife's hand dropped slowly from her husband's arm, and her eyes sank to the ground, as he refused the first request she had preferred since their married life of only a few short months.

"Stand my ground?" she repeated, in a low voice. "That I shall ever do, but I hoped you would be at my side."

"That is, for the moment, not possible, as you see. As for the rest, you have shown to-day that you know how to defend yourself. And I have no doubt that the hint which I found it necessary to give you, will bear fruit, and that you will, in future, be guarded in your answers. At any rate, you must stay here until I return."

Adelheid was silent. She saw that nothing was to be gained by further speech. Wallmoden stepped back to the writing-table and put aside his papers, and locked his drawers with his usual precision; then he took up the two letters, with their red checks, and folded them together.

"One thing more, Adelheid," he said, casually, "Prince Adelsberg was most noticeable in his attentions to you to-day; he was always near you."

"Do you wish me to keep him at a distance?" she asked, indifferently.

"No, indeed, only keep him within bounds, so that there will be no unnecessary talk. No harm will come to you from being in his company. We do not stand on the same plane as the burgers, and it would be ludicrous for me, in my position, to enact the jealous husband toward every man who pays my wife attention. I leave all that to your discretion; I have unbounded faith in your tact."

This sounded very reasonable, very temperate, and above all, very indifferent. No one could accuse Herr von Wallmoden of jealousy towards the young prince, whose undisguised admiration caused him no second thought; and, as he had just said, he had unbounded faith in his wife's tact.

"I will send these telegrams myself," he said. "Since the duke's arrival there's a telegraph office in the castle. You should ring for your maid, my child; you look tired and worn—good-night."

With that he left her, but Adelheid did not follow his advice. She returned once more to the window, and a bitter, pained expression lay on her face. She had never before felt so keenly that she was to her husband nothing more than a glittering bauble, to be exhibited by him to prove how wisely he had chosen a wife; she was to be treated with the greatest courtesy and politeness, because a princely fortune had been received from her hand; but as a woman she was to be refused the most trifling request with equal courtesy, because it did not suit his pleasure.

The night was dark, and the low clouds which surrounded the forest heights were black and heavy; only here and there, where a break occurred, was a star to be seen glimmering far and faint in the distant heavens. The face which peered out into the darkness had not the proud, cold look which the world knew, but a disturbed, anxious expression, lacking altogether that repose which was its chief characteristic at most times.

The wife had both hands pressed against her breast, as if in pain. She would have flown from that dark power which she felt was upon her. She had sought her husband's protection, had plead for it—in vain. He went and left her alone, and the other remained, with his dark, demoniacal eyes, with his voice and tones, which exercised such a singular, irresistible influence over her.

CHAPTER IX

October had come. It was autumn's reign. The leaves of the trees were richly colored with deep and varied hues. The landscape lay enveloped morning and evening in fog and mist, and the nights brought with them the hoar-frost, but the days, for the most part, were sunny and delightful.

Since the gay evening on which the whole country round had assembled, there had been no special festivities at Fürstenstein; all interest had centered in the hunt, which was, of course, of paramount importance to the men.

The duke, at his wife's instance, decided to have no other great or noisy entertainment at the castle. The duchess liked a change of faces in their little circle, but she courted the quiet and freedom from restraint which her mountain home brought her. There were frequent arrivals and various excursions, both by horse and on foot, through the mountain forest, and a goodly number always met around the princely board at night to discuss the pleasures and excitements of the day.

Adelheid von Wallmoden belonged, naturally, to this exclusive circle. The duchess, who had learned through some source, of her sister-in-law's insulting attitude toward the young wife, had been more amiable than ever, and had managed to keep Baroness von Wallmoden near herself whenever it was possible; the duke also, anxious to show all attention to the Prussian ambassador, seconded his wife's endeavors with zest.

Wallmoden was still in Berlin, though over two weeks had elapsed since he left the castle, and he had not yet been able to write definitely as to the date of his return.

One of the most frequent guests at Fürstenstein was Prince Egon Adelsberg, who was an acknowledged favorite among his princely kinsfolk, and his friend Rojanow was always included in the invitations sent to Rodeck. The prince's prophesies had proven true; Hartmut had descended upon them like a brilliant meteor. All eyes were turned upon him with admiration and wonder, and it pleased his new associates to have him soar above the old fashioned usages and customs of their monotonous Court life. He had read his 'Arivana' to the duchess at her request, and had scored a decided success. The duke had promised him that his drama should be brought out at the Court theatre, and the princess Sophie had made a special point of taking the young man under her wing.

The princely household followed, as usual, in the wake of their master, but willingly enough in this instance, for Hartmut won friends on all sides by his cordiality, good temper, and grace of manner and person.

The prince's hunting wagon stood before the castle of Rodeck. It was early in the day and the faint mist which yet hung over the hills concealed a bright, warm sun. Egon stepped out on the terrace dressed for the hunt, closely followed by the old steward, to whom he was speaking.

"So you want to see the hunt, too, do you?" he asked. "Of course, if there's anything to see, Peter Stadinger must see it. My valet has asked permission also. For that matter I believe all the inhabitants of the forest have turned out to-day with their whole families to go to the hunting grounds."

"Yes, your highness, they don't often have an opportunity to see such a sight," replied Stadinger. "The great Court hunts seldom take place in our woods. There's hunting enough around here to be sure, but then you never ask any ladies to Rodeck, and the ladies—"

"Are a great bore," interrupted the prince. "That's my opinion; but what are you prating about? You are generally down on the women, and unless they are over eighty don't want to see one of them around the place. Are you going back to your young and giddy days?"

"I meant the court ladies, your highness," said Stadinger impressively.

"'The court ladies,' can honor me with their company for a walk, but I'll never invite any of them to any hunt of mine, for I'm still a young bachelor."

"And why is it that your highness is still a bachelor?" responded the old servant reprovingly.

"Man alive, I do believe you are trying to get me married, like my old—like all the rest of the world. Don't waste any thought or time on me, for I won't marry."

"Your highness is wrong," remonstrated old Stadinger, who always gave his master the title once at least in each sentence, for he thought if he did have to read the prince a lecture every now and then, he must show him some respect while doing it, "and it is unchristian, too, for the marriage relation is a holy state in which it is well to live; your father, blessed be his memory, married—and so did I."

"Of course, and so did you. Yes, you are the grandfather of that lovely girl, Zena, whom you sent away in such shameless haste. By the way, when is Zena coming back?"

The steward appeared not to hear the question, but returned obstinately to his theme.

"Her highness, the duchess, and princess Sophie, are very anxious to see you married. Your highness should think it well over."

"Well, that's enough of your fatherly advice for one day. And it's no business of princess Sophie. By the way, as you are going to Bucheneck, where the hunt meets to-day, it's very possible that you will be seen and spoken to by some of the court."

"Very possible, your highness," agreed the steward, complacently. "Her grace often honors me with a little conversation, for she recognizes me as the oldest servant of a princely house."

"Well, if the princess should inquire by chance about the snakes and beasts of prey which I brought with me from my travels, you can tell her that I'm going to have them sent to one of my other castles."

"That is not at all necessary, your highness," replied the steward. "Your gracious aunt has obtained information about everything."

"Information? About what? Perhaps you have given it."

"I was questioned the other day at Fürstenstein. Princess Sophie was just returning from a walk and beckoned me to her to ask me a few questions."

"The deuce she did!" muttered the prince, who saw mischief. "And what answers did you give her?"

"'Your grace need feel no uneasiness,' I said, 'of living animals we have only monkeys and parrots at Rodeck, and there's never been a snake about the place; a sea serpent was coming, but it died on the way, and the elephants broke loose before they were shipped at all, and went back to their palm groves—so his highness told me. As to tigers, we have two, but they are stuffed, and we've only the skin of a lion in the large hall, so your grace can see that no harm will come from them.'"

"No, but enough will come from your tattle," said the prince, angrily. "And the princess, what did she say to it all?"

"Her grace only smiled and then asked me about the women employed here at Rodeck, and if all the girls in the region were not here. But I said," and Stadinger threw his head back proudly, "'all the women at the castle, your grace, were engaged by me. They are all industrious and honest; I have seen to that; but his highness ran away when he caught sight of them, and Herr Rojanow was more put out than the prince even, so the gentlemen never paid but one visit to the kitchen.' Her grace was very kind and gracious to me, and took leave of me very well contented, I could see that."

"And I'd be very well contented to send you to the devil, you old fool. To spoil it all with your long tongue," exclaimed the prince, furious now.

The old man, who thought he had done everything for the best, looked at his young master in perplexity.

"But I only told the truth, your highness."

"But the truth's not to be spoken at all times."

"Oh, I did not know that."

"Stadinger, you have a bad habit of answering back—perhaps you also told the princess that Zena had been in the city for several weeks?"

"Yes, your highness, she asked me about my granddaughter, particularly."

"What's the trouble with Stadinger now?" asked Hartmut, who came out at this moment, also attired for the day's sport, and who had caught the last few words.

"Oh, he's been making a first class fool of himself, that's all," explained the exasperated prince. The oldest servant of a princely house could not allow such an insult to pass.

"I beg your highness's pardon. I have not been making a fool of myself at all."

"Perhaps you believe it is I who have been doing it?"

Stadinger looked his young master well over and then replied, discreetly:

"I do not know, your highness—but it might be so."

"You're an old bear," cried the prince sharply.

"The whole forest knows that, your highness."

"Come on, Hartmut, there's nothing to be gained from this old ghost of the woods," said Egon half angry, half laughing. "First you place me in all sorts of embarrassments, and then you defend yourself by giving me a lecture."

With that he went off with Rojanow to the carriage. Stadinger remained standing in a respectful attitude, for he never meant to be rebuked for lack of respect to "his highness." It never occurred to him to yield an inch of ground; that was for Prince Egon to do, but not for Peter Stadinger.

Egon was almost of this opinion himself. He related what had occurred to Hartmut as they drove along, and with a comical despair he concluded:

"Now can you imagine what kind of a reception that most worshipful aunt of mine will give me? She evidently suspected that I wanted to keep her away from Rodeck. Now my morals are saved in her eyes, but at the expense of my love of truth. Hartmut, you must do me a favor; you must be my lightning rod. Expend all your power of fascination upon that imperious kinswoman of mine. Dedicate a poem to her if necessary, but at least shield me from the first fierce flashes of her anger."

"Well, I should have thought you weather-proof in that particular by now," said Rojanow smiling. "You must have had cause for forgiveness before this for such enormities. The duchess and the other ladies will be on horseback to-day, will they not?"

"Certainly; they could see nothing from the carriages. By the way, did you know that Frau von Wallmoden was an accomplished horse woman? I met her day before yesterday returning from a ride with her brother-in-law, the head forester."

"Ah, then we'll know where to find Prince Adelsberg to-day."

Egon, who had been leaning back comfortably, sat erect now, and said, as he gave his friend a searching look:

"Not so spitefully, I beg of you. You are not often in the company of the lady in question, I grant that, and you bear yourself as if you were only a looker-on at others, but I know you well enough to understand that you and I are very much of the same opinion concerning her, nevertheless."

"Well, and if we are—would you consider it a breach of friendship on my part?"

"Not in this instance. For the object is unattainable by either of us."

"Unattainable?" an ironical smile played around Rojanow's lips.

"Yes, Hartmut," said the young prince, half in earnest, half in jest, "the lovely, cold northern light, as you have named her, remains true to its nature. It gleams on the horizon distant and unapproachable, and the icy sea above which it shines is not to be broken through. The lady has no heart.

She is free from every feeling of passion, and that is what gives her her enviable security. Here you must acknowledge all your influence, all your boasted powers are frustrated by that icy breath; you are chilled through, and so you keep your distance."

Hartmut was silent. He was thinking of the moment in the tower room when he had begged for the bright blossom. She had refused him, but no icy breath had enveloped the young wife while she stood trembling beneath his pleading glance and words. He had seen her daily since then, but had seldom gone near her, but he knew that now, as before, she was under his influence.

"But, in spite of it all, I cannot tear myself loose from this foolish fascination," Egon went on in a dreamy tone. "It always seems to me that the ice and snow will disappear as if by magic, and warmth and light burst out in full bloom in their stead. If Adelheid von Wallmoden were still free—I believe I'd try the experiment."

Rojanow, who had been lost in thought as he gazed steadily into the mist which yet shrouded the hills, turned around suddenly and violently now.

"What experiment? Do you mean by that, you'd offer her your hand?"

"That thought seems to excite you greatly," said the prince, laughing out loud. "Yes, that's precisely what I mean. I have no such prejudice against trade as my respected aunt, who would go into convulsions over the very thought, and even you don't seem to take to the idea any too kindly. Well, you can both calm yourselves, his excellency her husband, has already secured the prize, and he'll never change her into a creature of warmth and light with those tiresome diplomatic speeches of his—but the man is happy; he has had no end of good luck."

"Call no man happy until his death," said Hartmut, half-aloud.

"A very wise remark, only not quite original," answered Egon. "Do you know that at times you have a look in your eyes which is positively alarming, like a demon. Forgive my saying so, but you looked this moment as if you were one."

Hartmut did not answer.

They were just turning from the forest into the broad road, and Fürstenstein, with its ducal flag flapping gaily in the morning wind, was plainly visible on its wooded height.

Half an hour later, their carriage rolled along the broad graveled carriage-way, where all was life and bustle. Every servant of the household was stirring; carriages and saddle horses were standing ready for the start, and nearly all those invited to join the hunt had arrived.

As the gay throng started on their way, the sun suddenly burst forth through the mist, and as it shone down on the glittering cavalcade just leaving the castle, it made a brilliant and impressive picture.

The duke and duchess rode at the head, closely followed by their numerous suite, and then came the many guests. All the younger women were on horseback, and the whole party were in full hunting costume.

Away they rode in the clear sunlight of a bright autumn morning. Over the hills and meadows and through the woods. Shots were fired on every side, and the flying deer broke through the thicket and across the clearing, while the whole hunting park resounded with the din of the sport.

The whole corps of foresters had been summoned by the head forester, who saw to it that no arrangements were lacking to make the day a success. He felt that this was peculiarly his affair, and that no mishaps of any sort should occur.

They arrived about midday at Bucheneck, a small hunting lodge belonging to the duke, which lay in the center of the forest, and which could offer shelter in case of any unfavorable change in the weather. To-day no such precaution seemed necessary, as the weather was glorious, only somewhat too warm for the season. The sun beat down almost too fiercely, as they took their breakfast in the open air.

With that exception, everything was a success, and the crowd which moved hither and thither over the broad, green meadow, near which Bucheneck lay, were in high spirits. The duke, who had handled his fowling piece with more than usual skill, was in the best of humors; the duchess chatted gaily with the ladies, and the head forester fairly beamed with pleasure, for the prince had congratulated him warmly upon his faculty for doing perfectly all he undertook. Frau von Wallmoden, who kept near the duchess, was the object of much attention; she was unquestionably the most beautiful woman there; the others needed for the most part rich toilettes and glittering gems to set off their beauty. Here in the clear light of the midday sun, clad in dark riding habits, which permitted neither color nor adornment, many paled who were at other times very attractive in appearance, but Frau von Wallmoden, with her slender figure and erect bearing, which seemed especially suited to the saddle, her clear skin, large, earnest eyes and wealth of blonde hair so simply coiled, was a picture at which to gaze with unmitigated pleasure. In short, the "northern light," as she was now commonly called at court, the prince having whispered the name, was the admired of all beholders, all the more so when it became known that the cold, statuesque beauty was soon to desert them.

Frau von Wallmoden had received a letter from her husband yesterday, stating that his diplomatic business was ended, but that affairs in North Germany connected with the Stahlberg manufactories would detain him for some time longer. It was whispered that there were to be many important changes, great improvements were to be introduced, and in all this Baron von Wallmoden as executor and guardian of the only son, would have a decisive voice. The length of his absence from the South Germany court would necessarily be uncertain, so he had asked his government for an extended leave, which had been granted, and had announced all this to the duke. He had written his wife at the same time, leaving her free to remain at Fürstenstein, or to join him at once and go with him to her old home to see her brother again; now, after two weeks, if she chose to leave, no "misconstruction" could be placed upon her departure. Adelheid had chosen without hesitation; she had announced to the duchess that she would leave on the following day.

Princess Sophie and her sister, together with some of the older ladies, had driven to Bucheneck in carriages, and the Princess Sophie's first anxiety had been to get hold of her nephew. But so far Prince Egon had managed to avoid her. He had been everywhere but in the neighborhood of his deceived aunt, until at last, losing all patience, she ordered a gentleman of the Court to bring Prince Adelsberg to her at once. This order was imperative, and Egon did not dare disobey it, but he took the precaution of having his "lightning rod" with him to get the first shock. Hartmut was by his side when he presented himself before the princess.

"Well, Egon, it's a great privilege to see your face at all to-day," were the first words. "You are in demand on all sides, it seems."

"But I am always at the service of my beloved aunt," Egon declared. His amiability was of no use to him on this occasion, however; the princess measured him with anything but a conciliatory glance.

"Whenever your knightly services are not needed in the interest of Frau von Wallmoden. You will have the opportunity of exhibiting a glittering example of chivalry and courage, when her husband comes back. You will learn to know and appreciate him better then."

"I appreciate him very highly now, as a man, as a diplomat and as 'his excellency.' Your grace must surely believe that."

"I believe you absolutely, Egon. Your love of truth is one of the verities upon which I pin my faith," said the lady, with biting irony. "For that very reason I was pleased to have the opportunity of a little talk with old Stadinger the other day. He's not so rusty after all, for his years."

"Poor fellow, he suffers greatly from weakness of memory," the prince hastened to assure her. "Stadinger forgets nearly everything—don't you know, Hartmut? What he declares most earnestly one day, is entirely forgotten on the next."

"I found, on the contrary, that his memory was very fresh; above all, this faithful old servant of your house is trustworthy, circumspect—"

"And rude," interrupted Egon, sighing. "You can have no idea of the incivility in which old Peter Stadinger's whole nature is steeped. He tyrannizes most terribly over Herr Rojanow and myself. I have thought seriously of putting him out of the way."

It is hardly necessary to say he had not thought of anything of the kind.

Princess Sophie, who was an autocrat, and who dealt most severely with her own servants, was inclined to be very lenient in this instance.

"You should not think of harming so faithful a creature," she answered. "A man who has served three generations of your race can be forgiven for slight eccentricities, especially when one thinks of the pleasant life which the two young masters of Rodeck lead him, for we all know they do not court company, but prefer loneliness."

"Ah, yes, loneliness," said Egon with feeling. "It is a great change after our eventful life in the East, and we enjoy it in full measure. I occupy myself principally—"

"With the taming of wild beasts," interrupted the princess, maliciously.

"No, with—with—reminiscences of my travels, which I recount to Hartmut, while he poetises a little, and composes melancholy odes from them. He's writing a little poem now on some reflection he heard your grace make."

The princess turned with a radiant smile to the young poet as she exclaimed:

"And have you really been able to use any nonsense which I may have uttered in a poem, Herr Rojanow?"

"Indeed, I have, your grace, and I am very grateful to you for your idea," replied Hartmut promptly. He had no idea in the world what the talk was all about, but was ready to second whatever his friend might suggest.

"I am delighted to hear it; I adore poetry, and think it the greatest of literary productions."

"You two will agree perfectly as to that," said Egon with admiration. Having accomplished his object, he escaped, leaving his friend to enter into a discussion with the princess, on the relative merits of poets and their inspirations.

The prince once more approached the duchess's little circle, where he was sure to find Frau von Wallmoden, and where he was far from the sound of his malicious aunt's voice.

The breakfast was ended, and the day's sport was about to begin in earnest. But since noon the bright, sunny weather had changed; the heavens were overcast, and there was a fear that one of the sudden, heavy storms which were frequent at this season, might come before the day was over.

The duchess, with some of her friends, had taken their stand upon a height, from which they thought they could obtain the best view, but the hunters took a sudden turn, and the lookers on were forced to follow.

It was at this juncture that a slight accident occurred to Frau von Wallmoden; her saddle girth broke, and she would have had a disagreeable fall had she not had the presence of mind to slip at once from her saddle to the ground. To follow the riders was now an impossibility, for her groom could not have obtained another saddle for her, so she decided to send the servant over to Bucheneck with the horse, and follow on foot, at her leisure.

It was a relief to her that this accident had occurred, it saved her the weary necessity of following the hunt to its close, and permitted her to drop for a time, in this solitude, the mask which she wore before the world, and which was at times becoming almost too heavy for her to carry.

Now that she was alone and unobserved, the cold, proud repose which had been so noticeable since her wedding-day, departed as a shadow, and she was a creature of another world.

Her features, which were an heritage from her father, and betokened a strong and determined nature, had become more rigid in the last few months, but over her face lay a new expression, one of pain and anxiety, as if some secret and hitherto unknown spring had been touched; the blue eyes lost their cold, passionate look, deep shadows lay in them, which told of strife and anguish, and the blonde head sank low, as under some unsupportable burden.

And yet Adelheid breathed more freely than she had done for many a day, at the thought that this was the last one at Fürstenstein. To-morrow at this time, she would be far away, and distance she prayed would save her from that dark influence against which she had been battling for weeks in vain, when she would no longer see those eyes whose power she dreaded, or hear the voice which bewitched her. When she had flown from the mysterious power which held her, she could conquer and utterly destroy it. God be praised!

The sound of the hunt grew each moment less distinct, and was finally lost altogether in the distance; but in the wood, near the elevation on which she stood, the baroness could hear crunching footsteps which told her she was no longer alone. She turned to go in an opposite direction, but as she turned, a man's form appeared among the trees, and Hartmut Rojanow stood before her.

The meeting was so sudden that Adelheid lost her self-possession.

She drew back as if seeking protection among the trees beneath which she had been standing, and stared at him with the eyes of a wounded animal watching the pursuing hunter.

Rojanow did not appear to perceive this. He bowed and asked hastily: "Are you alone, baroness? The accident was not serious, then?"

"What accident?"

"I heard you'd been thrown from your horse!"

"What an exaggeration. My saddle girth broke, and as I saw it in time I jumped to the ground, while the animal stood perfectly still—that was the accident."

"Thank God—I heard something of a plunge, a fall, and as you did not return to the hunting field I—"

He stopped suddenly, for Adelheid's glance showed him she did not believe his statement; he had probably met the groom and had questioned him. Now at last her self-possession returned, and she said very coldly:

"I thank you, Herr Rojanow, but your solicitude was altogether unnecessary. You should have reflected that the duchess would not have allowed me to remain unsought in the wood had so serious an accident occurred. I sent her word I was on my way to Bucheneck."

She would have passed by him now, but as he stepped aside, he said in a low voice:

"My dear madame—I have to beg your pardon."

"My pardon—for what?"

"For the favor for which I plead so hard and injudiciously. I only asked for a flower. Is my crime then so great that your anger must last for weeks?"

Adelheid remained standing, almost without knowing it. She was again under the influence of those eyes and that wonderful voice.

"You are mistaken, Herr Rojanow," she responded. "I am not angry with you."

"No? And yet you assume again that icy tone which is ever yours when I am near you, and now that you have heard my drama you make no sign of approval. You were present when I read it at Fürstenstein. I heard words of praise on all sides. Your lips alone were closed. From you I received no single word of commendation—will you deny it to me now?"

"I thought we were out for a hunt, to-day," said Adelheid evasively, "and this is neither the time nor the place to discuss poetry."

"We have both left the hunt for to-day; it's on its way now toward the Rodecker heights. Here is the true forest loneliness. Look at the perfect autumn landscape around us. It speaks to the heart of peace and forgiveness. Look at that placid sheet of water, a those heavy storm-laden clouds against the horizon—to me there is more poetry in this than in the crowded salons of Fürstenstein."

The aspect of the landscape had entirely changed since the morning hours, and a dull, gloomy light had taken the place of the bright, clear sunshine, beneath whose gleams the cavalcade had set forth so merrily.

The endless stretch of forest which lay before them was in its gayest autumn dress, but in the sombre light of the approaching storm, its brilliant leaves looked faded and faint. The deep reds and many tinted yellows of the foliage formed a beautiful picture, but these were the colors of decay and death, and told that the end of their life and bloom was not far distant.

Beneath them lay the little lake, dark and motionless, surrounded by high grasses and swamp reeds. It looked like another lonely sheet of water in the far northland—the Burgsdorf fish pond, and back from this little lake stretched a meadow green and marshy, from which, even now, a faint mist was rising, a mist, which as night came down, would change into a rain, while the will-o'-the-wisp in its endless sport and motion, would play in and out among the long green rushes, now gleaming, now disappearing—thus perfecting that far off picture of long ago.

The air was oppressive and sultry, and the distant clouds were forming deeper and darker heights against the horizon.

Adelheid had not answered Hartmut's question; she stood looking into the distance with face turned away from the man who was watching her, and yet she felt the dark consuming glance resting on her, as she had felt it so many times during the past few weeks.

"You are going away to-morrow, my dear baroness!" he began again. "Who knows when you will return—when I shall see you again. May I not beg for your verdict now, may I not ask whether my words have found favor in Ada's eyes?"

Again her name upon his lips, again that soft, veiled, passionate tone which she so feared, and which rang in her ear like the voice of an enchanter. She felt there was no escape, no chance for flight, she must look the danger in the eye. She turned to her questioner, and her face betrayed that she had decided to fight out the battle—the battle with herself.

"Are you interested in my verdict merely because I bear this name?" she said coldly and proudly. "It stands at the beginning of your poem, which by the way was sent me the other day by some mysterious hand, without name."

"And which you read notwithstanding?" he interrupted triumphantly.

"Yes, and burned."

"Burned?" The old savage expression came over Hartmut's face, that intense angered look which had evoked from Egon's lips the expression, "You look like a demon, Hartmut." The demon of hate and revenge burned once again in his breast as he thought of his recent insults from this woman's husband, insults which must be resented to the full. And yet he loved the woman before him as only Zalika's son could love, with a wild, consuming passion. But in this moment hate gained the mastery.

"My poor pages!" he said with unconcealed bitterness. "They, too, suffered in the flame; they were, perhaps, worthy a better fate."

"Then you should not have sent them to me. I will not and dare not accept such poems."

"You dare not, my dear Baroness? It is the homage of a poet which he lays at a woman's feet, and poets have had that right for all time. It is incumbent on you to accept such an offering."

The words were spoken in such a hot, passionate whisper that Adelheid trembled.

"Perhaps you pay homage to the women of your country in such words. German woman do not understand them."

"But you understand them," said Hartmut fiercely, "and you understand the fire and passion of my 'Arivana,' which rises above all laws and restrictions of this narrow, human life. I saw that on the evening when you turned your back on me, while the rest of the world applauded and came forward with their congratulations. Do not deceive yourself, Ada. When the god-like spark enters two souls, it bursts into flame whether they be of the south or the cold north, and that spark has ignited and burns in us both. All strength and will dies in its fiery breath, it extinguishes all else, nothing remains but that holy, sacred fire which illumines and blesses, even while it consumes. You love me, Ada, I know it; do not try to deceive me, and I love you beyond all power of speech."

He stood before her in the triumph of victory. Never before had his dark beauty shone forth so strongly, never before had his eyes glowed with such intensity, or his face expressed such passion and longing.

And he had spoken the truth.

The woman who leaned against the tree, trembling and deadly pale, loved him; loved him as only a pure, exalted nature can love. This cold, haughty woman, whom the world had named heartless, was swayed and torn by this, the first love of her young life.

She felt within her a passion to which she could no longer blind herself; the fiery breath, with all its fierceness, was blowing down upon her. Now came the crucial-test.

"Leave me at once, Herr Rojanow—this instant," she said. The words had a choked, scarcely audible sound, and they were spoken to a man who was not accustomed to yield when he felt himself the victor. He would have gone closer to her—but something in the young wife's eye, in spite of all, kept him within bounds. But he spoke her name again, and in a tone whose power he best knew:

"Ada!"

She shuddered, and made a protesting motion.

"Not that name. For you I am only Adelheid von Wallmoden. I am married; you know that."

"Yes, married to a man who is standing on the threshold of old age; who does not love you, and for whom you could feel no love even if he were younger. What does that cold, calculating diplomat know of love? The Court, his position, his advancement, is all in all to him; his wife is nothing. He exults over the possession of a treasure whom he knows not how to prize, and to whose happiness and peace he gives not a thought."

Adelheid's lips trembled. She knew only too well that all he said was true. She did not answer.

"And what binds you to this man?" continued Rojanow, coming closer. "A word, a single 'yes,' which you have spoken without knowing its significance, without knowing yourself. Shall you permit it to bind you for your whole life? Shall you allow it to make us both miserable for all time? No, Ada, love, that eternal, undying right of the human heart, must have its own. Men prate of guilt, others of destiny. It is destiny which is beckoning us to-day, and we must follow after. A feeble word cannot separate us."

At this moment a lightning flash parted the heavy, distant clouds, and cast a long, narrow, dazzling light over the great forest, and gleamed across Hartmut's face and figure where he stood.

Surely he was his mother's son now. He never looked more like her than at this moment, with his dark, destroying beauty, and his peculiar, passionate, demoniacal glance. Perhaps it was this glance which brought Adelheid to her senses, perhaps it was the something concealed behind all the fire and passion.

"A freely given and freely received word is an oath," she said, slowly, "and who breaks it breaks his honor."

Hartmut breathed hard; keen and cruel like a lightning's flash, came a memory to his soul, the memory of that hour in which he had freely given his word—and broken it.

Adelheid von Wallmoden looked straight at Hartmut now; her face was pale, and her voice trembled as she addressed him again:

"I wish you to cease this persecution, which has been going on for weeks now. You fill me with horror—your eyes, your words, your manner. I feel that everything which emanates from you is false, and no one can love that which is false."

"Ada." There was a tone of passionate entreaty in his voice, but hers had gained in steadfastness now, and she continued earnestly:

"And you do not love me. I have seen for some time that your pursuance of me was from hate, not love. You and your kind have not the capacity for loving."

Rojanow was silent from surprise. Who had taught her to read him so nearly aright?

He had not even acknowledged to himself how closely the love and hate were united in his breast.

"And you say this to the author of Arivana?" he exclaimed with bitterness. "My drama has been called the ode to love, and—"

"Then those who so named it have been deceived by the flimsy veil of oriental legend in which your figures are enveloped, they have seen the Eastern priest with the woman he loves succumb to an iron, inhuman law. Perhaps you are a great poet, perhaps you will astonish the world with your fame, but to me you are something else, for the passion and fiery language of 'Arivana' have taught me something of its creator; of the man who believes in nothing, to whom nothing in the world is holy, neither duty nor pledge, neither manly honor nor womanly virtue; who would drag the highest in the dust for the sport of his passion. I yet believe in duty and honor, believe in myself, and with this belief I bid defiance to the fate which you so triumphantly prophesy will enthrall me. It can drive me to death— but never into your arms."

She stood opposite him, neither trembling nor irresolute. All her secret struggles were over, and with each word one more link of the chain was loosened.

Her eyes met his, full and free; she feared their dark, baneful glance no longer—that mysterious power was broken; she felt it and breathed deeply, like one whose hour of deliverance had come.

Again there was a flash of lightning, noiseless, not followed by any thunder crash, but it seemed to open the heavens to their very depths. In the palpitating light one could see fantastic cloud pictures, forms which seemed to struggle and battle with one another as if borne by force before the storm, and yet the cloud-mountain stood immovable on the far horizon; and just as immovable stood the man upon whose dark countenance the lightning flash revealed a deep pallor.

His eyes had not turned from the young wife's face, but the wild glow within them was extinguished, and his voice had a strange sound as he said:

"And this is the sentence for which I begged. I am then, in your eyes nothing more than a—reprobate?"

"A lost man, perhaps—you have forced me to this avowal."

Hartmut stepped slowly back a few steps.

"Lost," he repeated in bitter tone. "That is probably what you think. You may be at rest, my dear madam. I will never approach you again; one has no desire to hear such words a second time. You stand so proud and firm upon your watch tower of virtue and judge so severely. You have no conception what a wild, desperate life can make of a man who goes through the world without home or family. You are right. I believed in nothing in the heavens above or on the earth beneath—until this hour."

There was something in his tone and in his whole bearing which disarmed Adelheid.

She felt she had no cause to fear a further explosion of passion, and her voice grew milder as she answered:

"I judge no one, but I belong heart and soul to another world, with other laws than yours. I am the daughter of a father whom I dearly loved, who, all his life long, trod but one path, the earnest, rigid path of duty. Upon this he raised himself from poverty and privation to wealth and honor, and he taught his children to follow in the same way, and it is this thought which has been my shield and protection in this hard hour. I could not endure it if I were compelled to lower my eyes before the noble image which my memory holds. Your father is no longer alive?"

There followed a long, oppressive pause. Hartmut did not answer, but his head sank under the words of whose crushing significance the questioner had no knowledge, while his eyes seemed to pierce the ground.

"No," he said at last, slowly.

"But you have the memory of him and of your mother?"

"My mother!" Rojanow broke forth wildly now. "Do not speak of her, in this hour—do not speak to me of my mother."

It was an alarming cry, a mixture of boundless bitterness, with reproach and despair. In it the mother was sentenced by her son, he felt her memory was but a desecration of this hour.

Adelheid did not understand him, she only saw that she had touched on a point which admitted of no discussion, but she also saw that the man who stood before her with his deep, dark glance, with his tone of despair, was another than he who had stood there a quarter of an hour before. It was a dark, fathomless mystery upon which she gazed, but she had no longer any fear.

"Let us end this interview," she said, earnestly. "You will seek no second one, I believe that; but one word more before we part. You are a poet. I have felt that in spite of everything, as I have learned to know your work. But poets are teachers of mankind, and can lead to good or to ill. The wild flame of your 'Arivana' springs from a life which you, yourself, seem to hate. Look yonder," and she pointed to the distant heavens inflamed now with the lightning's play. "Those are also flaming brands, but their beginnings are from above and they point out another way—and now farewell!"

Long after she had disappeared, Hartmut stood on the same spot as if rooted to the ground. He had answered no word, made no comment, only gazed where she had pointed, with fixed, hopeless eyes.

Flash after flash of lightning was now rending the heavens and the whole landscape was enveloped in a lurid glare which reflected itself in that little sheet of water so like the Burgsdorf fish pond; the long reeds and grasses swayed and bent above the water and the mist from the meadow rose above it all.

Under just such long, waving grass the boy had lain long ago and dreamed of the day when he should mount like the falcon from which his race had taken their name, always higher and higher into boundless freedom toward the sun, and now on a similar spot the sentence had fallen upon him like a judgment from heaven, and the will-o'-the-wisp on this lowering autumn night seemed in its spectral flashes to dance over the grave of false hopes and falser aspirations. The falcon had not mounted to the skies, the earth had held him fast. He had felt for some time that the intoxicating cup of freedom and of life which his mother's hand had poured for him was poisoned; there were for him no cherished memories to guard—he dare not venture to think of his father.

Darker and darker grew the heavens with their heavy, storm laden clouds, and wilder and fiercer was the struggle between those giant figures which were riven at every flash only to come together again with greater fury, and brighter and more vivid grew that mighty flame as it mounted higher and higher in the inky firmament.

CHAPTER X

The winter gaieties had fairly begun in the South-German capital, and in the exclusive court circle the artistic element played a prominent part. The duke, who loved and fostered art, took great pride in being accounted its patron, and strove to make his capital an intellectual and artistic centre. The young poet who had been received so favorably by the court, and whose first great work was soon to be produced at the court theatre, was an object of great interest to the little world. It was an almost unheard of feat for a Roumanian to write in the German tongue, even though it was admitted that, in this instance, the writer had received his education in Germany. Here, as at Rodeck, he was the bosom friend and guest of Prince Adelsberg, and many strange and wonderful stories were related of this friendship. But Hartmut's personality, above all else, created for him an enviable position no matter where he turned. The young, handsome and genial stranger, surrounded as he was with a halo of romance and mystery, had only to appear to have all eyes turned upon him.

Soon after the return of the court to the city, the rehearsals for "Arivana" began, and its author and Prince Egon had the matter in charge.

The latter entered so enthusiastically into the spirit of it all, that he made the lives of the director and theatre attachés miserable with his many and contradictory suggestions concerning the setting of the drama, a matter about which, it is unnecessary to add, they were much more capable of directing than he. At first they could not get an actress to suit them, but they finally secured the services of a young and favorite opera-singer named Marietta Volkmar.

The preparations for the performance, which they had intended originally to bring out late in the season, were now hurried forward with all speed, for royal visitors were expected at court, and the duke was most anxious that this weird and poetical drama with its Indian setting should be presented before them. Unusual honors to the poet were prophesied as a result of this spectacle.

Such was the condition of affairs when Herbert von Wallmoden returned to the court, and he was, naturally, painfully surprised.

He had asked his wife casually, while inquiring for others, whether the prince's Roumanian friend had yet left Fürstenstein, and she had answered in the negative. He had not expected Hartmut to leave at once, for the latter had declared most positively he would not. But Wallmoden imagined he would think it all well over, and when Prince Adelsberg left Rodeck that would end the whole matter. Under no circumstances would Rojanow appear by the prince's side at the capital where the ambassador had threatened to denounce him at once.

But Baron von Wallmoden did not understand the unyielding defiance of this man, who had indeed dared much. Now, upon his return from the north, he found this "adventurer" established on a very sure footing, in close intercourse with the court and society of the capital. It would be a most embarrassing matter to explain everything at this late day, when all were on the *qui vive* of expectation, and when the duke was so deeply interested both in the new drama and in its author. It would make a very painful impression in all circles. The experienced diplomat did not disguise from himself the fact that the duke would complain, and with reason, that all this exposure should have been made on the first day of the stranger's appearance rather than at this inopportune time. There remained nothing for it but to be silent and await developments.

Wallmoden had no thought of the danger which had threatened himself. He had not seen fit to tell his wife anything concerning his old friend Falkenried's history, and decided now that she had better know nothing more about Prince Adelsberg's friend than was known by their associates.

No conversation concerning Hartmut had ever passed between them save the one fleeting question and his wife's monosyllabic answer.

But he felt he dare keep silence no longer toward his nephew Willibald, for there would be a similar scene to that enacted by the mother at Hochberg if the son was surprised by the sight of his boyhood's friend.

The young heir had accompanied the Wallmodens to the southern capital, where he intended remaining a few days, when he was going on to Fürstenstein to see his betrothed, for the head forester had expressly requested that the September visit, which was so suddenly interrupted, should be finished later in the season.

"You were only with us a week," he wrote to his sister-in-law, "and I desire to see something more of my future son-in-law. Everything is in order again, I trust, in your much loved Burgsdorf, and there is little to do in November at any rate. So send Will to us, even if you cannot come yourself.

I will not take no for an answer. Toni is waiting to see her lover—so don t fail!"

Frau von Eschenhagen admitted that he was right, and she was glad enough to have Will go. He had made no further attempt to assert himself against her motherly authority, and appeared to have fully regained his reason again. He had grown quieter of late and since his return from Fürstenstein rushed with greater zest into all his agricultural pursuits; he had, take it all in all, behaved in a most exemplary manner.

On one point alone he remained obstinate, he would not discuss with his mother the "idiocy" of which he had been guilty and which caused their sudden journey home, and avoided all reference to the subject. Of course his mother understood how it was; he was ashamed of his sudden excitement, and of a passion which had been only momentary, and wanted to forget it and have her forget it, too, as soon as possible. As for the rest, he wrote regularly to his bride-elect, who responded most punctually. Frau Regine, who considered it her special prerogative, read all this correspondence, and declared herself satisfied with it. There was no sentiment, no declaration of affection, in these letters; they were quite practical epistles, telling of home matters in a homely fashion, but they evinced Will's intention to keep his word and marry his cousin on the day appointed, and now near at hand.

So Willibald was told that he could go and visit his bride; the permission was granted all the more willingly because Frau Regine knew that Marietta Volkmar must have returned to the city long since. Baron von Wallmoden and his wife had paid a flying visit to Burgsdorf on their way south from the Stahlberg factories, and Willibald was put in their care and was to spend a few days in the South-German Capital. During those few days in which he would remain in the ambassador's house, he was perfectly safe, his mother assured herself.

The baron found that it would be necessary to tell his nephew about his old friend at once. On the very day of their arrival, Hartmut Rojanow's name was mentioned several times in Willibald's presence. He asked promptly to whom the name belonged, and was answered, 'to a young Roumanian poet.' An unmistakable wink from his uncle was all that saved him from further questions.

Then when they were alone the ambassador explained to Willibald who and what this Hartmut Rojanow was. An adventurer of the lowest and worst type, whom he would soon expose and force to abandon forever the *rôle* which he was now playing with so little right, but with such signal success.

Poor Willibald shook his head in a dazed sort of way over this news. His old friend, for whom he had always had a warm and unchanged affection, notwithstanding the episode of ten years before, was near him now, and he dare not see him again.

Wallmoden was especially sharp and explicit about this, and made his nephew promise to say nothing about the matter to Frau von Wallmoden or his uncle von Schönau. But poor Willibald could not understand it at all; he needed time and quiet with this as with all other things, to comprehend them fully.

The day on which "Arivana" was to be produced, came at last. It was the work of a young and unknown poet, but the circumstances connected with its production were such that society was anxious to judge for itself of this work of the duke's latest protégé. The theatre was crowded to overflowing, and the ducal couple with their suite were early in the court boxes. Although no special announcement had been made, the evening was evidently looked upon as a festival occasion, and every one was attired *a la grande toilette*, the ladies vieing with one another in the richness and brilliancy of their dress.

Prince Adelsberg, who was in the ducal box, was as much excited as if he had written the drama himself.

His aunt, too, was greatly interested in the success of the evening's entertainment, and had been looking carefully over the play bill when he entered the box; she called him to her at once.

"Our young friend seems to have his whims like all other poets," she remarked. "What a singular caprice to change the name of his heroine in the last hour."

"But that is not the case," Egon answered. "The change was made long before we left Rodeck. Hartmut took it into his head that 'Ada' was too cold and clear-cut a name for the passionate character of his heroine, so he re-baptized her."

"But the name 'Ada' is here on the programme," interrupted the princess.

"Certainly, but it belongs to quite a different person in the drama now, one who only appears in a single scene."

"Then Herr Rojanow has made his alterations since he read it for us at Fürstenstein?"

"Only a few; the play is really quite unchanged with that single exception. Hartmut has added that scene with Ada in it, and I can assure your highness it's the most poetical thing he has ever written."

"Of course, everything your friend writes is wonderful in your eyes," his aunt answered, but her unusually gracious smiles showed that in this opinion she did not disagree with him.

The ambassador and his wife, who had only returned forty-eight hours before, sat in one of the large proscenium boxes. Baron von Wallmoden was anything but a willing guest of the court to-night, but he knew it was incumbent on him in his position to accept this evening's invitation. The duke had invited the whole diplomatic corps, and as the North German ambassador and his wife had dined at the ducal table that evening no excuse could be offered for declining the later entertainment.

Willibald had come too, to see and hear the work of his old-time friend; as his uncle was to be there, surely he had a right also. It did not please Wallmoden to have him there, but he could not well forbid his nephew's presence when he himself was present. Will, who had some difficulty in obtaining a seat in the parquette, unfolded the programme carelessly, when suddenly his eye caught the name of "Marietta Volkmar," and knew whom he was to see this evening. He folded the programme hastily and put it in his pocket; he regretted in this moment that he had come to the theatre at all.

Finally the performance began. The curtain rose, and the first act, little more than a prelude, was soon over. It was an introduction to the spectators, of that weird, fantastic, legendary world into which they were to enter, with Arivana, the sacred place of offering, the holy of holies, in the foreground.

The principal character in the drama, the young priest, who in the fanaticism of his belief puts everything earthly far from him, as unclean, appeared, and in a few masterly, powerful lines, pronounced his vow, by which, for him, for time and eternity, all earthly bonds were loosed, and he was committed heart and soul to the service of his God. The oath was taken, the holy flame blazed and waved on the sacrificial altar, and the curtain fell.

The applause, started at once by the duke, resounded on all sides. This work, about which so much had been said, was bound to be a success, in a certain sense, for this one evening at least. But there was something more than idle flattery in this applause. The spectators felt at once that, a true poet had spoken to them; the creation had already had the commendation of the court, but the public were carried away with it now. They were charmed by the diction, by the characters, and by the subject, and when the curtain rose anew, there was a look of silent expectancy on every face.

The drama now moved forward in majestic measure upon a scenic background as full of warmth and color as the language and characters of the piece.

The luxuriant vegetation of India, the fabulous pomp of her temples and her palaces; the men and women with their wild loves and their still wilder hatred; the rigid laws of their faith; all this was strange and fantastic, but the manner in which these men and women felt and acted was familiar to every one. They stood under the influence of a power which is the same to-day that it was a thousand years ago; the same in the tropics and in the colder climes of the north; the power of passion in the heart of man. It was indeed a doctrine of fire, and its burden was the inalienable right of passion to sweep away every obstacle, to break down every barrier of law and custom, of oath and pledge, which stood between it and its aim.

A right which Hartmut Rojanow well understood and illustrated in the exercise of his own unbridled will, which knew no law and no duty, and to which self-gratification was the highest good.

The awakening of this passion, its mighty growth and final triumph, was described in words of ravishing eloquence, and depicted in pictures which seemed drawn, now from the purest heights of ideality, and now from the depths of the pit. The poet had done wisely to drape his characters with the veil of an oriental legend, for under this covering he might express sentiments and present scenes, which otherwise would scarcely have been forgiven, and he did this now with a boldness which threw glowing sparks into the souls of those who heard him, and held them enthralled as if by some infernal spell.

By the close of the second act, the success of Arivana was assured.

The work was presented with a skill and perfection of acting never surpassed on any stage. The actors in the two principal *rôles* played their parts with a fire and perfection which could only have come from genuine enthusiasm. The heroine was no longer called Ada. That name was borne by a being who stood, strange and alone, in this restless world of surging passions; one of those half-fabulous creatures with whom the Indian legends people the icy summits of the Himalayas; cold and pure as the eternal snows which glisten in those lofty regions. She appeared only in one scene, and at the decisive moment of the drama, where she moved through the stormy action as if upon spirits' pinions, warning and exhorting, and Egon was quite right when he said that the words which the poet put into her mouth were the most beautiful of the whole play.

Suddenly the pure, white light of heaven breaks through the red glow of the drama; the scene is beautiful, but short and swift and fleeting as the zephyr's breath. The chaste form vanished to the snowy heights of her distant home, while here below from the river's moonlit shore rose the song of the Hindoo maiden—Marietta's soft and swelling voice; the cry of warning from above was lost in these sweet seductive tones. In the last act came the tragic ending, the judgment upon the guilty pair who suffer death in the flames. But this death was no atonement, it was rather a triumph, a glorious apotheosis, and out of the midst of the fire flamed high toward heaven the infernal doctrine of the unconditional right of passion. The curtain fell for the last time, and the applause, which had increased from act to act, rose now to a perfect storm. The house shouted for the author and would take no denial. At last Hartmut came forward, free from every trace of embarrassment, and beaming with pride and joy. He bowed his thanks to the public, which had held to his lips that night a cup of delight such as he had never before tasted. They are intoxicating, these first draughts from the goblet of fame! In the pride of victory the young poet cast a glance toward the proscenium box whose inmates he had already recognized.

He did not find what he sought.

Adelheid had leaned back in her chair and covered her face with an open fan. He saw only the cold, unmoved countenance of the man who had so deeply insulted him, and who now was the witness of his triumph.

Wallmoden understood only too well the mute language of those flashing dark eyes; they said to him:

"Dare to despise me now!"

At an early hour the next morning, Willibald von Eschenhagen entered the great city park, which, he had just declared to his uncle, he would explore for himself. This extensive, well-wooded park, which lay before the city's very doors, was well worth a visit, but Willibald took scant notice of its beauties as he hurried on in the keen November morning. He glanced neither to the right nor to the left, but strode on, striking into this path and now into that, frequently re-treading the very ground which he had left but a moment before.

Perhaps this brisk, aimless walk, would silence or stupefy the passion and excitement which were struggling for mastery within him.

Some of his excitement was due to seeing his old friend again, for he had been greatly moved at the sight of him. Fourteen long years he had heard nothing of Hartmut, had been forbidden even to mention his name, and now he stood before him suddenly in all the pride and glory of a rising poet's fame, wonderfully changed in appearance and manner, but yet the old Hartmut still, the same with whom he had so often frolicked and never quarreled in by-gone days. Even had he been unprepared, he would have known his dear old friend at a glance.

Wallmoden had been greatly disturbed and annoyed at the result of the previous night's performance. He had scarcely spoken as they drove from the theatre, and his wife had been equally taciturn. She explained that the heat of the crowded room had given her a headache, and in consequence retired at once upon reaching home.

Her example was followed by her husband, who, as he bade his nephew good-night, said:

"Do not forget our talk, Willibald. Be silent before every one, no matter who. You'll have to be on your guard, too, for the name of Rojanow will be on every one's lips for the next few days. He's had luck this time, like all adventurers!"

Willibald made no answer to this, but he felt that something beyond adventurer's luck had come to the author of Arivana. Under other circumstances he should have looked on this drama as something unheard of, inexplicable, without in the least understanding it, but last night he seemed to comprehend it all fully.

One could love without the consent of parent or guardian; such freedom was not confined to India alone—it often happened in Germany as well. A promise given thoughtlessly and blindly could be broken, but what then? Yes, then came the fate which Hartmut had pictured so beautifully, yet so vividly. Will was fully determined to transfer the lesson which Arivana had taught him to Burgsdorf. Surely the punishment invoked by the furious priestcraft, would be no worse than the vial of Frau von Eschenhagen's wrath.

The young heir sighed deeply as he thought of the second act of the drama, where, from the group of Hindoo maidens, the sacrificial figure steps forth. How lovely she looked in her soft, white, clinging garments, with the wealth of flowers in her dark curly hair. His eyes had never left her during the two or three times when she had appeared for a moment on the stage; then her song sounded forth from the shore of the moonlit river, the same clear, sweet voice which had captivated him in the little parlor of Waldhofen, and here again were the same old unholy feelings against which he had battled so bravely then.

And the worst of it was that he no longer considered them unholy.

The energetic walker came for the third time to a little temple which was open at one side and within which were seats inviting to rest, and a marble bust in the centre. Willibald stepped in and sat down, less from necessity for rest than with the hope he might in this seclusion get his disturbed thoughts in order.

It was about ten o'clock in the morning, and the grounds were almost entirely deserted.

Only a single pedestrian, a young man elegantly attired, lounged along slowly, and to the casual observer, purposelessly.

But he was on the lookout for some one, for he glanced with unconcealed impatience toward the winding walks which led direct from the city.

Suddenly he stepped quickly behind one of the pillars which supported the little temple, where he could see any one approaching without being seen himself.

About five minutes later a young lady walking briskly came along a narrow path which led past the temple. She was of slight, graceful figure, wore a dark, fur-trimmed mantle with cap and muff to match, and was glancing over a roll of manuscript as she stepped quickly forward.

Suddenly she gave a surprised cry, which had anything but a joyful sound, as the young man stepped in front of her.

"Oh, Count Westerburg."

The man bowed low as he exclaimed:

"What a happy accident! Who would have thought to find Fräulein Marietta Volkmar seeking the fresh air of the park at this hour."

Marietta stood still and looked the speaker well over from head to foot, before she answered, in a tone of mingled anger and contempt:

"I do not believe it is by accident that you so often and so persistently cross my path, Herr Count, although I have been very explicit as to the annoyance which your attentions cause me."

"Oh, yes, you have been very cruel to me," said the count reprovingly, but with unmistakable assurance. "You will not permit me to visit you, despise my gifts of flowers, hardly acknowledge my greetings when you meet me. What have I done to you? I have ventured to prove my devotion by laying at your feet a little tribute in the form of jewels, but you return them with—"

"With the explanation that I decline such insolent advances now and always," Marietta interrupted angrily; "that I will have no more of your brazen impertinences. You have waylaid me purposely to-day."

"Good heavens! I am only here to sue for pardon for my boldness," said the count, as he stepped, with apparent submissiveness, directly in front of her in the narrow path. "I know full well how unapproachable you are, and that no one guards her reputation more jealously than the beautiful Marietta."

"My name is Fräulein Volkmar," cried Marietta angrily. "Save such familiar speeches for those who appreciate them. I do not, and if you do not cease your importunities, I will in future claim protection against them."

"Whose protection?" sneered the count. "Perhaps that of the old woman with whom you live, and who is forever at your side! It is only when you go to Professor Marani that she is left at home; you do not regard the old singing master as dangerous. But that is the only time when you are without her."

"Except for a morning walk in the park, of which you are apparently aware. Get out of my path, please. I want to go on."

She attempted to pass him, but the count put out both arms to intercept her.

"You will at least, give me permission to accompany you, Fräulein? You can see for yourself the walks are lonely and deserted, and I'm bound to offer you my protection."

The park was indeed deserted; no sign of life in any direction, and the brave girl was secretly alarmed, but she answered, boldly:

"Do not attempt to follow me a single step. Your protection would be as unendurable as is your presence. How often have I to repeat that?"

"Ah, how angry she can get," said the count with a malicious laugh. "Ah, I must be repaid for those hard words. I must have a kiss from those rosy lips which speak so harshly."

He made a movement to take her in his arms, as the girl drew back, really alarmed now, but in the same moment he lay sprawling upon the sward, a heavy blow, well aimed, having thrown him to the damp ground, where he lay, a most contemptible object!

Marietta turned, more alarmed than ever, in the direction from which the blow had come, and the angry, hot expression on her face was succeeded by one of boundless surprise, when she saw who it was that had come to her aid so suddenly, and now stood by her side gazing grimly at the prostrate man whom he had put in this humiliating position with such evident satisfaction.

"Herr von Eschenhagen—you?"

Count Westerburg had in the meantime risen with some difficulty, and now advanced threateningly toward his new enemy.

"Sir, what do you mean by this? Who has given you the right—who has given you the right—"

"Stay where you are! Don't advance a step nearer this lady," interrupted Willibald, placing himself in front of Marietta, "or I'll send you flying under those trees, and you won't get up from the second blow as soon as you did from the first."

The count, who was neither very large nor very rugged, and who had felt already the weight of this young giant's fist, measured Willibald for a minute, but that was long enough to convince him that a hand to hand scuffle could only result one way.

"You will give me satisfaction—if you are capable of giving satisfaction," he began in a half-suffocated voice. "Probably you don't know that you have before you a—"

"A low scoundrel whom it will give me pleasure to discipline," said Willibald, composedly. "Remain where you are, if you please, or I shall be obliged to do it on the spot. My name is Willibald von Eschenhagen of Burgsdorf, and I am to be found at the residence of the Prussian ambassador, if you have anything more to say. I beg you to accept my protection, Fräulein, and I'll pledge myself that you'll not be insulted again."

And then something unheard of, almost past belief, happened.

Herr von Eschenhagen, without awkwardness or embarrassment, with the grace of a gentleman of the old school, offered Fräulein Volkmar his arm and led her away, without troubling himself farther about the low scoundrel!

Marietta had accepted his arm, but she spoke no word; as soon as they were out of hearing she began, with an agitation which was anything but natural to her: "Herr von Eschenhagen—"

"Yes, Fräulein?"

"I—I am very grateful to you for your protection. But the Count—you have insulted him deeply—he will challenge you, and you will accept his challenge?"

"Certainly, with the greatest pleasure," answered Will, and a smile broke over his face which proved that such a state of affairs would give him great gratification. His stupidity and obtuseness had disappeared, he felt he was a hero and deliverer, and was very well satisfied with himself. Marietta looked up at him in speechless surprise.

"But it is terrible that all this should happen on my account," she remonstrated. "And that it should be you, of all men."

The last remark did not please the young man.

"You evidently regret that, Fräulein," he said rather stiffly. "But under such circumstances you cannot always have what you want. I was near by, and you were forced to accept my services even though I do not stand very well in your esteem."

A flush crossed Marietta's face as she remembered the time when she had poured the vials of her wrath and contempt over this man who now came to her rescue so bravely.

"I was thinking of Toni and her father," she answered softly. "I am altogether blameless, but if I should be the cause of tearing you from your bride—"

"Then Toni would have to accept it as an intervention of Providence," answered Willibald, upon whom the mention of his betrothed seemed to make no impression. "One can but lose his life once, and there is no use looking on the worst side, either. Where shall I take you, Fräulein? To Park street? I think I heard you lived on that street."

She shook her head violently.

"No, no; I cannot walk, I shall call a carriage; there are some over there. I had meant to go to Professor Marani, to practice a new part, but I cannot sing now."

Willibald turned his steps in the direction where the carriages were standing, and they went on in silence until they came near them. Marietta stopped then, and turning to her escort, said anxiously:

"Herr von Eschenhagen, must it be? Can nothing be done?"

"Well, hardly. I knocked the count down, and called him a low scoundrel, and most fellows would regard that as sufficient grounds for a duel. But, don't you worry about it. The whole affair will be over to-morrow or next day, with only a couple of scratches to tell the tale, in all probability."

"And I shall have to wait two or three days in anxiety and uncertainty. Cannot you send me some news?"

Will looked down into the dark, tearful eyes, and a light came in his own such as had gleamed from them on the first day he saw the little "singing bird."

"When all is happily over, I'll come myself and bring you the news if I may?"

"Certainly, certainly. But if it should end unfortunately, if you should fall?"

"Then hold me in kinder remembrance than you have done hitherto," said Willibald, earnestly and cordially. "You took me for a coward. O, don't say a word, you were right; I have felt it bitterly enough, but I was accustomed always to obey my mother, who I knew loved me devotedly. But now you see that I know also how a man should behave when he sees a defenseless girl insulted, and I will avenge that insult—if need be with my blood."

Without waiting for an answer, he hailed a driver, assisted Marietta into the carriage, and repeated to the man the street and number which she gave him. She placed her little hand in his for a moment, and gave him a long look, then, as the carriage rolled away, she threw herself back on the cushions with a loud sob. Will looked after the carriage as long as it was in sight, then he threw his shoulders back and said, with a sort of fierce pleasure:

"Now, have a care, Herr Count. It will be a real pleasure for me to have a shot at you."

CHAPTER XI

The short November day was nearly over, and the twilight shadows were lengthening rapidly, when Prince Egon, returning from a short walk, entered his brilliantly lighted palace.

"Is Herr Rojanow in his rooms?" he asked a footman.

"Yes, your highness," the servant answered with a respectful bow.

"Then order the carriage for nine o'clock, to take us to the castle."

So saying Egon sprang quickly up the stairs, and hastened to his friend's apartments, which were on the first floor, not far from his own, and which were furnished with all the old-time magnificence of a princely house. A lamp was burning on the table in Hartmut's little study, and he himself, looking weary and dejected, was lying full length upon a couch.

"He of the laurel wreath is taking his rest," said the prince, laughing, as he entered the room and came quickly forward to his friend. "I can't find fault with you this time, for you haven't had a minute's rest to-day. There's something exciting in being the rising star in the poet's heaven, but it's hard on the nerves, I must admit. People are vieing with one another to do you honor. You certainly had an overwhelming reception to-day."

"Yes, and we must go to the court to-night," Hartmut answered in a tired, indifferent tone; evidently the prospect was not an enlivening one.

"We must, indeed. The high and mighty desire to do homage to the hero of the hour, my dear aunt at the head of them. You must know that she thinks she's the embodiment of soulfulness and poesy herself, and that she has discovered a responsive spirit in you Praise the Lord! She'll leave me alone for a while, and if she gets very deep in her illusions, she'll forget ail about the marriage plan, for the time at least; but you seem to be very indifferent to the ducal favor which, by the way, is quite pronounced. You hardly speak. Are you ill?"

"I'm tired. I wish I could escape from all the noise, and go to Rodeck."

"To Rodeck? That would be a fine place in the November mists and the damp, leafless forests. Ugh, it gives me the horrors."

"All the same, I have a great longing for the dreary loneliness, and I'm going there, too, after a few days; that is, if you have no objection."

"Well, I have very serious objections," retorted Egon crossly. "In heaven's name what's the matter with you anyway? Now when the whole city is wild over the author of 'Arivana' and your presence is demanded everywhere, you want to run away from all the glory and triumph, and hide yourself in a little, dark hole which is only bearable in midsummer. Such an idea is unheard of."

"For my own sake—I need quiet and rest—I will go to Rodeck."

The young prince shook his head. He was accustomed to have his friend do as he pleased without much heed to his remonstrances, and he knew no means by which he could combat this new whim; but it did appear to him a very unaccountable one.

"I believe my highly esteemed aunt knows what she's talking about sometimes," he said, between a joke and a reproof. "She said to me last night, in the theatre, 'Our friend has caprices like other poets.' I agree with her. What has come over you, Hartmut? Yesterday and to-day you were fairly beaming with triumph and joy, and now I have scarcely left you for an hour and return to find you in the depths of melancholy. Have you seen anything in the papers which has annoyed you? Something from the pen of a malicious, spiteful critic, I'll be bound."

He turned toward the writing-table, where the evening papers lay.

"No, no," Rojanow said, hastily, but he turned his face sidewise, so that it lay in the shadow. "All the papers mention 'Arivana,' and each strives to outdo his neighbor in writing complimentary things about me. You know I am of an uncertain temper, and am often cast down, without being able to give reason for my depression."

"Yes, but now when you are overwhelmed with praise, fairly extolled to the skies, such depression should be far from you. You really seem exhausted. That comes from the excitement we both have undergone during the past few weeks."

He bent anxiously over his friend, who stretched out his hand to him as if to atone for this sudden change.

"Forgive me, Egon. You must have patience with me—I'll be myself again in a little while."

"I sincerely hope so. My poet has much honor awaiting him, even tonight. I'll leave you now. Try and rest, and don't let any one else disturb you. You have three good hours before we need start."

The prince went. He had not seen the bitter smile on his friend's face when he referred to his triumphs and good fortune; and yet the prince had spoken the truth. Fame was good fortune and happiness, perhaps the highest in life, and Hartmut was willing to acknowledge that it was so, until an hour ago, when a bitter drop had mingled in his cup.

When the young man had entered his room an hour before, he had glanced hastily over the evening papers. A review of his work was to be found in each, and he read with interest the impressions which the drama had made: of its strength, and depth, and power, and how skillfully the young and talented Roumanian, Hartmut Rojanow, had outlined and elaborated his characters.

Then, as he turned the sheet, another name met his gaze, a name which, for the moment, deadened his very senses.

The article which caught his eye stated that the recent journey of the Prussian Ambassador to Berlin, had been on a matter of great significance. Herr von Wallmoden had had an audience of the duke immediately on his return, and they had discussed matters of the gravest importance, and now a high Prussian officer was expected, who was the bearer of certain special dispatches to the duke. It was evident that some weighty military affair was under discussion, and Colonel Hartmut von Falkenried would be in the city in a few days.

Hartmut let the paper drop from his hands; his whole body seemed to turn to ice. His father to be here in a day or two! Herr von Wallmoden would of course tell him all. The possibility of meeting him now seemed to resolve itself into a certainty.

"When you have made a great, proud name and future for yourself then you can stand before him and ask him whether he despises you or not," Zalika had said to her son on that memorable night when he had protested against breaking his word to his father. Now the first step toward this brilliant future had been taken.

Hartmut Rojanow already wore the laurel wreath, and that was enough, surely, to obliterate the past. It should and must be enough; and it was this thought which blazed from Hartmut's eyes as he looked toward the ambassador's box last night.

But could he look thus into his father's eyes? Despite all his defiance he feared those eyes, and them alone, in all the world.

He had partly decided to go to Rodeck, and then he picked up the paper again to see if any date was named for the distinguished officer's arrival. He felt within him a something—a secret and burning longing. Perhaps now when his great triumph was but just begun, the hour for reconciliation had come; perhaps, when Falkenried saw what the freedom and life for which his son had craved so long ago, had developed, he would forgive the boy for the sake of the man. He was his child still, his only son, whom he had clasped to his arms with such passionate tenderness on that last evening at Burgsdorf.

This memory brought with it a mighty longing in Hartmut's soul for those arms, for a home, for all that he had lost since those boyhood's days, which, despite their severity, had been so innocent, so peaceful, so happy.

The door opened, and a servant entered and extended a card on a salver. Rojanow made an impatient movement to take it away.

"Didn't I tell you I wouldn't see any one else to-day?"

"I told the gentleman that," explained the servant, "but he said he'd like Herr Rojanow to hear his name, anyway—Willibald von Eschenhagen."

Hartmut rose suddenly from his reclining position; he did not believe he had heard aright.

"What name, did you say?"

"Von Eschenhagen—here is the card."

"Ah—show him up. Hurry!"

The servant left the room, and a minute later Willibald entered, but remained standing, uncertain and hesitating, near the door. Hartmut had sprung up and was staring at him. Yes, these were the same old features, the dear face, the honest blue eyes of his youth's friend, and with a passionate cry of:

"Will! My own dear Will! Is it really you? You have come to me!" he threw his arms stormingly around his friend's neck.

The young heir, who little understood how his appearance just at the moment when old memories were welling up in Hartmut's brain, had moved his friend, was almost overcome by this reception. He remembered that Hartmut had always been his superior, intellectually, and how many times he had been made to feel this. He had thought that the author of

"Arivana" would have grown even more imperious and self-assertive, and now he was given this tender and overwhelming reception.

"Are you then so rejoiced to see me, Hartmut?" he asked, somewhat timorously. "I almost feared it would not be right for me to come."

"Not right, when I have not seen you for ten long years?" cried Hartmut, reprovingly. And then he drew his friend toward him and began to ask questions and chatter away with such genuine heartiness, that Will soon lost his shyness and could speak as of old to him.

He explained that he had only been three days in town, and was on his way to Fürstenstein.

"Yes, and you're to be married soon. I heard of your betrothal at Rodeck, and I have seen Fräulein von Schönau once. I wish you great happiness, old fellow."

Willibald took the wish for his happiness with characteristic coolness. He sat and gazed on the floor, and said in a low tone:

"Yes—my mother chose a wife for me."

"I can well believe that," said Hartmut laughing. "But you at least gave your 'yes' willingly."

Willibald did not answer, but seemed to be studying the pattern of the carpet intently; suddenly he asked abruptly:

"Hartmut—how do you go to work to write poetry anyhow?"

Hartmut repressed a smile with difficulty. "That is not easy to explain. I really fear I cannot answer you intelligibly."

"Yes, writing poetry is a curious thing," sighed Willibald with a sad shake of the head. "I tried it myself after I came out of the theatre last night."

"What! You've taken to poetry?"

"Haven't I, though," said Will with a lofty self-consciousness. "But," he added dejectedly, "I can't make it rhyme, and it hasn't the same sound as your verses. I have it in my head, but I don't suppose I have it just right. How did you begin yours? The commencement is the stumbling block. It's nothing very great or romantic, like 'Arivana.'"

"Addressed to her of course?" hazarded Hartmut.

"Yes, to her," Willibald admitted with a deep sigh; and now his listener laughed out loud and clear.

"Well, you are a model son, one must concede that. It's not unusual for a man to be engaged in response to a father's or mother's wishes, but your sense of duty is so strong that you fall in love with the girl and even go so far as to write verses in her praise."

"But they are not to her," cried Willibald suddenly, and with so sorrowful a face that Hartmut gazed at him dumbfounded. He believed that his friend was out of his mind, and Willibald's next statement quite overpowered him, without weakening this suspicion.

"I had a quarrel early this morning with an insolent fellow who attempted to insult a lady, Fräulein Marietta Volkmar of the Court theatre of this city. I struck him to the ground and I'd do it again if I had an opportunity;—him, or any one else who came near Fräulein Volkmar."

He had grown so excited, and rose, as he spoke, with such a threatening air, that Hartmut seized him by the arm and held him fast.

"Well, I've no intention of going near her, so you needn't shake your fist at me, old boy. But what have you to do with the opera singer, Marietta Volkmar, who has always posed as a very mirror of virtue?"

"Hartmut, have a care. You must speak respectfully of this lady to me. To make a long story short, this Count Westerburg has challenged me, and we're going to have a shot at one another, and I sincerely hope I'll leave him with a remembrance he won't soon forget."

"Well, you're making very fair progress in your romance, I must say," Hartmut answered with growing astonishment. "You've been in town two days, have had a quarrel with a stranger, who has demanded satisfaction, are the knight and protector of a young singer on whose account you are going to fight a duel. For God's sake, Will, what'll your mother say?"

"As it concerns an affair of honor, my mother will have no right to say anything," Willibald declared with true heroism. "But I will have to find a second here, where I am a stranger and know no one. Of course uncle Wallmoden knows nothing of the matter, or he would have the police interfere at once, so I resolved to come and ask you whether you would perform that service for me?"

"Ah, that's why you came?" said Hartmut in a pained voice. "I thought for the moment it was the old friendship which had brought you. But, all the same, I am at your service. With what weapons do you fight?"

"With pistols."

"That's an advantage for you. When we used to shoot at a target at Burgsdorf, you were a fine shot. I'll see the Count's second the first thing in the morning, and let you know of the arrangements at once; but I must write to you, for I won't enter Herr von Wallmoden's house."

Willibald only nodded. He had thought that his uncle's enmity would be returned in full by Rojanow, so considered it better to say nothing on the subject.

"Yes, write me," he answered. "You make what arrangements you deem fit. I have no experience in such matters, and leave it all to you. Here is the second's address. Now I must go. I have much to do yet—I must prepare for the worst."

He rose and held out his hand to his friend, but Hartmut did not see it. He sat with eyes fastened on the ground, as he said in a low, stifled tone:

"Wait a minute, Will—Burgsdorf is not far from Berlin—do you often see—"

"Who?" asked Will.

"My—my father."

The young heir was evidently embarrassed by the question; he had avoided the name of Falkenried all through the conversation, and he did not know that the father was expected in the city.

"No," he answered finally, "We don't see the Colonel at all."

"But he comes to Burgsdorf sometimes, does he not?"

"No—he keeps to himself, but I saw him by chance the other day with uncle Wallmoden in Berlin."

"And how does he look? Is he much changed in these last years?"

Willibald shrugged his shoulders: "He has certainly grown old. You would hardly recognize him with his white hair."

"White hair!" exclaimed Hartmut. "He is scarcely fifty-two years old—has he been ill?"

"No—not that I know. His gray hair came suddenly in a few months when he demanded that his resignation be accepted."

Hartmut grew pale and stared at the speaker with anxious eyes.

"My father wished to leave the army, he, heart and soul a soldier, devoted to his profession—in what year did that happen?"

"They would not accept it," said Will, evasively. "They sent him to a distant garrison instead, and for the last three years he has been minister of war."

"But he wanted to go—in what year was it?" Hartmut asked in a determined voice now.

"It was when you disappeared. He believed his honor demanded it. You should not have treated your father so, Hartmut; it nearly killed him."

Hartmut gave no answer, made no attempt to vindicate himself, but he breathed heavily.

"We'd better not talk about it," said Will, turning to go. "Nothing can be undone now, I'll expect your letter in the morning, and you'll arrange everything. Good-night."

Hartmut did not seem to hear his friend's words nor notice his departure; he stood and stared on the ground. A few minutes after Willibald had left the room he threw his head back, and passed his hand over his eyes.

"He would have resigned," he muttered, "resigned, because he believed his honor demanded it—no, no, I cannot see him, not now—I shall go to Rodeck."

The gifted poet, who had stood proud and triumphant before the whole world and received the laurel wreath of fame, dared not meet his father's eye—rather face loneliness and desolation.

Marietta Volkmar lived with an old kinswoman of her grandfather in a modest little house surrounded by a tiny garden, in one of those restful, retired streets which are fast disappearing from our large cities.

The two women, old and young, lived a quiet, uneventful life, which permitted no breath of gossip concerning the young singer; they were objects of interest and affection to the other inmates of the house, and Marietta's clear voice was a welcome sound and her bright young face a cheering sight, to the few who had apartments under the same roof.

For the past two days the "singing bird" had been dumb, and whosoever caught sight of her face, saw pale, tear-stained cheeks and swollen eyes. The people of the house could not explain it, and shook their heads over it until old Fräulein Berger said that Dr. Volkmar was ill, and his grandchild could not obtain permission just now to go to him. All this was true enough for the good doctor was suffering from a severe cold.

But it was no sufficient reason for Marietta's despondency, which had caused much comment among her fellow-workers at the theatre.

She stood at the window of the comfortable little living-room, having just returned from rehearsal, and looked out drearily into the quiet street. Fräulein Berger was stitching industriously by the little centre table, and looked up now at the young girl with a grave shake of the head.

"Child, why do you take the thing so hard?" she said, almost sharply. "You'll wear yourself out with all this anxiety and excitement. What's the sense of looking on the worst side?"

Marietta turned toward the speaker; she was very pale and there was a sob in her voice, as she replied:

"This is the third day and I can learn nothing. O, it is terrible, this waiting hour after hour for bad news." "But why need it be bad?" remonstrated the old lady. "Yesterday afternoon Herr von Eschenhagen, was well and happy. I went out myself at your desire and found he was out driving with Herr and Frau von Wallmoden. Perhaps the matter has been settled amicably."

"Then I'd have had news before now," the girl answered, hopelessly. "He promised me and he'd keep his word, I know it. If anything has happened, if he has fallen—I believe I can't live through it."

The last words sounded forth so passionately that Fräulein Berger glanced at the speaker frightened.

"Marietta, that sounds very unreasonable," she said. "It wasn't your fault that you were insulted, neither would you be to blame if your friend Toni's fiancé was shot. You couldn't really be more despairing if it was your own lover who was to fight."

A deep flush overspread the pale features of the girl for a moment, and she turned again toward the window.

"You do not understand, auntie," she replied in a low tone. "You do not know how much happiness I have had in the head forester's house, how humbly Toni begged my pardon for the insults her future mother-in-law heaped upon me. What will she think of me when she hears that her lover has had a duel on my account? What will Frau von Eschenhagen say?"

"Well, they can be easily convinced that you are blameless in the whole affair, and if it ends well, they need know nothing about it. I hardly know you, child, the last few days. You, who always laughed every care and anxiety away, to sit and mope and grieve. It's incomprehensible to me. You have hardly eaten or drunk a thing for two days, and wouldn't sit down to your breakfast this morning. But you must eat some dinner, and I must go and see to it at once."

With this the old lady rose and left the room. She was right, poor Marietta seemed indeed a changed girl. It was without doubt a painful, depressing feeling, that blame would undoubtedly rest upon her; her friends at Fürstenstein perhaps might never be made to understand the real state of the case, how innocent she was of any intention to wrong or even annoy them; her reputation, too, of which she had been so guarded; would not every paper be teeming with this "affair of honor," if either combatant were killed?

"If need be with my blood," these had been Willibald's last words to her and they rang in her ears. "O, God be merciful. Not that! not that!"

Suddenly a tall, manly figure turned the corner and came forward hastily through the little street, evidently in search of some special number, and as Marietta looked down she gave a cry of delight, for she recognized Herr von Eschenhagen.

She did not wait for the bell to be answered, but rushed out impetuously to open the door herself.

Her eyes were wet with tears, but her voice sounded clear and jubilant:

"You have come at last—God be praised!"

"Yes, here I am, safe and sound," Willibald replied, while his whole face glowed at this reception.

How they got back to the little sitting-room neither of them ever knew, but he had drawn her arm through his and led her in, while she feasted her eyes on his flushed, happy face. But now she noticed that his right wrist was bandaged.

"You have been hurt?" she said, in an anxious whisper.

"Only a scratch, not worth talking about," Willibald answered, with great cheerfulness of spirit. "I gave the count something worth remembering, though—a fine shot through his shoulder—nothing dangerous, but slow to heal, so that he'll have plenty of time for reflection. It's very satisfactory, very!"

"Then it's all over? I knew it."

"Yes, we met this morning at eight o'clock. But there's nothing to be anxious about now, Fräulein. It's all well over."

The young singer gave a deep sigh, as she said: "I thank you, Herr von Eschenhagen, I thank you from my heart. You have risked your life on my account, and I cannot be too grateful."

"There is no occasion for gratitude, Fräulein, but as I have faced a pistol on your account, you must, at least accept a little memento of the occasion. You must not trample this peace offering under your feet."

As he spoke he unwrapped—somewhat awkwardly, for he had only his left hand—a full blown rose and two buds from its cover of tissue paper.

Marietta's eyes sank and a flush of shame o'erspread her features as she took the flowers, without speaking, and pinned them on her breast; then she reached out her hand, as if begging for forgiveness; it was grasped at once.

"You are accustomed to receive gifts of flowers," he said almost apologetically. "I hear from all sides how much homage is paid you."

The young girl smiled, but smiled more sadly than joyfully.

"You have seen what manner of homage is done me at times," she said. "Count Westerburg is not the first against whom I have had to contend. So many men consider it perfectly legitimate to attempt liberties with any one who appears on the stage, and sometimes even those with whom one associates are not—believe me, Herr von Eschenhagen, my lot is not always an enviable one."

Willibald appeared surprised.

"Not an enviable one? Why, I thought you loved your profession, heart and soul, and that nothing could induce you to leave it."

"Certainly, I love it; but I am realizing each day, more and more, with how much that is hard and bitter I have to contend. My teacher, Professor Marani, says 'one must mount with the wings of an eagle, then he leaves all the dross far beneath him.' I think he is right, but I am not an eagle, I am only what my dear grandfather has often called me, 'a singing bird,' with nothing but my voice, and no strength to mount to dizzy heights. The critics have said before now that my acting lacked fire and strength, and I feel myself that I have little dramatic talent. I can only sing, and I'd much rather do that at home in our own green woods, than here in a golden cage."

The girl's voice had a worn, discouraged ring, very unusual in one so full of vivacity. The recent occurrence had brought her unprotected position before her most forcibly, and unconsciously she opened her heart to the man who had shielded her so bravely. He listened in astonishment to her sad words, but instead of showing any pity, his face and eyes fairly beamed with happiness and joy at her sad admission. He asked abruptly, almost roughly:

"You long to get away from here? You will leave the stage?"

Despite her troubles, Marietta laughed out at this question.

"No, indeed, I have no such thought. What would I turn to then? My dear grandfather has scraped and saved for years in order that I might receive a musical education, and it would be but a poor return for me to go back to him now, a burden for his few remaining years. He shall never know that his 'singing bird' longs for her woodland nest, or that she has hardships and insults to encounter here. I have more courage than that. I mean to fight it out, no matter how heavy the odds. So do not let them hear anything about my murmurings at Fürstenstein. How soon are you going there?"

A shadow fell across the young heir's happy face, and his eyes sank to the floor.

"I am going at two this afternoon," he answered in a strange, depressed tone.

"O, then grant me one favor. Tell Toni everything—everything—you hear? She has cause to blame us both. I shall write to her to-day, at once, and tell her about this unfortunate affair, and you will explain just how it happened, too, will you not?"

Willibald raised his eyes slowly from the ground and looked at the speaker.

"You are right, Fräulein, Toni must hear all, the whole truth. I had decided on that before I came here—but it will be a trying hour for me."

"Oh, no indeed, it will not," Marietta said hastily. "Toni is good and full of confidence; she will know that what we tell her is the exact truth, and that we were both quite guiltless in the matter."

"But I am not guiltless, at least toward Toni," said Willibald very earnestly. "Do not look so frightened, you would hear all later, so it is, perhaps, as well to hear it from my lips. I am going to Fürstenstein to ask Toni"—he hesitated and sighed deeply—"to give me back my freedom."

"Heaven help us! and why?" cried the young maiden, seriously alarmed at this declaration.

"Why? Because, feeling as I do, knowing that Toni has no place in my heart, it would be wrong to lead her to the altar. Because I know now what is the one thing needful to make a happy marriage, because," he stopped and looked at Marietta so steadily and so expressively that she could not fail to understand him. Her face flushed painfully; she drew back and made a hasty motion as if to prevent further speech.

"Herr von Eschenhagen, tell me no more."

"I cannot help it," Willibald continued, almost defiantly. "I fought it over and over in my own mind when I was alone at Burgsdorf, and honestly tried to keep my word. I thought it might be possible; then I came here and saw you again—the other evening in 'Arivana'—and then I realized that all my struggling had been in vain. I had not forgotten you, Fräulein Marietta, no, not for an hour, even while I was trying to persuade myself you must be forgotten, and I should not have forgotten you my whole life long. I will tell Toni all this frankly, and my mother, too, when I see her again."

It was all out at last. The man who could not stand alone at Fürstenstein, and for whom his mother had done all the talking and planning, spoke now, warmly and earnestly, from his very heart, as only a man can speak in such an hour. He had learned what liberty meant when his affections were aroused, and with this knowledge he had forever cast aside the dependence of habit and indifference.

He crossed the room to Marietta, who had gone back to the window.

"And now one question. You were very pale when you opened the door for me, and had been crying. Of course this affair was very painful to you. I can understand that, but—but were you the least bit anxious—on my account?"

He received no answer. There was only a low, stifled sob.

"Were you anxious about me? Only a little 'yes;' you cannot know, Marietta, how happy it will make me."

He bent over the maiden whose head had sunk so low, but he could not see the gleam of happiness which lighted up her face as she said softly: "I have been so anxious that life has hardly been endurable the past two days."

Willibald gave a laugh of exultation, and tried to draw her into his arms; she gave him one long look, and then released herself.

"No, no, not now. Go—I beg you."

He stepped back at once.

"You are right, Marietta. Not now; but when I am free, I shall come to you and beg for another 'yes.' Good-bye. God bless you!"

He was gone in an instant, before Marietta could collect her thoughts; and now the voice of her old kinswoman, who had entered the room a moment before, unperceived by its occupants, recalled her to herself.

"My child, what is this, what does it mean? Have you both forgotten—"

The excited girl did not let her finish; she flung her arms around her neck, and cried out, passionately:

"Ah, now I know why I was so angry when he allowed his mother to insult me and did not take my part. It grieved me so to think he was weak and cowardly, for I have loved him from the very first."

CHAPTER XII

Extensive preparations for the approaching social season were being made at the house of the Prussian ambassador. Wallmoden had entered upon the duties of his present official position early in the past spring, but his father-in-law's death following immediately after, and the summer coming on, he had as yet done nothing to discharge the social obligations incumbent upon him as the representative of a great government. The magnificent house which he had taken was furnished with great splendor. His marriage to an heiress made many pleasant things possible to him now, and his great desire was to make his residence one of mark in the southern capital. The following week he was to give his first reception, and in the meantime, numerous visits had to be made.

The ambassador was busily engaged, also, in attending to certain official matters of more than usual importance. With all his other cares he was secretly annoyed at the result of the production of "Arivana." If he had had any thought before of openly denouncing Hartmut Rojanow, such denunciation was now almost impossible.

This adventurer had been so praised and so lauded and admired for his poetical genius and talents, that just at present it was a matter of doubt whether any statement which Wallmoden could make would have much effect on the society and the court where the newly risen star was the hero of the hour. Hartmut had risked much against Wallmoden's threats—and won. The one thing which completed the ambassador's discomfiture, and made his position extremely painful, was the coming of Falkenried. It would be impossible to conceal his son's whereabouts and doings from the father, and Wallmoden dare not let him learn them from strangers. When they had met in Berlin, for a brief hour, neither knew of the journey to the South which the Colonel would have to take almost immediately. He was to be the guest of his old friend, for he also knew Adelheid very well; she and her brother had grown up under his eyes.

When Major Falkenried had taken command of a distant garrison ten years before, the little city where he was stationed had been very near the principal Stahlberg factories. The new major's reputation had preceded him; he was said to be a valiant soldier, devoted to the service, who, when not on duty, gave all his time to the study of military tactics and discipline, but who held all mankind, soldiers excepted, in abhorrence. He had a house and lived among men, but for the rest, he turned his back upon society and every one connected with it.

But the head of the house of Stahlberg took little heed of the gossip or of the major's attitude toward his fellow-men, and approached him without hesitation. The bitter, disappointed man, who shunned all the world, could not fail to admire in the manufacturer much that was akin to his own nature, and while their acquaintance never ripened into friendship, Falkenried understood and appreciated Stahlberg's rugged character, and in the years in which they lived near one another the Stahlberg house was the only one which he ever entered willingly. So he grew to know the children of the house intimately, and kept up his intercourse with the family after his return to Berlin. When Wallmoden married he felt that both he and Adelheid had been hardly treated by the Colonel, when the latter sent some plausible excuse for not attending the wedding. Adelheid knew little or nothing of the Colonel's fateful history. She supposed him to be childless, and had only recently learned from her husband that he had married very young, been divorced from his wife for many years, and was now a widower.

Eight days after the return of the Wallmodens, as Adelheid was sitting at her writing table late one afternoon, Colonel Falkenried was announced. She rose at once, threw down her pen and hastened to greet her old friend.

"How glad I am to see you, dear Colonel. We received your telegram, and Herbert was just about to start to the station to meet you himself, when he received a summons from the duke and had to go at once to the castle, so we could only send the carriage for you." Her greeting was warm and cordial, such as an old friend of her father might have expected, but Falkenried, while not exactly distant, was certainly not hearty. He took the extended hand, but his manner was cold and earnest, and he said indifferently, as he took the chair offered him: "Well, we can talk to one another until his return."

The colonel had changed, changed so greatly as to be past recognition. Were it not for the tall and erect bearing he would be taken for an old man. The hair of this man in his fifty-second year was snow white, his forehead was deeply ploughed with furrows, and the deep lines in his face told of sorrow beyond all hope of cure. The countenance, which had once been so full of expression, had a staring, uncomfortable look now, and his manner bespoke a reserve and repression which could not be penetrated. Regine's expression, "The man seems turned to stone," was only too true.

One could not help forming the impression that the good or ill of his fellow creatures were both matters of supreme indifference to him; he lived only in the fulfillment of the duties of his profession.

"I have disturbed you, Ada," he said, using the old name which he had always heard in her father's house, as he threw a glance at the half-finished letter on the writing table.

"Oh, there's plenty of time," his hostess answered carelessly. "I was only writing to Eugen."

"Ah, yes; I saw him day before yesterday, and he sent his love to you."

"I knew he would go to Berlin on purpose to see you. He has not seen you for over two years, and neither have I, except for the moment, as we passed through Berlin. We did hope you would come out to Burgsdorf while we were there, and Regine felt sorely vexed that you did not accept her invitation."

The colonel looked at her gloomily. He knew, too well, the bitter memories associated with the place. He had only been there a couple of times since his return to Berlin.

"Regine understands how much my time is occupied," he answered evasively. "But to return to your brother, I want to speak to you about something, Ada, and I am not sorry we are alone. What is the matter between Eugen and his brother-in-law? What has happened?"

A shade of embarrassment crossed Adelheid's face at this question, but she answered carelessly: "Nothing especial, only they don't exactly understand each other."

"Not understand one another! Wallmoden is almost forty years your brother's senior, and he's the lad's guardian, too, for two years more, until Eugen attains his majority. So the boy had nothing to do but obey orders for that brief space."

"Of course, but Eugen, while warm-hearted, is impetuous and inconsiderate, as he has always been from a small boy."

"That's a pity! He'll have to change all that when he assumes the responsible position which is awaiting him, if he expects to follow in his father's footsteps. But there seems something more than that the matter here. I made a passing allusion to your marriage, Ada—that it had surprised me a little, more especially as I had known your husband so well, and had not imagined you were so ambitious. Whereupon Eugen turned on me and defended you in the warmest manner. Said you had been sacrificed for him, and left me quite bewildered by his passionate words and insinuations."

"You should not have paid any attention to him," said Adelheid, with noticeable uneasiness. "Such a young hothead sees the tragical side of everything. What was it he did say?"

"Really nothing. He said you had made him promise to say nothing without your permission, but that he hated his brother-in-law. What does it all mean?"

The young wife was silent; this talk was anything but pleasant to her. The colonel looked at her searchingly, while he continued:

"You know it is not my habit to force myself into others' secrets. I take little interest, now-a-days, in the doings of my neighbors, but the honor of my oldest friend is called into question by the insinuation of a boy. I had no patience with Eugen, and told him to go to Wallmoden and threaten him if he had anything to say. His answer was: 'O, Herr von Wallmoden would explain the thing by calling it diplomatic; he has shown himself a great diplomat. Ask Ada, let her tell you her experience.' So I did as he bade me, I asked you, but as you will say nothing, I have no alternative but to speak to your husband. For I cannot keep silence concerning such insulting remarks."

He spoke without excitement, in a measured, cold tone, as if, while a matter of no moment to himself, he felt it his duty to interrogate his friend's wife.

"Pray don't mention it to Herbert, I beg of you," Adelheid said, hastily. "I will tell you myself. Eugen has been carried away by his temper; he has taken the affair too much to heart from the beginning. There was nothing dishonorable in it."

"I supposed that when Wallmoden had to do with it," the colonel interrupted with marked emphasis.

Adelheid lowered her voice, but she avoided the colonel's eye as she continued:

"You know that I was not engaged to Herbert until after our year's residence in Florence. My father was very ill and his physicians ordered him to Italy for the winter. We went to Florence for a couple of months; our farther movements were to depend upon my father's condition. My brother accompanied, us and when the winter set in he was to return home. After a few weeks we took a villa just outside the city, and lived, of course, a very retired life. Eugen saw Italy for the first time under very sad and depressing circumstances; it was very trying for him, a mere boy, to sit day after day in a sick room, so I seconded his request to be allowed to go to Rome for a few weeks, and obtained the desired permission for him. I ought never to have done so. But I did not know how great was his inexperience or into what it would lead him."

"Which means that he plunged into frivolous pleasure or dissipation while his father lay on his death-bed," the Colonel interposed harshly.

"Do not be hard on him. My brother was scarcely twenty years old, and while he had a loving father, he had a severe one, who had brought him up with such strictness that this little breath of freedom proved too much for him. The young German, with no worldly experience whatever, was enticed into a circle where play ran high, and where, as was afterwards proven, cheats and gamblers plied their vocation. Eugen in his ignorance saw nothing of all this; he lost considerable sums, and at last one night the club was raided by the police. The Italians resisted them and a scuffle ensued, into which Eugen was drawn. He only defended himself, but in so doing severely wounded one of the police, and he was arrested with the others."

The Colonel had listened in silence to Adelheid's agitated recital, but he showed neither interest nor emotion as he said severely: "And poor Stahlberg had to live to see his son, whom he imagined a model, come to this!"

"He never knew it. It was only a momentary seduction, a boy's misstep through ignorance, which will never be repeated; Eugen has given me his word of honor for that."

Falkenried laughed out suddenly, such a bitter, mocking laugh, that the young wife looked at him in alarm.

"His word of honor. Certainly, why not? It is as easy given as broken. Are you really so credulous that you would take the word of such a boy?"

"Yes, I am, indeed," Adelheid answered earnestly, as she looked reprovingly into the face of the man whose bitterness she could not understand. "I know my brother; he is his father's son in spite of everything and will not break his word."

"It is well for you you can still trust and believe; for me such days were over long ago," said Falkenried, scowling, but in a milder tone. "And what happened then?"

"My brother had word sent to me at once. 'Do not tell father, it would kill him,' he wrote. I knew better than he that it would do so; my father was far too ill then to bear any excitement. It was hard for the moment to know what to do, for we were strangers in a strange land. Then I thought of Herbert, who was at that time ambassador to Florence. We knew him slightly at home, and he had called upon us in Florence, and offered his services or those of his attachés if we should desire anything. Since we had taken a house he had been to see father frequently, and came now immediately in answer to my request. I had reliance in him, and told him all, asking for advice and help, and he gave me both."

"At what price?" asked the Colonel, suddenly, with darkening face.

"No, no; it is not as you think, or as Eugen will persist in believing. I have not been forced. Herbert gave me my free choice. He explained to me that the matter was much more serious than I had thought, that all sums lost at play must be paid, and that the affair might yet assume serious proportions on account of the wounding of the policeman. He explained that it would be very embarrassing for him in his position, to be personally mixed up in such an affair. 'You desire me to save your brother,' he said. "Perhaps I can do it, but I place my present position, and my whole future at stake by so doing, and one hardly cares to do that for any one less than a brother, or brother-in-law!"

Falkenried rose with a start and paced the room once, then he stood before his friend's wife, and said in an angry tone:

"And in your deadly anxiety, naturally you believed him?"

"Do you mean that it was not so?" questioned Adelheid.

He shrugged his shoulders as he answered:

"Possibly. I understand little of diplomatic considerations, but I know that Wallmoden showed himself a greater diplomat than ever in this hour. What answer did you give him?"

"I begged for time, it had all come on me so suddenly. But I knew not a moment was to be lost, so the same evening I gave Herbert the right to rescue his brother-in-law."

"Naturally," muttered Falkenried with keen contempt. "Wise Herbert."

"He left for Rome at once," continued Baroness von Wallmoden, "and returned eight days later with my brother. He had succeeded in getting Eugen off without making him conspicuous; his name was not even mentioned in the papers as connected with the affair. How Herbert did it I never knew. He spent money like water, and he told me later that he pledged half his fortune to cover the gambling debts."

"That was very magnanimous, when he was about to gain a million by the sacrifice. And what did Eugen say to this—transaction?"

"He did not know of it at the time, for he returned at once to Germany, as had been arranged before. Herbert came to the house now, daily, and my father grew to like him, and when Herbert finally proposed to him for my hand, I was thankful that the affair had taken the turn it had, and my father imagined he had been paying court to me all this time. But Eugen was not to be deceived. As soon as he heard of our betrothal, his suspicions were aroused, and he wrung the truth from me. Since then he has reproached himself continually, and has a hatred for Herbert, notwithstanding my repeated assurances that I was not coerced, and have had no cause to regret my marriage, and that I find in Herbert an attentive, considerate husband."

Falkenried looked searchingly in her face as if he would read her inmost thoughts.

"Are you happy?" he asked at last, slowly.

"I am contented."

"That is much in this life; we are not born to be happy. I have done you an injustice, Ada. I thought that the glitter of court life, the opportunity to marry a baron and an ambassador had tempted you to become Frau von Wallmoden, but I find instead—I am sorry, Ada, that I did you an injustice."

He extended his hand as he spoke, and in the motion there was a plea for pardon.

"Now you know all," said Adelheid with a deep sigh, "and I beg you not to discuss the subject with Herbert. You see for yourself he did nothing dishonorable. I repeat to you he used no force, my love for my brother was the only force. I could not have expected Herbert to exert himself as he had to do in Rome—for a stranger."

"If a woman had come to me under such circumstances, I should have saved her brother—without stipulations," Falkenried exclaimed.

"Ah, you—I would have followed you with a light heart."

These words disclosed unconsciously how hard had been the struggle within this girl's breast. If a sacrifice had to be made, far easier to make it to the dark, gloomy, rigid man who, notwithstanding all his bitterness and hardness, she could trust implicitly, than to the polite and attentive husband who had taken advantage of her inexperience and fear.

"You'd have had a sad lot in that case, Ada," the colonel answered with a shake of the head. "I am one of those human beings who can give or receive nothing more in this world; life was over for me long ago. But you are right, it is better for me not to discuss this matter with Wallmoden, for if I gave him my opinion—but he is and ever will be a diplomat."

The conversation was over and Adelheid rose and said in her usual quiet tone:

"And now shall I show you to your room? You must be fatigued after your long journey."

"No indeed, I'd be a poor soldier to be worn out by a night's travel. In the service something else is expected from us."

He bore no marks of fatigue; as he stood, broad and tall before her, his muscles and sinews seemed made of steel, it was only the face which was old and haggard. The eyes of the young wife followed him thoughtfully as he again paced the room. She noted the furrowed forehead, so high and broad under the white hair. It seemed to her she had seen it somewhere else, only the locks were dark and curly, and beneath the brow were strange, large eyes, which illumined a face of southern beauty. But surely the forehead on which she gazed was strangely like that across which the sudden wave of passion had passed on that memorable day of the hunt, even to the deep-set blue veins which stood out so prominently in the temples. It was a strange, unaccountable, fascinating resemblance.

A few hours later the two old friends were seated together in Wallmoden's private study. The host had dreaded this hour, but now the tale was told and the impression which it made on the Colonel anything but what his host had expected. He had told of Rojanow's sudden appearance at Fürstenstein, of the sensation which his drama had created in the city, of his wandering life with his mother during past years, and of Zalika's death. Falkenried had leaned back in the chair, his arm resting on the window sill, and listened to the whole long story without movement of form or feature, without a question, without a comment; he hardly seemed to hear, he was indeed made of stone.

"I believe it is right to tell you all this now," concluded the ambassador. "Hitherto I have not troubled you with the knowledge which has come to me from time to time, but now you must learn all I have to tell and how the land lies."

The Colonel did not change his position, and his voice betrayed no emotion as he replied: "I thank you for your good intentions, but you could have spared yourself the trouble. What do I care for this adventurer?"

Wallmoden had not expected such an answer, and looked keenly at his friend as he continued:

"I deemed it necessary to tell you because of the possibility of a meeting. Rojanow plays a conspicuous part here and is to be met with everywhere. The duke is greatly taken with him; you will be very apt to come across him at the castle."

"And what then? I know no one who bears the name of Rojanow, and he will not dare to know me. We will pass one another as strangers."

Wallmoden watched his friend's face closely while he was speaking; he wondered if all feeling was dead, or if this intense coldness and indifference were assumed.

"I believed you would have taken the news of your son's re-appearance differently," he said, half aloud. It was the only time he used the word "son;" he had called him Rojanow in telling the story, and he did it with a purpose now. For the first time there was a movement from the window, but it was a movement of anger.

"I have no son, bear that in mind, Wallmoden. He died that last night at Burgsdorf, and the dead return no more."

Wallmoden was silent, but the colonel stepped up to him and laid his hand heavily on his arm.

"You mentioned just now that you felt it your duty to tell the duke, but consideration for me had kept you silent so far. I have but one thing left to guard in the wide world, the honor of my name, and such an explanation on your part would stain it forever. Do what you think is best. I shall not prevent you, but—I must then do what I think best."

His voice sounded hard as ever, but there was a tone underlying his words which fairly frightened the ambassador.

"For God's sake, Falkenried, what do you mean?"

"Do as you choose. You diplomats have peculiar ideas of honor at times, with which ordinary mortals may not agree—I leave it to you."

"I shall be silent, I give you my word," answered Wallmoden, to whom Falkenried's words were enigmatical, for Adelheid's confession was unknown to him. "I had really decided on that before you came. The name of Falkenried shall not be exposed to scorn or derision through me."

"Well and good, then we need not discuss the subject farther," said Falkenried. Then, after a short pause, he began on quite a different subject.

"You have prepared the duke for what I bring him? What does he say about it?"

Here was again the old, iron impenetrability which closed the door against all inquiry. The change was a welcome one to the ambassador, who was here, as elsewhere, the diplomat, and disliked nothing more than unnecessary candor and straightforwardness, and who would never have thought of giving all this information to Falkenried, had not the danger of his friend learning it elsewhere been very great. Now no matter what happened, he could say to the father, "I told you. I warned you." Even the duke could not find fault with a man for sparing an old friend. "Wise Herbert" understood how to answer them all.

Colonel Falkenried's stay was limited, and there was so much to be done that he had scarcely time to breathe.

Audiences with the duke, consultations with prominent military officials, hours spent with certain members of foreign embassies, all these had to be crowded into a few days. Wallmoden was scarcely less in demand until everything was arranged. The ambassador, and more especially Colonel von Falkenried, had reason to be contented with the result, for they had acquired everything which they demanded for their government, and could count with full reliance on the duke. It was whispered that some matter of more than ordinary import was on the tapis, but none of the gossipers knew what, and the few who did know kept their own counsel.

The author of "Arivana" was the favorite of the day, and people began to discuss his very erratic behavior. Almost immediately after his glittering triumph he had turned his back upon all who had done him homage, friends and sycophants alike, and gone to the "wilderness," as Prince Adelsberg explained to every one; where that wilderness lay, no one knew, for Egon had given his word to his friend that he would not reveal his retreat, and Hartmut had promised in return that as soon as he had had a little quiet and rest he would come back. So no one knew that Herr Rojanow was at Rodeck.

Baron von Wallmoden's carriage was drawn up on a cold, dark morning before the door of the Prussian ambassador's residence.

This time the drive was to be a long one, for servants brought out furs and robes and piled them on the seats. The ambassador, who had just risen from his breakfast, was taking leave of the Colonel.

"Well, good-bye until to-morrow night," he said, holding out his hand. "We'll be back by that time, anyway, and you'll remain for several days yet."

"Yes, as the duke has requested it," answered the Colonel. "I sent my report off at once to Berlin; so a few days either way doesn't matter now."

"Of course not. And they'll certainly be well satisfied with your reports, too. But we've had a few hot days with little time for rest. Thank God, everything is arranged and we can breathe again! I feel that I am free to leave the city now for twenty-four hours, so Adelheid and I will go to Ostwalden."

"Ostwalden is the name of your new country seat? I remember, you mentioned it yesterday, but I did not understand just where it was situated."

"It lies about ten miles from Fürstenstein. When we were there in September, Schönau called my attention to it. It is situated in the most beautiful part of the celebrated forest, and suits me exactly. They asked a ridiculous price for it, but since my return I've decided to take it and am going there now to make some final arrangements."

"Ada does not appear too well pleased with your choice. She seems to dislike the neighborhood of Fürstenstein," said the Colonel. But Wallmoden shrugged his shoulders indifferently.

"Just a whim, nothing more. In the beginning Adelheid was in raptures over Ostwalden, and then later she raised every possible objection to the place; but I had gone too far to retreat. I shall in all probability remain some time at my present post, and want to avoid long journeys in the summer. So that a country seat which can be reached in four hours from town possesses great attractions in my eyes. The castle has been sadly neglected of late years, and I'll have to make many altertions. But I have my plans for rebuilding and altering all arranged, and am going to make it one of the finest places in the country."

He talked with great satisfaction over all he was to accomplish at Ostwalden. Herbert von Wallmoden had possessed but a small fortune of his own, and had been forced to live very circumspectly all his life long, in consequence. But now he could give free rein to his desire for splendor and display, and could talk of fine homes in city and country without thought of the outlay, or any consideration either for the whims of the young wife whose fortune he was spending with so lavish a hand.

Perhaps Falkenried thought of all this as he listened to his friend grown almost enthusiastic on the subject, but he said nothing. He had grown more silent and stonier than ever, if that were possible, during the last few days. And when he did ask a question concerning the every-day affairs of life, one felt it was merely mechanical, and that he scarcely cared whether he received an answer or not.

Now as Adelheid entered the room, fully equipped for her journey, he turned to her and offered his arm to escort her to the carriage. After he had helped her in it, Wallmoden entered, and as the coachman cracked his whip, said:

"We'll be back to-morrow without fail—good-bye."

Falkenried bowed and stepped back. It mattered little to him whether they came back to-morrow or not, all friendships were over for him. But as he entered the house again, he said:

"Poor Ada, she deserved a better fate."

Everything was going on in the usual quiet fashion at Fürstenstein. Willibald had been there for a week. He was two days later than he had expected to be; but he had met with a slight accident, and his hand was hurt, so he told his uncle; and this was perfectly satisfactory, and not at all alarming, as the hand was nearly healed now. The head forester found his son-in-law changed since his last visit, and changed for the better, too. He had become much more earnest and decided than formerly, and seemed so well satisfied with his daughter, von Schönau thought.

"I believe Will will turn out to be a man, yet. How much he improves without his mother to stand by to command and dictate."

As for the rest, Herr von Schönau had no time to trouble himself with the lovers. The duke, during his stay at Fürstenstein, had made many changes and innovations upon the established order of things in the forestry, and it required both zeal and watchfulness on the part of the head forester to set things straight again, and bring his subordinates back to the old regime. He saw Antonie and Willibald daily, and noticed that they were much together and seemed to understand one another perfectly, so he did not concern himself much about them.

In the meantime there had been much anxiety and alarm in the house of Dr. Volkmar.

The doctor's sickness, which had not at first been regarded as serious, had suddenly taken an alarming turn, and owing to his age the worst was feared. His granddaughter was telegraphed for in hot haste, and she, after obtaining permission from her manager, who gave her part in "Arivana" to an understudy, hurried home at once.

It was at this time that Antonie showed her sincere, unobtrusive attachment to her childhood's friend. Day after day she went to the Volkmar cottage, to comfort and cheer Marietta, who hung in an agony of anguish and suspense over her grandfather's bed. Willibald found it necessary to go with his cousin and do what he could. All this seemed natural enough to the head forester, who was sincerely attached to the Volkmars, and felt a great desire to show more than an ordinary amount of attention to "the poor little thing" who had been so cruelly insulted in his house. He had it in for his sister-in-law when he should see her again.

At the end of three dreadful days the doctor's strong constitution asserted itself, and hopes of his recovery were entertained. Herr von Schönau was as rejoiced as any of the family, and rubbed his hands with a satisfied air when Toni, on the fourth day, reported a marked amendment in the doctor's condition.

But a thunder-storm from the north was descending upon them all. Suddenly, without any announcement, Frau von Eschenhagen appeared in their midst. She had wasted no time in the city with her brother, but came on directly from Burgsdorf, and descended like a veritable thunder-storm upon her brother-in-law, who was in his own room reading the papers.

"Bless us—is it you, Regine?" he cried, really alarmed. "This is a surprise. Why didn't you send word you were coming?"

"Where is Willibald?" was her only response in an incensed tone. "Is he at Fürstenstein?"

"Of course, where else would he be? He wrote you of his arrival, that much I know."

"Let him be called—now, this minute."

"What's the matter with you, Regine?" asked the head forester, noticing for the first time her intense excitement. "Is Burgsdorf burned to the ground? I can't bring your Will to you now, this minute, for he's not here just now, he's over at Waldhofen—"

"Probably, at Dr. Volkmar's. In that case she's there too."

"What 'she?' Toni has gone over as usual to be with Marietta; that poor little girl has been in despair for the past few days. And I want to have a word with you, Frau sister-in-law, while we are on this subject. How could you have spoken so cruelly to Marietta, in my house, too. I didn't hear of it for some time after, but I can tell you I—"

A loud, angry laugh interrupted him.

Frau von Eschenhagen had thrown aside her bonnet and cloak, and she now strode angrily to her brother-in-law's chair.

"Do you still reprove me because I did my best to put an unclean thing out of your house? You have always been blind. You would not listen to me—and now it is too late."

"I believe you're gone clean mad, Regine," said Herr von Schönau solemnly. He didn't really know what to think. "Control yourself long enough to tell me what the trouble is."

For reply Regine unfolded a newspaper and pointing to a certain paragraph said tragically:

"Read!"

The head forester began to read, and he, too, soon became excited, and grew red and angry as he read on. The paper was a weekly, published in the South-German capital, and the article which excited their joint wrath read as follows:

> "We have just learned that a duel with pistols was fought early last Monday morning, in one of the unfrequented suburbs of our city. The opponents were the well-known society gentleman, Count W., and a young North German landlord, W.v.E., who is the nephew and has been for the past few days the guest of a very prominent member of the diplomatic circle. The cause of the quarrel which resulted in the duel was a member of the court theatre company, a young singer who has, until now, enjoyed a good reputation. Count W. was wounded in the shoulder, and Herr v.E., who has left the city since, received a trifling wound in the hand."

"That goes beyond anything I ever heard," cried the head forester, in a towering rage. "My future son-in-law fights a duel on Marietta's account. What was the quarrel about? What do you know about it, Regine? My papers don't mention it."

"But mine do. You'll find it in yours if you look them over well. I caught sight of the article yesterday, and started at once, without even staying over to see Herbert. Evidently he knows nothing about it yet, or he'd have sent me word."

"Herbert'll be here to-day; in an hour or two now," said von Schönau, while glancing hastily over the papers. "He was going to Ostwalden with Adelheid, he wrote me, and would return to town by way of Fürstenstein and spend an hour with me. Perhaps he is coming to tell me about it, but that doesn't change anything. What's the matter with Will, has he gone mad?"

"Yes, that he has," answered Regine, all excitement again. "You sneered at me, Moritz, when I warned you your child would suffer from association with an actress. That such a thing as this could happen never entered my head until the moment when I discovered that Willibald, my own, only son, was in love with this Marietta Volkmar. I tore him from the danger and returned at once to Burgsdorf. That was the reason of our sudden flight. I did not tell you for I thought Will was only dazed for the moment, and would soon recover his reason again. The boy seemed to have done so, or I would never have trusted him to come here without me. I put him in Herbert's charge and felt perfectly sure that all would be well. He could only have been in the city three or four days at most, and well must he have spent his time."

She threw herself back in an easy chair, worn out and anxious as well as angry, while the head forester walked up and down the room angrier than ever now.

"And that's not the worst of it," he cried. "The worst is the game which the rascal has been playing with me and my poor daughter since he came here. My poor child has been running to Waldhofen day after day to give what comfort and aid she could, and Willibald has always accompanied her to comfort Marietta too—oh, its atrocious! Your model son has turned out well, I must say, Regine."

"Perhaps you think I intend to shield him!" Regine answered spitefully. "He shall stand before me, shall stand before us both, and speak. That's what I have come for. He shall learn to know me!"

She rose as though ready now for the attack, and her hearer, who was muttering angrily to himself, said aloud:

"He shall learn to know us both!"

Just then, in the middle of their excitement, the door opened, and the poor, ill-treated fiancé, Antonie von Schönau entered the room quiet and composed as ever, and said as she went toward her aunt:

"I heard from the servants of your unexpected arrival, dear aunt—I am so glad to see you."

Instead of any answer or word of greeting from her aunt the same question from both sides sounded in her ears.

"Where is Willibald?"

"He'll be here in a few minutes, he waited to give some direction to the castle gardener; he does not know his mother is here."

"To the castle-gardener! Doubtless he wants some more roses," Frau von Eschenhagen broke out afresh, while the father held out both his arms to Toni and said, in a trembling voice:

"My child, my poor, deceived child, come to me. Come to your father's arms."

He would have drawn his daughter into his arms, but Regine stepped before him and said in a husky voice:

"Be composed, Toni, you will have a fearful blow from your false lover; you will despise him and his deceptions from your very soul."

This sudden sympathy had in it something alarming, but fortunately Toni had never been troubled with weak nerves; she released herself now from this double embrace, and drew back from them both as she said, with quiet decision:

"I could not do that, for Will is beginning to please me better now than he has ever pleased me before in his life."

"So much the worse," interrupted her father. "Poor child, you know nothing, suspect nothing. Your lover has fought a duel, and for a woman, too."

"I know it, papa."

"For Marietta," screamed her aunt.

"I know it, dear aunt."

"But he loves Marietta," they both cried out with one voice.

"I know it all," declared Toni in her quiet, drawling tone. "Have known it for a week."

The effect of this declaration was so depressing that the two angry parents were dumb, and looked at one another stupefied. In the meantime Toni continued with the utmost composure:

"Will told me all about it just as soon as he got here; and he spoke so simply and with such true heartedness that he made me weep from very sympathy; then a letter came from Marietta begging my pardon, and it was so loving and penitent in its tone that I was deeply moved. There was nothing for me to do but to give back my lover his freedom."

"Without asking us?" interposed her aunt.

"No questions were necessary in this case," Antonie answered, quietly. "I cannot marry a man who declares to me that he loves another woman. So we dissolved our engagement without any further discussion."

"Indeed, and I learn it now for the first time. You two have become very independent, all at once," cried the head forester, enraged.

"Will meant to explain to you the next day, papa, but after such an explanation he felt he could not remain here longer, and just then Marietta was called home by her grandfather's illness. She was nearly broken hearted when she thought he would die, and Will felt he could not leave her until he knew what would be the result of the illness. So I said to keep silence until the danger was over, and then speak. We have both gone daily to the cottage to cheer poor Marietta. They are so grateful to me and call me the guardian angel of their love."

The young girl seemed quite affected by this thought, and took her handkerchief to wipe the tears which were welling up in her eyes.

Frau von Eschenhagen stood stark and stiff as a statue.

Schönau had folded his arms, and said with a deep sigh:

"Well, God bless you for your magnanimity, my dear child. So everything is as if it had never been. But you have been very generous in your statements, one must acknowledge that. You have taken it very quietly, and seen your betrothed make love to another girl before your very eyes."

Antonie nodded her head. She was greatly pleased to play the *rôle* of guardian angel, and she found no difficulty in so doing for her affection for Willibald had been very mild from the beginning.

"There was no talk of love making, papa. Dr. Volkmar was far too ill," she explained. "We had all we could do to comfort poor Marietta, who was dreadfully alarmed. You can see for yourself now that I have not been deceived and that Will has been outspoken and honorable throughout. It was I who advised him to be silent for a few days, particularly as it was a matter which only concerned us two, and—"

"Oh, that is what you thought. Then it does not concern us at all?" the head forester interrupted angrily.

"No papa, and Will thought with me that in such a case there was no use in troubling the parents—"

"What did Will think ?" asked Frau Regine, who at this unheard of assertion thought it was time to take part in the conversation again.

"That one should love before one marries, and Will is right," Toni declared with unwonted vivacity. "When he and I were engaged, there was no talk of love. It was all settled for us, but that'll never happen to me a second time. I see now for myself what it means when two people love one another with their whole hearts, and how greatly it has changed and improved Will. Now when I marry I must be loved as Will loves Marietta, and if I can't find a man who will love me devotedly, I'll remain single all my life."

And with this declaration and with a decisiveness in which nothing was lacking, Fräulein Antonie von Schönau tossed her head back, and walked out of the room leaving her father and aunt in anything but an enviable state.

Herr von Schönau turned to his sister-in-law and said in a subdued but angry tone:

"Your son has been going ahead beautifully, Regine. Now Toni declares she will be loved devotedly, too; this is the beginning of fine, romantic ideas in her head, and Will seems to have them all down fine by this time. I verily believe he has done his own proposing this time."

Frau von Eschenhagen did not heed his ironical remarks; she sat gazing vacantly into space, but the look on her face was not pleasant to see.

"I'm glad you can see the comical side," she said after a pause. "I confess I look another way."

"That won't help you much," Herr von Schönau answered. "When a model son begins to rebel, that's the end of it. It's hopeless trying to change him, particularly when he's in love. But I am very curious to see Will genuinely in love, and to hear what this paragon has to say for himself."

His curiosity was to be gratified at once, for just at that moment Willibald put in an appearance.

It could be seen at a glance that he had heard of his mother's arrival and was prepared to face her. The young heir did not hang back diffidently this time, as he had done when he hid the roses in his pocket two months before. There was something in his bearing which told he was prepared for combat.

"There is your mother, Will," began the head forester. "You must be greatly surprised to see her."

"No, uncle, I am not," the young man answered, but he made no attempt to approach his mother, who stood like a threatening cloud, and whose voice was an angry growl as she asked:

"Perhaps you know, then, why I came?"

"I imagine why, mother, even though I do not know where you obtained your information."

"The newspapers keep us advised—there, read that," and his mother handed him the newspaper from the table. "But Toni has been here and told us all—do you hear—all!"

She spoke the last words in a tone of annihilation, but Willibald did not seem at all disturbed by them, and answered very quietly:

"Well, then, in that case, there's no need for my saying anything. Otherwise I should have spoken to my uncle this afternoon."

That was too much. Now the cloud broke with thunder and lightning, and the storm descended with such violence upon the head of the sinning son that there seemed nothing less for him to do than to sink into the ground as a creature too debased to live; but he did not sink; he bent his head before the driving tempest, and when his mother stopped a moment—she had to take breath—he looked up quietly and said:

"Mother—will you allow me to speak now?"

"Oh, you are ready to speak? That is really remarkable," Schönau interrupted with a sneer. He felt he had not been kindly used by his daughter and her lover. Willibald began to speak, at first hesitatingly and slowly, but, as he went on, his voice strengthened, and his courage returned.

"I am very sorry to have grieved you, but I could do nothing else this time. I was as innocent of any desire to fight a duel as was Marietta. She was followed in the park by an impertinent fellow who insisted upon pressing his attentions upon her; she was alone, unprotected. I saw what happened and knocked the fellow down for his pains. He sent me a challenge which I would not, and dare not decline. I have only Toni's pardon to beg for loving Marietta, and that I did immediately upon my arrival. She knows all, and has given me back my freedom. We understand and respect one another much more since our betrothal is at an end, than ever we did before."

"Well, this almost passes belief," exclaimed the head forester angrily. "We did not force you; you could have said no, either of you, if you had desired."

"Well, we do it now," Willibald answered, so decidedly and quickly that his uncle looked at him quite bluffed. "Toni sees as well as I that a mere marriage by arrangement is not right, and when one has felt the bliss of loving he must marry the object of that love and no other."

Frau von Eschenhagen, who had recovered her breath by this time, felt the sting of these last words. It had not entered her thoughts that one betrothal had been broken in order that another might be arranged, but now the fearful possibility struck her.

"Marry;" she repeated, "who would you marry? Would you marry that Marietta, that creature—"

"Mother, you must learn to speak of my future wife in a different tone—" said her son, in so earnest and decided a manner that the enraged woman was dumbfounded. "As Toni has released me, I am at liberty to love Marietta, and Marietta's character is blameless, of that I have had proof. Who vexes or insults her must answer to me—even if it be my own mother."

"See, see, the boy's getting on bravely," cried the head forester, whose sense of justice overcame for the moment his anger. But Frau von Eschenhagen was far removed from any instinct of justice. She had believed that her mere presence would have subdued her son, and now he defied her in this manner. His very appearance was different, and this enraged her the more for she realized how deep and strong was the feeling which could thus have changed him.

"I will spare you the trouble of calling your own mother to account," she said with intense bitterness. "You are of age and are the heir of Burgsdorf, and I cannot prevent you doing as you choose. But on the day when you bring Marietta Volkmar to Burgsdorf—I leave it."

The threat had its effect; Willibald moved back a step as he said excitedly:

"Mother, you are speaking in anger."

"I speak in full earnest. As soon as an actress enters that house as mistress, where I have lived and ruled in honor for thirty years, and where I had hoped to lay my head down for my last, long sleep, I leave it forever. So take her to Burgsdorf if you wish—you have your choice between your mother and the actress."

"But Regine, don't be so unreasonable," remonstrated Schönau. "You should give the poor fellow some chance and not leave him such a hard choice."

Regine did not heed his remonstrance, she stood there, white to the very lips, her eyes fixed upon her son. She repeated impressively:

"Decide which it shall be—she or I."

Willibald had grown pale, too, and an expression of deep pain lay on his face as he said gently: "That is hard, mother. You know how dearly I love you, and what a grief it will be to me if you should leave me. But if you are so cruel as to leave me no option, then," he straightened himself and finished with great decision, "then I choose Marietta."

"Bravo!" cried the head forester, who quite forgot that he was a sufferer also. "Will, I can echo what Toni said, you please me better now than you have ever done in your life. I really feel very sorry you are not going to be my son-in-law."

Frau von Eschenhagen had not been prepared for such an answer. She had built upon her old power and strength, and now it lay at her feet a wreck.

She was not the woman to yield, however; had it cost her her life she would not have bent her stubborn will then.

"Very well, then, we are done with one another," she said shortly, and turned to leave the room without heeding her brother's whispered words, as he rose to follow her. But before they had reached the door, it was opened hastily by a servant, who said excitedly:

"The steward from Rodeck is here and wishes—"

"I have no time to be bothered now," interrupted Schönau sharply. "Tell old Stadinger I am engaged upon important family matters and—"

He did not finish, for Stadinger, who had followed the servant stood in the doorway, and said in a suppressed tone:

"I come upon a family matter, Herr von Schönau, but it is a sad one. I cannot wait, but must speak with you at once."

"What is it? speak out!" said the head forester. "Has any misfortune happened to the prince? He's not at Rodeck?"

"No, his highness is in the city, but Herr Rojanow is here and sent me. He begs that you and Herr von Eschenhagen come down at once to Rodeck, and," he glanced at Frau von Eschenhagen, of whose arrival he had not heard, "and my lady should come, too."

"But what is it, what has happened?" cried the forester, seriously alarmed now.

The old man hesitated; he seemed not to know how to break his bad news gently. At last he spoke.

"His excellency Baron von Wallmoden is at Rodeck—and the baroness, too."

"My brother?" Regine cried apprehensively.

"Yes, my lady. His excellency was thrown from his carriage and now he is unconscious at Rodeck, and the physician whom we summoned in haste, says his condition is very serious."

"God help us! Moritz, we must go at once," exclaimed Regine.

Schönau had already rung and he ordered horses and carriage to be got ready at once. "And now, Stadinger, tell us how it happened."

"The Herr Baron was on his way from Ostwalden to Fürstenstein," began Stadinger. "The way lay through the Rodeck lands, not far from the Castle. Our forester, who was in the woods close by with some of the men, fired a couple of shots at a deer which started out of the thicket and ran across the road just in front of His Excellency's carriage. The horses shied and started off, and the coachman lost control of them. The forester, who reached the road at that moment, heard the Frau Baroness say to her husband: 'Sit still, Herbert! for God's sake, don't move!' But the baron must have lost his head, for he stood up and made one spring. Of course he did not know where he was going, and fell with great force against a fallen tree. Just a few yards farther on, at a bend in the road, the coachman succeeded in pulling up the horses. The baroness, who was not hurt at all, only shaken a little, hastened at once to her husband, but the poor gentleman was badly hurt, and was unconscious. The forester and his men brought him to Rodeck. Herr Rojanow did everything that was necessary, and then sent me in hot haste for you!"

In the presence of this new disaster, all dissensions ceased, and Toni was summoned and orders were hastily given, and as soon as the carriage was ready the head forester and Frau Regine hurried off. Willibald and Stadinger followed them at once, but as they descended the stairs, the former held back for a moment and asked in a whisper:

"What did the physician say? Did you hear anything?"

The old man shook his head sadly and answered in a subdued tone:

"I stood by when Herr Rojanow questioned him in the hall. There is no hope. The poor baron won't live until night."

CHAPTER XIII

The little hunting lodge of Rodeck, which lay so white and silent in the snow of that first December day, had seldom been witness to so great an excitement as that occasioned by Baron Wallmoden's accident. It was about noon when the two foresters appeared with their unconscious burden in their arms. Hartmut Rojanow had seen at a glance what was to be done. He had the injured man taken at once to Prince Adelsberg's room, sent off a messenger for the nearest physician, and gave intelligent orders concerning the sick man's treatment until the doctor should arrive.

Then, when the physician told him there was no hope, he dispatched old Stadinger to Fürstenstein. Frau Regine only arrived in time to see her brother die. Wallmoden never recovered consciousness after the fearful shock of his fall; he lay upon the bed silent and motionless, breathing with difficulty, and recognizing no one, and an hour later all was over.

Toward evening Herr von Schönau and Willibald returned to Fürstenstein. Before starting for Rodeck a telegram had been dispatched to the embassy telling of the accident, and now the head forester sent another announcing its fatal termination.

Fran von Eschenhagen remained at Rodeck with her brother's widow. The corpse would be taken to the city early in the morning and until then the two women would remain with it. Adelheid, who had faced the danger so bravely, and had done her duty, though there was little to do at her husband's death bed, now when all was over, seemed to lose her strength. She was bewildered by the sudden and terrible occurrence.

Hartmut Rojanow stood at his window in the second story, and glanced across the desolate, bare forest, which, with its snowy mantle, had a ghostly, uncanny look.

The night came down quickly, and the stars shed a faint light over the tall, leafless branches. Yesterday the first snow storm of the season had come, and everything as far as eye could reach was enveloped in an icy mantle. The great level park before the castle was knee deep with snow, and the broad branches of the fir trees bent to the earth with their heavy white burden. The stars came out one by one and dotted the heavens with their clear, quiet light, while far to the north a faint rosy glow tinted the distant horizon like a first morning greeting in the eastern sky. But it was night, a cold, icy winter night, upon which no gleam of a new day could have fallen.

Hartmut's eyes rested on the distant shimmer, but he heeded not its light; all was dark and gloomy within him this night. He had not spoken to Adelheid von Wallmoden since the memorable day in the forest, until he met her to-day walking beside her bleeding and unconscious husband, whom they were bearing to his death bed. The moment forbade everything but action, and Rojanow had not attempted to enter the sick room, but had waited outside for the physician's reports. Neither had he showed himself when Frau von Eschenhagen appeared, but he had spoken later with Herr von Schönau and Willibald. Now all was over, Herbert von Wallmoden was no longer numbered among the living, and his wife, his widow, was free!

Hartmut breathed heavily at this thought, but it brought him no joy. His feelings were changed since that hour when he had staked his all and lost, for he loved this woman now, madly. This sudden death had showed him the chasm which yawned between them, a chasm no less because Adelheid's marriage bonds were broken. Her aversion had been for the man who believed in nothing, and to whom nothing was sacred, and that man was as great a scoffer, as great an unbeliever to-day as ever.

He had pleaded for forgiveness in the character to which he had given her name in "Arivana," but that Ada had disappeared again in the heights above after giving her warning cry, leaving to their fate the creatures she had exhorted, with their earthly passionate hates and loves. Hartmut Rojanow could not force the wild blood in his veins to run in quiet grooves, he could not bend to a life of strict and narrow duty, and he would not! What were the use of all those gifts which he felt were his, if they did not lift him out of the old ruts, did not raise him above the duties and limits of the commonplace world? He knew well that those great blue eyes urged him to follow the paths which he hated so bitterly, and which, he told himself over and over again, he could never take.

The rosy shimmer yonder over the forest had grown deeper as it mounted higher in the heavens. Unmovable it shone in the north, mysterious, far and high—the great northern light in its dawning splendor!

A roll of carriage wheels and sound of horses' hoofs coming at great speed waked Hartmut from his dream. It was past nine, who could be coming at so late an hour? Perhaps the second physician, who had been sent for early in the day, but had not yet answered the summons; perhaps some one from Ostwalden, where the news had been sent late. The carriage turned into the broad road, and came on crunching and cracking over the icy ground, and drew up under the wide porte cochere at the side of the house. Hartmut, who was virtually master of the place, left his room and hastened to see who had come or what was wanted.

He had taken but a step or two down the stairs which led to the entrance hall, when he stopped suddenly and held his breath with a gasp. There sounded a voice which he had not heard for ten long years. It spoke in a low, subdued tone, and yet he recognized it at the first word.

"I come from the Prussian Embassy," the new-comer explained. "We received the telegram early this afternoon, and I started at once. How is he? Can I see Herr von Wallmoden?"

Stadinger, who admitted the stranger, answered in a low tone. Hartmut did not hear what he said, but could imagine from the next words:

"Then I come too late!"

"Yes, sir; the Baron died this afternoon." There was a short pause, then the stranger said:

"Take me to his widow; tell her it is Colonel von Falkenried."

Stadinger led the way, and a tall figure wrapped in a military cloak followed him; the man watching on the stairs could only recognize the contour of the figure. The two had long since disappeared in the room beneath, and yet Hartmut stood grasping the ballister, and looking down into the semi-darkness with vacant eyes. When Stadinger came out again, Hartmut retraced his steps slowly to his own room.

For a quarter of an hour he paced restlessly up and down. He was having a hard, fierce struggle with himself; he had never yet bent his pride, never been able to yield, and he must bend and bend low before this deeply injured father; this much he knew. But the longing, the burning longing to see and be with him again, finally gained the victory.

He threw back his head with sudden decision. "No, I will be no coward. I will not avoid him. Now that we are under the same roof, within the same four walls, I will venture. He is my own father and I am his son!"

From the castle clock of Rodeck sounded forth ten slow, heavy strokes. Without in the forest all was still, and within was the silence of death. The old steward and the servants had all gone to bed, as had also Frau von

Eschenhagen. She had had a long journey without rest, and one painful excitement after another on this never-to-be-forgotten day, and now nature demanded rest. Lights yet glimmered from a few windows, and these belonged to Colonel von Falkenried's and Frau von Wallmoden's rooms, which were only separated by a long, narrow ante-chamber.

Falkenried was to accompany Adelheid to the city to-morrow. He had seen her and Regine, and then had stood for a long time beside the body of his old friend, who had parted from him with a careless good-by but yesterday; who had been so full of plans and projects of his hopes and ambitions for the future. Now everything was at an end. There he lay, cold and stiff upon the bier. Falkenried stood at the window in his own room; even this fatal accident had not moved him from his icy calm; he had long looked upon death as a happy release. Life was hard, very hard—but not death.

He gazed out into the silent winter night. The whole northern sky was aglow with the dark red flame which started out of the darkness like a sheet of fire. The stars blinked faintly, as through a purple veil, and far beneath them all the earth lay cold and white and still.

Falkenried was so deeply wrapt in thought that he did not notice the opening and closing of the door of the adjoining room. Softly his own room door opened, but he did not look up nor see the tall figure standing on the threshold.

The Colonel still stood by the window, though his face was but half turned toward it, and the flickering of the candle on the table shone across it. How deep and sad were the lines around the mouth; how fearfully furrowed the high forehead beneath the white hair. Hartmut shuddered unconsciously—he had not thought to find the change so great nor so painful. This man who was yet in his prime, looked old, so old. And who had worked this change? Several minutes passed in silence, then a sound was heard in the room, half aloud and breathless; only one word, but that one full of inexpressible tenderness:

"Father!"

The colonel started as if a voice from another world had fallen on his ear. Then he turned slowly, but with an expression as though he expected really to see a vision from the spirit-land.

Hartmut took a few quick steps forward, and then stood still. "Father, it is I. I come—"

He was silent, for now he met his father's eyes—those eyes which he so dreaded; and meeting them, he was robbed of all courage to speak farther. His head sank and he was silent.

Every drop of blood seemed to have left the colonel's face. He had not known that his son was under the same roof with him, and was totally unprepared for the meeting. But he made no outcry, showed no sign either of anger or weakness. Still and stark he stood and looked upon him who had once been his all. At last he raised his hand slowly, and pointed toward the door:

"Go!"

"Father, hear me."

"Go, I say!" The order sounded threatening this time.

"No, I will not go!" cried Hartmut, passionately. "I know that reconciliation can only come in this hour. I have wronged you deeply; how deeply, how severely, I feel now for the first time. But I was only a boy of seventeen, and it was my mother whom I followed. Remember that, father, and forgive me, forgive your own son."

"You are the son of the woman whose name you bear; you are no son of mine. No one devoid of honor can be a Falkenried."

The words were almost too much for Hartmut. The blood mounted hot and wild to his brow—the brow so like his father's—and it required all his strength to keep himself under control.

The two believed themselves to be alone in the silence of the night, for all in the castle had retired to rest. They did not know that they had a witness. Adelheid von Wallmoden had not retired to rest. She knew that sleep would not come to her eyes, which had witnessed the dreadful accident which left her a widow. Still clad in the dark traveling dress which she had worn on that fateful journey, she sat in her room, when the colonel's voice sounded on her ear. With whom could he be speaking at that late hour? He knew no one, and yet his voice had a strange, threatening sound. Puzzled and uneasy, the tired woman rose and stepped into the ante-chamber which separated the two rooms, to see who it was. She had no desire to overhear any conversation. She had a nervous feeling that something new might have happened. Then a voice which she knew only too well, said "Father," and that one word revealed to her what the next few words confirmed. Like one possessed she stood still and listened to all which came to her through the half-opened door.

"You make this hour very hard, father," Hartmut said, laboring to control his voice, "but I think I hardly expected anything else. Wallmoden has told you about me, I feel sure, and what I have sought, and how I have succeeded. I bring you the poet's wreath, father, the first which has fallen to my share. Learn to know my work, let it speak to you, then you will realize how impossible it was for a man of my temperament to live and breathe under the restrictions of a profession which was death to every poetic feeling; then you will forgive your unruly son for his boyish trick."

Hartmut Rojanow was himself again, and spoke with his old domineering pride. His arrogant self-consciousness clung to him even in this hour. He was the author of "Arivana," who acknowledged neither obligation nor duty.

"The boyish trick," said Falkenried in a harder voice than ever. "Yes, that's what they called it in order to make it possible for me to remain in the service. I called it something else, and many of my comrades with me. You would soon have been an ensign, in a few weeks you would have been fleeing from the flag you had sworn to defend—I have never known such another case. You had been well and carefully educated and I had striven to instill into your mind the keenest sense of honor. You knew only too well what you did, you were no longer a boy. He who flees like a thief in the night from the service of his country is a deserter; he breaks his word and he does not know what honor means. That is what you did! But it comes easy for you, and such as you, to do such things."

Hartmut bit his lips and his whole body trembled at these merciless words. His voice had a hollow, half suffocated sound as he answered:

"Listen, father, I cannot bear that. I have bowed before you, have plead for forgiveness, and you drive me from you. It is the same cruel hardness with which you once drove my mother away. It was your severity alone which was accountable for her erratic life after you thrust her from you and for mine through hers."

The colonel folded his arms and an expression of withering contempt played round his lips.

"And you heard all this from her own lips? Possibly! No woman falls so low that she reveals to her son the disgraceful truths of her life. I would not soil your soul at that time with the truth, for you were yet innocent and pure. Now you will understand me when I say that my honor demanded the separation from your mother. The man who had stained it fell by my hand, and she, as you know—I put her from me."

Hartmut grew deadly pale at this revelation. He had never known this, never dreamed of such a thing, had in fact, believed that it was his father's cruel disposition which had separated husband and wife.

The image of his mother whom he had so dearly loved, was suddenly and ruthlessly despoiled of its purity and its charm, and in its place came the desolating conviction that she whom he had trusted and followed had been his destruction.

"I would have protected you from the poisonous atmosphere of such an influence," continued Falkenried. "Fool that I was! Even without her persuasion you were lost to me. You had your mother's features, and it was her blood which flowed in your veins, and sooner or later you were bound to come to your own. You became what you are—a homeless adventurer who knows neither fatherland nor honor!"

"That is too much!" cried Hartmut, almost wild now. "I will not be so insulted by any one, not even by you. I see now that no reconciliation between us is possible. I will go, but the world will judge otherwise than you. It has already crowned me, and I will force from it the recognition which my own father denies me."

The colonel looked at his son, and there was something frightful in his glance; then he said, slowly and distinctly, in his icy tone:

"Better be careful that the world does not learn that the 'laurel crowned poet' was suborned in Paris for over two years—as a spy."

Hartmut started back as though shot.

"I? in Paris? you must be out of your mind."

Falkenried shrugged his shoulders contemptuously:

"Still acting a comedy? you need give yourself no trouble; I know all. Wallmoden laid before me the proofs of the game which Zalika Rojanow and her son played in Paris. I know the sources from which the money came on which you lived after she had lost her fortune. She was greatly sought after for her peculiar accomplishments, for she was very skillful. He who paid the highest price—secured her services!"

Hartmut was completely overwhelmed.

This then was the solution of Wallmoden's riddle. He had not understood the ambassador, and had thought his insinuations of a different nature.

He could understand his mother's hypocrisy now, her evasions, her kisses and flatteries when he pressed her with questions. This last was indeed the worst of all—and the last vestige of respect for her who had borne him died within him as he listened to his father's recital.

The silence which ensued was awful. It continued for several minutes, and when Hartmut spoke again his voice seemed to have lost all sound, and the words came brokenly—scarcely audibly—from his lips:

"And you believe that I—that I—knew it?"

"I do," the colonel answered shortly.

"Father, you cannot, you must not believe that, it would be too terrible. You must believe me when I tell you that I had not the slightest premonition of such a disgrace. I believed that part of our fortune was saved, I did indeed—you must believe that, father."

"No, you did not," responded Falkenried, more coldly than ever. Hartmut threw himself upon his knees.

"Father, by all that is sacred in heaven and earth—oh, do not, do not look at me that way—you will drive me mad. Father, I give you my word of honor—"

A wild, hideous laugh from his father interrupted him.

"Your word of honor—you gave that at Burgsdorf. Let us end this comedy; you cannot deceive me. You leave me with one lie, you return to me with another. You have become the genuine son of your mother. Go your own way, and I'll go mine. But one thing I tell you, I command you! Never venture to connect the name of Falkenried with the dishonored name of Rojanow. Never let the world know who you are. Remember this warning, otherwise my blood be upon your head—for I will make an end of it all."

With a cry of despair, Hartmut sprang up and would have rushed to his father, but the latter held him back with his hand.

"Perhaps you think that I love life. I have borne it because I must, and I felt that it was my duty. But there is a point where duty ends, you know it now—so act accordingly."

He turned his back to his son and stepped again to the window. Hartmut spoke no word; in silence he turned and left the apartment.

The ante-chamber was not lighted, but the dim, distant light from the northern sky fell upon the face of a woman, who stood pale as death near the window, and whose eyes gazed with a look of indescribable anguish at the face of the miserable man who entered the room. He saw her, and a single glance told him that she knew all. His cup was full! The woman whom he loved had been a witness to his terrible humiliation.

Hartmut never knew how he succeeded in leaving the castle; he only knew that he was suffocating within four walls and must have air. But when he realized where he was and who he was, he was lying in the deep snow at the foot of an old fir tree. It was night in the forest, a cold, icy night, the heavens were illuminated with a deep red glow which centered in the north and sent up its long, gleaming sheet of flame.

It was summer again, the sultry July days were half over.

The forest trees cast long, cool shadows from their green and sombre depths, while the sunbeams danced in and out among the branches through all the silent, bright days.

Ostwalden, the estate which Herbert von Wallmoden had purchased immediately before his death, had been empty and deserted until within the past few days, when the young widow, accompanied by her sister-in-law, Frau von Eschenhagen, had arrived. Adelheid had left the South German capital soon after her husband's death, and had gone to her old home accompanied by her brother, who had hastened to her side as soon as he heard of the sad accident. Her short marriage had only lasted eight months and now in her twentieth year she wore the weeds of widowhood.

Regine had been easily persuaded to accompany her sister-in-law. She had never changed her ultimatum regarding her return to Burgsdorf, and it is needless to add, Willibald had not changed. Adelheid asked her to go home with her and she had gone, feeling that her threat had as yet borne no fruit.

Frau von Eschenhagen believed she could effect a revolution of feeling in Willibald's heart by this move. But his newly acquired firmness had not been fleeting, though he tried every argument to persuade his mother to return to Burgsdorf and to think kindly of his future wife—but all to no purpose. Regine had no thought of yielding an inch, and now, mother and son had not seen one another for many months.

There had been no formal betrothal to Marietta. Willibald felt that he owed his cousin and uncle the consideration of not having a second betrothal follow so closely upon the first. Then Marietta's contract with the Court theatre bound her for the next six months, and as her engagement was a secret there, it was thought advisable to keep it so until she had left the theatre forever. The young singer had but just returned to her grandfather's house, where Willibald was also expected soon. Frau von Eschenhagen knew nothing of all this, or she would hardly have accepted an invitation which brought her into the neighborhood of Waldhofen.

The day had been hot and sunny, but the late afternoon hours brought a refreshing breeze, and swayed the drooping branches of the trees which overhung and shaded the road leading from Ostwalden through the Rodeck forest. Along this road, two men were trotting their horses; the one in gray jacket and hunting cap was the head forester, Herr von Schönau, the other in a light summer riding suit, which set off his slender figure to advantage, was Prince Adelsberg. They had met accidentally, and soon discovered that they were bound for the same place.

"I did not dream of meeting your Highness here," said Schönau. "I understood you were not coming to Rodeck at all this summer. I saw Stadinger day before yesterday and he certainly didn't expect you then."

"Stadinger made a great hue and cry because I came upon him so unexpectedly," answered the prince. "To hear him you'd think it was his own castle and I was intruding. And then I walked from the station, and he considered that a most undignified proceeding. But the heat at Ostend was unbearable; the sun just poured down on the strand, and an irresistible longing came over me for my own cool forest home. Thank the Lord, I am rid of the heat and noise of that Babel at last."

His Highness had not cared in this instance to tell the truth. A certain attraction in his immediate neighborhood, of which he heard accidentally, had started him from the North Sea at a moment's notice. Stadinger in a report which he sent his master concerning certain matters at Rodeck, had mentioned that preparations were being made at Ostwalden for the reception of the young widow. And it was in consequence of his own gossipy letter that the steward was disagreeably surprised by the prince's sudden appearance. The head forester seemed somewhat sceptical about the prince's fancy for his "cool forest home," for he said banteringly:

"Then I am greatly surprised that our Court remains so long at Ostend. The duke and duchess are there, and Princess Sophie with a royal niece, a kinswoman of her late husband, I hear."

"Yes, with her niece." Prince Egon turned suddenly and looked at his companion.

"Herr von Schönau, I see you are about to congratulate me. If you do I'll demand satisfaction on the spot, right here in the middle of the forest."

"I don't intend to get into any difficulty with you," laughed his hearer. "But the papers speak very openly of an impending betrothal at Court, and that the duchess and Princess Sophie are charmed with the prospect."

"My beloved aunt has many desires which I fear will never be gratified," said the prince, coolly. "Her obedient nephew doesn't always fall in with her views, and that's the case in this affair. I went to Ostend because I had to; in other words, because the duke invited me, and I could not refuse; but the air did not agree with me, and I prize my health above all things. I didn't feel well from the first, so at last I resolved—"

"To break loose," interrupted the head forester. "That was very like your highness, but how will you calm your kinsfolk at Court?"

"Oh, well, I can make it all right with them if they feel aggrieved. As far as that goes," continued the prince, with seeming frankness, "I made up my mind last winter to spend part of the summer here, and when Stadinger wrote me that some alterations were going on, I determined to come on to Rodeck myself to superintend them."

"Superintend the putting up of a new chimney?" questioned the head forester in surprise. "The old one smoked last winter, so Stadinger determined to put in a new one, but that don't require any attention from you."

"What does Stadinger know about it ?" said the prince angrily. He wished the "old bear" would hold his tongue about what went on at Rodeck. "I have many changes in view. We are pretty near our destination, I see."

With that he started his horse on at a faster gait, and the head forester followed his example, for Ostwalden lay before them. The great building which Herr von Wallmoden would have made so magnificent, had he lived, was an old, rambling castle, with two high towers, one on either side, which gave the building a very picturesque appearance, surrounded as it was by a wild, partially overgrown park. The present mistress of the place, so it was said, intended to make few changes, but she would not sell the place. What mattered a country-seat more or less to the heiress of the Stahlberg millions.

The gentlemen found on their arrival that Frau von Wallmoden was walking in the park, and Frau von Eschenhagen was in her room. The young prince announced that he would seek the lady of the house, while the head forester turned his steps toward his sister-in-law's room.

He had not seen Regine since the previous winter. As he entered the room he said in his wonted hearty manner:

"Here I am. I didn't think it worth while being announced to my sister-in-law, although she does avoid my house with contempt. I don't believe in hunting pretexts for quarrels, so have ridden over in this hot sun to have an explanation."

Regine reached out her hand to him. A passing glance would reveal no change in her in these last six or seven months; she was the same strong, determined woman as ever. But there was a change, nevertheless. Heretofore her severity and harshness had always been tempered by a certain winning cheerfulness, but that was gone now. She had not yielded, but—she had suffered. She was estranged, perhaps forever, from her only son, who was the idol of her mother's heart.

"I have nothing against you, Moritz," she said heartily. "I knew you would be true to the old friendship in spite of all that you and your daughter were made to suffer; but of course it is very painful for me to go to Fürstenstein; you must see that."

"On account of the broken engagement? Well you can console yourself about that. You saw and heard at the time how good naturedly Toni took the matter. She played the *rôle* of guardian angel much better than that of sweetheart, and she wrote you several times that she had no regrets and so did I. But, I am sorry to say, our assurances have amounted to nothing."

"No, but I know how to appreciate your rare generosity."

"Rare generosity!" repeated her brother-in-law laughing. "Well, perhaps a jilted bride and her father do not always want to speak a good word for a recreant lover, but that is not the case this time, and who knows but we may be able to persuade the mother to see as we do. Toni and I have both remarked that Will never was a man until now, and that—forgive me, Regine, but I must say it—he owes his manhood to little Marietta."

Frau von Eschenhagen's brow darkened at this remark; she did not see fit to answer it though, but showed that she wanted to avoid further discussion by asking, in a changed tone:

"Has Toni come back yet? I heard from Adelheid that she had been visiting in the city, but was expected any day."

Herr von Schönau, who in the meantime had ensconced himself in a comfortable chair, answered:

"Yes, she came home yesterday—and with an escort, too. She brought a young man with her who was to be her future husband, she declared, and as he declared so too, with great positiveness, there was nothing left me but to say, yes and Amen."

"What's that? Toni engaged again?" exclaimed Frau Regine in surprise.

"Yes, this time she did it all herself. I knew nothing of it. But you see, she took it into her head that she must be loved to distraction; nothing less romantic would do for her. Well, Herr von Walldorf seems to answer all her requirements. He related to me with the greatest satisfaction how he fell on his knees and assured her he could not live without her, and how she gave him a similar touching assurance, with more to the same effect. Yes, Regine, the day has gone by when we can keep the children in leading strings. When they get ready, they want to choose their own partners for life and I must say they're not far wrong."

The last sentence was uttered with seeming carelessness, but Regine understand it fully. Thoughtfully she repeated:

"Walldorf? The name is strange to me. When did Toni meet him?"

"He is a friend of my son and came home with him on his last visit. As a result of that visit, I met the mother, and she invited Toni to spend a few weeks with her, and that's where all the courting was done. But I have no reason to feel dissatisfied. Walldorf's a handsome fellow, and lively, and head over heels in love; he seems a little light and frothy now, but that will disappear when he gets a sensible wife like Toni. These model sons are not always to my taste; they get too skittish when they break loose. We have an example of that in Will. Walldorf will resign in the Autumn. I won't have my Toni marrying a lieutenant; I will buy them an estate and they will be married at Christmas."

"I am greatly rejoiced on Toni's account," said Frau von Eschenhagen, heartily. "You take a great load from my heart by this news."

"And now," said the head forester, nodding to her, "you should follow my example and take a load from the heart of another betrothed couple. Be reasonable, Regine, and give in. Little Marietta is a dear, good girl, if she has sung in a theatre. Every one speaks highly of her. You need never be ashamed of your daughter-in-law."

Regine rose suddenly and pushed her chair back with a violent movement.

"I beg you, Moritz, once for all, to spare me such requests. I will stand by my word. Willibald knows the conditions under which I shall return to Burgsdorf. If he does not fulfill them, we are better apart."

"It will be a long time before he will do that," said her brother-in-law, dryly. "When a man is asked to abandon the woman he loves for a mother's whim, he's not apt to do it if he's made of the right stuff."

"You express yourself very freely," said Frau Regine, angrily. "But what does a man know of a mother's love or of the gratitude of children? You are all an ungrateful, heedless, selfish—"

"Hold! I have something to say for my own sex," von Schönau began excitedly. Suddenly, however, he leaned forward and said in a changed tone:

"We haven't seen each other for seven months, Regine, so don't let's quarrel the very first day we meet. We can do that any time, you know. We won't discuss that obstinate heir of Burgsdorf, but speak of ourselves. How do you like life in the city? To me you hardly seem contented."

"I am very well contented," declared Regine with great decision. "All I miss is the work; I am not accustomed to an idle life."

"Of course you miss it. You always have been at the head of a great establishment, and that's where you should be now, so I—"

"Don't begin again, I beg you."

"No, I don't mean Burgsdorf this time," said von Schönau, looking down at his riding boots. "I only meant—you're all alone in the city, and I'm all alone at Fürstenstein, and when Toni marries, it will be very weary. Would it not be better—oh, I've said it all to you before—perhaps you won't, perhaps you have a better offer in view, but—wouldn't it be better to have a triple instead of a double marriage?"

Frau von Eschenhagen looked darkly on the ground and shook her head.

"No, Moritz, I never was less in the humor for marrying than now."

"Another refusal!" cried the head forester impatiently. "This makes the second time. First you would not have me because you had your son and your beloved Burgsdorf to look after, now you won't have me because you are not in the humor. Humors have nothing to do with marrying, only common sense; but when a woman hasn't any sense, and is too stubborn to—"

"You're in a very flattering mood, I must say," interrupted Regine, thoroughly aroused now. "It would be a very peaceful marriage, with you wagging your sharp tongue all the time."

"It wouldn't be peaceful. I never expected that," Schönau declared, "but neither would it be monotonous. I believe we could endure one another. Now, once for all, Regine, will you have me or will you not?"

"No, I don't care to enter into a marriage of endurance."

"So be it!" cried the head forester, furious now as he jumped up and seized his hat. "If it gives you such pleasure to be eternally saying no, why say it. Willibald will marry and he is right, and now I'll do everything to hurry on his marriage just to annoy you." So saying he left the room in a violent temper, slamming the door behind him as he went, while Frau Regine remained behind equally irritated. These two were apparently fated to quarrel whenever they met; it seemed a necessity of their natures, but no quarrel was so bitter that peace could not be established at their next meeting.

In the meantime Prince Adelsberg had found Frau von Wallmoden in the park. He begged her to continue her walk, and now the two were sauntering under the cool dark shadows of the great lindens, whose spreading branches protected them from the sun's rays, which beat down so fiercely on the neighboring meadows.

Egon had not seen the young wife since her husband's death. He had made a formal visit of condolence at that time, but Eugen Stahlberg had received him in his sister's stead, and immediately after the brother and sister had left for the North. Adelheid still wore deep mourning, but Prince Egon thought the sombre attire and black veil under which her fair hair gleamed like a halo, only enhanced her beauty.

His glance frequently sought the fair young face, and each time he asked himself what change had come over it; he felt there was a change, but could not define wherein it lay. Egon had only seen her when her cold, proud reserve held every one in check. Now all coldness had disappeared, he saw and felt it, and yet there seemed a mystery about her which he could not unravel.

She could not be grieving for a husband old enough to be her father, who, even had he been nearer her own age, was of a cold, guarded nature, and could not inspire the love of a fresh young girl. And yet there was something in the face which told of sorrow, of a deep and voiceless woe.

"If this icy exterior could be broken through one would find warmth and life beneath," Prince Egon had declared more than once, half jestingly. Now this transformation had been partially effected, slowly, almost imperceptibly. But this soft, half-pained expression, which had taken the place of the haughty, cold one, this sorrowful glance, gave the young widow the one charm which had been lacking—gentleness.

The conversation had been about trifling every-day matters, inquiries and answers concerning the court and the harmless gossip of the day. Egon repeated the story he had already related to the head forester about the heat of Ostend, and his desire for solitude in his little woodland home. His listener's fleeting smile showed him that she was as incredulous as Herr von Schönau had been; perhaps she too had read the newspaper statements concerning the royal niece at Ostend. He was angry, and was puzzling his brain to know how he could broach the subject, and correct the error into which the papers had led her, when Adelheid asked suddenly:

"Will your highness be alone all summer at Rodeck? Last year you had a guest with you."

A shadow darkened the prince's face, and he forgot the correction which he was about to make concerning his reported betrothal.

"You mean Hartmut Rojanow?" he said very seriously. "He will scarcely join me; he is in Sicily at present, or was, at least, a couple of months ago. Since then I have not heard from him, and don't even know where to write."

Frau von Wallmoden stooped to pluck a flower which grew in her way, as she said quietly:

"I believed you were in constant correspondence with one another."

"I hoped to be when we parted, but the fault is not on my side. Hartmut has become an unsolvable riddle to me lately. You witnessed the glittering success of his 'Arivana' on that first night; which success has been repeated in many cities since then; the drama has fairly taken the people by storm, and the poet who has done it all flees from the world, even from me, and buries himself, God knows where. I cannot understand it. Upon my soul, I cannot understand it."

Adelheid plucked the petals of her flower as they walked on slowly, then said in a low tone, as she looked with intense interest into the prince's face:

"And when did Herr Rojanow leave Germany?"

"In the beginning of December. Shortly before that he had gone to Rodeck to spend a few days; that was immediately after 'Arivana' was brought out. I thought it was a whim of the moment and said little, but suddenly he came back to me in the city in a state of excitement which fairly frightened me, and announced that he was going to leave Germany and travel. He wouldn't listen to reason, wouldn't answer a question, and was off like a thunder-bolt. He had been gone weeks before I heard from him again; since then I have had some letters, few and far between. He was in Greece for several months, then he went to Sicily, and now for two months I have been waiting anxiously for news."

Egon spoke in an anxious tone. No need to ask how painfully this separation from his dearest friend affected him.

He little knew that the woman by his side could have solved the riddle for him. She knew what drove poor, unsatisfied Hartmut from land to land, knew the blemish that soiled the poet's name. This was the first news she had heard of him since that fatal night at Rodeck, when all had been revealed to her.

"I presume poets are formed of different clay from common mortals," she said slowly, as she scattered the leaves before her. "That's the only reason one can ascribe for their vagaries."

The young prince shook his head sadly.

"No, it is not that; his peculiarities spring from some other source. I have felt confident for a long time that there is something dark and mysterious in Hartmut's life, but I never could ascertain what it was. He would allow no allusions to his past. I have often broached the subject, but he resented all reference to it. There seems to be a veritable sword of Damocles hanging over him, and when in some happy moment he thinks he has escaped, he looks up, and there it hangs as usual gleaming above his head. I was more impressed than ever with that idea when he last parted from me, he was so excited—almost insane—nothing could hold him back. I cannot tell you how sad I am about him. For more than two years we lived together. I learnt to know and appreciate his warm heart, and responsive, genial nature. Now everything is desolate and dreary without him, and all the rich coloring seems to have gone out of my life."

They had reached the limit of the park and remained standing for a moment now. Before them lay a long stretch of meadow with a hot afternoon sun streaming down on it, while a background of forest-clad mountains rose high and green in the distance. Adelheid had listened silently, and now her sad glance rested on the far mountain heights. Suddenly she turned and held out her hand to her companion.

"I believe you to be a very self-sacrificing friend. Herr Rojanow should not desert so true a comrade. Perhaps you could save him from this—sword of Damocles."

Egon could hardly credit his senses.

This warm hand pressure, the sad, tender glance from the eyes brimming with tears, and the almost passionate earnestness with which she spoke, surprised and enchanted him. He grasped her hand and pressed it with fervor to his lips.

"If I could ever do anything for Hartmut, I would do it gladly. Rest assured your plea for him will spur me on. While I am here you must allow me the neighborly privilege of coming to Ostwalden frequently. Do not say no for I am all alone at Rodeck, and I came here solely for the purpose—"

He stopped suddenly, feeling that the time had not yet come when he could reveal to her why he had come, and he saw that no such confession would avail him now. Adelheid drew her hand back quickly, and stepped back; for a moment the old icy manner was upon her again.

"Of avoiding the heat and noise of Ostend; so you have already explained." She said very coldly.

"That was only a pretext," responded the prince earnestly. "I left Ostend because of certain reports which were being circulated concerning me. When I saw myself figuring in the newspapers, I determined to make an end of it. These reports were altogether groundless, as far as I was concerned. I give you my word for it, Baroness."

He had at least taken advantage of this opportunity to explain how untrue were all rumors concerning his engagement to his aunt Sophie's niece. Frau von Wallmoden was distant and formal as she replied:

"Why does your Highness deem it necessary to make this declaration to me? It was only a report, I fancy. It is understood, I believe, that you have resolved never to give up your freedom. I think we must return to the castle now? You say my brother-in-law has come with you, and I must see him."

Egon turned with her, and as they sauntered back resumed his light, gossipy chatter. As soon as possible he made some excuse for leaving, and as Adelheid bade him good-bye, she gave him a courteous invitation to call again, and that was to him the important thing.

"My cursed hastiness!" he muttered, as he rode away. "I'll keep away for a couple of weeks. As soon as any one approaches a step near, she turns into ice again"—but here the prince's face lighted—"but the ice is beginning to melt. I saw it and felt it in her tone and glance. I will have patience—the prize is worth a struggle!"

Egon von Adelsberg little thought that every glance, every tone had been inspired by the memory of another, and that the invitation to repeat his visit had only been spoken because the fair chatelaine of Ostwalden hoped to hear from her guest the news of a distant wanderer.

CHAPTER XIV

It was midsummer in the warm and pleasant month of July, when the world, which lay in such dreamy, peaceful repose, was suddenly awakened in affright as from a deep sleep. From the Rhine to the sea and back again to the Alps, there blazed an unearthly lightning flash followed by distant thunder-roar, and from the west the heavy war cloud descended upon the land; while the cry of "War! War! War with France!" re-echoed throughout all Germany.

It came like a whirlwind upon the South Germans,—tearing men from their homes, changing plans so carefully laid, and parting many who made them, forever. Where all had been so calm but one short week before, everything was now confusion and excitement. At Fürstenstein where the daughter of the house was happy with her lover, all was bustle now, for the lover must leave at once to join his regiment. At Waldhofen where Willibald was expected, he appeared suddenly in hot haste to spend with Marietta the few days which intervened before he marched to the front. At Ostwalden, Adelheid was making hasty preparations to start for the North, in order that she might clasp her brother once more in her arms, before he, too, joined the troops. Prince Adelsberg had left at the first sound, and was in the city as soon as the duke. The world had changed its face altogether in a few short hours.

Willibald was in the little garden of Waldhofen, speaking earnestly and impressively to the old doctor, who sat upon the rustic bench, but who hardly seemed persuaded by the younger man's eloquence.

"But, Will, it seems very precipitate," he said, shaking his head, "your betrothal to Marietta has never been made public, and now you are going to be married. What will the world say?"

"Under existing circumstances the world will say it was the proper thing to do," Will answered, emphatically. "Though we need not care what it says. I must go to the war, and it is my duty to make Marietta's future secure before I go. I couldn't endure the thought that she'd have to return to the stage if I should die, nor be left to the tender mercies of my mother; the fortune which I shall inherit is in her hands, and she will guard it carefully.

I have only the estate of Burgsdorf, which if I should die, goes to a distant branch of the family. According to the old family law and custom, however, the widow of the heir has a rich dower. I want Marietta to have my name, and I can then go to the field feeling assured that her future will be well provided for."

He spoke quietly but with determination. The indifferent, dull Willibald, was not to be recognized in this energetic man, who knew what he wanted, could give clear, sound reasons, and was determined to have his wishes fulfilled. He had gone through a hard but thorough school in these last six months in which he had been alone. He had had to fight against many obstacles, but the manliness and independence within him had asserted themselves for all time. Even in appearance he was changed for the better, and the head forester was right when he said that Will was a man at last.

Dr. Volkmar could not say him nay; he knew, alas, only too well, if that war took Marietta's lover from her, she would be friendless, penniless and alone, and a load was lifted from his heart at the thought of her future being assured. He made no further objections, but only said:

"And what does Marietta say? Is she willing?"

"Certainly. We decided the question last evening, after my arrival. I didn't alarm her by telling her I might be killed, or bother her with anything of that kind. There will be time enough for that should anything serious happen, but I did tell her that if I was wounded my wife could come to me and nurse me. That decided the matter. We will have a very quiet wedding, of course."

The young fellow's face clouded over as he spoke, and he sighed deeply.

"No, we don't care to have a gay wedding when the mother's blessing cannot follow the bridal pair to the altar. Have you really done everything you can, Will?"

"Everything," Willibald answered, earnestly. "Do you think it is a light matter to do without my mother on such a day? But she left me no choice, and I must bear it. I must take the necessary steps at once. I had the forethought to bring such papers as were needed with me."

"And do you think it possible to have all the arrangements for the marriage made in a few days?" asked the Doctor, doubtfully.

"Certainly. I will attend to all the formalities that are necessary, so that there will be no difficulty. As soon as we are married, Marietta will go with me to Berlin, where we will stay until I am ordered to the field, then she can return to you."

Dr. Volkmar rose and held out his hand, saying:

"You are right, it is the best thing to do under the circumstances. Well! well! my singing-bird, so you are willing to be married off-hand as this lover of yours wishes?"

The question was put to Marietta, who had joined them at the moment. Her face bore traces of recent tears, but her eyes lighted with a smile as Willibald clasped her hand in his.

"I won't be long away from you, and you are willing, are you not?"

The old man's glance was half of pain, half of pleasure, as he thought how little these two knew of life and its dark shadows, which had closed in around him so long ago. He said in a trembling tone, "Well, marry, and God be with you! I give you my blessing from the bottom of my heart."

The simple preparations were to be made with all speed, and the marriage to take place as soon as possible. Willibald, to whom the head forester had already confided his daughter's engagement, felt that there was no need of delay now, out of respect to his cousin Toni.

Toward evening Dr. Volkmar went to visit some patients, and the betrothed pair, who had had but little opportunity to see one another, settled themselves for a long, quiet talk. The future was dim and fraught with fear and dread, but the present belonged to them, and in that thought there was happiness despite everything.

They whispered together in the shaded room, talking the old sweet lovers' talk, and so thoroughly absorbed in one another that they failed to hear some one cross the hall with slow, hesitating steps. Then the rustle of a woman's gown attracted their attention, and they looked up and sprang to their feet as they looked.

"My mother!" cried Will in an alarmed but joyous tone, putting his arm around Marietta as he spoke, as though to protect her, for his mother's face wore its hardest, most forbidding look. Without appearing to notice the young girl she turned her face to her son.

"I heard from Adelheid that you were here," said she in a hard, dry tone, "and I thought I would come and ask you how things were going on at Burgsdorf. Who have you left in your place during your absence? No one can tell how long the campaign will last."

The joyful expression on her son's face disappeared; he had hoped for another greeting from his mother's unexpected appearance.

"I have provided for possibilities as well as I could," he answered. "The greater part of the people will have to go, too, and the inspector is off already; there is no question of substitutes now. So the work will be, of necessity, limited, and old Merton can oversee it."

"Merton's an old sheep," said Regine, in her most decided tone. "If he has the reins, things will come to a pretty pass at Burgsdorf. There's nothing else for it, but for me to go and see to it."

"What! You will go?" Willibald cried, but his mother cut him off sharply.

"Do you think I'd let everything you own go to ruin while you were in the field? Burgsdorf will be safe in my hands, you know that. I have had charge for many a long year, and I'll take my old place until you return."

She still spoke in a hard, cold tone, as if she would stifle all warm feelings, but now Will took his sweetheart in his arms and came close to her.

"For my worldly possessions, mother, you have a care," he said reprovingly. "But for the best and dearest I possess you have neither word nor glance. Have you really only come to say you will return to Burgsdorf?"

Frau von Eschenhagen's lips trembled; she could retain her forced composure no longer.

"I came to see my only son once more before he went to the war, perhaps to meet his death," she said with painful bitterness. "I had to learn from others that he was come to take leave of his future wife, but not to take leave of his mother, and that—that I could not endure."

"We were coming!" cried the young heir, excitedly. "We were coming before we left here to make one last attempt to win your heart. See, mother, here is my love, my Marietta—she waits for a friendly word from you."

Regine gave a long look at the lovers, and a pained expression passed over her face as she saw her son draw Marietta's head down on his breast, while the girl's happy, blushing face spoke of trust and love never to be shaken. Motherly jealousy had a last, sharp struggle against her better nature, and then, conquered by love and justice, disappeared forever. Frau von Eschenhagen stretched out her hand to the young maiden.

"I have grieved you sorely, Marietta," she said half aloud, "and have done you great injustice, but you have repaid me by taking my boy from me, my boy, who loved no one but his mother until he met you, and now loves none but you. I believe that makes us quits."

"O, Will loves his mother as much as ever," cried Marietta eagerly. "I know only too well how much this separation has cost him."

"Well, there, we will have to endure one another on his account," Regine responded, with an attempt at joking which was far from successful. "We will both be anxious enough about him in the days to come, when he is in the field—ah," with a deep sigh, "there'll be sorrow and care enough then. What do you say, child? I believe we'll bear it better together."

She held out both arms, and in the next moment Marietta lay sobbing upon her breast. There were tears in the mother's eyes, too, as she leaned over to kiss her future daughter. Then she said in her natural sturdy tone:

"Do not weep. Keep your head in the air, Marietta. A soldier's sweetheart must be brave, remember that."

"A soldier's wife," corrected Willibald, as his face grew bright. "She is to be a soldier's wife before I march."

"Then Marietta will belong by right to Burgsdorf," said the mother, seemingly not at all surprised at this news, which she took very kindly. "No demurrers, child. The young Frau von Eschenhagen has nothing farther to do with Waldhofen except to visit her grandfather. Or perhaps you are afraid of the stern mother-in-law? Ah, I know you think he will protect you," with a nod toward her son, "although he is not at home. He would even declare war against his own mother if she didn't meet his little wife with open arms."

"But she will always do that, I know it," exclaimed her son, with a happy laugh. "When my mother once opens her heart, then everything she does is right."

"Ah, now you can flatter," said Regine with a reproving glance. "You will come to your future home at once, Marietta! As to the management of affairs, you need not bother your head about that. I'll take care of everything, for a little thing like you wouldn't know where to begin, and candidly, I wouldn't allow any one to have a voice in the management of Burgsdorf while I lived there. If I decide to live elsewhere that's another matter; but I can see already that Will will want you to live like a princess all your days. I can but pray that he'll return to us whole and sound."

She threw her arms around her son and they embraced more warmly than they had ever done in their lives before.

A quarter of an hour later, the head forester, coming in hastily to see the old doctor, found the three in earnest conversation. He gave Regine a look, to which she responded by saying:

"Well, Moritz, am I still the personification of obstinacy and unreasonableness?" and she held out her hand to her brother-in-law. But he did not take it. Her second refusal but the week before was still fresh in his mind, and he turned to the others now, saying:

"So you're to be married at once, I hear? I met Dr. Volkmar and he told me all about it, so I came over to offer our services to the bride, but as Willibald's mother is here, there's little for me to do."

"Ah, your services will be heartily welcome, uncle," said Willibald cordially.

"Well, well, I won't be sorry to see my nephew married," said the head forester, kindly. "You've become a very romantic young man of late. Toni's caught the fever, too, and nothing would do but that Walldorf and she should be married at once; but I put my foot down on that. I said the circumstances were quite different, and that I had no intention of being left all alone like a cat."

He gave another grim look at Regine, but she went up to him and answered him cordially:

"Come now, Moritz, don't growl; let us be happy and without strife for once. You see I did say yes, to my boy at least, when I found his heart was set on Marietta."

The head forester looked at her gravely for a moment, then he seized her hand and pressed it warmly, as he said:

"Yes, I see, Regine, and perhaps you'll repent ere long of your no in another matter, and give a yes instead."

The old steward of Rodeck stood in his master's dressing-room in the Adelsberg palace. He had come to the city to receive instructions from the prince before the latter left for the field. Egon, who wore the uniform of his regiment, had just finished giving the old man his orders, and said, finally:

"And keep everything in good order at Rodeck, I may possibly be able to spend a few hours there before I start, though the order to march may come any day. How do you think I look as a soldier?"

He stood back and straightened himself as he asked the question.

He was a handsome man, and his tall, slender figure appeared to great advantage in the rich uniform which he wore. Stadinger looked at him with eyes full of admiration.

"You're magnificent!" he said. "It's a pity your highness has to go as a soldier!"

"What do you mean? Am I not heart and soul a soldier? Service in the field won't be any too easy, but I'll soon get accustomed to it. Nothing should be difficult when it's one's duty."

"No, your highness thinks a great deal about duty; that's why you left Ostend when your honored aunt had arranged a marriage for you, so suitable in every particular, and that's why you—"

"You old rascal!" said the prince. "There's one thing I shall miss in the field, and that's your insinuations and sermons. By the way, remember me to pretty little Zena when you get back to Rodeck. Is she there now?"

"Yes, your highness, she is there now," said the old steward with emphasis.

"Naturally, because I'm marching to France. But I'll tell you a secret. I'm going to be a model of reason and virtue when I come back and then I shall marry."

"Really?" said Stadinger with delight "How rejoiced the whole court will be!"

"That's as it may be," said Egon. "It's more than probable that the whole court will be in a rage, especially my aunt Sophie. But you be silent, Stadinger; don't breathe a syllable while I am away. Who knows but I may never return to you—think kindly of me, old fellow."

Stadinger's eyes were filled with tears as he turned to go, and he said:

"How can your highness talk that way? It's not likely an old worn-out man like me would be left, and you, so handsome, so young, so gay be taken. That's not according to nature."

"Well, well, I did not mean to sadden you, you old ghost of the woods!" said the young prince reaching out his hand. "We'll think of victory and not of the slain, but if both should come together it would not be so hard."

The old man knelt and kissed his young prince's hand.

"I would I could go with you," he said, half aloud.

"I've no doubt of it," said the prince laughing. "And you wouldn't make a bad soldier either, despite your old gray head. This time the young ones have to go, and the old ones stay at home. Good-bye, Stadinger," and he shook him heartily by the hand. "What! You're not crying' You ought to be ashamed of yourself. Away with all tears and sad forebodings. You'll read me many a lecture yet."

"God grant it," said old Peter, with a heavy sigh. He gave one glance at the bright, handsome face, and looked at the moist eyes; then he went away with sad, drooping head. He realized for the first time, poor old man, how deep his highness had crept into his heart.

The prince glanced at the clock.

He had an engagement soon but not for an hour yet, so he picked up the newspapers containing the latest war rumors.

There was a quick, decided step in the next room; Egon looked up surprised. Servants did not step thus, and visitors were always announced. This visitor needed no announcement as every servant in the palace knew, and all doors were thrown open to him.

"Hartmut, is it you?"

Egon started forward in joyful surprise as his friend entered, and threw himself upon his breast.

"You are again in Germany, and I had no warning of it? You bad boy, to keep me two whole months without any news! Have you come to see me off and say good-bye?"

Hartmut had not responded cordially either to the greeting or embrace; he was gloomier than ever, and there was no sign of joy in his face over this meeting.

"I have come directly from the station," he said. "I almost feared I would not find you, and so much depended on my doing so."

"Why didn't you write or telegraph that you were coming? I wrote to you at once when war was declared. You were in Sicily, were you not?"

"No, I left there as soon as the war seemed to me inevitable, so I did not get your letter. I have been in Germany a week."

"And only come to me now?" said Egon reprovingly.

Rojanow paid no heed to his friend's reproof; his eyes were fastened on his uniform with consuming jealousy.

"You are already in the service I see," he said hastily. "I, too, am anxious to enter the German army."

Nothing he could have said would have surprised Egon so effectually. In great astonishment he stepped back a pace.

"In the German army? You, a Roumanian?" "Yes, and that is why I come to you; you can make my entrance possible."

"I?" said the prince, his amazement increasing each moment. "I'm only a young lieutenant myself. If you are really in earnest you must apply to some high officer in command."

"That I have done already, in various places, in the neighboring states, but no one will take a stranger. A hundred questions are asked, above all one is treated with suspicion and distrust; no one seems to understand my decision."

"To speak openly, Hartmut, neither do I," said Egon earnestly. "You have always shown the greatest aversion to Germany. You are the son of a land whose court circles have always followed French manners and customs; the people have always been closely allied to France, so the distrust and suspicion are easily explained. But why do you not go to the duke in person, and prefer your request? You know how much he would do for the poet who wrote 'Arivana.' All you will have to do will be to obtain an audience, and that will be granted as soon as your name's sent in. An order from him would silence every objection."

Rojanow's eyes sank to the ground, and his dark, frowning brow grew blacker as he answered:

"I know it, but I can ask nothing of him. The duke would ask the same questions as the others. I dare not refuse him an answer, and I could not tell him the truth."

"Nor me?" asked the prince, as he stepped up to his friend and placed his hands on his shoulders. "Why do you wish to fight under the German flag?"

Hartmut drew his hand across his brow as if to smooth out something, then he answered with a gasp:

"Because it means deliverance or—death."

"You return as great a mystery as when you went away," said Egon, shaking his head. "You have avoided my questionings; can you not tell me your secret now?"

"Only get me into the army and I'll tell you everything!" cried Rojanow, feverish with excitement. "I care not under what conditions, only get me in the army. Don't speak to the duke or to any of the generals, only get me into some subordinate command. Your name, your kinship to the reigning house will make your recommendation of great value. They will not be captious when Prince Adelsberg solicits a place for a friend."

"But they'll be sure to ask me the same questions they asked you. You are a Roumanian—"

"No, no!" exclaimed Rojanow, passionately. "Have you never seen, never felt that—I am a German?"

The effect of this declaration was not so great as Hartmut had feared.

The prince looked steadily at him for a minute, then he said:

"I have thought that for some time. The man who wrote 'Arivana' never learned the German language as part of his education; it was born in him. But you bear the name of Rojanow—"

"That was my mother's name, she belonged to a Roumanian Bojarin family. My own name is—Hartmut von Falkenried."

"Falkenried? That was the name of the Prussian officer who came from Berlin with the secret despatches to the duke. Is he a kinsman of yours?"

"He is my father."

The prince glanced sympathetically at his friend, for he saw how it wrung his very soul to make this confession. He felt that here lay hidden a family drama, and desirous to avoid all show of curiosity concerning it, he only said:

"Take your own name as the son of your father; then every regiment in Prussia will be open to you."

"No, that would close them forever—I ran away from the cadet academy over ten years ago."

"Hartmut!" There was atone of horror in the exclamation.

"Ah, you are like my father. You regard me as a criminal. You who were reared in freedom know naught of the severities and restraints of that institution, of its tyrannies, to which every one within its walls has to bow in blind obedience. I endured it as long as I could, then I left it, for my soul demanded freedom and light. I appealed to my father in vain; he but tightened the chains—so I tore them apart and went away with my mother."

His manner was wild and excited as he told his short, fateful story; but his eyes, anxious and watchful, never left his listener's face. His father, with his fierce, severe code of honor, had cursed him, but his friend, who adored him, who had professed such a deep admiration for his genius, surely he would understand him, and how he had been driven to take such a step. But this friend was silent now, and in his silence lay his sentence.

"And you, too, Egon?" In the tone of the questioner, who had waited a long minute, and waited in vain for some word, there was inexpressible bitterness. "You, who have so often said to me that nothing should hamper the poet's flight, that he must break all bonds which would bind him to the earth. That's what I did, and it's what you would have done in my place."

The young prince drew himself up proudly, and answered decisively:

"No, Hartmut, you are in error there! I would perhaps have escaped from a severe school,—but from military service never!"

There were again the same old hard words he remembered as a boy— "the military service"—"the service of arms!" All the blood in his body rushed to his head.

"How did it happen you were not an officer?" continued Egon. "The cadets are promoted while very young in the north! Then in a few years you could have resigned. Just at the age, too, when life was beginning, and been free—with honor."

Hartmut was dumb; that was what his father had said to him once, but he would not wait. The barriers were an obstruction, and he threw them down, not recking that he trampled duty and honor in the dust at the same time.

"You do not understand how many things pressed upon me at the time," he explained with difficulty. "My mother—I will not complain, but she has been my fate. My father was divorced from her when I was little more than a baby, and I thought she was dead. Then suddenly she appeared in my life and I was tossed and torn by her hot mother love and her extravagant promises of freedom and happiness. She alone is accountable for my broken word—"

"What broken word?" asked Egon, excitedly. "You had not yet taken the oath?"

"No, but I had promised my father to return, when he permitted me a last interview with my mother."

"And instead of doing so, you ran away with her?"

"Yes."

The answer was almost inaudible, and then followed a long pause. The young prince spoke no word, but a deep, bitter pain lay on his sunny face, the bitterest of his lifetime, for in this minute he lost the friend he had loved so passionately.

Hartmut began again, but did not look at his friend while he spoke.

"Now you understand why I will force myself into the army at any price. On the battle-field I can expiate my boyhood's offense. When I saw in Sicily that war was imminent, I flew in haste to Germany. I hoped to be able to enter the service at once. I did not dream of the difficulties which I should encounter; but you can help me if you will."

"No, I cannot," said Egon, coldly. "After what I now know it would be an impossibility."

Hartmut grew pale to his very lips as he stepped excitedly before him.

"You cannot? That means you will not."

The prince was silent.

"Egon"—there was a tone of wild entreaty in his voice. "You know I have never asked a favor of you, this is the first and last, but now I beg, I implore your friendship. It is my release from the fatality which has followed me since that hour. It means reconciliation to my father, reconciliation to myself—you must help me!"

"I cannot," repeated the prince, solemnly. "The repulses which you have received are hard to bear, I doubt not, but they are right. You have broken faith with your country and with duty. You fled from the service—you, an officer's son—so it is closed against you—and you must bear it."

"And you say all this to me, so quietly, so coldly?" cried Hartmut fairly beside himself now. "This is a matter of life and death to me. I saw my father for the first time in over ten years at Rodeck when he hurried to Wallmoden's death bed. He scourged me with contempt and fearful words. That was what drove me from Germany and sent me roaming through foreign lands, for his words went with me and changed my life into hell. I hailed the war cry as my release. I would fight for the land I had once deserted. But you, you, who alone can open the door, shut it in my face. Egon, you turn from me; only one course is left!"

He turned with a movement of despair to the table on which the prince's pistols lay, but the latter pulled him back in affright:

"Hartmut! Are you mad?"

Egon was pale too, now, and his voice trembled as he said:

"I cannot let that happen, I will do my best to get you into some regiment!"

"At last I thank you!"

"I cannot promise anything, for I must keep it from the duke. He leaves to-morrow for the seat of war. If he learns later that you are in the army, the excitement of war may prevent him asking the why and wherefore. But it will be several days before I can know anything definite. Will you be my guest until then?"

The prince had recovered his self-possession, and spoke as usual to his old friend; but Hartmut understood the undertone in this question.

"No, I will not remain in the city; I will go to the forestry at Rodeck. You can send me word there, and I'll be in the city in a few hours."

"As you please. Will you not go to Rodeck castle?"

Hartmut give him a long, sorrowful glance.

"No, I will stay at the forestry. Farewell, Egon."

"Farewell!"

So they parted without one pressure of the hand, without one cordial word, these two who had been more than brothers, and as the door closed between them Hartmut knew that he had lost the dearest friend of his life. Here, too, he had been judged and sentenced! Surely his punishment was being meted out to him with no scant measure!

CHAPTER XV

A dark, misty vapor enveloped the forest like a veil, and from time to time the rain fell in torrents. The tree tops swayed in the wind, and the raw, wet atmosphere reminded one of November rather than of midsummer.

The mistress of Ostwalden was in her forest home and alone; she had received news from her brother telling her he would march at once, and as her journey to Berlin to see him would be futile, she had been persuaded to remain in the south until after Willibald's marriage. The marriage had been a very quiet, simple affair, and Marietta had accompanied her husband to Berlin, where he was to join his regiment, and when he marched, she was to go to Burgsdorf, where her mother-in-law was again established.

Early one morning Prince Adelsberg drove over to Ostwalden.

He had obtained a day's leave that he might give some necessary orders at Rodeck, but it was toward Ostwalden not Rodeck that he ordered the horses' heads to be turned. He came to say good-bye to Adelheid, whom he had not seen again since that first visit.

When he reached Ostwalden, he found its mistress away on some errand of mercy, and he was ushered into a reception room to await her return. He paced the room restlessly, thinking of many things, of the struggle for life or death which lay before him, of the morrow's march, but mainly of the beautiful woman whose face had warmed with fire and sympathetic light while discussing his friend, of her dignity, her goodness and gentleness, and his heart was filled with the hope that he might take with him some word, some assurance to make him feel that when the strife was over he could return to peace—and her. He had no foreboding that the warmth and fire had not been from sympathy with him.

But in spite of everything, a shadow lay upon the sunny young face. It was not the war which troubled him, he went into that heart and soul, with no presentiments, and with all the ardor of youth. He dreamed and planned a happy future when all the excitement and turmoil were over.

Then the door opened and Frau von Wallmoden entered.

"I beg your pardon for keeping your highness waiting so long," she said after the first greeting. "The servants told you, perhaps, that a member of the household was dying."

"I heard that one of the men about the place was very ill," Egon answered as he hastened toward her.

"Yes, poor Tanner. He was formerly a tutor somewhere in this neighborhood, but his health failed, and Herr von Schönau recommended him to my late husband. He has been here ever since we bought the place. He told me the other day how thankful his mother was that he had so easy a position. Since Herr von Wallmoden's death, nothing further has been done towards a library here, and Tanner was to have had special charge of that, so that except to act as my secretary occasionally, there has been literally nothing for him to do. Only yesterday I obtained the necessary papers for him to enter the army, and he was all enthusiasm over the prospect. This morning he had a severe hemorrhage, and now the physician says he cannot live an hour. It seems terrible to see a young life cut off so suddenly without any warning." The young mistress sighed deeply as she finished her sad little story.

After a minute's pause, Egon said quietly:

"I have come to say good-bye. We march to-morrow or next day, and I could not go without seeing you once again. I am fortunate in finding you here; some one said you were going away."

"Yes, I go to Berlin at once. Ostwalden is too isolated; I want to be near the centre where I can receive the latest news at this exciting time. My brother fights for the flag, you know, and I must be where I can hear from him."

Again there was a short pause, and the prince was thinking how he should say what lay nearest his heart, when Frau von Wallmoden asked a question, speaking indifferently, but with a slight falling in her voice.

"When I last saw your highness you were in doubt about your friend's whereabouts. Has he given any signs of life yet?"

Egon's eyes fell to the ground, and the shadows which had disappeared when the baroness entered the room, come back now, darker than ever.

"Yes!" he answered coldly. "Rojanow is again in Germany."

"Since the declaration of the war?"

"Yes, he came—"

"In order to enter the army? O, I knew it!"

The prince looked at her in great surprise.

"You knew it, baroness? I supposed you only knew Hartmut through me, and considered him a Roumanian!"

The young widow's face flushed as she realised how unwise she had been to make this outcry, but she answered quickly:

"I learned to know who Herr Rojanow was last winter when he was at Rodeck. I have known his father, however, for many long years, and the—I take it for granted that your highness knows the whole story?"

"Yes, I know it all," said Egon in a hopeless tone.

"Colonel Falkenried was a near friend of my father, and a constant guest at our house. I had never heard of his son, and took it for granted that he was childless, until that frightful hour at Rodeck, on the day of my husband's death. I was witness to the painful conversation between father and son."

The young prince breathed more freely; and an uncomfortable, suspicious feeling was set at rest for the moment.

"Now I understand your interest and sympathy," he responded. "Colonel Falkenried is to be pitied indeed."

"Why he?" inquired Adelheid, struck by the hard tone. "And how about your friend?"

"I have no friend. I have lost him," cried Egon with a passionate burst. "What he told me two days ago made a break between us, but what I have since heard has parted us forever."

"You judge a seventeen year old boy—he could not have been much older—very severely."

There was deep reproof in Adelheid's voice as she spoke, but the prince shook his head passionately.

"I'm not speaking of his flight, or his broken word, though they were both bad enough, considering he was an officer's son, but what I learned yesterday—I see, my dear madam, you do not know the worst. How should you? I should not have spoken."

"I beg your highness," began Adelheid again, "to tell me the truth. You say that Rojanow has come back to enter the army. I am not surprised. I expected it, for it was the only thing left for him to do to expiate his old fault. Does he march beneath our colors yet?"

"So far he has not been able to gain admission, and I have been saved a fearful responsibility," said Egon, with intense bitterness. "He endeavored to get into several regiments but was refused every time."

"Refused? And why?"

"Because he dared not acknowledge himself a German, and all strangers, especially Roumanians, are regarded with suspicion, and with justice, too. We can't be too cautious now, for fear of spies!"

"For God's sake, what do you mean by that?" exclaimed Adelheid, who began to see toward what Egon was drifting. He sprang up now in great excitement and came over to her side.

"If you wish to know, then listen to me. Hartmut came to me and desired me to use my influence to get him into one of our regiments. I refused at first, but he finally forced me to promise to do my utmost with a threat which I now think he had no intention of carrying into execution. I kept my word, and went at once to a general officer whose brother had but recently returned from Paris where he was secretary of our legation. This gentleman was present at the time of my visit, and as soon as he heard the name of Rojanow, asked many questions and then told us—I cannot speak of it—I have loved Hartmut more than any one else in the world, have almost adored him, his talents, his genius, and now I learn that this friend, who was all in all to me, is but a miserable, low wretch. He and his mother served as spies—spies, think of it—in Paris. Perhaps he would do the same in our army, and that was his object in striving to be admitted."

He laid his hand over his eyes if to keep out the horrible picture.

There was something inexpressibly sad in the young man's face and manner as he told how his idol had been shattered. Adelheid rose, and supporting herself against a chair, spoke in an eager, excited, trembling tone.

"And what did he say when you accused him?"

"Rojanow, do you mean? I haven't seen him again and do not intend to. It is better to spare both him and me. He is at the Rodeck forestry awaiting an answer from me. I sent him three lines telling him what I had learned, without one word of comment. He has the letter by this time, I suppose, and that will be sufficient explanation."

"God help him!"

"You speak sympathetically," said the prince, sneering.

"Yes, for this is not the first time I have heard this terrible accusation. His father threw it into his face during their interview."

"Well, when his own father acknowledged the disgrace, surely—"

"He is a sadly injured, deeply embittered man, and could have no unbiased judgment; but you, Hartmut's friend, who stood so near him, should shield him from such an imputation!"

Egon looked with astonishment at the excited woman.

"That evidently seems an easy matter to you," he said slowly. "I could not do it. There was too much to condemn in Hartmut's life; he told me much himself that had seemed mysterious before, and I can find no excuse, no extenuating circumstances for his actions. Even his denunciation of—"

"Of his mother! She was the sword which hung over his head. It was she who destroyed her son! But he knew nothing of the shameful depths to which she had sunk; he lived with her but she concealed her life from him. I saw it, I knew it when his father hurled the dreadful accusation at him; he was as one struck by lightning. There was truth in the man's despairing cry. Whatever his youthful misdemeanors, his punishment in that hour balanced them all. His flight, his broken promise, have robbed him of a father, and of his dearest friend; but though they turn against him I will believe in him. Yes, to the death! Their charge is untrue, he is an innocent man."

Adelheid was in a state of intense excitement now, her cheeks were aflame, her voice and manner had that intense passion which love alone can give. Egon stood and looked at her. There it was, the awaking to love and life, of which he had so often dreamed; the sea of ice had melted forever, but for another.

"I will not venture to decide whether you are right or not, my dear madame," he said, in a spiritless voice, after a second's pause. "I only know one thing. Whether Hartmut be guilty or innocent, he is to be envied in this hour!"

Adelheid drew back with a start. She understood the significance of his words, and her head sank before his pained, sorrowful glance.

"I came to say good-bye," continued Egon, "and to ask one question, one favor—but it is fruitless to ask it now. I have only farewell to say to you."

Adelheid raised her eyes, in which the hot tears were standing, and held out her hand to him.

"Good-bye," she said. "Good-bye. May Heaven protect you!"

The prince shook his head, and said with bitterness:

"What does it matter? I had thought to return—do not look at me so pleadingly. I have made a great mistake. I see it now, and I will not annoy you with my moaning, but Adelheid, I would willingly fall if I could but inspire for a moment the feeling and passion which you reserve for another. God bless you! Good bye!"

He pressed her hand and was gone.

A dreary afternoon. The wind had risen since the morning hours, and whistled ominously through the tall forest trees; the clouds grew darker and heavier, and the damp air was growing rawer and colder every moment. The sunshine of yesterday was forgotten in the gloom of to-day. The fresh green leaves, torn by the rising storm from the tall, waving branches, fell in a swirl at the feet of the tall, dark man, who, with folded arms, leaned against an old tree, utterly oblivious to the tempest which was gathering about him.

Hartmut's face was deadly pale, and on it there lay a strange, unearthly quiet; the fiery light was gone from those speaking eyes, and his hair lay wet and heavy upon his forehead. The storm had whirled his hat from his head, but he did not notice it, neither did he know that a heavy shower had drenched him to the skin. After wandering about in the woods for hours, he had at last found this spot—a fitting place to accomplish his purpose.

He had waited with feverish expectancy the message from Egon, and it had come. No letter, only three lines with the signature, "Egon, Prince Adelsberg," but these three lines, for him who received them, meant—the end of all things. Thrust out forever and despised! The friend his heart held dear asking neither for confirmation nor denial, but condemning him unheard.

The crash of a mighty branch which had been broken in the whirlwind, aroused Hartmut from his brooding. He was not alarmed, and turned his head slowly to look where the heavy branch had fallen. Only a few feet from him—why had it not struck him and ended his misery in a moment? How welcome was the thought of death. Such fatalities follow only those who love life. He who seeks death must accomplish it with his own hands. He took his gun from his shoulder and set the stock firmly in the ground and felt over his breast for the right place. He looked up at the veiled heavens, then down at the little lake with the deceptive, marshy meadow-lands beyond, with the old gray mist hovering over it as usual.

He seemed to see again the will-o'-the-wisp darting in and out, that spirit of the marsh at which he had often gazed in the long ago over his mother's shoulder, and while listening to her seductive words. He gave no second look to the sky, no sign was in the heavens to-day to lead him up to higher planes. One shot through the heart and all would be over.

He moved his hand to touch the trigger, when he heard a voice call his name. It was a quick, desperate cry, and a figure tall and slender, enveloped in a dark storm cloak, rushed before him. The gun fell from his hands as he looked up to see Adelheid's face, white and despairing, looking into his own.

Several minutes went by before either of them spoke. It was Hartmut who broke the silence finally.

"You here, my dear madame?" he asked, forcing himself to speak quietly. "Why are you abroad in such unseemly weather?"

Adelheid looked at the weapon which had fallen at her feet and shuddered.

"I might ask you the same question," she answered.

"I started out for a hunt, but this is no day for sport. I was just emptying my gun, when you—"

He did not finish, for her pained, reproving glance told him that all subterfuge was useless—he broke off and gazed gloomily before him. Adelheid too, abandoned any attempt at an ordinary conversation. Her voice was trembling and her face white as death, as she said: "Herr von Falkenried—God help us, what would you have done?"

"That which would have been finished now, had you not interfered," said Hartmut, in a hard tone. "Believe me, dear madame, it would have been better if accident had brought you here five minutes later."

"It was no accident. I was at the Rodeck forestry and heard that you had been gone several hours; a terrible suspicion took possession of me and drove me to follow you. I was almost certain I should find you here."

"You were seeking me? Me, Ada?" His voice trembled with emotion as he asked the question. "How did you learn that I was at the forestry?"

"Through Prince Adelsberg, who was with me to-day. You received a letter from him this morning?"

"No, only some intelligence," responded Hartmut, with drawn lips. "The few short lines contained no word directed personally to me, only business, only a communication which the prince thought necessary to make—I understood it!"

Adelheid was silent; she had felt sure that those few lines would be as death to him. Slowly she stepped toward him in the shadow of a great tree, the wind blew so fiercely that it was a necessity to have such protection as the trees could afford; Hartmut did not seem to notice its increasing fury.

"I see that you know what those few lines contained," he began again, "but it was not new to you. You heard it all at Rodeck. Ada, when I saw you standing in the shimmering, ghostly light on that frightful night, and knew that you had seen me trampled in the dust—even my own father, who loathes me, would have been satisfied with my punishment."

"You do him injustice," said Frau von Wallmoden, earnestly. "You saw him only when he was thrusting you from him with such iron relentlessness. I saw him afterwards when you had disappeared. He broke into the wildest anguish and I caught a glimpse of the father's heart which loved his son above all else on earth. Have you made no effort since then to convince him?"

"No, he would believe me as little as did Egon. He who has once broken his word destroys all belief in himself, no matter though he afterwards give his life in defense of truth. Had I met my death upon the battle-field, perhaps his eyes and Egon's would have been opened. Now when I fall by my own hand, the few who know my life will say, 'it was his guilt which drove him to despair, and forced him to commit the deed.'"

"No," said Adelheid softly, "one would not say it. I believe in you Hartmut, despite everything."

He looked at her, and through the gray hopelessness of despair a gleam of the old light shone forth.

"You, Ada? And you tell me this on the very spot where you condemned me? At that time, too, you knew nothing—"

"That was why I had a horror of the man to whom nothing was holy, who knew no law but his own passions; but when I saw you pleading at your father's feet, I felt fate rather than guilt had led you astray. Since then

I have known that you could not throw aside that unfortunate heritage of your mother. Rouse yourself, Hartmut! The way which I showed you then is yet open. Whether it leads to life or death—it leads onward and upward."

Hartmut shook his head darkly!

"No, that has all gone by now. You do not know what my father did for me with his frightful words, what my life has been since then; but I will be silent, no one would understand. I thank you for your belief in me, Ada. My death will be easier."

"God help us! You dare not do it."

"What value has life for me?" said Hartmut with great excitement. "My mother has marked me with a brand as of seething iron, and that mark closes every door to atonement, to salvation. I am alone, condemned, thrust out from my own countrymen. Why, even the poorest peasant can fight; that right is denied only to the criminal without honor, and such I am in Egon's eyes. He fears that I would only join with my own countrymen to betray them, to—be a spy!" He put his hands over his face, and his last words died out in a groan. Then he felt a hand laid gently on his arm.

"The stigma lies in the name of Rojanow. Abandon that name, Hartmut. I bring you that for which you so ardently long—your admission to the army."

Hartmut gazed in unutterable astonishment at the speaker.

"Impossible! How could you?"

"Take these papers," said Adelheid, drawing out a long sealed envelope which she carried under her cloak. "You will answer the description of Joseph Tanner, twenty-nine years old, slender, dark complexion, dark hair and eyes. It's all right, you see; no one will question your right with these papers."

She handed him the envelope which she held with a convulsive grasp, as if it were a costly treasure.

"And these papers?" he asked doubting yet.

"Belonged to the dead! They were given me for one who will not use them now, for he died to-day; and I will be forgiven if I save the living by their use."

Hartmut tore open the envelope, the wind nearly blew the papers from his hand, so that it was with difficulty he could master their contents, while the baroness continued:

"Joseph Tanner had a small office at Ostwalden. This morning he had an unusually severe hemorrhage and died an hour after. Poor fellow, he had only time to leave a message with me for his old mother. I shall send her everything belonging to him, except these papers, which I, myself, obtained for him, and these I have kept for you. We rob no one; they would be of no use whatever to the mother. A severe judge might question my right, but I take all responsibility. God and my fatherland will forgive me."

Hartmut folded the papers carefully and hid them in his breast, then he threw the wet locks back from his broad forehead, his father's forehead, for that mark of the Falkenried blood was patent to the most careless observer.

"You are right, Ada. I can never thank you enough for what you have done to-day, but I will strive to deserve it!"

"I know that. God guard you from danger, and now good-bye."

"No, you cannot wish that for me!" said Hartmut sadly. "This battle of life and death into which I go can ease my own conscience of a load, but my father and Egon will never know, if I live, that I have fought for my country, and the old stain will still be there. But if I fall, then you can tell them that I fought under a strange name, and am at rest, perhaps under foreign soil. They will at least have some respect for my grave."

"You would fall?" asked Ada, with sad reproof in her voice. "Even if I tell you that your death will be mine too?"

"Yours, Ada?" he cried excitedly, "and do you no longer turn in abhorrence from my love, from the fate which threw us together? To possess you would be my highest glory, for you are free. Such joy comes to me now, only for a single fleeting minute, and then ascends again to unattainable heights, like the prophetess of my drama who bore your name. No matter; it is with me now in this moment of parting."

He drew her to him and pressed a kiss on her brow, while she broke into a passion of tears on his shoulder.

"Hartmut, promise me that you will not seek death."

"No, but it will seek me! Good-bye, my own, good-bye."

He tore himself from her, and rushed away through the storm. She stood still, leaning in her turn against the old tree, whose branches tossed their arms and kept time to the moaning and shrieking winds which played at hide and seek through the leafy foliage. But suddenly in the west, through a rent in the angry clouds, shone a purple ray. It was only for a minute, only a single lost beam of the descending sun, but it lighted up the woodland height and beamed across the face of the departing man, as he turned back once to wave a last adieu. Then the dark clouds met again, and hid the light—the last greeting of the setting sun.

The red, flickering firelight lit up the interior of a small house which had formerly been the home of a signal man, but now served as headquarters for the officers of the advanced guard. The room made anything but a comfortable impression, with its cold, rough, whitewashed walls, low ceilings and narrow barred windows; the heavy logs of wood which blazed and crackled in the clumsy stone fire-place, threw out a grateful warmth, for the weather was bitter cold and the ground covered with snow. The regiments which lay here were little better off than those before Paris although these belonged to the army of the South.

Two young officers entered the room, and one, as he held the door open for his comrade, said with a laugh: "You'll have to stoop here, for the entrance to our villa is somewhat out of repair."

The warning was not unnecessary, for the tall figure of the guest, a Prussian Lieutenant of Reserves, had need to stoop to avoid the loose, overhanging plaster. His companion who was doing the honors, wore the uniform of a South German regiment.

"Permit me to offer you a chair in our salon," he continued. "Not so bad after all, considering everything; we'll have worse than this before the campaign is over. You are looking for Stahlberg. He is at an outpost near here with one of my comrades, but he'll certainly be back soon. You won't have to wait above fifteen minutes."

"I'll wait with pleasure," responded the Prussian. "Eugen's wound was not very serious, I judge. I looked for him in the hospital and heard that he had gone on a visit to the outpost, but would probably be back shortly, so I thought I'd come over and see him at once."

"The wound was but a slight one, a shot in the arm, but not deep; it's almost healed now, but Stahlberg cannot use it in active service for some time yet. You are acquainted with him?"

"Oh, yes, I was a kinsman of his sister's late husband. I see you do not remember me. My name is Willibald von Eschenhagen. I have met your highness several times in past years."

"At Fürstenstein!" exclaimed Egon with animation. "Certainly, now I remember you well, but it is wonderful what a change the uniform makes in one's appearance. I didn't recognize you at all at first."

He cast an admiring, surprised glance at the tall, handsome man whom he had once ridiculed as a cabbage grower, but who looked so brave and manly in his military dress. It was not the uniform which had so altered Willibald; love, camp life and entire change from the old monotonous existence had done it. The young heir was no longer a "weak tool," as his uncle Schönau had called him, but a brave, determined, genuine man.

"Our former meetings have been but fleeting," the prince went on, "so you must forgive the liberty if I offer you my congratulations; you are betrothed, I believe to—"

"I believe your highness is laboring under a mistake," Willibald interrupted him, with some embarrassment. "When I last saw you at Fürstenstein I was to be the future son of that house, but—"

"That's all changed," interrupted Egon, laughing. "I know all about it from a comrade of mine, Lieutenant Walldorf, who is to marry your cousin, Fräulein von Schönau. My words had reference to Fräulein Marietta Volkmar."

"Now Frau von Eschenhagen."

"What! you are a married man?"

"And have been for five months. We were married just before I marched, and my wife is at Burgsdorf with my mother."

"Then I can congratulate you upon your marriage. But seriously, Herr Comrade, I ought to call you to account for your robbery of an artist from our midst. Please tell your wife that the whole city is in sackcloth and ashes over her loss."

"I will tell her, although I think the city has no time for such light sorrows now. Ah, there are the gentlemen! I hear Eugen's voice."

There they were, true enough. They entered just as Willibald ceased speaking. Young Stahlberg greeted his friend with a joyous cry of surprise. They had not seen each other since the war began, though they were in the same army corps. Eugen's arm was in a sling, otherwise he looked well and happy. He had none of his sister's beauty, neither had he the strength and earnestness of expression which had been her legacy from their father. The son seemed, to judge from his appearance, of an amiable and yielding, rather than a strong nature; but notwithstanding all this he resembled his sister strongly, and that was the secret of Egon's friendship for him. His companion was a handsome young officer, with keen, merry eyes, and as he stepped into the room the prince introduced him to Willibald.

"I need not fear a duel when I mention your names to one another," he said laughing. "You'll have to meet some day. Herr von Eschenhagen— Herr von Walldorf."

"Bless me! I at least declare for peace!" cried Walldorf gaily. "Herr von Eschenhagen, I am rejoiced to know my future wife's cousin, who got ahead of us at the altar. We, too, wanted a marriage from the saddle, but my future father-in-law assumed his fiercest look and declared: 'First conquer, and then marry.' Now we've been doing the former for the last five months, and when I go home again I'll see to the latter."

He shook Toni's cousin warmly by the hand, then turning to the prince, said:

"We have something here for you. Orderly from Rodeck, present yourself before his highness, Herr lieutenant, Prince Adelsberg."

Through the open door came a tall figure which Egon recognized as that of his old, gray-haired steward. He closed the door cautiously, and came forward into the room.

"Saints preserve us, it's Peter Stadinger!" It was, indeed, old Peter who stood in front of his master. He was not unknown to the other officers, either, for they all greeted him with a shout.

"Well, we must have lights now, that your highness may have a good view of this old 'ghost of the woods,'" cried Walldorf, as he lit two candles and placed them with comic gravity before the old man. Egon laughed as he said:

"You see, Stadinger, what a prominent personage you are, and how much I talk about you; now I'll present you in all form; here, gentlemen, is Peter Stadinger, noted for his unfailing incivility and his everlasting moral lectures. He thinks that I need both to keep me in order and even here in the field he has followed me in order that he might keep up the friendly custom. I trust he pleases you, my masters—now you can let me go, Peter."

But instead of obeying this order, the old man held his two hands all the more firmly, while he said in a tone of deep emotion: "Ah, your highness, you cannot know how anxious we have been about you at Rodeck."

The prince answered him impatiently: "Indeed, and that's why you have run away and left things at sixes and sevens at Rodeck, despite all my solemn charges? I had not thought you would be so neglectful of duty."

Stadinger looked at him quite puzzled.

"But I came on receipt of your letter telling me to do so. You wrote me to fetch Lois from the hospital, so I started at once. I saw the boy this morning, and found him as gay as he could be, but he can't be moved for a week, the doctor said; then I am to take him home. What your highness, and Lois, and all the rest from Rodeck would have done if I had not stayed home to guard and control—God alone knows."

Egon drew his hand back impatiently.

"I am Herr Lieutenant here, and have no other title but my military one, remember that! and here you are as meek as a lamb, when I counted on a fine sermon for the benefit of us all. Lois, gentlemen, is the grandson of this old growler, a fine, brave fellow, and he has a sister as sweet as a peach. But her grandfather sends her away regularly the minute I set foot in Rodeck. Why didn't you bring Zena with you, and let her see a little of the world?"

The old man, notwithstanding his desire for peace, threw back his head at this interrogatory, and answered with all the old acerbity:

"I believed your highness had no time for folly now."

"You made a mistake then. We lead the wildest kind of a life in the army, and when I go home again—"

"Your highness has promised to marry," finished the steward in such an impressive manner that the officers all shouted. Egon joined in, but something was wanting in his merriment, and in his answer too.

"Yes, yes, I've promised that, sure enough, but I have many matters to settle in the meantime, I'll keep my word in ten years, or perhaps in twenty—perhaps never!"

Stadinger listened to his highness's words—not for worlds would he have obeyed the order to call him Herr lieutenant—and his face darkened.

"I almost thought as much, for when your highness really does plan for the future your plans don't last twenty-four hours. Your blessed father married, and I married, and all men marry, and it's the only way to cure you of your foolishness, and—"

"Now gentlemen, the sermon's coming," laughed Egon good-naturedly. He was not far wrong, for Stadinger spoke his mind as usual, and to the point too, so that before he finished the officers felt he had the best of it against the prince. After half an hour's chatter, Willibald and Eugen Stahlberg rose to go. As they bade good-night to the prince he said:

"You push on to-morrow, I hear?"

"Yes, we march to R——— at daybreak to meet Major General von Falkenried and his brigade. We'll be some days on the way, I fancy, for the whole of this region is infested with the enemy, and our next move will depend upon theirs," answered Willibald.

"Then tell the general, Will, that I'll be there at latest in a week," said Eugen. "It's pretty bad to have to stay behind on account of a scratch that's not worth talking about. In another week I'll be all right. I don't care what the doctor says, and I hope to join my regiment before you take R———."

"We'll have to be active now," said Egon, "for resistance doesn't continue long where General von Falkenried commands. He's always first with his men and has been victorious beyond belief. It seems as if no difficulties were too great for him to surmount."

"He seems to stand at the head," answered Lieutenant Walldorf. "He may take R———- while we are lying here idle; perhaps he has taken it already. No news can reach us with the enemy between."

He rose to accompany his departing comrades a short distance, while the prince remained behind by the fire. He folded his arms and looked vacantly at the burning logs, but the expression of his face was not in accord with the gaiety he had exhibited before his friends. It was dark and gloomy, and all light and happiness seemed gone out of it. He had forgotten Stadinger's presence until the latter gave a little cough, then he turned and said:

"Ah, you are there yet, are you? Tell Lois I asked for him, and that I will see him to-morrow some time. I'll see you again, of course, for you'll have to wait several days for him. You didn't think we had such a fine time here, did you? No need to take life hard just because we may lose it any day."

The old man looked keenly at his master.

"Yes, the gentlemen were jolly enough, and you were the ring-leader, but—your highness is not gay now."

"I? What's the matter now? Why shouldn't I be gay?"

"I don't know, but I see you are not happy," declared Stadinger. "When you were at Rodeck with Herr Rojanow you were quite different. As you stood looking into the fire just now I could see that something lay on your heart."

"Don't bother me with your observations," exclaimed Egon impatiently. "Do you think I should never have a serious thought, when it may be we go into battle to-morrow?"

Then he resumed his old position, and Stadinger, though silent, was unconvinced. He knew full well that something was the matter with his master, that it was no thought of battle which clouded his sunny face. The door opened and Lieutenant Walldorf entered without closing it.

"Come in," he cried to some one behind him. "Here's an orderly from the seventh regiment with some information. Come in, orderly!"

Walldorf repeated his invitation to enter in an impatient tone. The soldier who stood on the threshold of the door had hesitated, and made a movement to retreat into the darkness again. Now he obeyed; he remained close to the door, his face in the shadow.

"You come from the outpost yonder on chapel mountain?" questioned Walldorf.

"At your service, Herr lieutenant."

Egon, who had turned round indifferently when the soldier entered, started as he heard the voice. He took a hasty step forward, then halted suddenly, as if he remembered something, but his glance embraced the stranger with a look almost of horror. He was, as far as one could see in the semi-darkness, a tall young soldier wrapped in the coarse mantle of the private, with a helmet over his closely cut black hair. He stood stiff and immovable, and gave his message minutely. His voice had a suppressed, almost suffocated tone.

"I come from Herr Captain Salfeld!" he announced. "We have seized a suspicious looking man, dressed as a peasant, but probably from the relief corps, who was sneaking into the fortress. There was some writing found on him."

"Come over closer," ordered Walldorf sharply. "I can't hear you over there by the door."

The soldier obeyed at once, and stepped up to the officers. The firelight gleamed full upon the face, which was pallid, and on the tightly compressed lips, but not on the eyes, for they seemed fastened to the ground.

Egon's hand seized the hilt of his sabre with convulsive grasp; it was all he could do not to cry out, while Stadinger stared at the man with wide open eyes.

"There was some writing found on him, but it was of no consequence, nor what he told by word of mouth either. Now the Herr Captain wants to know whether he shall send the prisoner here, or to headquarters, for he thinks there is more in the papers than meets the eye."

There was nothing uncommon in this message. Suspicious characters were arrested daily, particularly from the relief corps, but Prince Adelsberg hesitated, as if he feared the sound of his own voice, then he gave the answer:

"Tell the Herr Captain to send the prisoner here. We relieve the guard in two hours, and he can be taken on to headquarters at once."

"I hope we can make the churl say something," said Walldorf. "Many a coward loses his hold when he knows there's a court martial ahead of him. Well, we'll see."

The soldier stood waiting for his dismissal; not a muscle of his face moved, but he never lifted his eyes. Egon had recovered himself now, and he asked, in his coldest, most distant tones:

"You belong to the seventh regiment?"

"At your service, Herr lieutenant."

"Your name?"

"Joseph Tanner."

"Forced into service?"

"No, a volunteer."

"Since when?"

"Since the thirtieth of July."

"You have been through the whole campaign?"

"At your service, Herr lieutenant."

"Very well. You can take my message to the Captain."

The soldier saluted and left the room. Walldorf had been a little surprised at this examination, but gave no second thought to it. He looked after the retreating figure and said as he shrugged his shoulders: "The men on Chapel hill have the devil's own time. They have no rest day or night, and have to exert themselves to the utmost. The poor fellows have to work in the hard frozen trenches until the sweat runs from their faces and their hands are covered with blood. Fighting is the only relief they get."

He stepped into another room to order the watch for the expected prisoner, and to make some additional arrangements. Egon threw open the window and leaned out—he felt he was suffocating. Then he heard Stadinger's voice behind him in a half-whisper as though he were too frightened to speak out loud.

"Your highness!"

"What is it?" the prince answered without turning around.

"But didn't your highness see—?"

"See what?"

"The orderly, who was just here—that was Herr Rojanow, as sure as he lives and breathes."

Egon saw that presence of mind was necessary here; he turned and said coldly: "I believe you see ghosts!"

"But, your highness—"

"Nonsense! only a passing resemblance. I noticed it myself. That's why I asked the man his name. You heard him say his name was Tanner!"

"Yes, but it was Herr Rojanow for all that," said Stadinger, whose sharp eyes were not to be deceived. "To be sure the black locks were gone, and the proud, independent manner, but his voice was, the same!"

"Do cease your senseless chatter," said Egon violently. "You know very well that Herr Rojanow is in Sicily, and now you find him in an orderly of the seventh regiment. It is really laughable."

Stadinger was silent; everything that he said was laughable or impossible. The prince was only vexed because he had discovered that his friend was only a common soldier. To be sure the Herr Rojanow of Rodeck, who ordered every one around, even the prince himself, and the orderly whom Lieutenant Walldorf ordered to come forward because he didn't speak loud enough, were as far apart as heaven and earth. If it had not been for the voice!

"Then your highness, you think—" Stadinger began again.

"I think you're an old ghost-hunter," said Egon gently. "Go to your quarters and get a good night's rest after your journey; otherwise you'll be discovering resemblances throughout the whole garrison—good-night!"

Stadinger obeyed, and left for his own quarters at once. He shook his head as he went—he was by no means satisfied with his master's peremptory dismissal of the subject.

The prince paced the little room in great excitement as soon as he was alone. His former friend had forced his way into the army notwithstanding. Joseph Tanner! He remembered perfectly to whom the name had belonged, and knew only too well whose hand had opened the way for Hartmut. What will not a woman do for the man she loves, what price will she not pay? She had even sent him into danger in order that he might be reconciled to life and himself.

Jealousy, fierce and wild, filled Egon's heart at these thoughts, and above all rose the fearful suspicion of the man's fidelity to his flag and country. Was his presence at the dangerous outpost an answer to suspicions, or was it a cloak to hide secret machinations?

Then the prince thought of the pale, dark face which had been so dear to him, and with a motion of torture, he tried to put the memory from him. He knew, none so well, Hartmut's intense pride, and this pride was dragged in the dirt day after day in the degrading position which he occupied.

He had heard of the ceaseless labor on Chapel hill, of the days and nights employed in digging trenches, of the worn bodies, the bleeding hands. That was what Rojanow did now, the same Rojanow who had had a city at his feet one short year before, who had been the honored guest at princely boards, whose successful work had not only placed the laurel wreath on his brow, but had brought him a fortune as well. And besides all this, he was General von Falkenried's son.

Egon's breast heaved violently as he thought of it all. Then his lost confidence came back to him slowly, and banished the unjust doubts. Hartmut was atoning now for his boyish folly. As for the rest, his mother, and she alone, was to blame.

It was about nine o'clock in the evening when the prince left his quarters in order to visit the commandant. He did not go on an affair of service, but in answer to an invitation from the general, who had been an old friend of his father, and had looked after the son, since the campaign began, with fatherly solicitude. Egon would have given much to be alone this evening, for his meeting with Hartmut had moved him deeply, but a soldier has little time for brooding, and an invitation from a commanding officer must not be set aside.

As the young prince went into the house he met an adjutant coming out, who explained breathlessly that there was bad news, but that the general would tell him all.

The general was alone, and was pacing the room in great excitement, gesticulating and muttering as he went.

"Ah, Prince Adelsberg, is it you?" he exclaimed, halting in his walk as Egon entered the room. "I can't promise you a pleasant evening, for we have had intelligence which destroys all sociability for us to-night."

"The adjutant said something about trouble," answered Egon. "What is it, your excellency? The despatches at midday were very favorable."

"I only got the news an hour ago. The man you sent to headquarters to-night as a suspicious character had it all. Do you know what he had with him?"

"Captain Salfeld sent word he had papers of little importance, apparently, but thought they might contain some secret advices; of course, a spy would not carry anything in writing that looked suspicious on the surface."

"Well, the papers were most important. The man was a coward, naturally, and when he was threatened with a bullet, he revealed all, and, alas! we cannot doubt the truth of his statements. You may remember a few lines on a slip of paper which read that one had better in an extreme case follow the heroic example of the commanding general before R——-."

"Yes, I didn't understand that, for the fort will have to surrender soon. General von Falkenried said he hoped to take it to-morrow."

"Yes, and I fear he will do it!" answered the General, excitedly.

"You fear, your excellency?"

"Yes, there's been treachery, there's been foul villainy at work! They will surrender the fort, and then as soon as their garrison have been taken off as prisoners of war, and our men occupy the citadel, it will be blown up."

"God help us!" cried the young prince, excitedly. "Cannot General Falkenried be warned?"

"I fear we cannot possibly do it. I have already sent warnings by two different ways, but our direct course to R——— is cut off. The enemy holds the mountain pass, and it is quite impossible for the messengers to reach the place in time."

Egon was silent for a moment.

The pass was obstructed by the enemy. He knew that Eschenhagen's regiment was going forward to open it, but that would not be done for a day or two.

"We have thought of everything," continued the general, "but there isn't the faintest hope of doing anything. Falkenried will force them to close, he never turns back, and then he and hundreds, yes, thousands, of his men, will perish."

He began his walk again, too excited to keep still. But the young prince stood by helpless; then a sudden bright thought entered his mind.

"Your excellency?"

"Well?"

"If it were possible in spite of everything, to send the despatches by the mountain path—a good rider could get to R——— by to-morrow morning; to be sure he'd have to ride for life or death—dash right through the enemy."

"What folly! You are a soldier and should know that such a course would be madness. The boldest rider would be shot down before he had been gone an hour."

"But if one could find the man who would make the attempt? I know a man who would do it."

The general scowled at the young man.

"Do you mean that you would venture upon this useless exposure? I forbid it, once for all, Prince Adelsberg. I pride myself upon my officers' bravery, but I cannot permit any such senseless experiments."

"I do not mean myself, your excellency," said Egon, earnestly. "The man whom I mean is in the seventh regiment, and is at this moment on outpost duty on Chapel mountain. It was he who brought me word of the prisoner."

The general shook his head thoughtfully.

"I tell you it's impossible, but—who is the man?"

"Joseph Tanner."

"A private?"

"Yes, a volunteer."

"You know something about him?"

"Yes, your excellency; he is perhaps the best rider in the whole army,—bold to a fault and capable enough, in case of necessity, to act with the caution of an officer. If the thing can be done, that man'll do it."

"And you believe—it's a terrible responsibility to ask a man to ride to sure death—you believe the man will do it freely—willingly?"

"I'll swear he will, your excellency."

"Then I dare not refuse, though it's a fearful venture. I'll send for Tanner at once."

"May I take the order to him?" interrupted Egon, quickly. The general turned in surprise and looked at him.

"You, yourself, do you mean? Why?"

"Only to save time. The way which Tanner must take lies over Chapel mountain; before he'd get to headquarters and back again to his starting place an hour would be lost."

There was nothing to be said in answer to this, and yet the general felt there was something about the whole affair which he did not understand. A common soldier rarely undertook, voluntarily, a mission which drove him into the arms of death, but the old warrior asked no further questions, he only said: "You will be responsible for the man?"

"Yes," said Egon, quietly but emphatically.

"Good, then you can give him all the necessary instructions; there is one thing more; he must have credentials if he ever reaches our own posts, for any detention would be fatal where every minute counts."

He turned to his writing table, and after setting his seal to a paper, handed it to the prince.

"Here are the necessary papers, and these are the despatches for General Falkenried. Let me know at once whether Tanner was willing to go or not."

"I'll let your excellency know immediately."

Egon hurried to his own quarters, where he ordered his horse to be saddled. In five minutes he was off for Chapel mountain.

Chapel mountain, which the German troops had so christened from the little church which stood on its summit, was one of a subordinate range of hills, which traversed the country in the region where the army corps of the South were quartered. The little church lay desolate and lonely, half buried in the deep snow. Priest and sacristan were gone long since, and the house of God bore traces of demolition, for a deadly battle had been fought on this height. The walls were standing and part of the pointed roof; the rest had been carried away by shot and shell, and the wind whistled through the shattered windows. Ice and snow covered the surrounding wood, and a faint half-moon lit up the whole with a ghastly, uncertain light.

It was a bitter cold night, like that memorable one at Rodeck. A deep red flame lit up the horizon, but it was no northern light this time, no purple glow to lessen the gloom, it was the signal of war, the deep, blood-red flash such as went up from every village and hamlet in Germany, rousing men to action, waving them on to battle and—to death!

A single guard stood at one of the lonely outposts—Hartmut von Falkenried. His eyes were fixed on distant watch fires which from time to time sent up their showers of sparks to heaven. In the distance, warmth and light, here, ice and night. The cold which had been intense all day strengthened with the night, and seemed to freeze out all life from the solitary watch on duty. True there were other sentinels, at various posts, but they were not accustomed to winters in the Orient or in Sicily. Hartmut had spent no winters in the north since his boyhood's days, and the cold seemed to freeze the very blood in his veins.

A deadly languor came over him, which was not the forerunner of sleep; it crept into the limbs and closed the heavy eyelids. He fought it off bravely, but it would return again and again as the icy air grew colder. He knew what it meant and struggled bravely against it. Surely he would not freeze to death.

His glance turned, as if seeking strength, to the little half-ruined house of God. What were church and altar to him? He had cast all belief from him long ago. Death was an eternal night, and life alone could give him all he wished, full expiation of his early fault, the woman he loved, the poet's crown, his father's blessing! But here he stood at his post waiting an inglorious death, which he felt would meet him ere the night was over. He would not swerve from duty, death might seek him and find him—on guard.

Then in the distance he heard steps and voices which came nearer; they waked him up from the lethargy into which he had fallen. He aroused himself and grasped his gun more firmly, though he knew it was some one from his own regiment. What was it? The hour of redemption was close at hand though he knew it not. A few minutes later a corporal with another man stood before him.

"Picket! Orders from headquarters brought by an officer!" cried the corporal. The relief had come! The man who but a second since stood on the bleak, dreary shore of despair, felt himself recalled to life at the sound.

He started to follow the corporal, when the other man, an officer also, stepped forward.

"Let the corporal go on. I wish to speak to you alone, Tanner. Follow me!"

Prince Adelsberg, who wished no witnesses, stepped into the little church, and Hartmut followed him. The pale moonlight entering through the open window showed only disorder and confusion. The roof had been pierced by a cannon ball, which had shattered pulpit and desk as well; only the little altar, in its quiet niche, remained undisturbed.

Egon stepped into the middle of the room, then he turned and said:

"Hartmut!"

"Herr lieutenant?"

"Drop that now; we are alone. I did not think we would see one another so soon again."

"And I hoped it would have been spared me, too," said Hartmut gloomily. "You come—"

"From headquarters, I heard that you were on picket duty on Chapel mountain. A fearful night for such a service."

Hartmut was silent. No need to say that had he not been roused it would have been his last. Egon glanced uneasily at him; despite the uncertain light he saw how exhausted and spent the man before him was as he leaned against a pillar as if needing support.

"I came with a commission which you can accept or not as you see fit," he began again. "The thing is almost impossible, would be altogether so for any one but you. You have the courage, but whether, after all your exertions you have the strength, is another question."

"A quarter of an hour of warmth and some refreshment will bring back my strength. What is it?"

"A ride of life and death. To take some intelligence to R——— through the mountain pass just where the enemy lies."

"To the front!" cried Hartmut; "that's where—"

"General Falkenried is with his brigade. He is lost if the news does not reach him. We put the means of saving his life in the hands of his son!"

Hartmut grasped his friend's arm. He was all excitement and anxiety in an instant.

"I can save my father? I? What has happened? What am I to do?"

"Listen. The prisoner which you sent to us this evening has made some terrible revelations. The fort is to be blown up after the surrender, as soon as the French garrison are out and our men are in it. The general has sent two messengers—but they take round-about ways and will never reach there in time. Your father intends to seize the fort to-morrow. He must be warned in time, and there's but one way. The news must go through the mountain pass which the enemy hold; that is the only chance to reach our friends. But that way—"

"I know it. Our regiment marched through it two weeks ago before the enemy had taken it," cried Hartmut.

"All the better! You must of course lay aside your uniform."

"I only need exchange my cloak and helmet. If I had stayed here I'd have been dead in a few hours; now if I ride fast enough I have one chance. If I only had a good horse."

"That is ready for you, I brought my own Arabian, Sadi, with me. You know him well, have ridden him often. He'll fly like a bird on a night like this, he'll need no whip to spur him on."

The conversation was whispered in stormy haste, and the prince handed him the papers.

"Here is the general's order which you present when you reach our sentinels, and here are the dispatches. Take a half hour to get some warmth and strength into your body, then you can start."

"Do you think I want rest or warmth?" cried Hartmut, the old Hartmut again. "When I break down now it will be from the enemy's bullet. I thank you Egon for this hour, in which you have at last, at last, exonerated me from a fearful suspicion!"

"And in which I send you to your death," said the prince gently. "We must not hide the truth from ourselves—only a miracle can save you."

"A miracle?" Hartmut's glance sought the altar which the flickering moonlight revealed. He had ceased to pray long years ago, and yet in this moment a hot, speechless prayer went up to Heaven for strength to accomplish this miracle. "If I can only save my father then I am content!"

In the next second he turned, and Egon, who had put new life into him and given him back his courage, said gently:

"And now let us say good-bye! God bless you, Hartmut!"

The two friends clung to one another in a last embrace. All that had come between them was lost sight of forever, and the old, warm love was mightier than ever in this last hour, for they both felt that it was a farewell for all time.

Scarcely fifteen minutes later a rider dashed out of the camp. The slender Arab's hoofs hardly touched the ground over which it sped; in a wild gallop it went on over the snow-covered ground, through the ice-clad forest, over frozen streams, on, on, into the mountain pass!

CHAPTER XVI

The following day brought clear, frosty weather. The intense cold had abated and the sun shone out warm and bright. Eugen Stahlberg and Lieutenant Walldorf, free from duty for the time being, were in Prince Adelsberg's quarters. Walldorf had been thrown from his horse the previous evening, and his hand had been injured, and this prevented him from going out with his company, as Egon had done. The gentlemen were waiting for the return of their princely comrade, who must be back soon now, and as they waited, they teased and guyed old Peter Stadinger, who was on duty early at his master's quarters.

The young officers had heard nothing of the news which had been learned over night at headquarters, they were as merry as could be, and indulged in much raillery over old Peter's lectures to his master. But the old man said little in answer to their banter this morning; his master was long in returning, and Stadinger had reached the age when he borrowed trouble, and it rested heavily upon him. Finally Walldorf got out of all patience with him and said:

"I believe, Stadinger, you'd like to strap the prince on your back and take him off to Rodeck with you. The camp is no place for anxiety or alarm, remember that."

"Then the prince had to reconnoitre to-day," added Eugen. "He has to make a detour from Chapel mountain to the valley beneath and through the ravine, in order to see what the outlook is. We'll probably have a pleasant exchange of civilities with the French gentlemen within the next few days, and we want to be ready for them at all points."

"But there's plenty of chances for them to shoot now, isn't there?" asked the old man with such anxiety that the officers had to laugh aloud.

"Yes, there's chances enough to shoot," Walldorf asserted. "You seem to be afraid of a gun. You're safe from any stray shots here!"

"I?" the old man straightened himself; he was deeply insulted. "I wish to God I could be in the midst of it all."

"Yes, you'd stay by the prince, and when you saw a bullet coming you'd give his coat a pull and say: 'Be careful, your highness, here comes a bullet.' That would be great fun."

"Herr Lieutenant," said the old man so earnestly that their merriment was silenced, "you should not talk so to an old hunter, who has climbed time and again to the mountain's summit, and shot, and killed too, where he had scarcely room to plant his foot. It is only here that I am so anxious and discouraged—I would the day were well over."

"We were only in fun," said Eugen good naturedly. "Of course you're not afraid of a shot, one only has to look at you to know that. But don't come to us with your presentiments and misgivings; after men have stood under a shower of bullets they don't heed croakings. When we're all home again I am going to visit my sister at Ostwalden and we'll be good neighbors, you and I. The prince is very fond of his hunting castle at Rodeck, is he not? But you can banish your gloomy thoughts, for here he comes."

There was a quick step without on the stair; the old man gave a relieved sigh, but when the door opened it was only Eugen's man who appeared.

"Isn't his highness coming?" asked Walldorf; but Stadinger gave the man no time to answer. He had glanced at his face, only a glance, then he started forward and seized his hand half-frantically.

"What is it? Where—where is my master?"

The man shook his head sadly and pointed to the window; the two officers hastened to it, but Stadinger lost no time in looking; he rushed out of the door and down the steps and across the little yard, and sank down with a piercing cry beside a litter which two soldiers were carrying, and upon which a tall, youthful form was stretched.

"Silence!" said the surgeon, who accompanied the sad little procession. "Control yourself, the prince is badly wounded."

"I see that," said the old man, huskily. "But his wound is not mortal? Tell me it's not mortal!"

He glanced up at the physician with a look of such despair, that the latter had not the heart to tell him the truth. He turned to the two officers who had followed Stadinger, and answered their questions instead.

"A bullet in the breast," he said in a whisper. "The prince desired to be brought to his own quarters, and we have been as careful as we could, but the end is nearer than I thought."

"No hope then?" asked Walldorf.

"Not the slightest."

The men were already lifting their burden to carry him into the house, when the physician motioned them to put him down.

"Wait! The prince wants to speak to his old servant, I think. A few minutes here or there doesn't matter now."

Stadinger saw and heard nothing of what was going on around him, he saw only his master. Egon appeared to be unconscious; the blonde hair was thrown back, the eyes were closed, and under the mantle with which the man had covered him was the blood-soaked uniform.

"Your highness!" said the old man in low, heart-rending tones. "Look at me, speak to me! It is your old Stadinger."

The well-known voice found its way to the dying man's ear; he opened his eyes slowly, and a faint smile crossed his face as he recognized his faithful servant.

"My old ghost of the woods," he said softly; "and you are with me at the last."

"But you'll not die, your highness," murmured Stadinger. His whole body was in a tremble, but he never took his eyes from his adored master. "No, you will not die, you will not die.'"

"Do you think it is so hard?" said Egon quietly. "Yesterday you were quite right, a burden was on my heart, now it is light. Take a greeting to dear Rodeck, and the forest, and to the lady of Ostwalden."

"To whom? To Frau von Wallmoden?" asked Stadinger, thinking he had not heard aright.

"Yes, tell her I send her my last greeting; she must think of me sometimes."

The words came slowly, brokenly, from the lips which would so soon refuse to do further service, but there was no mistaking their full significance. Eugen was startled when he heard his sister's name, and bent over the dying man, who looked into the countenance which so resembled Adelheid's, and again a smile lighted his face. Then he raised his head and laid it heavily on the breast of his old ghost of the woods, and the sunny blue eyes closed forever.

It was a short, painless battle with death, a peaceful falling to sleep. Stadinger hardly breathed while life remained in the body of him he had nursed as a babe and cherished as a man, but was to lose forever now. When all was over the old man lost control of himself, and threw himself in despair on the body of his beloved master, and sobbed like a child.

Yonder, on the other side of the mountain-pass, the clear, bright winter sun lighted up the citadel which had just surrendered to the German troops. The garrison which had occupied it were marching off prisoners of war, while a portion of the victors were already on their way to the fort.

General von Falkenried, surrounded by his staff, was standing in the market-place of the little city, and was just on the point of marching to the fortress. The helmets and guns of the men gleamed brightly in the morning sun as they marched in solemn order toward the citadel.

General von Falkenried, who had been giving various orders, now turned to his officers and gave the signal to move forward.

At that moment a rider came dashing down the main street at a mad galop. His noble horse was covered with sweat and froth, and his flanks were bleeding from the sharp spurs which had been pressed into his side. The rider's face was covered with blood, too, which evidently came from a wound in the forehead which had been hastily bound with a cloth. As if fleeing before a storm, he heeded naught in his path, but rushed on in his mad ride toward the market-place where the commanding general was to be found.

Just a few steps from his goal the horse's strength gave out and he fell. But in the same instant the rider had sprung from the saddle, and hastened to the commander-in-chief.

"I come from General M— —."

Falkenried drew a sharp, quick breath; he had not recognized the blood-stained face, he only knew that the man must have come on some important mission, but the tone of the man's voice gave him some premonition of the truth.

Hartmut swayed for a moment and put his hand to his head—it seemed as if he, like his horse, would succumb at the last moment; but he gathered himself together for a final effort.

"It is a warning from the general—there is treachery, the citadel is to be blown up as soon as our men are in it—here are the dispatches."

He tore the dispatches from his breast and handed them to Falkenried. The officers were startled by the unexpected news, and gathered around their chief waiting the corroboration or denial of the statement just made, but a strange sight met their eyes. Their general, who never lost his presence of mind, no matter how unexpected or how dreadful the calamity which he faced, stood gazing at the orderly as if a ghost had risen from the earth, still holding the unopened dispatches in his hand.

"Herr General, the dispatches!" said one of the adjutants, half aloud. He understood his leader as little as did the others. It was enough to bring Falkenried to his senses. He tore open the dispatches and learned their contents in a second, then again he was a soldier who thought of nothing but duty. He gave his orders in a loud, clear voice, the officers hurried hither and thither, cries of command were given, and signals sounded in every direction, and a few minutes later the division marching to the fortress was brought to a standstill, while the withdrawing garrison was also brought to a sudden halt.

Now the alarm signal was sounded from the citadel. Neither friend nor foe knew what it signified, only the newly conquered fort must be evacuated at once. The orders were carried out promptly. Despite the haste there was no disorder; the troops turned to march back to the city as they marched from it.

Falkenried still stood in the same place issuing orders, receiving communications, while with glance and word he watched and guided all. But he found a minute's time to turn to his son, he to whom he had given no sign of recognition.

"You are bleeding—your wound must be bound."

Hartmut shook his head.

"Later; first I must see the retreat and know we are saved."

The fearful excitement kept him up. He swayed no more, but watched with feverish impatience every movement of the troops. Falkenried looked at him, then he said:

"Which way did you come?"

"Over the pass."

"Why, the enemy hold it," cried the General.

"Yes—they hold it."

"And yet you came that way?"

"There was no choice; we only knew it last night, and I had no time for any other."

"That's a piece of heroism without parallel," said a high officer, who had just come up with a communication and heard the last words. "Man, how did you dare to run such a risk?"

Hartmut was silent; he raised his eyes slowly, and looked at his father. Now he was not afraid to meet those eyes, and in them he read that he was absolved.

But even the strength of him who has ventured all—and won, has its limits.

His father's face was the last he saw, then a bloody veil covered his eyes; he felt the blood again, hot and wet, running down his face, and all was night to him as he sank to the ground.

There was a roar and a shock which made the whole city quake and tremble. The citadel whose outline rose bold and clear toward the blue heavens seemed suddenly to be turned into a seething, glowing crater, vomiting flame. Within the bursting walls a very hell seemed to gape, as the shower of stones rose in the air only to sink again in the fiery hollow, and, as the gigantic wreck burned and blazed, it made one mighty pillar of fire reaching to the very heavens above—a vengeful, hideous flame of death.

The warning had not come a moment too soon. In spite of all precautions there had been some victims who lived in the immediate vicinity of the citadel and could not be reached, who were either blown to pieces or severely wounded; though in comparison with the fearful calamity which might have occurred and would have paralyzed all Germany, the loss was slight.

The General with his officers and all his troops were saved.

The General, with his wonted foresight and energy, had taken every precaution to avoid the terrible catastrophe, while his coolness, his example, had done more than anything else to inspire both officers and men to action. But now, when his duty as commander-in-chief was done, he had his rights as a father.

Hartmut had been carried, when he fell, to a house near by, and lay unconscious on his narrow cot. He neither saw nor heard his father, who stood with the surgeon by his side.

Falkenried looked earnestly at the pale, worn face and closed eyes, then he turned to the surgeon and said:

"Do you consider the wound mortal?"

The physician shrugged his shoulders.

"The wound of itself is not, but the strain and excitement of that fearful ride, the loss of blood, and the terrible night—I fear, General, there's little hope for the brave fellow. We must be prepared for the worst."

"I am prepared!" said Falkenried earnestly, then he kneeled and kissed his son, whom he had only found, he feared, to lose again; as he rose two hot tears fell on the death-like face.

But the father had no time to stay by his son. He must be up and doing. After a few minutes he left the room, leaving repeated injunctions with the doctor not to relax his watchful care for an instant.

The General's staff and many other officers were waiting in the market-place for their commander. As they waited they talked of the man who had ridden through the jaws of death to save them all; none knew his name, but he had come through the mountain pass, had faced a revengeful and infuriated foe, with death on all sides, and had reached them in time.

When the general appeared they surrounded and questioned him at once concerning the brave stranger.

Falkenried had his usual earnest look, but the settled gloom of his face was gone forever, and in its stead was an expression which those around him had never seen before. His eyes were wet, but his voice was firm and clear as he answered:

"Yes, gentlemen, he is severely wounded, and perhaps the ride which saved us all was his death ride. But he has done his duty as a man and a soldier, and if you would know his name, he is my son—Hartmut von Falkenried."

The old manor house of Burgsdorf lay peaceful and quiet in the summer sunshine. Its young master, who had been away from it for a whole year had just returned to it and to his young wife, for the war was over.

The great estate had not suffered during his long absence; it had been well cared for. The mother had taken the reins in hand again, and had governed as of old with judgment and a watchful eye, but she now resigned them willingly to her son, and declared her intention of taking up her residence in Berlin.

She looked well and happy to-day as she stood upon the broad stone veranda talking with her son who was by her side. He had never before seemed so handsome in her eyes, for his military life and discipline had given him a fine, stately bearing. She might well feel that he had gained something with which her education had not provided him, but she would not have admitted that for the world.

"So you intend to build?" she asked.

"I had thought of it."

"The old house in which your father and I lived is not good enough for your princess, whom you must needs surround with all possible glitter and splendor. Not that I care. You have the money to do it with. If all these fine doings please you, well and good. It's nothing to me, thank God."

"Don't try to be so severe, mother," laughed Willibald. "If a stranger heard you he'd think you were the worst kind of a mother-in-law. If Marietta's letters had not given me assurance enough that you spoiled her, your own actions every day would do so."

"Now and then one plays, even in old age, with a pretty doll," Regine answered dryly. "And your wife is but a fragile doll. Do not imagine she'll ever be a capable housewife—I saw at a glance that she hadn't it in her to manage here."

"You are quite right," answered her son eagerly "The work and the management of the estate are my care and mine alone, and I shall never bother Marietta with them. One takes pleasure in work too with such a sweet little singing bird by his side and in his heart."

"Willibald, I don't believe your head is right yet," said Frau von Eschenhagen with her old acerbity. "Who ever heard a sensible man, a married man and a landed gentleman, speak in such a manner of his wife, 'A sweet little singing bird.' You've been learning that from your bosom friend, Hartmut, whom you all think such a great poet."

"No mother, that's my own poetry," said Willibald, defending himself. "I never wrote but one poem, and that was on the night when I saw Marietta play. I gave it to Hartmut and asked him to change it a little and make it read more like his. I'll tell you what he said in answer. 'Dear Will, your poem is very beautiful and full of feeling; but you'd better let it remain as it is. The public would in all probability not appreciate the lines as they deserve, and your wife will value your work better without any rearrangement by me.' That was my bosom friend's judgment."

"It served you right; what had you, a landlord, to do with verses?" cried Regine sharply. Just then the door from the dining-room opened, and a dark curly head peeped out, while a fresh voice said playfully:

"May a poor subject have a moment's speech with her most gracious majesty?"

"Come here with you," said Frau von Eschenhagen, but the invitation was unnecessary, for the young wife was already in her husband's arms, while he, drawing her to him, whispered something in her ear.

"There you begin again," said his mother. "Some people never grow tired of folly."

The young wife turned toward her mother-in-law and said:

"You mustn't forget that we had no honeymoon when we were married, and so we are taking it now. You know from experience that one is permitted an extra share of happiness during that time."

Frau Regine shrugged her shoulders. Her honeymoon with Herr von Eschenhagen of blessed memory had been of another kind.

"You received a letter from your grandfather, did you not, Marietta?" she said, changing the subject. "Good news?"

"The very best. Grandpapa is quite well, and is delighted at the thought that he'll be here with me in another month. He writes that it's the quietest summer he has known for a long time around Waldhofen. Rodeck has been desolate and deserted since the prince's death. Ostwalden is closed and Fürstenstein will be empty soon, too. Toni is to be married in two weeks, and then uncle Schönau will be all alone."

The last words were spoken in a peculiar tone, and Marietta gave her mother-in-law an odd glance, which the latter did not notice; she only said:

"It does seem singular for Hartmut and Ada to spend the first weeks of their marriage here in that little villa when they could go to the great castle at Ostwalden or one of the Stahlberg palaces."

"They wanted to be as near the general as possible," said Willibald.

"Well, in this case, Falkenried could have gotten leave and gone to them. God be praised! The man seems to live again since he has his son with him. I knew better than any one how the boy's flight struck him, for he fairly worshipped his son, notwithstanding his severity. That famous ride which saved his father and his troops, absolved him from all his boyhood's errors, for which, after all, his mother alone was accountable."

"If we only had some wedding festivities in the family," said Marietta. "Will and I were married without any, because the war had commenced, and now when the war is happily ended, Hartmut and Ada are married just as quietly as we."

"My child, when a man has gone through all that Hartmut has endured, he has little desire for gaieties," said Frau von Eschenhagen, earnestly. "Besides, he has by no means recovered his strength yet. You saw how pale he was when they were married. Adelheid's first marriage was very different from her second one. Her poor father gave her away, although he was so ill, and she in her train and lace and diamonds looked like a queen; but her face was pale and cold. Now, she seemed like a different creature as she turned with Hartmut from the altar in her simple white silk gown and gauzy veil. I have never seen so peaceful, so happy a face! Poor Herbert! He never possessed his wife's love."

"Who could love so old a man? Always with his diplomatic coat and manner on, too. I shouldn't have been able to do it, I'm sure," cried Marietta, thoughtlessly.

Her mother-in-law, who held her brother's memory sacred, said tartly:

"Such an opportunity would never have come in your way. A man like Herbert von Wallmoden would scarcely have chosen you, you little insolent thing—"

The little insolent thing threw her arms around Frau Regine's neck, and said, flatteringly:

"Now, don't be angry, mamma! I wouldn't exchange my Will for all the great ambassadors of the world, and neither would you."

"You're a little minx," said Regine, striving to look as severe as ever. "You know very well that one can't be angry with you long. Oh, there'll be a petticoat government at Burgsdorf from this time on, such as the place has never witnessed before. Will's a little ashamed before me yet, but as soon as I'm gone he'll surrender at discretion."

"Why do you cling to that idea, mother?" said Willibald, reprovingly. "Why do you want to go when all is love and peace between us?"

"Just for that reason I go, that peace may continue; we need not discuss it, my son. I must always be first where I live and work. You must be that now, and we wouldn't pull together. Until now we have been distressed and anxious about you, not knowing what hour would bring tidings to break our hearts. That's all over, but I'm not so old that I must be set aside as useless. Wherever I am I must be the head, and for that reason I am going."

She turned and entered the house, while her son gazed after her and gave a troubled sigh.

"Perhaps she is right," he said, "but it will be hard for her to be without duties or occupation. Enforced quiet will be very hard for her, I know. You should have begged her to remain, Marietta."

Marietta laid her head on his shoulder and looked up smiling:

"O no, I'll do something better. I'll have a care that when she leaves us she will not be unhappy."

"You? What will you do?"

"Only a simple thing—have her get married."

"What do you mean?"

"O, Will, to be so wise and yet see nothing," said his wife with her old sweet silvery laugh. "Have you no idea why uncle Schönau was in such a bad humor when we met him in Berlin, and urged him to visit us? Your mother didn't invite him because she feared another proposal; he understood that, and it made him furious. I saw them at Waldhofen the time of our marriage, and I knew he would have been very glad to have a similar ceremony performed for himself, only your mother said him nay. Don't put on such a face, Will; you look exactly as you did the first day I saw you."

Her husband was gazing at her in boundless astonishment. He had never dreamed of such a possibility as his mother marrying again, or his uncle either, for that matter. It struck him now as a most excellent arrangement.

"Marietta, how wise you are!" he said, looking with admiration at the smiling girl, who was beaming with satisfaction at the manner in which her news had been received.

"I'm wiser than you think," she declared triumphantly, "for I have set the wheel going. I took occasion to let uncle Schönau know that if he stormed the fort again, a complete surrender might follow. He said he had no intention of being refused again, but you'll see him sooner than you think. In fact he's in the house now, came half an hour ago, but I determined to say nothing about it before mamma—here he is now!"

The head forester stepped on the terrace just in time to hear the last words.

"Yes, here I am," said Herr von Schönau. "It's all your little wife's fault, Will, that I am at Burgsdorf. I'm here at her suggestion, and if that mother of your's is not obstinate and unreasonable and pig-headed as usual—why I'll marry her."

"I pray to God you may, uncle," answered Will, to whom this summary of his mother's wonted characteristics was very singular, to say the least.

"Yes, so do I," agreed Schönau, "your wife thinks—"

"I think that you shouldn't lose a moment," cried Marietta, "Mamma has just gone to her sitting-room and knows nothing of your arrival. Will and I will remain behind, and if the worst comes to the worst call on us. Forward, march!"

With these words she gave him a push, and the sturdy, broad shouldered man turned at her bidding, saying to Will, who entered the house with him:

"They are all commanders whether they be large or small—it's born in them, I suppose."

Regine von Eschenhagen stood at the window of her cosy room looking out upon her beloved Burgsdorf, which she was to leave in a few days. Though she had said so decidedly she would go, the decision had been no light matter to her. The strong, active, capable woman who had been mistress here for thirty years and over, dreaded the quiet and inactivity of city life, of which she had had some slight experience at the time of her quarrel with her son. She dreaded going back to it now, though she knew it was but just and fitting to leave Willibald and his wife alone, and she had the courage to do what was right. She heard the door open and turned to see the head forester enter the room.

"Moritz, you here?" she said, surprised. "It was very sensible of you to come."

"Yes, I'm always sensible," answered the head forester, with his usual lack of tact. "You didn't have the grace to invite me, but I thought I'd come in person to invite you and your children to Toni's marriage. You will come to Fürstenstein, will you not?"

"Certainly we will come, but we were surprised to hear it was to take place so soon. I thought you were going to buy them an estate first and settle the matter more slowly!"

"No, they wouldn't wait or listen to reason. Our warriors make great demands when they come home covered with glory. Walldorf said to me quite coolly: 'You know you said first conquer then marry. Well we have conquered; now I shall marry without any delay. The estate can wait, the land won't run away, but we must be married now!' Of course Toni seconded everything he said. What could I do? I let them name the day then and there."

Frau von Eschenhagen laughed.

"The young are in a hurry to marry, though they have plenty of time to wait."

"The old have none to spare, though," said the head forester promptly, glad of so good a chance to get on the subject near his heart. "Have you reflected enough over our little affair, Regine?"

"What affair?"

"Why, our marriage. I trust you are in the humor for it now." Regine turned away somewhat embarrassed.

"How you do love to take one by surprise, Moritz."

"So that is what you call taking by surprise?" cried the head forester, irritated. "Over five years ago I asked you to marry me, then last year a second time, and now for the third time, so you have had plenty of time to consider the matter. Yes, or no? If you send me away this time I'll never come again, understand that!"

Regine did not answer, but it was not indecision which made her hesitate. Notwithstanding her hard, unyielding nature, deep down in her heart there had always been a warm feeling for the man who was to have been her husband long years ago, for Hartmut von Falkenried. When he had turned from her she had married another, for she had no thought of leading a desolate, useless life; but the same feeling of bitter woe which had entered the young girl's heart was in the heart of the older woman to-day and closed her lips. She stood silent for a few minutes, then cast the sweet, sad memory from her forever, and gave her hand to her brother-in-law:

"Well then, yes, Moritz! I will make you a good and true wife."

"Thank God!" said Schönau earnestly, for he had feared her hesitation would result in a third refusal. "You should have said that five years ago, Regine, but better late than never. It's all right at last."

And with these words the persevering man folded her in his arms with affectionate tenderness.

The sun shone down warm and bright on the meadow land and penetrated even into the forest depths. It fell across the pathway of General von Falkenried and his son and daughter, who were sauntering along under the high firs on the way which led to Burgsdorf.

Falkenried did not seem the same man he had been for the past ten years. The war which, despite its victories and final triumph, had made so many old before their time, had affected him apparently in a different manner. His white hair was thin over his deeply furrowed brow, but his features had life again, his eyes had fire and expression, and one saw at a glance that this was no old man, but one in the zenith of his strength and power.

Falkenried's son had not fully recovered his strength yet, and his face showed traces of great suffering. The war had not left him younger, on the contrary he had grown older; his pallid face, and the broad, red scar on his forehead, told a tale of their own. For months after that fearful night he had lain at death's door, but with returning life and strength all traces of the old Hartmut, of Zalika's son, disappeared forever.

It seemed as if, in casting from him the name of Rojanow, he cast with it the unholy heritage of her who had borne him. The dark curly locks were beginning to grow again over the high, broad forehead, so like his father's.

The young wife by his side, so beautiful, so winning always, was lovelier than ever now, for joy and happiness had set their seal on her bright, girlish face! Who would recognize in this slender, graceful figure, clad in a simple, summer frock, the proud, cold court beauty in her laces and jewels? The smile, the tone in which she spoke to her father and husband, Frau von Wallmoden had never known, for it was Ada Falkenried who had learned it.

"You can go no farther to-day," said the general, standing still. "You have a long walk back, and Hartmut is not strong enough for much yet. The physician was very decided about his not exerting himself."

"If you only knew, father, how hard it was to be mistaken for an invalid when I am getting so well and strong again," said Hartmut. "I am getting strong enough—"

"To bring on a relapse by your folly," his father answered. "You have never learned patience, and it is altogether owing to Ada that you are as strong as you are."

"If it hadn't been for her there would be no Hartmut to-day," said her husband, giving her a glance of tenderest love. "I believe the case was almost hopeless when she came to me!"

"The physicians at least gave no hope, when I telegraphed for Ada in response to your cry. The first minute you recovered consciousness, you called for her, to my boundless astonishment, for I did not know you even knew one another."

"That hardly seemed fair to you, papa, did it?" As she glanced up laughing into her father's face, he drew her to him, and kissed her forehead.

"You know best what you have been to Hartmut and me, my child. I thank God for bringing him back to me through your nursing. And you are right in detaining him here, although the physician says he could travel now. He must first learn to know his fatherland and his home to which he was so long a stranger."

"First learn?" said Ada, reprovingly. "What he read to you and to me to-day shows that he has long since learned it; his new poem breathes a different spirit from his wild, passionate 'Arivana.'"

"Yes, Hartmut, your new work is certainly fine," said his father, as he reached out his hand to his son. "I believe the fatherland will yet honor my boy in peace, as well as in war."

Hartmut's eyes lighted as he returned the warm hand pressure. He knew what such praise from his father's lips signified.

"Good-bye," said the general, kissing his daughter. "I'll go on from Burgsdorf to the city, but in a few days we'll meet again. Good-bye, children."

As he disappeared through the trees, Hartmut led Ada toward the Burgsdorf fish-pond. When they reached it they stood gazing down on the still sheet of water which lay so placid and clear in its setting of water lilies and reeds.

"Here, as a boy, I played for hours with Will," said Hartmut softly, "and here my destiny was decided for me on that fateful night. I realize now, for the first time, all that I did to my father in that fearful hour."

"Ah, but you have repaid him for all his suffering," answered Ada, as she laid her hand on her husband's arm. "The world, too, has forgotten your boyhood's folly. That was proven by the words of praise and congratulations which poured in upon your father from all sides about his heroic son."

Hartmut shook his head. "That was no heroism, it was despair. I did not think I should succeed. No one thought so; but even had I fallen, the enemy's bullet would have redeemed my honor. Egon understood that, and that was why he put my salvation in my own hands. When we two said good-bye in the little ruined church on that icy winter's night, we knew we should never meet again, but we both thought I would be the victim, for I rode to almost certain death. But a spirit-hand seemed to lead me, and in the hour in which I reached my goal, poor Egon fell. You need not hide your tears, dear. I have no jealousy of the dead."

"Eugen brought me his last greeting," said the young wife, the hot tears standing in her eyes. "And poor Stadinger wrote me, too, of his master's last words. I fear the old man won't live long; his letter sounded as though he were heart-broken."

"My poor Egon!" Hartmut's voice told how deep was his sorrow for his loss. "He was so sunny, so amiable always. He seemed created for a long, cloudless life. Perhaps you would have been happier by his side, Ada, than with your wild, stormy Hartmut, who will so often vex you with the dark shadows of his life."

Ada glanced up at him, smiling through her tears.

"I have only one love, and that is my wild, stormy Hartmut, and I know no greater happiness than to be his wife!"

Wood and water lay quiet in the afternoon sunshine. The old firs stood dark and tall, while the reeds whispered softly to one another, and thousands of sunny sparks danced on the water. Far above, in the heavens to which the boy had once longed to mount like a falcon, the sun rode on his glorious course. In splendor he shed his rays on all beneath—mighty, eternal and glorious source and promise of life and joy.